W9-AWC-323

THE SILENT ROSE

"Do you have any idea how insane this all sounds?" Jonathan crossed the room to the place beside her.

"I know." A hard lump rose in Devon's throat. She cared about Jonathan Stafford. She didn't want him looking at her the way he was now. "I'm not sure what the truth really is, but I have to find out. I wish I'd never gone into that house, but I did. I can't turn my back on this now. I can't—and I won't."

"Damn you!"

Tears stung Devon's eyes and began to trickle down her cheeks. Jonathan saw the wetness and some of the hardness seeped from his features.

"I don't believe for a moment that any of this is real. I hate the fact that what you're doing may wind up hurting my family." He moved closer. "I know I'm going to have to stop you, that I should stay as far away from you as I possibly can. Then I look at you, watch the way you smile, and all I can think of is how it might be to kiss you."

His thumb moved back and forth across her jaw and Devon trembled.

"I don't know how I'm going to stop you, but I *can* find the answer to this." He tilted her head back and settled his mouth over hers, fitting their lips perfectly together.

Don't do this, her mind screamed. *You know what he's after!* But it made no difference. From the moment he had touched her, Devon was lost.

BOOK YOUR PLACE ON OUR WEBSITE AND MAKE THE READING CONNECTION!

We've created a customized website just for our very special readers, where you can get the inside scoop on everything that's going on with Zebra, Pinnacle and Kensington books.

When you come online, you'll have the exciting opportunity to:

- View covers of upcoming books
- Read sample chapters
- Learn about our future publishing schedule (listed by publication month *and author*)
- Find out when your favorite authors will be visiting a city near you
- Search for and order backlist books from our online catalog
- Check out author bios and background information
- Send e-mail to your favorite authors
- Meet the Kensington staff online
- Join us in weekly chats with authors, readers and other guests
- Get writing guidelines
- AND MUCH MORE!

Visit our website at
http://www.zebrabooks.com

THE SILENT ROSE

Kat Martin

Zebra Books
Kensington Publishing Corp.
http://www.zebrabooks.com

ZEBRA BOOKS are published by

Kensington Publishing Corp.
850 Third Avenue
New York, NY 10022

Copyright © 1994 by Kat Martin

All rights reserved. No part of this book may be reproduced in any form or by any means without the prior written consent of the Publisher, excepting brief quotes used in reviews.

If you purchased this book without a cover, you should be aware that this book is stolen property. It was reported as "unsold and destroyed" to the Publisher and neither the Author nor the Publisher has received any payment for this "stripped book."

Zebra and the Z logo Reg. U.S. Pat. & TM Off.

First Pinnacle Printing: November, 1994
First Zebra Printing: August, 1999
10 9 8 7 6 5 4 3 2

Printed in the United States of America

FROM THE AUTHOR

Dear Readers,

Although I love writing historical romance novels and intend to write many more in the future, *The Silent Rose* is the first in a series of contemporary romantic suspense novels that will also be coming your way. For a number of years, it has been my dream to write stories about ordinary women who have had extraordinary experiences—something beyond the norm that they simply can't explain. I believe most women, including me, as well as a number of men have had moments such as these, though perhaps they have never mentioned them for fear they would not be believed. I'm hoping readers will be able to relate to stories like this one and enjoy a very sexy romance as well.

The second book in the series, *The Dream,* will be out next year. If you like Devon and Jonathan's story in *The Silent Rose,* I hope you'll watch for Jack and Genny in *The Dream,* and that you enjoy!

All best wishes,
Kat

One

The raindrops spattered against the windshield with the same monotonous rhythm as they had the day before, but today the swish of blades against glass seemed grating instead of soothing, eerie instead of pleasant. The biting wind blowing in off the Connecticut coastline was no colder this afternoon, no more chilling, yet it somehow seemed so.

As the rented Lincoln Town Car sped along the deserted stretch of country road on its journey to the small New England town of Stafford, Devon James tried to ignore her uneasy feelings. Anxiety had gripped her since early that morning. It was nothing she could put her finger on, probably just coincidence.

At least that's what she told herself over and over as the hours dragged slowly past. Still, she felt as if something strange was about to happen.

Something unaccountable.

Something dreadful.

"You're awfully quiet." Michael Galveston's voice cut through the silence in the car and the sounds of the storm outside. Michael was Devon's fiancé. They'd been engaged for more than two years. "I hope nothing's wrong."

So do I. Devon forced a smile using the same valiant effort it took to push her uneasiness away. "I'm just a little tired, that's all."

Who wouldn't be? she thought, hooking a lock of her shoulder-length pale blond hair behind an ear. Three days of Darnex Management conferences, three days of playing corporate future-wife, three days of working to pass inspection by the other vice-presidents' spouses—and of course their not-so-subtle insinuations that Michael might not really intend to marry her, since they had been engaged for so long.

Devon had politely ignored their thinly veiled disapproval, though it made her insides churn. If only she could tell them it was she, not Michael, who kept postponing the wedding. Make them understand her uncertainties about marrying him, since they were so different—about marrying anyone, in fact.

"I'm just not ready yet, Michael," she had told him again last month.

"I don't like this, Devon. People are beginning to talk. I've tried to be patient. I've put up with all your insecurities, all your self-doubts, but I won't wait much longer. Either we get married by April fifteenth, or we're through." That was the date of their first meeting over two years ago. Long enough for a courtship, according to Michael.

Knowing him as she did, she knew he meant it. She was surprised she'd been able to hold him off as long as she had.

The car swerved to avoid a downed tree branch, and Devon started, her hand automatically gripping the armrest to steady herself. She felt tense and nervous in a way she hadn't since the endless days and nights of her divorce. Was it Michael and the pressure he was bringing to bear? What was this uneasy feeling that had gripped her since dawn?

"You're not starting your period, are you?" With a look of condemnation, Michael swung his hazel eyes in her direction, staring at her a little longer than he should have, considering the storm and the wetness of the road. "This is supposed to be a romantic evening. I don't intend to sit around and watch you brood."

"No, Michael, I just got over my period. I'm really just tired. I'll be fine as soon as we get there and get settled in." At least that's what she hoped.

Michael reached over and patted her knee. "You're not still worried about Mrs. Corbin, are you?"

Another vice-president's wife. They all seemed so much alike she found it hard to tell them apart.

"As soon as we're married, she'll accept you as part of the family. I'll grant she can be catty at times, but you'll win her over." Another knee pat. "I have all the faith in the world."

Devon just nodded. She doubted she'd ever win any of them over. She was so different, more of a loner. It wasn't that she didn't like people; she just worried that they might not like her. In a lot of ways she was shy, and she'd always been a little bit off-beat. An "everybody's out of step but Devon" sort of person. She didn't think she could ever be the "team-player" a corporate wife was expected to be.

Still, she loved Michael. He had been good to her, helped her when she needed it. And sacrifices had to be made in any relationship.

"How much farther?" he asked.

"Just a few more miles, I think."

"You think?"

"Well, it doesn't look far on the map."

For a moment he seemed disgruntled, then with an effort, he smiled. "Sorry, baby. I guess I'm a little tired, too."

He was trying hard to be polite, and go along with Devon's plans for a romantic interlude, which she was certain he saw as a prelude to her eventual surrender to his wishes. Michael fully expected her to set the date for their wedding any day now. And he was used to getting his way.

With his light brown hair, hazel eyes, and finely shaped features, Michael Galveston had always been attractive to women—and they had usually done his bidding. He flaunted his authoritative manner, and for a while they found that attractive, too. Devon had. Now she often found his overbearing ways more irritating than exciting. Still, he was good to her and, oddly enough, she really believed he loved her. Which, after being married to Paul, made up for some of the things about him she found difficult to accept.

Looking at his handsome profile, and the subtle air of confidence Michael wore like an expensive shirt, Devon thought of the women who would have jumped at the chance to marry him. She thought of her own reluctance and figured her postponements must have somehow fit into his plans. Until now. With his recent promotion to vice president in charge of marketing, a fiancée would no longer do. Michael needed a wife, and in most ways Devon fit his image of the perfect corporate spouse.

She smiled as she recalled the way he'd once described her, "tall, blond, statuesque, and always well-groomed." In truth, her fine, pure features were those of a Scandinavian. But because she'd been adopted, she had no way of knowing her national origin for sure. She had graduated from New York University instead of Smith or Barnard, but she had earned a degree in literature and graduated with honors, and in the last few years had become one of the nation's leading authors of women's fiction.

Her family background was hardly suitable, by Michael's third-generation, almost-old-money standards, but in some ways, she figured, having been raised in the sort of blue-collar family that had made America great, then forging her way to the top carried a certain mark of accomplishment. After all—Devon James was a self-made woman. Who better to stand behind that bastion of American life—the corporate executive—than just such a woman?

Or at least that was how Michael saw it.

On top of that, Devon's novels earned a great deal of money. They were called introspective and intelligent. Michael was willing to overlook the fact that she was a year and a half behind schedule on her current project and people were beginning to doubt her long-term staying power.

Sometimes she even doubted it herself.

As she sank back against the tufted red leather seat, Devon's musings faded with the absorbing patter of the rain. The big dark blue Town Car slowed, and Michael turned down the main street of the small seaport town of Mystic. It overflowed with tourists in summer, but late fall was the off-season. The sidewalks were empty, except for people whose errands demanded they be out, their collars turned up against the wind.

The rain had washed the pavement clean, and the air smelled damp and musty. The Lincoln's headlights reflected off the asphalt as they crossed the drawbridge over the neck of the bay and drove cautiously through the rapidly growing mud puddles. When they spotted the small metal sign that pointed toward Stafford, Devon's anxieties returned. Subtly at first, then stronger as the minutes passed and they neared the all-but-abandoned, once-busy town.

A hundred years ago, Stafford, Connecticut had been a village of wealth and power, the center of the Stafford family shipbuilding empire. Today, all that was left of the once-thriving town was a general store whose weathered sign was peeling and almost unreadable, a gas station with one of those old-fashioned pumps you sometimes saw in museums, a rustic restaurant famous for its lobster, and the Stafford Inn, once the Stafford family mansion, now the bed and breakfast where she had reserved a room.

It had been Devon's idea from the start. Something different from the oh-so-efficient plastic hotels like the towering Hyatt they had stayed in during the Boston conference. Instead of subsisting for three days on overcooked scrambled eggs and the usual rubber chicken that always left her stomach uneasy, they would enjoy carafes of good wine and plates of sharp cheddar cheese. Then an evening at one of the finer Mystic restaurants not too far away, followed by a restful night's sleep in a deep feather mattress.

Tomorrow they'd awaken to a sumptuous home-cooked breakfast of raisin granola muffins with real peach preserves, fresh-squeezed orange juice, and hot old-fashioned oatmeal. The travel brochure had made the place sound so delightful Devon just couldn't resist.

Michael had reluctantly agreed. He wasn't into moldy old houses, he had firmly pronounced, as if she couldn't have guessed, but if it made her happy . . .

Devon sighed. April fifteenth didn't seem nearly far enough away.

They drove down the narrow winding lanes that made up the town of Stafford, and at last they rounded the corner onto Church Street. The windshield wipers grated as the rain began to thin. Michael pulled the car up in front of the three-story white-pillared mansion and turned off the ignition. Without the noise of the engine, the storm outside grew louder. The tops of the trees bent over and the wind outside whistled through the branches, filling the car with an eerie whirring that seeped in, though the windows were rolled up tight.

Devon listened to the sound, almost a keening, and her sense of foreboding seemed to swell. Her heartbeat quickened and her chest grew tight. She tried to tell herself she was being silly, that it was only the wind and the rain, but something said it was more than that. The apprehension she felt seemed to come from somewhere inside her, to grow and mushroom till it stole the very air from inside the car.

"I'll get the luggage," Michael said. "You go on in before you get wet."

With a sudden unwelcome fervor, Devon wished this were another of the times they had done what Michael wanted instead.

She watched him get out of the car, push the remote button to unlock the trunk, and lift the lid. The rain had thinned to a bone-chilling drizzle, but the wind still howled, and the flat gray overcast looked even darker than before.

Instead of going inside, Devon rounded the car and leaned into the trunk. "I won't need much." Ignoring her tapestry hanging bag, she picked up the small matching overnight case, repacked in Boston in readiness for their brief, one-night stay. "If I carry this, you won't have to come back out in the rain."

Michael nodded and picked up his two big, belted leather bags. He was a tall man, well-built, but not very muscular. He had gained a little weight since his promotion. Devon figured with the rich food and five-o'clock martinis he would probably gain a little more as the years went by. But Michael would never be fat. He was far too vain for that.

Devon skirted the four-foot hedge that encircled the mansion and stepped onto the narrow cement walkway, as Michael followed close behind. The house loomed large and imposing ahead of her, dwarfing its neighbors—smaller houses which had obviously been built years later on portions of the original Stafford land. In comparison, the mansion looked like a grand old matriarch whose children had not quite come up to par.

Devon's high-heeled boots clicked on the shiny wet surface, each footfall echoing hollowly. The wind whipped strands of her pale blond hair and calf-length gray wool skirt, and the odd keening sound whistled eerily through the trees. Devon's palms began to sweat.

What in God's name is the matter with me?

She pulled her gaze from the swaying, wind-whipped cypress back to the walkway leading up to the mansion, draping a sleek lock of damp blond hair over an ear so she could see. In its day, the house had been lovely. Twin Doric columns supported a rounded front porch that jutted out protectively over two tall white-painted doors. But Devon noticed the paint was peeling badly and the stone steps leading up to them were cracked and in need of repair. Thin-bladed grass jutted from between the spaces, though the yard around them had recently been mowed.

"Is this your idea of an *elegant turn-of-the-century mansion by the sea?*" Michael asked, repeating the words she had read to him from the brochure. "Needs a good paint job, if you ask me."

"I thought it would be charming, and it is." That was a lie. There was nothing the least bit charming about the Stafford Inn. It was huge and uninviting, cared for—*tended* might be a better word—but not to the fine specifications Michael expected. Still, she was tired of his condescending attitude and determined to make the best of things, even if he wasn't.

Michael climbed the wide porch steps and Devon followed. The front door was ornately carved. Though badly weathered, it looked huge and imposing. When Michael rang the doorbell, the chimes sounded old and heavy and dull, just like the mansion itself.

At first Devon wondered if anyone was home. Then the eye-level miniature door serving as peephole swung wide. "It's about time you got here," said a woman's voice through the opening. "I was beginning to think you weren't going to come."

The hostile greeting set even Michael aback. "We told you we'd arrive before six—isn't that right, Devon?" She nodded. "It's only five-forty-five."

The tiny door closed, old brass locks clanked and grated, and the big door swung wide. "I'm Mrs. Meeks. Ada Meeks. The others have already arrived. Come on in."

What others? Devon wanted to ask, but didn't. Because the moment she stepped into the interior she wanted to turn tail and run. The huge foyer was empty. Overhead hung a slightly dusty chandelier, its once-lovely crystal prisms no longer glistening. And beneath her feet lay a scratched but clean-swept inlaid parquet floor.

There was no one in the sparsely furnished salon where a burgundy horsehair sofa with a small Hepplewhite table beside it rested against one stark white wall. The floors were bare, except for a worn but still-serviceable Oriental carpet. And an old brass floor lamp, with a red-fringed shade, sat in the corner beside an antique plush velour overstuffed chair.

There was no one in the dining room either. Just a long mahogany table to which several leaves had been added, and eight mahogany chairs, only five of which matched.

There was no one—yet Devon felt certain there was.

This is insane, she found herself thinking. *There is nothing in this house to be afraid of.*

"Follow me," Mrs. Meeks said. "You'll be sleeping in the yellow room on the third floor upstairs. It's the only room we've got left." Her officious tone said if they'd gotten there earlier they could have had better accommodations. The brochure said there were only six bedchambers, which was one of the reasons Devon had chosen the place.

Michael grunted and cast her a glance of despair, but picked up his bags and waited for Devon to pick up hers. Like soldiers being assigned to their barracks, the two of them followed Mrs. Meeks toward the massive mahogany stairway at the back of the foyer. As they marched along single file, Devon's eyes rested on the back of the small woman's head.

Ada Meeks couldn't have been more than ten or twelve years Devon's senior. A woman perhaps in her early forties. Though her mouse-brown hair had already begun to gray, her face was relatively unlined, and her skin looked smooth and supple. Yet the woman's bent posture and dour expression—even the sound of her voice—all made her seem much older. On first impression, Ada Meeks could have easily passed for sixty.

They reached the second-floor landing and walked down the hall, passing a huge room dominated by a canopied four-poster bed. Like the rooms downstairs, this one, too, looked Spartan, but the flowered spread matched the curtains, the paint was new, and so was the carpet. The couple who were unpacking inside, swung the heavy door closed, leaving only the muffled sound of their voices. The other bedroom doors were closed, but occasional sounds of occupancy drifted through the heavy paneled wood.

"We're workin' on the place a little at a time," Mrs.

Meeks explained. "Just put a new bath in the yellow room where you'll be stayin'. It's got the nicest fixtures in the house."

Michael's sigh of relief was almost audible. He hated old bathrooms worse than just about anything. Always a meticulous dresser, he liked to groom himself with as little trouble as possible. Devon didn't really blame him, though she had always been a bit more flexible. Often she preferred the warmth and charm of older accommodations to the efficiency of more modern ones.

Michael shifted the strap of his heavy leather suitcase as they reached the foot of the second staircase, this one a quarter of the width of the first, obviously leading up to what had once been the servants' quarters just below the attic. Michael looked none too pleased.

"You're sure you have nothing else available?"

"Not a thing." They climbed the stairs in silence, as Devon more and more regretted her decision to come here. There was an oppressive atmosphere in the house, a sort of thickness that seemed to pervade the place and ooze from every doorway.

The yellow room was nice enough, small but adequate, furnished with a queen-sized bed and several pieces of white wicker furniture. It was clean, though Spartan like the others, but in this part of the house the ceilings angled lower and the small dormer windows gave a feeling of airlessness to what little space there was. Devon wrinkled her nose at a slightly musty odor she couldn't quite name.

"This do?" Mrs. Meeks asked.

Michael wanted to say no; she could see it in the set of his shoulders, the tension in his jaw. "Devon?" he asked, surprising her, though she shouldn't have been. He was wearing his martyred expression.

"It's fine, Mrs. Meeks."

"Will you be goin' out?"

"We'll be dining out, yes," Michael answered.

"Then you'll need a key to get back in the front door." Fishing into the pocket of her calico apron, the broad-hipped woman brought out a big brass skeleton key and a smaller room key, and handed them to Michael. "Try not to wake up the household when you get home."

When Michael merely nodded, Devon's green eyes went wide with surprise. By now he should have had the woman soundly relegated to her position. She was there to wait on him, not the other way around. Michael usually made that plain from the start. She wondered why in this case he hadn't.

"I don't like this place," he said as soon as the heavy door had closed.

"To tell you the truth, neither do I," she finally admitted. "But we're here now, it's storming outside, and I'm too tired to lug this stuff back to the car and leave."

"Why don't we put our clothes away and drive into Mystic for dinner? By the time we get back, we'll be ready for bed. As long as the mattress is decent—" He sat down and tested its firmness, which seemed to pass his inspection. Then he glanced toward the open door on one yellow wall and noticed with satisfaction the gleaming white porcelain tub and shiny pale yellow linoleum. "At least the bathroom is new."

Michael picked up his leather garment bag, walked across the room, and opened a small door less than five feet high that led into the closet, which was narrow and ran the length of the room. Old brass coat hooks protruded every two feet from cedar wainscoting that, unlike the rest of the room, had never been painted.

Devon noticed that the musty odor increased as soon as Michael opened the closet door. It smelled bitter and acrid, a little like creosote, she thought as the distasteful odor drifted toward her. She glanced at the closet and felt a prickling across her skin. When Michael finished hanging up his clothes, Devon discreetly walked over and closed the closet door.

"I'm sorry about this, Michael. I had hoped this would work out better."

Michael took her hands, fine-boned and slender, and pulled her close. He bent his head and kissed her. "Next time I'll take care of the arrangements."

Devon only nodded. Fighting with him rarely did any good. And the oppressive little room had done nothing to lift her spirits—or to remove her sense of dread, which had been growing steadily since the moment they had stepped through the door.

The evening went better than Devon had expected. For once Michael made up his mind to accept things instead of trying to change them. And after they left the house, both of their moods grew lighter. Michael pressed her about the wedding date, just as she expected, but she surprised herself by giving him the answer he wanted.

"Why don't we get married on our anniversary?" she suggested.

"April fifteenth?"

"Yes. It's the day we met, that makes it special, doesn't it?"

"What day of the week is that?" He pulled his burgundy leather daytimer out of his breast pocket and checked the calendar. Devon felt a twinge of disappointment. Romantic sentiment aside, Michael would want it to be on a weekend, while she wouldn't care when or where they got married, as long as it made them both happy.

"Saturday. Perfect." He smiled and took her hand. "I'll get Mother started on the arrangements right away."

Mother. She could have guessed that was what he would want. No cozy chapel, no romantic elopement. Then again, what did it matter?

"Fine," she agreed, suddenly seeing the practical side. She really couldn't afford the time it would take to plan things, anyway. She was already behind in her writing, and now that the marriage was in fact going to happen, she realized she didn't really care all that much how they went about it.

Not the way she had the first time. When she'd married Paul James, she had wanted things to be perfect. A long white wedding gown with a heavy lace train. A huge church with stained-glass windows filled with hundreds of guests. It had taken a third of her father's savings to pay for the extravagant affair, but he had wanted to make her happy. And she was—deliriously so. She would never forget the thrill she had felt, walking down the aisle on her father's arm, or the love in her heart for her mother when she spotted the gleam of tears on the thin woman's cheeks.

And Paul had been handsome and so very charming.

Four years later she was divorced.

"We'll have to start working on the guest list," Michael said, jarring her out of the past.

"I hope you'll try to convince your mother to keep it simple."

"Simple is hardly in Mother's vocabulary. But I'll do my best." Michael seemed so pleased Devon wondered why she hadn't given in sooner. He practically beamed all the way back to 25 Church Street. Even Devon felt a sense of relief. The decision at last had been made. On April fifteenth she would become Mrs. Michael Galveston—corporate vice-president's wife and dedicated *helpmate.* That's what Michael called it.

She never told him how much she loathed the expression.

"Mrs. Michael Galveston," she repeated softly. It had an odd, unfamiliar ring, but she would get used to it. Besides, she hadn't been Devon James for the past two years.

Michael opened the car door and helped her out. Sharing his umbrella, they dashed through the rain, which had started again with a vengeance, and up onto the porch. The brandy they had sipped after dinner had both of them feeling mellow, and Devon yawned behind her hand.

"Sleepy?" Michael searched his pocket for the heavy brass door key.

"Bushed."

"Me, too." Using the ancient skeleton key, Michael turned the lock, and they stepped into the foyer.

When he closed the door, the dull thud echoed behind them, and Devon's heartbeat quickened. Michael turned back toward the stairs, but neither of them started in that direction. Though a small dim lamp had been left burning in the salon, casting a faint yellow glow to light their way, something held them back.

"I don't like this place," Michael whispered, voicing Devon's thoughts exactly. "It seems so . . ."

Evil. That was the word that leapt into her mind, and goosebumps raced across her skin. "Ghosts of the past," she teased, but Michael didn't laugh, and Devon wasn't really teasing.

"Let's go upstairs." Michael draped the neck of his black umbrella over one arm and took her hand.

Devon followed, anxious to reach the sanctity of their small attic bedroom. They climbed the stairs in silence. Michael's hand held hers a little tighter than she was used to. He worked the smaller brass key in the lock on their door, and they stepped inside to find the bed turned back and a wicker desk lamp lit, turning the yellow room even more yellow. With the rain beating down on the roof above their heads and pattering lightly against the windows, it felt less hostile in here. Almost cozy. Even a little romantic.

Michael must have felt it, too. Setting his umbrella aside, he turned her into his arms and kissed her. Not the simple, loving, good-night kiss she expected, but a long, sensuous, exploring kiss that seemed a bit out of character for Michael.

Maybe it was setting the date for their wedding. Maybe it was the brandy. Whatever it was, it felt different and exciting. Devon kissed him back, opening her mouth to let his tongue slide inside. Michael's hands cupped her bottom, and Devon slid her arms around his neck. He worked the buttons at the front of her jacket then slipped his hand inside her bra to cup a breast. Unbuttoning her skirt, he pushed it down her hips to the floor, pulled her slip off, and unhooked the back of her bra.

Michael's every move felt sensuous and exciting, different than it ever had before. Devon couldn't remember when making love with Michael had been so heady. Certainly not in the beginning, when she'd felt guilty about being with a man besides Paul. Certainly not in the last few weeks, when they'd both been working too hard and she had been having all sorts of doubts about their relationship.

But tonight, in this small attic bedroom, Michael's touch seemed right somehow. He kissed her again and slid his fingers through the curly blond hair at the juncture of her legs. He found her wet and ready for him—burning for him in fact.

Michael left her long enough for them to dispose of their clothing, then settled himself beside her on the bed. He kissed her again, deeply, passionately, his mouth and hands seducing her with an expertise she hadn't known he had. His fingers warmed her, stirred her, blotted all but the pleasure he was creating. *Why hadn't it been this way before?* she thought, feeling a feather-soft touch on her breast, a teasing stroke against the inside of her thigh. *Why hadn't they* done *this before?*

Devon's response increased and so did Michael's. She ran her hands across his shoulders, laced them in the fine brown hair on his chest, then ran her tongue across his nipple. Her mind felt drugged and heavy with passion. The room seemed to recede, leaving only the queen-sized bed and the man whose fingers touched her—everywhere.

All at the same time.

Devon started, disoriented for a moment, then she inwardly smiled. It was crazy what a woman's fantasies conjured. She could almost imagine there were two sets of hands on her body. Four hands touching instead of two. Four hands skimming and teasing, and sliding in and out of her. Four hands moving down her thighs, kneading her buttocks, teasing her nipples. It was crazy, but never had she felt more erotic sensations.

In the eye of her mind, she could almost see the hands moving, and the more she saw them, the more they aroused her. What harm could there be in pretending it was so? Why not enjoy herself, give herself over to the sexual experience?

Instead of fighting the image, she reveled in it. Two men were making love to her, not just one. Two men, one imagined, one real. She let her mind drift, let each touch become separate. And that's when she noticed—or at least imagined she did.

One set of hands was familiar: Michael's practiced movements, doing the same sort of things he always did. Smooth-skinned fingers, manicured nails. But the other hands felt different. Blunt fingers slid into her, callused palms moved down her thighs. Blunt, gentle fingers, loving fingers. Teasing, caring, almost worshiping. Nothing like Michael's. Yet the most sensuous hands she had ever felt.

Michael parted her legs and slid inside her while the hands skimmed over her body. *It's a fantasy,* she told herself. *Enjoy it.* And so she did. She let the hands heighten Michael's penetration. Let them touch places no one had touched before. Let them slide in and out, probing, easing, driving her to frenzy.

"Michael," Devon whispered, close to climax, feeling it build to a degree she had rarely experienced and certainly never with Michael. She started to tremble and waves of pleasure washed over her. The fingers didn't stop their magic, just kept moving and touching, making it sweeter. Michael came, too. With such a pounding urgency, she thought he would never stop.

She clutched him tighter, but it wasn't Michael she saw in the eye of her mind. It was a thick-chested, dark-complected man, rough yet gentle. *A working man, a foreigner,* she thought, but didn't know why. His hands were blunt and callused, thick, beefy hands that could destroy at a whim, but when they touched her, they were the gentlest hands she had ever felt.

He's Portuguese, she thought insanely, my dark passionate lover. It was crazy and she knew it, but as Michael slumped against her, gleaming with perspiration, and the hands said their fleeting good-bye, it didn't seem crazy at all.

"That was incredible," Michael said, almost with reverence.

"Yes." They lay quiet for a while, Devon refusing to let go of her fleeting images. Then Michael rolled from the bed and went in to shower. He always showered afterward, and expected Devon to join him. Devon sighed. She would rather have savored the closeness and stayed where she was, but she gave in as she always did and swung her long legs to the floor.

When they had finished and he opened the bathroom door, they found the light had gone off in the bedroom.

"How did that happen?" he asked, staring into the darkness.

"Probably a loose bulb." She started for the lamp but Michael stopped her.

"Leave it. We don't need it any longer. Go get in bed."

Devon stretched out on the mattress, and Michael switched the bathroom light off. He took two strides into the darkened room—and froze. Devon stopped breathing. *Couldn't* breathe. Could not possibly.

There wasn't a speck of light in the room, not the merest flicker, yet huge swirls of blackness moved in front of her eyes. They seemed to be growing, spreading toward them, surrounding them.

Michael switched the light back on. He looked pale and shaken, and his hand gripped the doorjamb as if he needed something solid to hold him up.

"Michael?" Devon whispered, sure he had felt it, too.

He simply walked toward her, leaving the bathroom light on, stark and white behind him. From her position on the bed, the glare of it hit her full in the face, but the idea of turning it off seemed so abhorrent she never gave it the slightest thought.

Michael merely slid between the sheets and rolled to his side. He didn't mention the light, which still shined brightly, just plumped his pillow and closed his eyes. It took a very long time for his breathing to slow, another forty minutes—by the clock beside the bed—for him to drift into a restless slumber, but at last he was breathing evenly.

Devon wasn't. She had lain in the same position for the past half hour, afraid to turn over, petrified to close her eyes. Something was out there. She knew it as surely as she knew Michael lay sleeping. And if she let it, whatever it was would come after her.

Two

Anxiety, she told herself firmly. It had happened before, though not for some time, and she'd been uptight for the past three days.

This place was supposed to be restful, a haven where she could relax. Instead the house had only increased her tension. It was probably nothing. Just a result of too little sleep, too much strained conversation, too much worrying about her book.

The too-rapid pounding of her heart was a symptom of anxiety. Just like the perspiration on her palms, the tingling sensation in her limbs. Anxiety caused fear—the doctor had told her that. It was common in cases of stress. Her first attack had happened six months after Paul had left her. Their marriage had been a mistake, he had said. He wasn't ready to settle down. He needed time to "find himself," to "get his head on straight." Marriage just "wasn't his thing."

Devon had fallen apart. Marriage to her meant forever. Her parents had been married for thirty-five years. They never understood why he had left her. Devon certainly didn't. And she had loved Paul.

When the symptoms began, she had been certain she was having a nervous breakdown. Thank God for Ernie Townsend, the psychologist she had secretly picked out of the yellow pages, afraid her parents would find out, knowing they believed "shrinks" were for rich people whose only sickness was a need for someone to bore with their problems.

Dr. Townsend had shown her the whys of anxiety—though not that much was known—and how to control it. Devon was so determined to put it behind her that it hadn't taken long. Afterward, she felt she understood herself better. Still, occasionally the attacks reoccurred, usually after a weekend much like this one, though each one had been milder than the last.

All except this one. The symptoms were the same—the pounding heart and sweating palms, the adrenaline pumping through her veins. They were the age-old symptoms of fear—the body making ready for fight or flight.

But this fear went beyond anything she had suffered before. What she felt in the room was nothing less than stark, all-consuming terror.

Devon closed her eyes and tried to force herself to relax. Immediately her heartbeat increased and she found it difficult to breathe. Thoughts swirled into her mind. Ugly thoughts of death and terror. Images of people, distraught, anguished, of hurting and dread and lung-bursting efforts to breathe. Her eyes flew open. What had she seen? What was it that swirled toward her in the darkness behind her eyelids? What images was she fighting to hold at bay?

This is crazy, she told herself. You don't believe in ghosts. But that was exactly what she found herself thinking. There was something in this room. Some presence that hovered at the edge of the light. Something so sinister, so evil it took her breath away.

Devon rolled to her side, but she didn't close her eyes. Couldn't force them to close, though she wanted to desperately. Every minute in the room seemed to grow longer and heavier. Michael tossed and turned beside her. She had rarely seen him so restless. Did he sense it, too?

If it hadn't been so late, she would have awakened him—begged him to take her out of this room, out of this house. He would laugh at her, tell her it was just her imagination—wouldn't he? She wasn't so sure.

She glanced at the tiny red neon numbers on the clock beside the bed. Two o'clock. It seemed as if she'd been lying there for six or seven hours. How would she make it till dawn? Maybe if she closed the bathroom door a little, the light wouldn't be quite so bright and she could fall asleep.

Forcing her limbs to function, she got up from the bed, padded silently toward the light, and pulled the door halfway shut. Even that much darkness sent her heart slamming hard against her ribs.

"Anxiety," she repeated, climbing back into bed. But the longer she lay awake—the longer she felt this awareness, this sense that something was wrong—the more certain she became that it just wasn't so.

Devon took several long deep breaths and tried to slow her pounding heart. God, she needed some sleep. By three o'clock her eyes felt so heavy she could barely keep them open. When they finally drifted closed, she jolted awake with such a shot of fear she nearly screamed. Her palms were damp with perspiration and her stomach churned with menace.

There was nothing abstract about this terror. It had weight and substance; she could feel it with every nerve ending in her body. Something sordid and deadly, that would hurt her if she let it, maybe even hurt Michael. It wasn't her imagination. It was real.

Four o'clock. Devon's back ached from the tension she

felt in her limbs; her neck and shoulders were stiff and sore. She wanted to sleep—dear God, how she wanted to sleep. Her eyelids felt swollen and heavy, urging her to close them. Her pulse had returned to normal; the rain sounded soothing. If only she could get some rest . . .

Something stood at the foot of the bed—Devon was dreaming, she was sure. She had finally fallen asleep and now she couldn't open her heavy-lidded eyes. The room seemed dimmer than she remembered, the bathroom door stood open just the slightest crack.

The vision in her dreams drifted toward her, gliding effortlessly—a woman in a long full dress the color of the darkness. She was old and gray-haired, though Devon wasn't quite sure how she knew. The image was dim and wavering. The woman turned in Devon's direction, leather-faced, yet not really frightening. Devon searched her features but couldn't quite see them. Just one dark eye that watched her.

Where the other eye should have been there was nothing but an empty black hole.

Devon bolted upright, a scream lodged tight in her throat. Her heart thumped painfully, and her body glistened with sweat. Even the sheets felt damp. She glanced at the bathroom door. Just as in her dream—if indeed it had been one—it sat open only a crack. With her body still throbbing with the remnants of fear, Devon sagged back against the pillow, exhausted from lack of sleep and desperately wishing this terrible night would end.

She looked at the red neon numbers, which had begun to look as ominous as everything else in the room. Five o'clock. It would be daylight soon. Michael lay beside her, the covers bunched well below his hips, his hair mussed, his arms akimbo. He'd been nearly as restless as she had been still.

Michael must have felt her eyes on him, for he woke with a start. Running a hand over his face, he rubbed his reddened, sleep-weary eyes, tossed back the covers, and made his way to the bathroom. When he returned, he left the light on but partially closed the door, leaving only the crack of light that had been there before.

"Having trouble sleeping?" he asked.

"Yes," she said bluntly. "I'll be glad when it's morning."

Michael just grunted. Rolling away from her, he punched his pillow and eventually his breathing became deep and regular, though he still tossed and turned. Devon kept thinking of the woman in her nightmare—or whatever it had been. The frightening image hovered at the edge of her mind, yet somehow the old woman seemed more curious than sinister. If indeed she *had* been more than a dream. She wasn't infusing the atmosphere with evil. That presence still lingered in the darkness just a few feet away.

And Devon wanted to know what it was.

With grim determination, she closed her eyes and forced them to remain closed. The images were back, swirling and taunting, threatening something too sinister to name. She let them come closer, though her fingers gripped the sheet at her side and twisted it into a hard, tight ball.

Who are you? she asked into the silence of her mind and the blackness around her. *What are you?*

But no answer came, just this rolling, suffocating weight that settled on her chest and threatened to crush her.

Devon took a steadying breath and whispered the comforting words she had learned as a child. "The Lord is my Shepherd; I shall not want. He maketh me lie down in green pastures; He leadeth me beside the still waters. He restoreth my soul; He leadeth me in the paths of righteousness for His name's sake. Yea, though I walk through the valley of the shadow of death, I shall fear no evil, for Thou art with me."

The words eased the tightness in her chest, and the images and her fear slowly receded. Only a vague uneasiness remained, along with the hazy impressions she had gathered. When she opened her eyes, a faint gray light lit the windows. Dawn at last had arrived. With weary gratitude, Devon's eyelids slid closed and she drifted into a fitful sleep.

Several hours later, feeling dull and exhausted, heavy-lidded and drained, Devon forced herself to get up. Already awake, Michael swung his feet to the floor and walked toward the bathroom. She noticed the door was tightly closed.

"I hope to God the food in this place is better than the accommodations," Michael said, turning the knob and shoving it open. His light brown hair, usually as neat in the morning as when he went to bed, looked matted and dark with perspiration from his night of restless sleep, and his face appeared puffy and gray.

Devon knew she looked even worse. "So do I." She brushed tangled strands of pale blond hair from her face and forced herself to stand up. Padding naked across the floor, she picked up the clothes strewn carelessly about the room—very unusual for Michael—and walked over to the closet. The musty smell remained, she discovered as she opened the door, but not nearly as strong as it had been the night before.

Resting her palm against the jamb, she reached for a hanger, but her hand groped unsuccessfully into the darkened interior. Unconsciously her eyes closed and her fingers tightened on the hundred-year-old wood. Like watching a motion picture behind her eyes, images flashed through her mind. Devon's hand began to tremble and she clutched the doorframe tighter. *Dear God, this can't be happening!* But every nerve cell in her body said it was.

The images she had seen last night reappeared, their impressions even stronger. How could she *see* all of that? How could she *know?* She only felt certain that she did.

It took an effort of will to pull her hand away. When she succeeded, she felt light-headed and her fingers trembled as they had the night before. As she battled her thoughts, Devon remembered something she had read by Sir Arthur Conan Doyle, a man who believed strongly in the supernatural: "There is a difference between knowing something and *knowing* something." For the first time in her life, Devon understood exactly what he meant.

She glanced at the closet. Whoever had lived in the house had opened this door more than once, and it had never been painted. The varnish that covered the narrow strips of wainscoting were yellowed with age, but whatever impressions had been made in the deep reddish grains must have remained—assuming such things could happen.

She couldn't remember where she had read about such occurrences, impressions from the past left by the energies of people long dead—impressions that hadn't been disturbed, sometimes for centuries. Psycho-something-or-other was as close as she could recall.

Like a lot of people, Devon found the paranormal fascinating—yet at the same time it repelled her. And scared her.

She counted herself among the vast number of people who'd had a few unsettling experiences they couldn't explain, but up until now hadn't really considered them supernatural. She had read only as much as the average person—newspaper stories that jumped out at her, magazine articles that often seemed fairly well documented. She wasn't sure she believed any of it—and it always made her uneasy—still, she tried to keep an open mind.

Devon sank down in the chair and worked to sort through her impressions—those she had gathered just now, and those she had stored throughout the long, exhausting hours of the night.

She hadn't wanted to believe the terrifying thoughts that had swirled through her head. All night she had tried to think of a rational explanation. Now she was convinced that the images she had perceived were real. If only they weren't in such a jumble.

Michael opened the bathroom door. "You ready to get in here?"

Devon nodded and walked across the room.

The shower felt soothing. It eased the kinks from her neck and shoulders, soothed her aching bones and restored her mind to some semblance of order. Wildly, insanely, she knew what had happened in this house, in this room. Or at least thought she did. The presence—or whatever it was—had been real. She corrected herself. Not just one, if her theory proved true, more than one presence. How many exactly she didn't know.

Devon dried her hair and applied her makeup, using a little more foundation than usual to cover the dark gray smudges beneath her green eyes, the hollowness in her cheeks below her high cheekbones. Her blond hair shined and curled nicely, but it pointed up the waxy color of her skin, making her look wan and pale and exhausted.

Feeling a sudden burst of temper, Devon snapped her compact closed with a little too much force. She was angry, furious, in fact. And why the devil shouldn't she be? She'd been up all night, kept awake by God-only-knew-what. Her romantic evening had turned into a nightmare. The thought made her madder. Damn these people! She could bet they knew what went on in this room—in this whole damned house! Yet they let people come here—encouraged them to come. It was inexcusable. Obscene!

She stalked into the bedroom and found Michael watching her curiously.

"Are you all right?" he asked.

"No," she snapped. "I'm not all right." At his look of surprise, some of her anger fled. She wasn't mad at Michael. "I'm sorry. This certainly isn't your fault. I'm just tired, I guess." *To say the least.* "I didn't sleep at all last night."

"I'll be glad when we're out of here."

Devon couldn't have agreed more. Watching him pack, folding each item carefully then neatly putting it away, she thought again about the agonizing night she had suffered. While Michael rolled up his ties and settled them in an orderly fashion next to his shoes, she dressed in a pair of black wool slacks and pulled on a bright yellow sweater. When she glanced in the mirror, catching her reflection against the paler hue of the walls, she almost took it off.

She would never feel the same about yellow again.

Devon turned to Michael. The decision she had been pondering all morning had at last been made. "There's something I want to tell you, Michael. Something I wouldn't have mentioned if it had happened a few days ago."

Michael fastened the shiny brass locks on his suitcase. "You haven't changed your mind about the date of the wedding? The more I think about it, April fifteenth is perfect. The weather should be nice. We could honeymoon in the

Bahamas"—his brows drew together—"unless of course you're worried about finishing your book." He resented her writing, somehow felt threatened by it. And the hours involved took too much of her time away from him, he believed.

"It's nothing like that, it's . . ." She walked over to the window, wishing she could see more of the ocean that shimmered grayly in the distance between two old houses that probably hadn't been there when the Staffords had lived in the mansion. It still looked dull and cloudy outside, but the rain had stopped and the sun occasionally broke through the overcast.

For the first time, she noticed at the base of the outside stairs, a rose garden, bare and thorny, the stalks of each bush thick and gnarled with age. She wondered who had planted it, who cared for it now.

"Something happened to me last night, Michael," she finally said, turning to face him. "Something I can't explain, but I believe it's the truth and I want you to hear it."

Michael eyed her curiously. "Go on."

"Once or twice since I started writing and a couple of times after my divorce . . . odd things have happened to me . . . unexplainable things." She looked at him and saw his discomfort, but decided to plunge ahead. If they were going to be married, she should be able to talk to him. "I never really paid much attention before, just chalked it up to coincidence, but now I . . . What I'm trying to say, Michael, is that I think something terrible happened in this house."

"Last night?"

"No. A long time ago. I want to tell you what I believe it was, and then I'm going to find out if it's true."

Michael just looked at her.

"There was a child who died here. A little girl, I think, no more than four or five years old. I could see the image so clearly. Long black hair, one of those old-fashioned dresses that came to the middle of her calves, high-button shoes. The clothes were definitely old. Maybe the late eighteen-hundreds."

Michael said nothing. She took it as a good sign.

"I think the child did something bad. Not really terrible, just something her parents didn't approve of. They punished her—no," she corrected, sensing that was wrong, "the father punished her. He was a very strict disciplinarian. Too strict. I think he locked the child up—maybe in that closet." She pointed across the room to the door she had carefully closed. "I think the little girl suffocated." Devon felt a catch in her throat as she said the last word.

"That's crazy," Michael said.

"I know. This whole thing is crazy, but I still think it's true."

"I'll admit I don't like the place. I'll even admit I felt something . . . something . . ."

"Evil?" she supplied.

"Well, I . . ." Michael sighed and raked a hand through his light brown hair. "I couldn't say what it was; I just didn't like it."

"Everything was so jumbled," Devon said. "I felt someone's presence . . . or dreamed it, I'm not sure. An old woman. I think she may have lived here when she was younger. Something bad may have happened to her, too."

"Come on, Devon, surely two people couldn't have been murdered here."

"Not murdered. Definitely not murdered. Maybe . . ." She looked at Michael, caught his frown, and decided she had told him enough already. She turned to face him more squarely. "By the way, did you close the bathroom door last night?"

"You were awake when I got up. I closed it part way."

"It was closed when we got up."

"Well, I didn't close it."

"That's what I thought."

"What are you talking about, Devon? Are you trying to tell me you think this place is . . . haunted?"

She could dodge the issue, call it something he might be more willing to accept. "Yes."

"I don't believe in ghosts and I'm surprised you do."

"I hadn't really decided one way or another until last night. Now I'm convinced."

"Well, I'm not, and I hope to hell you don't expect to tell this crazy story to anyone else."

"I intend to write it all down. In fact, I'm going to do that before we leave this room. Then whatever I find out will either confirm or deny what I've written. If I'm wrong you can laugh about it for the next twenty years. If I'm right . . ."

"I don't like this, Devon."

"It won't take more than fifteen minutes."

Michael seemed disgruntled, but didn't press the issue. "I'll take the bags down."

"I'll bring mine down as soon as I've finished. I'll meet you in the foyer."

Michael shoved the door closed with his foot, descended the two flights of stairs, crossed the foyer, and continued toward the front door.

"Will you and your wife be joining us for breakfast, Mr. Galveston?" It was Ada Meeks, hands resting on a pair of wide hips.

Michael started to say no, that they were more than ready

to shake this place, but the aroma of fresh-baked bread drifted toward him and his stomach growled. He could probably eat and be finished by the time Devon got done with her crazy note-taking, or if she came down sooner, she could join him. They might as well fill their bellies.

"I'll be in to eat just as soon as I load my bags. I'm not sure about my wife." *Wife,* he repeated inwardly at the graying woman's nod. Devon wasn't Mrs. Michael Galveston yet, but she soon would be.

He shook his head at the thought of her latest tomfoolery. Trust Devon James to attract a roomful of ghosts!

If he hadn't been so out of sorts, he might have smiled. Devon had always been off-beat, a bit different from everyone else. It was one of the things that had attracted him to her in the first place.

It was one of the things he most wished he could change.

Even the night they had met had been out of the ordinary. He had gone to a party on the West Side with Bill Medders, one of his friends. The small apartment was filled to the rafters with every sort of weirdo from old hippies to heavy-metal artists. Not exactly Michael's usual style, but Bill was sleeping with the girl who lived in the apartment, Christy Papaopolis, and Michael had nothing better to do that night.

He'd been standing near the front door, talking to Christy and Bill, when Devon walked in. He would never forget that moment. The breath he'd just taken suddenly stuck in his lungs, and even after they'd been introduced, he had trouble remembering what he was about to say.

She was wearing an expensive silk blouse that matched a sleek blue leather mini that bared her long shapely legs well above the knee. Devon had extended her lovely long-fingered hand and smiled at him almost shyly. With her silky blond hair and peaches-and-cream complexion, she was gorgeous, but that hadn't been the attraction. It was the lost look, the near desolation, that Michael had seen in her pretty green eyes.

Knowing Christy, he would have expected Devon to have been an easy lay. Instead, she refused him three times before she even agreed to a date.

"I've just been through a divorce," she told him on the third attempt. "I'm not ready for another relationship."

"It's just a date, Devon. Coffee and a movie. That's not too heavy, is it?"

They'd had a good time, which seemed to surprise her. She agreed to see him again, and on the second date he took her to dinner, a quaint little French restaurant he knew on the Upper East Side—not really his favorite, but he figured she'd like it. Eventually he won her trust, and they started going out often. Even then, it had taken him three long months to seduce her.

He thought about last night and felt himself harden. God, she could be a pistol. Last night proved that. They had never had sex like that before.

Not even in the beginning. Though Devon never suspected, for a while he'd continued to date other women. But little by little it became apparent that no one else could come close to her. And it wasn't just her looks. Devon had a warm, caring nature, and she was far more generous than most of the women he had known.

True, she was a little too sensitive to suit him, a little too intelligent, a little too perceptive, but she listened to what he had to say—really listened—and she really seemed to care.

Devon had her faults, all right, everyone did. After what she'd been through with her ex-husband—the late-night carousing, the booze, and the women—she lacked self-confidence, but in a way that suited him just fine. She rarely argued with him and usually gave in to his wishes.

He thought of her now, up in that bedroom, writing down her crazy notes. As soon as he got her in the car, he'd tell her what she could do with them, and she had better listen.

Ghosts. Shades of Devon's friend Christy, head guru to the local weirdos anonymous.

True, the house had been eerie, more ghoulish than any place he had ever been. So what? That didn't mean someone had died in there. It didn't mean the house was full of spooks!

Michael tossed his leather bags into the trunk, closed the lid, and headed back to the mansion. *Bed and breakfast,* he corrected. Give him a nice clean Hilton every time.

Walking back up the steps, he opened the massive front door, almost surprised to find it unlocked. His stomach growled as he walked into the dining room. Granola or whatever, it smelled delicious. He hoped like hell it would improve his dismal mood.

He hoped like hell his coming confrontation with Devon would go as smoothly as he planned.

Three

Devon found Michael sitting at the long mahogany table in the dining room. All the chairs were filled with guests except the one next to him. Ada Meeks sat at the head of the table, wearing her usual bland expression, and at the sight of her, Devon's temper soared all over again. How many other people had experienced the kind of night she had? How could the woman let it go on?

"I decided I was hungry," Michael said, explaining his slight detour from their scheduled departure while he stood and pulled out her chair. "The food smelled so good I thought we'd go ahead and eat before we left."

Devon glanced at the table. Homemade raisin granola muffins, hot oatmeal, and real peach jam, just like the brochure had promised.

"That sounds like a good idea." She didn't add that she wasn't about to leave until Ada Meeks answered some of her questions.

Devon sat down and took a sip of the fresh-squeezed orange juice sitting beside her old-fashioned flowered plate. Around the table, silverware clattered and clanked, but no one said a word. Devon glanced across at the others. Eight people sat at the breakfast table, eating their food like robots. None of them looked particularly rested.

"Everybody get a good night's sleep?" she asked with a hint of sarcasm she hadn't intended.

Not one of the other guests—a man in a polyester leisure suit and his too-plump wife, a young Oriental couple, and a dark-suited businessman—looked up to answer. Michael nudged her leg in silent warning.

"Good morning, Mrs. Meeks." Devon flashed a smile she didn't mean. A voice inside her warned that she had better make this look good if she wanted any help from the dour-faced woman who ran the place.

"Good morning," Mrs. Meeks said.

Devon surveyed the room. "Such a beautiful old house. How long have you lived here?"

"My husband Edgar and I came here almost five years ago. It was pretty run-down, but we fell in love with it the moment we saw it."

"You've done wonders with it. Could you tell us a little of its history?"

For the first time Ada Meeks warmed. "House was built in 1899 by a man named Florian Stafford. The Stafford family—they were Stafford Shipbuilding then—practically owned the town. Built huge ships right down on the shore. Employed most of the people hereabouts—still do, in one way or another. Mr. Stafford and his brother William were both sea captains."

"I presume he was married," Devon said casually.

"Mary Louise Bennington, she was his wife."

"Any children?"

"No. They were childless the whole time they lived here."

Michael nudged her under the table, and Devon fought a rush of embarrassment. Anxiety after all.

"Well, actually they did have one child," Mrs. Meeks

amended. "It died when it was little. No one knew much about it."

Devon nudged Michael, whose hand had stilled on the spoon midway to his mouth.

"Was it a girl or a boy?" Devon asked.

"Little boy named Bernard."

Michael nudged Devon and finished his bite of oatmeal. Devon leaned back in her chair, torn between disappointment and relief. Then she felt Michael's breath beside her ear.

"You know," he said, "in the eighteen-hundreds, little boys and little girls both wore long hair and dresses."

If a knife had struck her in the ribs, the jolt could not have been more fierce. Dear God, it was possible. The picture came to her again. Doll-like, but not exactly feminine. Little Bernard Stafford. There was a rightness to it. Yes, the child could indeed have been a boy.

"Kind of an interesting story," Mrs. Meeks was saying. Michael looked as though he wished he'd kept his mouth shut. "Captain Stafford was grief-stricken somethin' awful when that little boy died. Poor Mary couldn't console him no matter how hard she tried. 'Course they weren't living here when it happened."

Devon sagged again, and Michael looked relieved.

"They were livin' down the street in the old original Stafford mansion. This was a churchyard then."

"A churchyard?" Devon repeated.

Ada Meeks nodded and swallowed the bite of muffin she'd been chewing. "The boy was buried here."

"What do you mean *here?*" Michael asked, setting his cereal spoon aside.

"I mean right here. Captain Stafford bought the whole darned block a few years after it happened. Built his house on top of the little boy's grave. When we started to remodel, we found Bernie's tombstone down in the basement. Strange what people will do in their grief."

Devon gripped the edge of the table, fighting the chills that stole along her arms and down her spine.

"Are you telling me," Michael said, "that this place is built over a cemetery?"

Something flickered in Ada Meeks's eyes. Any warmth that had been there fled. "I don't know much about it. If you'll all excuse me, I've got a couple of things left to do." Shoving back her chair, she hauled herself up and walked out the door into the foyer.

Devon waited a moment then followed her out. Michael stared after her as if she had lost her mind.

Part of her wondered if indeed she might have.

Devon found Mrs. Meeks standing in the foyer beside the guest book, which lay open on a small marble-topped table. She glanced up at Devon's approach.

"You finished with your breakfast already?" Mrs. Meeks asked.

"It was delicious, but I never eat breakfast, so I wasn't very hungry." Only part of that was true—she didn't usually eat breakfast, but after her sleepless night she was starving. "We really enjoyed our stay, Mrs. Meeks." Another bald-faced lie. She'd never been good at it, but these lies stemmed from a sense of desperation. "The house is quite lovely."

Mrs. Meeks beamed. "It's furnished just as it was when the Staffords lived here. So far as it goes, that is. A lot of the pieces are still missing. Funny thing about that—" She wiped her hands on her calico apron, a habit Devon had noticed. "Why, just the other day, I went to a yard sale down the block. Wasn't really there to buy anything, just sort of gawking, I guess. See that lamp over there in the corner?"

She pointed to the red-fringed brass floor lamp Devon had seen in the main salon. "Saw it sittin' there on the grass beside a stack of old phonograph records. Just had to have it. When I got it home, one of the neighbors—old Mrs. Davis—she's ninety-two—said it was the Staffords' favorite lamp. She said I'd put it right where it was when they used to live here. Fact, she said most of the furniture was exactly where it was before."

Goosebumps snaked down Devon's spine. "I see." It was all she could manage.

"We've even got the same kind of dog," Ada added as a long-bodied, sleek brown Dachshund waddled up near Devon's low-heeled black shoes. "A dash hound, or whatever they call them. I guess little Bernard used to have one just like him. Though somebody said the boy didn't treat him too well."

Bernard kicked the dog, Devon thought with a dizzy, off-balance, slightly surreal sensation, *and his father punished him by locking him up in the closet.* Down at her feet, the dog grumbled, almost as if he agreed. Devon's hands began to tremble as she looked again at Mrs. Meeks. How could she possibly know that? Did something in the house want her to know? And if it did, why had it chosen her?

"How would Mrs. Davis know a thing like that?" Devon asked. "If the house was built in 1899 and Bernard was already dead . . . ?" She let her words trail off and picked up the pen beside the guest book—anything to steady her shaking fingers. She wrote her name, but when she reached the part that asked for her address, she hesitated, then penned just three words, *New York City.* It was crazy, but she didn't want whatever existed in the house to know where she lived.

"People in this town been here for generations," Mrs. Meeks told her. "They haven't got a lot better to do than repeat a little gossip, even if it's a hundred years old."

"Have there been any unusual . . . occurrences . . . reported in the house?"

Mrs. Meeks gray-brown brow shot up, her look turning wary. "What kind of occurrences?"

You know very well what kind, Devon thought, fighting her temper again. There was something furtive in the woman's manner that made her more certain than ever that Ada Meeks knew about the presence in the house, or at least had her suspicions. "I'm talking about objects moving, apparitions, that sort of thing."

"You're not a newspaper reporter, are you?"

"No, just curious. Last night—"

"What did you see?" Mrs. Meeks cut in a little too quickly.

"I don't know that I saw anything. I just sort of felt it."

Ada shrugged her plump shoulders and glanced evasively away. "Once a lady said she saw an old woman in a rocking chair."

Devon's heart speeded. "An old woman?"

Mrs. Meeks nodded. "Lady thought it might be Annie Stafford—she was Cap'n Stafford's niece. Her mama died in childbirth, so when her father's ship went down, the girl moved in here with Mary and Florian, her aunt and uncle."

"How old was she?"

"Thirteen." Ada shook her head. "That caused quite a stir, I'll tell you. Rumor was Cap'n Stafford treated her no better than a servant."

And the servants' quarters were up on the third floor. "Annie slept in the yellow room." It wasn't a question.

"So they say. Lived here most of her life. Moved out for a while, but after Florian and Mary died, the house became hers and she moved back in."

Devon thought of the note pad in her suitcase sitting on the floor in the dining room, the words she had inscribed on the paper almost as if someone had guided her hand. Words about a lonely young girl who had also suffered in this house.

"Annie lived with them," Devon repeated, "but the captain and Mary never had children of their own—after Bernard, I mean."

"There wasn't much chance that happening. They slept in separate rooms on the second floor, if you catch my drift."

She caught it all right. "Is that Captain Stafford's picture?" Slightly faded, black and white oval portraits in polished mahogany frames hung on the wall above the guest book.

"That's Florian and Mary. He was a handsome man, can't ya see? All the Stafford men got those dark good looks. Mary was real quiet spoken, but Florian was a powerful, imposing kind of man. Most of the town was afraid of him."

I'm beginning to understand why. She looked again at the picture, at the smooth black brows and dominant cheekbones, at the intense black eyes, narrowed just enough to give the impression of disapproval. Cold, assessing eyes and yet the face remained compelling in a way she couldn't explain.

"How old was Florian when his son died?"

"Late twenties."

"And when Annie came to live here?"

"Late forties, I think. It was nearly twenty years later that his brother died."

A strong, imposing man reaching midlife who hadn't had sex in years. And a vulnerable young girl under his total control. The hurriedly scrawled words in her notebook read, *He hurt her.* Later Devon had written, *She hated him.*

"Is that Annie?" Devon pointed to a smaller portrait a few inches below the larger ones.

"That's her. Pretty little thing, wasn't she?" With her blond hair piled into saucy little curls on the top of her head, a softly curving smile, and warm dark eyes, Annie Stafford was indeed a lovely young girl. "Lots of folks remember Annie, though she was pretty much of a recluse."

"That's her, too." Devon pointed to a second small picture, this one far different from the first. Even the faded lines of the photograph couldn't disguise the tight, drawn look of Annie's features—nor the hesitant, guarded vagueness in her eyes that hadn't been there before.

"That was taken five years later," Ada said.

"Who owns the house now?" Devon asked.

"Jonathan Stafford. Great-great-grandson of Sheridan Stafford, Florian's uncle. He's the only Stafford still in the boat-building business. Since neither William nor Florian had children, most of the family wealth wound up with him."

Why did that name sound so familiar? "What else can you tell me?"

Mrs. Meeks's look turned guarded at Devon's too-probing tone. "Why you askin' all these questions?"

"I told you I was curious. That's all there is to it."

"I gotta go."

"One last thing," Devon pressed. "Did anyone ever mention anything about the closet in the yellow room? It has an odd, sort of musty smell. I got the feeling something might have happened in there."

"Nobody's said anythin' about the closet in the room you slept in. Sometime back a man and his wife who slept in the green room beside it said they couldn't sleep till they closed the closet door. Lady said something about a box. Said she kept seein' it in her dreams, over and over. It's all a bunch a hogwash, you ask me. Just gets people all stirred up about nothin'."

"A box?" Devon repeated, rolling the word around on her tongue. *Not a box, a trunk. A big old-fashioned steamer trunk with a dark green paisley lining.*

"That's what she said."

"But not in the yellow room, the room next door?"

"In the closet in the room next door," Mrs. Meeks corrected. "Course that closet goes through to both rooms—at least it did until we walled it off."

Devon swayed on her feet and steadied herself with a hand on the marble-topped table. "I see."

"Listen, Mrs. Galveston—"

"My name is James. Devon James." Why it seemed important she didn't know. She only knew she wasn't married to Michael yet, and until she was it was time she stood on her own.

"Well, *Miss James,* I hope you aren't plannin' to cause any trouble. We don't need any bad publicity like we got before."

"When was that?" Devon asked in surprise, which put an abrupt end to the conversation.

Mrs. Meeks puffed up like an overprotective mother hen. "I'm through answering your damnable questions. I think you and your friend had best be on your way." Looking more hostile than ever, Ada Meeks turned and trudged off, leaving Devon staring after her.

When Michael walked up and silently touched her arm, Devon jumped three inches.

"God, you scared me." Her hand came up to her breast as if it could calm her racing heart.

"Sorry." But he didn't really look concerned.

"I'm ready to leave if you are," she told him. "The sooner we get out of this place, the better I'll like it."

Several other guests beat them to it, looking just as relieved to escape the house as she no doubt did. She wondered if any of their nights had been half as bad as hers.

Michael picked up the bag she had left in the dining room, took her arm and led her across the foyer. Their footsteps rang on the battered parquet floors. Outside on the porch, Devon paused on the steps to look back at the house. She thought of the children and what might have happened to them—what she *believed* had happened to them. An ache rose up in her throat, and with a jolt of surprise, she realized that part of her wanted to stay. She felt it like a yearning, like desperate fingers grasping her and begging her to remain.

Turning away, she felt as if she were abandoning a loved one. But she forced her feet to move down the steps and along the narrow walk toward the car where Michael stood waiting.

With one last glance at the mansion, her eyes moved up to the small dormer windows in the third-floor attic bedroom. Windows into a past she could only imagine. When she did, she felt the same unwanted tightening in her chest, the same awful pounding of her heart she had felt the night before. Today the feeling swelled with an incredible sadness, and even a mist of tears.

She looked again at the window. For a fleeting instant she thought she glimpsed a figure, then realized it was only the shadow of a branch against the panes.

There was so much she didn't know, so much she would have to find out. Part of her demanded she discover the truth.

Part of her wanted to walk away from the house and never look back.

Jonathan Barrett Stafford took the manila folder he'd been reading, and set it on top of the pile that sat on the corner of his huge teakwood desk.

"I told you I didn't want to be disturbed," he told Allison Whitman, the girl filling in for his personal secretary, Delia Wills, off with a bout of the flu. It was only nine o'clock, but God, he missed her already.

"I'm sorry, sir. It's a Mrs. Meeks calling from Connecticut. She says it's imperative she speak to you at once."

Jonathan sighed. "All right, go ahead and put the call through." With more than a little impatience, he punched the speaker button on his ivory telephone, almost as indispensable as Dee. With a clock and a calculator, the phone had a memory list of a hundred commonly called numbers, a redial feature, a recorder, and a radio. He hadn't bought the model with the miniature TV screen. Jonathan never watched TV.

"What is it, Mrs. Meeks?" He spoke into the speaker and didn't try to hide his annoyance. He faced a ten-hour day and a full schedule of meetings tomorrow.

"It's that James woman, Mr. Stafford. She's been snoopin' around town again, askin' questions all over the place. She's gonna make trouble, I can feel it. You gotta put a stop to her, and the sooner the better."

Jonathan picked up the phone, his fingers gripping the receiver a little tighter than he meant to. "She hasn't been out to see Aunt Stell, has she?"

"Not that I know of. But she's bound to find out sooner or later."

"You shouldn't have talked to her in the first place. I've warned you about that before." He could almost hear Ada's pique on the telephone. She was a crotchety old woman, considering she wasn't really all that old.

"Damnable girl had a way about her. Seemed so nice and friendly. How was I to know she'd be like all the rest?"

"Next time keep your mouth shut and we won't have the problem."

"That's a laugh," Ada grumbled. "You've been tryin' to keep things quiet for years. Just keeps flarin' up. Damned bad for business, that's for sure."

"You just see that she doesn't get back inside the house," Jonathan warned. "I'll take care of the rest of it." *And personally see to Miss James.*

"Whatever you say." Ada rang off without a good-bye and Jonathan did the same.

The woman wasn't one of his favorite people, but she loved the old family mansion, had rescued it from ruin and done wonders with the place. Since the original Stafford estate was little more than a burned-out shell, the house on Church Street remained the scant legacy of the past the Stafford family had left. Jonathan intended to protect it as he should have done long ago.

And no one was going to dredge up those ridiculous stories that had sprung to life three years ago—nor drag his family name through the mud again.

* * *

Michael Galveston stepped out of the dented yellow taxi in front of Devon's brownstone apartment on East Seventy-eighth between Lexington and Third. Though the building was old, it had been renovated to perfect condition. Graceful stone pillars shadowed the entrance and big granite lions guarded the stairs as he approached.

Michael preferred glass and chrome to stone and wood. Once he and Devon were married, she'd be living in his high-rise condominium—no furnace problems, plumbing you could count on—it wouldn't take a smart girl like Devon long to get used to the advantages of an ultramodern apartment. Michael smiled at the thought.

He pressed the intercom button, and Devon's warm voice answered.

"It's me," he said flatly. He had come here on a no-nonsense mission; he intended to set the tone right from the start.

Devon buzzed him in, and he walked through the lobby, ignoring the flames in the hearth of the marble-manteled fireplace, the cherrywood paneling and elegant tapestry-upholstered sofa and chairs. Black leather and smoked glass—that's what a man needed—clean and simple, no muss no frills. Michael took the elevator up to the second floor. The damned old mahogany antique was slow. It would have been faster to take the stairs. The brass and etched glass elevator door slid open. He crossed the hall to Devon's apartment. She opened the door before he knocked.

"Hello, Michael."

"Devon." He bussed her cheek with a dutiful kiss. "I've missed you." They hadn't seen each other since the fight they'd had in the car on their way back from Stafford. He still couldn't believe Devon intended to go through with her incredible plan.

"Would you like a drink?" She closed the door behind him.

"Scotch and soda. Make it a double." While Devon walked to the antique walnut sideboard she'd converted to a bar, Michael threw off his muffler, unbuttoned his coat and tossed it off. He accepted the leaded crystal tumbler she handed him; the ice cubes clinking expensive notes against the glass as he walked over to the burgundy overstuffed sofa. The room was an eclectic mixture of old and comfortable new. It had a definite designer's touch—just the right blend of colors, a perfectly placed contemporary art piece here and there, several wonderful old paintings. But Devon had done it herself.

She sat down on the sofa, and Michael sat in the chair across from her. He wanted to have a serious conversation, and he didn't want Devon's feminine appeal distracting him. He glanced in her direction. Tonight she wore a loose-fitting bright red caftan that covered her long shapely legs all the way to her slender ankles. Heavy wooden earrings dangled from delicate ears that framed a face Michelangelo would have loved.

No wonder the VPs' old-biddy wives always treated her so coldly. Jealous, that's what they were. The execs were green with envy just to know he'd been in her bed. He'd definitely move up a notch in their eyes when he married her.

Michael leaned forward in his chair. "You aren't going to like what I have to say, Devon, but it just can't be helped."

Devon set the glass of white wine she'd been sipping down on the delicate Queen Anne table in front of the sofa.

"Oh?" She arched a fine blond eyebrow, a look Michael recognized as one of irritation. He'd expected as much; she'd just have to get over it. "And what, exactly, is that?"

"I've come to lay down the law, Devon. You're going to stop all this foolishness about haunted houses and you're going to stop now. Neither of our careers can stand the ridicule if this leaks out—and it's bound to, sooner or later."

"Maybe *your* career can't stand it—I'm a writer, I'm supposed to write about intriguing events."

"That doesn't include haunted houses."

"Why not?"

"Because it's a bunch of bull, that's why. Because people will think you're crazy."

"I don't care what people think. I'm writing this story, Michael. I'm going to find out what happened in that house, and I'm going to tell people about it."

"Why, dammit? Why is it so damned important?"

"Because I have to know if . . ."

"If what?" he pressed, knowing exactly what she was thinking. "If you're having another breakdown? If you were seeing things up in that room that weren't really there?"

"I never had a breakdown. I had anxiety. There's a world of difference and you know it."

He knew it, all right, but Devon wasn't really all that sure. He knew she worried that one day all the pressure she worked under might send her over the edge. In truth, it worried him, too.

"Call it whatever you like. You've been acting crazy since the moment we left that house. Working twelve hours a day, writing letters, calling people. Your father says you've made two trips up to Stafford in the last two weeks. He's worried about you, and he doesn't even know about *little Bernard.*

You're obsessed with this insane ghost story, and you're letting it ruin our relationship."

"If something like this can destroy it, maybe there wasn't much to it in the first place."

"You can't mean that."

"I do mean it."

She did, he could see it in the set of her slender shoulders, the way she looked him in the eye. He wanted to call back his words.

Then he thought of his years with Darnex Management, the nights he had worked late, the hours he'd spent on the weekends when everyone else had gone to the shore, the company parties he'd attended when he felt so tired he could drop. All that would very likely go by the wayside if the bosses found out his soon-to-be wife believed in *ghosts*. Damn her, he'd be the laughingstock of the company.

"Listen, Devon, you've got to think this thing through. You know what could happen if you keep this up."

"What do you mean?" She picked up her glass and nervously took a sip.

"I've seen the way this thing has affected you. For the first few days, you couldn't even talk about it without crying."

"Something like this is very traumatic."

"Why don't you admit it, Devon? This is damned hard for you to handle and it's going to get worse."

"No it isn't. Eventually, I'll be able to be more objective."

"And what if you can't?"

"I don't care. I'm going to write this story—no matter how hard it is."

"If you won't think of yourself—or me—think about

your mother and father. What in God's name are they going to say?"

Devon laughed, her voice a little too shrill. "I'm not a child, Michael. When it comes to this, I don't care what they say. For once, I have to be true to myself. I can't just let this go, whether they approve of what I'm doing or not."

"You'll hurt them, Devon. You know how worried they were about you after Paul left. They'll be sure you're having a relapse—and the truth is, you very well might be." It was an unfair tactic and he knew it, but he was feeling a little bit desperate.

"That's what you think, isn't it, Michael? That I imagined all of this? That it was just more of the same sort of thing that happened to me before?"

"It could be, Devon. The doctor told you it could happen again."

"It wasn't anxiety, Michael. Do you honestly believe that everything I told you was just some sort of eerie coincidence?" She set her wineglass down a little too hard and the glass rang loudly on the wooden tabletop. "You've seen my notebook. Those words were written *before* I talked to Mrs. Meeks. Is all that stuff about the young girl a coincidence, too?"

Michael shifted in his chair. "I'll admit it's . . . disconcerting, but there's bound to be a logical explanation. Given enough time, you could probably find it."

"Great. That's exactly what I'm trying to do."

Michael slammed his fist against the arm of his chair and came to his feet. "That is not what you're trying to do! You're trying to do just the opposite. You think that house is haunted and you're bound and determined to prove it."

"I have to."

"Why, for God's sake?" She didn't want to tell him, he

could see by the way she avoided his eyes. "Tell me the truth."

Devon lifted her chin. Wide green eyes locked on his face and her soft lips thinned in determination. "Because Bernard and Annie want me to."

Michael felt the air whoosh from his lungs. He sank back down in his chair. "That is the craziest thing you've said so far."

Looking uncomfortable and defensive, Devon picked up her wineglass, but this time she didn't take a drink. "I knew that's what you'd say, which is exactly why I didn't tell you in the first place."

"I want you to stop this, Devon. Before it goes too far."

"And if I don't?"

How far should he push her? he wondered. But he really had no choice. "If you don't—our engagement is off."

Though she didn't seem surprised, Devon took a sip of her wine, playing for time, perhaps. "That's what I thought you'd say." When she set the glass back down and came to her feet, Michael came to his.

"I had hoped we could talk this out," he said. "Straighten things out between us and put things back to normal."

"I have to do this, Michael. If you can't accept that, there is nothing more to say."

Michael rested his half-finished Scotch on the table beside Devon's wineglass. "I have a good deal of faith in you, Devon. Given a little more time, I'm sure you'll see reason. When that happens, I'll expect you to give me a call."

He started toward the door but Devon stopped him. Looking resigned but definitely upset, she slid off the two-carat solitaire she wore on her third left finger and handed it to him.

Michael shook his head, refusing to accept it. "You'll

come to your senses, Devon. I'm sure of it." He brushed her lips with a kiss. "You know I love you."

She nodded. Tears welled and slipped down her cheeks. "I know."

Michael pulled open the door and stepped into the wood-paneled hallway. Devon watched him until the elevator doors rumbled closed between them. Michael smiled to himself. It hadn't gone quite the way he had planned, but then Devon never had been that predictable. In the end, however, he felt certain she'd do as he asked. It might take a little more persuasion, a little more pressure, but sooner or later, Devon would give in to his demands, just as she always did.

Michael felt better already.

Four

Devon brushed the tears from her cheeks with the back of her hand. She had known Michael would disapprove. She had even known he might break their engagement. Still it hurt to end a relationship that had gone on for almost two years.

She sniffed back another round of wetness. She'd expected to be upset if they parted. What she hadn't expected was to be so profoundly *relieved.*

After all, she loved Michael Galveston. From the moment she'd met him at Christy's party, Michael had been kind to her. He had listened to her when she needed someone to talk to, flattered her as Paul never had, and in a subtle, supportive way, helped her back on her feet. She'd been attracted to his clean-cut good looks and take-charge attitude, at that time needing someone she could lean on.

Devon loved Michael—she just wasn't *in love* with him.

And just as she had feared, all her doubts about marrying him had resurfaced the moment they had returned to the city.

In the days they had been apart, she had gone over their relationship with an objective eye. Her work on the Stafford project—and Michael's outright objections to it—had forced her to examine their compatibility as she never had before. Was Michael what she wanted in a man? Was she the right woman for him? The answers came up a resounding no.

In that same course of time, she thought about what she had experienced that night at the inn. The incident had affected her profoundly, forcing her to think about death for the first time, and about life—all of life—especially her own.

Something had happened to her in Stafford. Good or bad, whatever it was, it gave her a sense of purpose, a shot of determination, and the ability to think more clearly than she had in years. It was important, this work she was doing. Perhaps the most important work she would ever do.

Unfortunately, as Michael had pointed out, it wasn't going to be easy. The experience she'd had in the yellow room had been far more traumatic than she had first thought. If she accepted what had happened as the truth—which she was determined to do—then maybe other things that happened in life weren't just coincidence either. The thought was more than a little disturbing. It was downright frightening.

Devon crossed the living room and sat down at the antique French desk in the corner. She wrote her books using an IBM computer in her office down the hall, but this delicate carved writing desk she used for personal correspondence, paying household bills, and storing miscellaneous legal papers.

Picking up the envelope resting on the dark green leather inset, she opened it and pulled out the letter she had received from Stafford the first week after the incident. It had come from the Town Clerk's office in nearby Groton, since Stafford had become too small to continue keeping records of its own.

For a five-dollar fee, they had given her a copy of a hand

written registration—since actual certificates were not in use at that time—of Bernard Randall Stafford's birth, and a second five dollars bought the same sort of document showing his death a little less than five years later.

The first registration merely confirmed the child's date of birth, April 21, 1893, and stated the names of his mother and father. The second document showed the date of death, May 26, 1897, and listed the cause as scarlet fever.

Another two-hour trip to Stafford to search old newspaper records at the local historical society had turned up nothing more than an obituary notice, and a time and place of burial—the Methodist cemetery located then at 25 Church Street. Devon also planned a trip to the Groton library to search for articles that might mention an outbreak of scarlet fever, or to make a renewed search of the probate records for additional deaths with scarlet fever listed as the cause, since before the advent of penicillin, the disease was often fatal.

In her heart, she didn't believe she would find anything to confirm the certificate.

"The Staffords owned most of the town," Mrs. Meeks had said. Their shipyard had been the main source of income for most of the people who lived there. Even today the Staffords had power and influence. How far would people go to protect the family who controlled their livelihood? Doctoring a few simple records might not seem like a high price to pay.

Devon reread the information on the small white slip of paper. *Bernard Randall Stafford.* She could see the small dark-haired child as clearly as if it stood there. The image made her chest grow tight and it suddenly felt a little hard to breathe. The overwhelming fear she had experienced in the yellow room seemed to lurk at the edges of her mind, surfacing whenever her thoughts swung in that direction. It would take months to complete the work on this project, months of dealing with a subject she had always abhorred.

The delicate cream and gold French-style telephone on the desk rang sharply, jolting Devon from her thoughts.

"Miss James, please, this is Jonathan Stafford." The voice on the line, clearly one of authority, sounded deep and decidedly male.

"This is she."

"Hello, Miss James. I'm sorry to be calling so late, but it's been brought to my attention that you have some sort of . . . interest . . . in the Stafford Inn."

What was it she heard in his tone? "You might say that," Devon answered cautiously.

"I was hoping we could get together and discuss it."

She glanced at the ornate grandfather clock ticking loudly just a few feet away. "As you said, it's awfully late."

"Not tonight. I tried to phone you earlier, but you were out." There it was again. A note of irritation that infused the pleasantly spoken words.

"I had some shopping to do."

Actually she had been visiting the New York University library, looking for information on Stafford Shipbuilding. Now she knew why Jonathan Stafford's name had sounded so familiar. Stafford Shipbuilding—today Stafford Enterprises—was a huge corporate conglomerate specializing in marine equipment. Though only one branch of the company still built and sold boats, they owned dozens of other closely related businesses. As head of the family-owned company, Jonathan Stafford was one of the wealthiest men in the country.

"Since my schedule is extremely full, how about lunch?

Would noon tomorrow be convenient? We can meet at Le Cirque. It's one of my favorites."

Devon had never been there. If Jonathan Stafford was trying to persuade her, he was certainly using expensive bait. "All right."

"My driver will pick you up at eleven-thirty."

"That'll be fine."

"Good-bye, Miss James, until tomorrow."

"Good night," she said to the resonant, masculine, slightly intimidating voice. It took several minutes after she hung up the phone to realize he hadn't asked for her address, though her number was unlisted. But then a man like Jonathan Stafford would have the power to obtain that information with very little effort.

Florian Stafford would have had that kind of power, too.

Jonathan stared down at the wide green eyes looking up at him from the picture on the jacket of the hardbound book on his desk. If the photograph was anywhere near accurate, Devon James would be stunning.

According to the short blurb beneath the picture, she had been twenty-seven at the time of publication. Since *Journeys* was two years old, she'd be twenty-nine today. The remarks mentioned that her degree in literature was from New York University and that she'd had two other novels published. Both *Journeys* and *Quest,* her previous work, had hit the *New York Times* bestseller list.

Of course, Jonathan knew all of that already. That and one helluva lot more. In fact, by the time he got through, he'd know just about everything there was to know about one Devon Lynn James, successful novelist, divorcée, and currently his number one pain in the ass.

He looked down at the page in front of him on the top of the open manila file. Though Devon's natural parents were listed as unknown, her adoptive father, Patrick "Paddy" Fitzsimmons, was a New York City beat cop, a third-generation Irishman and a rounder. Eunice Fitzsimmons was a housewife, according to the neighbors, a very good mother to her adopted daughter and only child. From what Derek Preston, the investigator assigned to the matter, had learned so far, Devon and her parents were still very close. A few years back, she had moved them into a luxury apartment not too far from their old neighborhood.

That was after her divorce, just over three years ago. Devon had met her ex-husband, Paul James, during her studies at the university. They had married and Paul had gone on to complete a law degree. Jonathan hadn't found out much about what had happened to end the marriage, but he intended to.

He shoved the file aside and leaned back in his chair, stretching his long legs out in front of him. He couldn't speak for the woman he studied, but his own divorce had been almost a relief, though he still felt guilty about the cause—working sixteen hours a day with little or no time for his family.

He had married Rebecca Winston, a girl of twenty-three, when he was twenty-eight, a little over ten years ago. Their son, Alex, had been born two years later. Two years after that, Becky had filed for divorce, entering into what became a bitter financial and custody battle. Then before the divorce was final, Rebecca had been killed.

The automobile accident had returned Jonathan's son to his care, which he had desperately wanted, but Becky's death dealt a bitter blow to them both.

By that time, Jonathan no longer loved her. He hadn't

since the first bloom of their marriage had faded, or maybe not even then. Still except for his sister when he was younger, Rebecca was the only woman he had let himself get close to. After Becky's death, he found himself missing her occasional phone calls, though they usually wound up arguing, or her small attempts to make amends for the trouble she constantly caused.

A soft rap sounded at his door, then it swung open. "Beggin' your pardon, sir." His driver, a Britisher named Henry Milford, stood in the opening, chauffeur's cap in hand. "You told me to come up for you at ten."

Jonathan nodded. He'd been working hard since six o'clock that morning. He had a big day tomorrow; he looked forward to a nightcap, a few minutes reading—which reminded him to take home Devon James's book—and a good night's sleep.

He only wished Alex would be waiting at the apartment, instead of sleeping in his narrow bed at the clinic a few miles away. He thought about stopping by to see Akemi, his Japanese mistress. She was always there waiting, and she could certainly help ease some of his tensions. But his mind and body seemed at odds on that particular idea.

"Auto's right out front, sir," Henry said with his British lilt.

Wearily, Jonathan picked up the hardbound novel and followed Henry into the darkened hall. Tomorrow he'd delve deeper into his problem with the James woman. He wanted at least one of his problems to come to a quick and final end.

Devon pushed through the heavy wooden doors in the lobby of her brownstone and stepped out onto the porch.

Just as Jonathan Stafford had promised, his driver waited beside the open door of a long black stretch limousine.

Devon descended the stairs, crossed the sidewalk, and slid into the wide, comfortable back seat.

"My name is 'Enry," the chauffeur said, leaving the *H* off his name, his voice an odd mixture of British and American. "If there's anythin' you need, miss, you just let me know." After a reassuring smile, he closed the door with the solid thud that accompanies a well-built auto, and Devon leaned back against the buttersoft gray leather seat.

Outside the dark-tinted windows, the icy November breeze blew papers into the gutters as the car sped down Madison toward Le Cirque on Sixty-fifth. In concession to the cold, Devon had worn a softly pleated ankle-length burgundy Dior knit suit, which fell narrowly over her hips. The jacket came just to her waist with round gold buttons that closed up the front, and a printed burgundy silk scarf swirled loosely around her throat.

She looked good today and she knew it. It gave her the feeling of confidence she somehow knew she would need.

The car pulled up at the curb in front of the restaurant, and Henry opened her door.

"Mr. Stafford will be waiting inside, miss."

"Thank you, Henry."

The restaurant oozed old-money elegance, she noticed as the doorman held open the door. Soft lighting, warm wood, and fresh flowers. The maitre d' started forward, but another, taller man in an expensive navy blue double-breasted suit stepped in front of him.

Devon's breath caught. She would have recognized Jonathan Stafford in a room of a thousand people. He looked just like the photograph she had seen in the foyer of the mansion on Church Street. Only Jonathan looked even taller than Florian, and far more imposing. Even their eyes looked the same, bold and compelling, yet somehow unreadable.

"Hello, Miss James." His smile seemed deceptively warm. "I'm Jonathan Stafford." Long brown fingers enveloped her hand in a gesture that felt solid and steady and entirely too confident.

"I'm happy to meet you." Happy wasn't quite the word. *Overwhelmed* would be more like it.

Standing well over six feet tall, with wavy blue-black hair and eyes an unusual grayish blue, Jonathan Stafford was one of the darkly handsomest men she had ever seen. Unfortunately, he seemed to know it. With wide shoulders that angled to trim hips and a pair of long lean legs hardened with muscle that even his well-tailored pants couldn't hide, he looked far more athletic than the usual corporate executive. Black wing-shaped brows, a smooth forehead, and prominent cheekbones echoed the power and wealth he exuded.

Michael would have been green with envy.

"I saw your picture on the cover of your book," Jonathan explained, having read her surprise that he had recognized her so quickly. "It didn't do you justice."

Amazingly Devon felt her face grow warm at the unexpected compliment. "Thank you."

"*Journeys* is a very good book, I might add, though I'm not quite finished. I've read all of your work."

Devon struggled to keep her dismay from showing. "I'm surprised a man as busy as you would be able to find the time."

"I spend a lot of hours on airplanes."

"Your table is ready, Mr. Stafford." The maitre d' arrived

with a flourish of gold-tasseled menus. "Are you ready to be seated?"

"Yes. Thank you, Isaac."

The maitre d', a graying man, very stiff-postured with slightly hooded eyes, smiled his acknowledgment. It was obvious Jonathan Stafford was a regular. It became more obvious when they'd been taken to a corner table that appeared to be the best in the house.

"Have you been here before?" Jonathan asked, once they were seated.

"No, but I've been wanting to come for some time. It's lovely."

"The murals on the walls are reproductions from the Singerie in the Château de Versailles."

"Are you interested in art, Mr. Stafford?"

"Jonathan," he insisted, "please."

"Then you must call me Devon." She smiled at him, intrigued by his dark good looks. Thinking of Florian, she was at the same time slightly repelled. When the waiter arrived to take their drink orders, Devon ordered a glass of white wine and Jonathan ordered a Perrier. "You don't drink, Mr. Stafford?"

"Jonathan," he corrected, assessing her with eyes that missed nothing.

"Jonathan."

"Not during the day. I've a very busy schedule."

"So do I, but I figured I could use a little fortification."

He smiled at that, a bright, charming smile that almost looked sincere. He could have posed for a Pepsodent ad, she thought, with a trace of amusement that withered as his odd gray-blue eyes swung to her face.

"I often make people nervous. It's a hazard of being the

president of the company. Since you don't work for me, you have nothing to worry about."

She wasn't so sure about that. She felt instantly attracted to him, noticing little things like the darkness of his skin above the brilliant white of his collar, the way a small scar on his left hand disappeared beneath the cuff. And she also felt wary. It was dangerous, this attraction, especially toward a powerful man like him.

"As to your question about my liking art," he said, "the answer is yes. I collect whenever I can find the time. I'm particularly fond of Oriental watercolors."

Devon smiled. "I collect contemporary impressionists. I love the light and warmth of the paintings, and the beautiful use of color. Of course, I've been known to buy just about anything I feel has merit and happens to catch my fancy."

Jonathan seemed a bit surprised. She wondered if he believed a fiction writer's interests were too shallow for something as sophisticated as art. That thought made her consider the kind of impression *she* had been making on him. Obviously, it wasn't all that favorable, a fact which irritated her more than it should have.

"Why have you invited me here?" she asked, with a little less subtlety than she had intended. The waiter arrived with their drinks before he could answer. Devon took a nerve-calming sip of wine. French, possibly a Pouilly Fuissé, and exceedingly good. She should have known.

The short balding waiter left them alone, and Jonathan opened the menu. "You should try the lamb and *pâté de campagna.*" He watched her over the rim. "It's one of their specialties."

Devon started to do as he suggested, just as she would have with Michael, but something in his manner warned her not to. "I'm sure it's very good, but it sounds awfully heavy. I usually eat something lighter."

Jonathan smiled in that disconcerting way of his, and Devon glanced down at her menu. Though she could no longer see him, she could feel his eyes on her and wondered again at his thoughts. When she was ready to order, the balding waiter who had brought their drinks materialized out of nowhere like one of the Stafford ghosts.

"I think I'll try the *sole au vin,*" Devon said, "with the goat-cheese salad to start."

"Striped bass, butter lettuce salad, lemon juice instead of dressing." Jonathan handed both of their menus to the waiter, who hurried away to do his bidding.

"Lemon juice instead of dressing—my, but you are health-minded." For a moment Jonathan looked at Devon oddly. It seemed few people questioned his wishes, even in light conversation.

"Wait till you see what I order for dessert," he teased, surprising her—and maybe even himself.

They made pleasant conversation until their salads arrived, then Devon's curiosity surfaced. "I think it's time you told me why I'm here, Mr. Stafford." He caught the pointedly formal note, but this time he didn't correct her.

Instead, he set his fork aside and pinned her with a gray-blue glance. "I want to know why you're digging up information on my family, Miss James. I want to know why you've been making those trips to Stafford."

"I should think that would be obvious. I'm working on a story."

"A novel?"

"Not exactly. More of a family biography."

"Isn't that a little out of your usual line of writing?"

"A little."

"And it's my family you've chosen." The blue left his eyes; they looked gray, hard, and totally disapproving.

"Maybe you should be flattered."

"Well, I'm not. Frankly, Miss James, I have quite enough trouble staying out of the limelight."

That was an understatement. Volumes had been written about Stafford Enterprises and the dark, secretive man who ran the corporation like some unrelenting ruthless steel giant. She'd spent more than four hours and had barely scratched the surface. Eventually, she planned to know all there was to know about Jonathan Barrett Stafford.

"I suppose you've spoken to Mrs. Meeks," she said.

"Several times." The disapproving note remained, though he seemed to be trying to hide it.

"Well then, in a way I'm glad you proposed this meeting." She toyed with the napkin in her lap, grateful he couldn't see this small sign of her nervousness. "You see, Mr. Stafford, I'd like to get more background information on the subject and so far it's been difficult. If I could just speak to you about your family—"

Jonathan shook his head. "I'm sorry, Miss James, I'm afraid that's out of the question. I wish I could help you, but I can't." Regret shadowed his face, but there was something else in his eyes. Devon suddenly believed that underneath his sympathetic expression, Jonathan Stafford was angry.

"I'm a man of privacy, Devon." His voice held a hint of entreaty that hadn't been there before. "It's difficult enough for me to find. If you write about my family, the papers will have a field day. Surely a woman of your intelligence can see where all this could lead. I had hoped you'd be willing to let the matter be."

Devon just smiled. Jonathan Stafford was good. Very good. But Devon made a living by studying people's expressions, their body language, the hidden signs other people might miss. All writers did. Someone else might succumb to Jonathan Stafford's cultivated charm and overwhelming presence, but Devon wasn't fooled for a moment.

"Just exactly what *matter* is it, Mr. Stafford, that we are discussing?"

Only a tiny inflection near his jawline revealed his displeasure. He watched her a moment, gauging her, trying to read her thoughts. Some invisible sign brought the waiter to remove their plates. While the little man worked, Jonathan sipped his Perrier, but his eyes remained on her face.

She wondered with a hint of irritation if she passed his slightly insolent inspection, then noticed his gray-blue eyes had moved down the front of her jacket to where her small breasts pushed against the fabric, and a different, slightly appreciative smile touched the corner of his lips.

It was the first honest smile she had seen, faint as it was, and unwillingly Devon felt an odd rush of warmth. Her fingers trembled at the hint of desire in those penetrating depths, and she tightened her hold on the napkin in her lap.

Jonathan must have realized what he was doing, for a bland look smoothed his features and he straightened a bit in his chair. "If we're going to discuss this further, Miss James, I'd rather not do it here. How about dinner, say . . . day after tomorrow?"

Though she felt more uncertain than ever, she needed information and Jonathan Stafford might have it. Not even her unwanted awareness of him, the almost palpable tension she experienced in his presence could have kept her away. "All right, Mr. Stafford."

"Jonathan," he corrected, his charming, Stafford, cultivated smile back in place.

"Jonathan," she repeated, unable to wrest her eyes from that dark, compelling face. She remembered the subtle flash of interest she had read in that face just moments before, and a tendril of heat unfurled in her stomach.

Then she thought of the anger he hid beneath his good looks and charm, thought of Florian Stafford and the violence she believed he, too, had cloaked beneath a cool facade—and wondered just how much alike the two men really were.

Five

Jonathan Stafford leaned back against the gray leather seat of the long black limousine. The interior still smelled new, a pleasant association of money and power and personal accomplishment. Built into the back of the panel to his right, soft blue lights lit buttons that regulated the climate control, stereo system, and television—the latter had never been turned on.

Jonathan settled farther into the soft gray leather, trying to let go of the tensions he had built up during the day. He had worked late again tonight, going over the account of Carstairs International, a huge corporation that owned Pacific American, the nation's largest small boat building company, one of Stafford's biggest customers. For the past three weeks, Tri-Star Marine had been dogging Carstairs's heels, hoping to sell them a new line of plastic fittings.

Kelovar was non-corrosive, they argued. It would hold up better than the forged and stamped metal castings supplied by Holidex Industries, a Stafford Enterprises corporation. If the product was half as good as Tri-Star boasted, Holidex was in trouble. So far, Jonathan hadn't been able to discover much about it, but he would. There was little about his competitors that he didn't already know.

The limousine rounded the corner onto Madison, passing a newly opened Brentano's Bookstore. The shop was dark now, lit only by the dim white glow of a few fluorescent lamps, but he could still make out the row upon row of newly released hardbound books on display in the window. Devon James's book rode on the seat beside him. He fingered it absently, unable to see her picture on the back in the darkness of the car, but remembering clearly her image, sleek and fair and sensuous, from the top of her shiny blond hair to a pair of delicate ankles above slender feet with fine high arches. Time and again, during the course of the day, his thoughts had strayed just as they did now, from his business dealings to the woman who'd been such a surprise at lunch.

Devon James was all he'd expected—and nothing he'd expected at all.

He had speculated on her intelligence. Her novels revealed a sharp inquisitive mind and she appeared to have one. He had been right about her looks, though as he had said, the picture on the book jacket didn't do her justice. He'd never meant the over-used flattery more.

But she seemed far more shrewd than he would have guessed, and far more perceptive. Though a number of his business associates and most of the women he knew succumbed to his practiced charm with little effort on his part, Devon had sensed the anger he worked to disguise. She had seen his false smiles for exactly what they were, and that more than anything intrigued him.

That and the fact she had a softness about her he hadn't expected, something she apparently worked very hard to hide.

Or at least he'd thought so at the time.

Perhaps it was just her looks that had captured his interest. Tall, graceful, and elegant, with prominent cheekbones and a soft coral mouth. She had the lean-boned refinement of a prize thoroughbred, yet he hadn't missed her subtle curves, shapely legs, and small upthrusting breasts. He'd caught himself wondering whether her nipples were pink and tight, or coral and pouty, the way he remembered her lips.

Jonathan felt his body stir. He couldn't remember when a woman's looks had affected him as much as hers did. Even in the restaurant he'd grown hard several times just watching the way her tongue touched the corner of her mouth, or licked something from the bowl of her spoon. Considering the circumstances, he found his reaction decidedly unpleasant.

And probably responsible for his out-of-the-blue idea of inviting her to dinner.

Jonathan had known from the start it would probably take more than a single encounter to convince Devon James not to write her book, but inviting her to dinner at his apartment—that had been the height of folly. No, he corrected, the height of pure unadulterated lust. Now he'd have to deal not only with his unwanted desire for her, but also with the unwanted invasion of his privacy.

Over the past three years, the peace and quiet of his home had become all important, a special place away from the harsh realities of the world, a place where he and his son could be together. Even Akemi had been there only once.

He thought of the petite Asian woman as he sat there. Up until lately, he'd been content with Akemi and their slightly impersonal relationship. Beautiful, intelligent, and attentive, Akemi understood his needs yet never interfered in his life, in his business. She was happy with the luxury apartment he provided, the generous allowance, and the freedom he permitted, all but making herself available to other men.

"We're 'ere, guv'nor," Henry said, pulling the car to the curb.

Jonathan smiled faintly. Henry's occasional Cockney lapses never ceased to amuse him. He glanced out the tinted window at the towering glass structure at Seventy-sixth and Madison. "So we are." Without waiting for Henry to open the door, Jonathan swung it wide and stepped out onto the sidewalk.

"I've a meeting across town at seven," he said through the chauffeur's open window. "You'd better be here by six."

"Aye, sir." Henry pushed the power button, and the glass rolled up, sealing him inside. He honked the horn at a cabby who came a little too close to suit him, then he stepped on the gas, and the long black car lurched away from the curb.

The man was definitely one of a kind, Jonathan thought, picturing Henry bulling his way through traffic. Amazingly, in the five years the man had been his driver, none of Jonathan's cars had ever received the slightest dent.

Smiling at the thought, Jonathan turned toward the high-rise, waved briefly at the red-and-beige uniformed doorman who stood with his back to the wind. Jonathan crossed the sidewalk, and pushed through the revolving glass door.

The lobby had been done in expensive beige marble. Ornate gilt-framed pictures lined the walls, and thick beige carpet covered the floor. Passing the security desk with the briefest of nods, he walked beneath the crystal chandeliers toward the elevators.

He used his key to unlock the apartment and opened the door to find Akemi waiting in the marble-floored entry, holding a snifter of brandy in a small brown hand.

"Good evening, Jonathan." She rose on tiptoes and kissed him full on the mouth, leaving the taste of cool mint mouthwash and a hint of the gin she usually drank, pink ladies, her favorite. A whiff of perfume, a delicate blend of rose and spice, drifted up from her pink silk kimono. With her assistance, Jonathan shrugged out of his cashmere overcoat and accepted the brandy she offered.

"Arigato," he said in Japanese, which, like French and Spanish, he'd come to speak quite well. Akemi led him into the living room, and he sank heavily down on the overstuffed white silk sofa, stretching his long legs out in front of him.

She rounded the sofa, came up behind him, and began to massage his shoulders. Her tiny hands were surprisingly strong for a woman no more than five feet tall. Weighing an even hundred pounds, with long black hair that fell nearly to her waist, and big black almond-shaped eyes, Akemi Kumato had finely formed lips and a small upturned nose. Her skin was the color of coffee laced with cream and just as warm.

"You feel much too tense, *aijin.* Why don't we get in the whirlpool and afterward I will give you a massage?"

Jonathan released a weary breath. That's what he'd come for, among other things, and it sounded better by the moment.

He glanced at the tiny woman, silently imagining the evening ahead, and his body began to respond. Akemi was a disciplined lover, well-schooled in the art of pleasure. So was he. In the years he had known her, they had given each other hours of enjoyment. Akemi had provided a respite from his long days at work, the problems he faced with his child, and his terrible sense of guilt for what had happened to him.

Though he wasn't in love with her and she most certainly didn't love him, when he was with her, he felt serene. At least he had until lately. Only in the past several weeks had he begun to grow restless, to question whether what little he shared with her was enough. Then again, he had no inclination for commitment. With his heavy load of responsibilities, he just didn't have the time.

"Come." Akemi smiled at the obvious interest that pressed against the front of his pants. She urged him off the sofa. "The bath is almost ready."

He followed her into the bedroom, tugging at his tie and pulling it off, then shrugging out of his shirt. Naked to the waist, he felt Akemi's breath on his skin as she worked a flat copper nipple between her small white teeth. Her hands splayed on his chest then ran expertly over his pectoral muscles, making them flex and tighten.

Akemi unbuckled his belt, worked the zipper on his slacks, and slid them down his thighs. As he stepped out of them, her hand cupped his sex through the narrow cotton briefs he wore, and his shaft grew harder still. She knew exactly how to touch him, where to touch him, had known long before he met her.

While he finished undressing, Akemi did the same. With unhurried movements, deliberately provocative, she eased out of her pink kimono and pulled the mother-of-pearl inlaid combs from her long black hair. Left to her preference, she dressed American, but she knew the embroidered robe pleased him, and she did her job well.

Naked, they walked into the marble bathroom and climbed into the huge Jacuzzi tub. Akemi poured in a liberal dose of perfumed bubbling bath oil, and the rushing water built soft white mounds of foam that clung to the curly black hair on his chest. The scent of roses filled the room, and the two dark-haired images on the mirrored walls fogged over with steam.

"You are quiet tonight, *aijin.* Something is the matter?"

"Something. Tension perhaps. Probably just worry."

"You wish to speak of it?"

If it had just been business, he might have. Akemi listened well—it was part of what was expected. And there was no censure, no disagreement with whatever it was that he said.

Sometimes he wished there were.

Most of the time, like tonight, he figured it was probably just as well. Worry about Tri-Star Marine and their efforts to win the Carstairs account, troubled thoughts about his son and what might happen if Devon James continued delving into his affairs, and his unexpected and unwanted attraction to her, were subjects he hoped to forget—at least for the moment.

"Right now I just want to relax." Against his will, an image of Devon's lovely face, smiling up at him softly, rose sharply into his mind. His shaft, already hot and pulsing, stiffened and throbbed even more.

"Do not worry, *aijin,* I am here to help you." Akemi smiled, much as his image of Devon had, her soft lips curving seductively. Beneath the sudsy water, her hand ran up his thigh to stroke his sex. Her mouth found his, her tongue slid inside, and her long black hair teased his nipple. When her arms went around his neck, he pulled her roughly onto his lap, his hand coming up to capture a breast.

A little surprised at his urgency, Akemi reached for a bottle of scented ginseng oil, just one of a number of small colorful containers filled with lotions, oils, and body gels used to heighten and prolong the act of sex, poured some into her palm, then spread the liquid around her nipples to make them stiffen and tingle. Jonathan usually helped her, arousing her slowly to the passion he demanded, readying her for the practiced game of seduction they always played so well.

Instead he urged her legs apart and drove into her swiftly, one sure thrust that drew a gasp of surprise from the small dark woman he had entered. Moving with long, hard strokes, he drove her to climax just seconds ahead of his own, then lay back against the slick wet marble.

"Jonathan?" Akemi said, her voice a little uncertain. Then the soapsuds drifted apart and she saw that he still remained hard beneath the surface of the water. She smiled with the confidence of a woman who knows the value of her charms. "It has been too long since we have made love with such passion."

Jonathan absently stroked her breasts, then pulled her mouth down to his for a kiss. He didn't bother to tell her it was his fascination for the tall blond woman he had met some hours earlier that had whetted his appetite so well.

Devon sat curled on her burgundy overstuffed sofa, her bare feet tucked under her, legal pad in hand, a pencil between her teeth as she went over the notes she'd been writing. She was revising her list of possible sources, adding new avenues of research, anything and everything she could think of that might help her discover the truth of what had happened in the house at 25 Church Street.

Earlier she had been thinking of her lunch with Jonathan Stafford, recalling the handsome man himself with far more clarity than she would have liked, recalling as well the overwhelming effect he'd had on her. It was the last thing she wanted and so she had, at least for the moment, successfully pushed those thoughts away.

She made another note in the margin of her notebook, then shoved the pencil into the knot of pale blond hair atop her head. Twice during the past two weeks, she had been to the Office of the Town Clerk in Groton, purchasing copies of any documentation that might concern Florian Stafford, his wife Mary, their small son Bernard, Anna Mae Stafford, or any other members of the Stafford family.

Her third visit had ended on a somewhat sour note when she made the mistake of asking if there had ever been any rumors concerning Bernard Stafford's death—or any tales of hauntings at the Stafford Inn. Betty Warton, the town clerk, a slight, graying woman with thin lips and a tight unfriendly smile drew herself up a good three inches, snapped closed the huge, dusty old leather volume Devon had been scanning, and carted it away.

"Ghosts," she grumbled on her return. "There never has been such a thing, never will be—and studying those old records isn't gonna make it so."

"I don't suppose there's anything I've missed," Devon asked, knowing it was pointless now.

"You've gone over every volume with a fine-tooth comb and spent a small fortune on hand written copies—surely that's enough."

"It'll be enough when I've gathered the information I need to know about the Staffords and what happened to that little boy."

"Well, I never!" Betty hefted the heavy volume and marched toward the stairs leading to the basement where the book had been stored.

Devon didn't really care. She had all the information Groton had to offer, including a copy of Florian Stafford's will—which had proved quite interesting.

Besides the usual sorts of items—*my saddle horse to my faithful servant, Robert Lawton, for his loyal years of service, my antique wooden cigar box to my friend, Jedediah Sim-*

mons, because he has always admired it—she discovered that Florian's portion of Stafford Shipping reverted to the oldest living Stafford male, at that time a man named Marshall Stafford, whom she later discovered was Jonathan's great-great-grandfather.

Mary Stafford, Florian's wife, received a large monthly stipend, all of Florian's personal property unless otherwise bequeathed, as well as a life estate, allowing her the use of the house for the balance of her living years.

Surprisingly the privilege extended to his niece, Annie, before the property reverted to the Stafford family holdings. To Annie, he also bequeathed: *the small gold locket that belonged to my mother, in hopes she will know the special place she held for me.* It seemed a little incongruous, considering what Devon believed had happened between the two of them. Then again, maybe it wasn't. How much guilt had Florian suffered from the unwanted intimacies he pressed on a thirteen-year-old girl? Maybe as much or nearly as much as he'd felt from killing his son.

Devon once more scanned her list, drawing a line through the words at the top, *Probate Records.* That task had been completed, and she had used the information she acquired in Groton to diagram the Stafford family tree. Except for Annie, who lived in the town until the late 1970s, Barrett and Estell Stafford, Marshall's children, had been the last of the family to be born and raised there, living in a remodeled version of the original Stafford mansion until the late 1920s.

Devon had been surprised to discover that the place had burned nearly to the ground three years ago. She wasn't yet sure who had been living in the house at the time, or even if it had been occupied. But she had found records that mentioned the names and addresses of family members living in New York, and they had been easy enough to locate. Jonathan Stafford, a younger sister named Madeline, his aunt Estell Stafford Meredith, and Jonathan's son Alexander appeared to be the only members of the family living today.

She glanced down her list of things to do. She had done enough research on the novels she had written to know exactly how to go about gathering the necessary information. Her list was already extensive.

She'd been over it again and again, adding to it each day and dividing it into two columns: one dealing with genealogy—information on the Stafford family itself, the other dealing with the paranormal—ghosts, hauntings, extrasensory perceptions—all the things she felt particularly uneasy about yet knew she would have to explore.

The top of that list was headed with a single name—*Christy Papaopolis.* Michael always called her "the head guru." Christy had been the first person Devon had phoned when she returned to New York from Connecticut—the only person she could count on not to think she was crazy.

Christy had listened with rapt attention and immediately suggested they return to the mansion for another night in the yellow room. Devon's insides churned at the thought. She was hardly ready for that—she wasn't sure she ever would be. But Christy had offered her help, and Devon intended to accept it.

They were scheduled to meet tomorrow afternoon at a place called the Insight Book Store, one of Christy's hangouts. She was supposed to introduce Devon to "people who understood the metaphysical—people who could help."

Devon glanced at the clock, saw how late it was, cursed herself for letting the time slip away, and jumped to her feet. Jonathan Stafford's driver would arrive in less than an hour. Why in God's name hadn't she decided on something to wear?

Devon hurried down the hall and into her bedroom, a sunny enclosure with molded ceilings and a four-poster canopied bed. It was decorated largely in white with accents of pale blue. The furniture was Queen Anne-styled dark mahogany. Two of her impressionist paintings, a Francis Donald and a Walt Gonske, each of bright blooming flowers, hung on the wall to the right of her dresser.

Stripping off her clothes as she walked along, Devon reached the bathroom, turned on the shower, and climbed in. Surely, the excitement she was feeling was only a result of her nervousness. But in truth, she knew it was not. Jonathan Stafford was an incredibly attractive man. His dark intriguing face and tall athletic body were the stuff of women's dreams. She would have to be blind or a fool to deny it.

Still, he was a little too smooth, a little too polished to really hold any appeal. He was also far too confident. He knew the allure he held for women—she could read it in his eyes whenever he looked at her. Until recently, she would have been afraid to subject herself to that kind of magnetism.

Just like Paul, she would have thought. Women fell at Paul's feet—she just hadn't realized he was accepting what they offered until it was too late. Jonathan Stafford had those same incredible good looks—even more so. To top it off, he had money, power, and charm. Women probably climbed all over themselves fighting to get in his bed.

She pondered that, thinking of the articles she had read about him in recent newspapers and magazines. Surprisingly, he was rarely seen out with a woman. Twice she'd seen pictures of him with a small, expensively dressed

Asian woman, but little mention was made of her, and they were never linked together in the tabloids. All in all, he seemed to keep his personal life out of the public eye as much as possible.

Whatever the outcome of the evening, he was an intriguing man, Devon thought as she climbed out of the shower, toweled herself dry, then walked to the mirror and began to apply her makeup. And she wanted to look her best for the occasion.

What should she wear to a powerful, wealthy, attractive man's apartment when her goal was to woo that man into helping her with a project he was certain to oppose? Something black, she decided, simple, elegant, not extravagantly expensive, but not a Macy's bargain-basement special either.

She smiled to herself, wondering what Jonathan Stafford would think if he knew she often shopped there when money got tight, mixing their inexpensive clothing with some of the more extravagant items she had purchased at Saks or Bonwit Teller in better days.

Devon dressed carefully in a simple St. John black knit sheath, low-backed and knee-length, a pair of black hose, black suede heels, a string of pearls and small pearl earrings.

She had just dabbed a hint of White Shoulders, inexpensive but still her favorite perfume, behind each ear when the intercom buzzed and Henry announced his arrival.

Devon took a deep breath and exhaled it slowly. "Stay calm," she told herself in the mirror. "He's just a man, for God's sake. This is business." He might be powerful and attractive, but he wasn't a monster like Florian Stafford. She glanced once more in the mirror. "And he certainly isn't interested in you."

* * *

The kitchen smelled of steamed rice and chicken stock, ingredients Jonathan had been using to cook the meal to come. It was a large room, mostly white, with the latest in modern appliances. The huge stainless-steel professional gas range was his favorite.

Jonathan checked the temperature on the oven, lowered it a little, then left the kitchen and walked into the mirrored dining room. A simple, Oriental-style arrangement of a single bare maple branch and several artfully arranged, rust-colored leaves sat in the center of the long black lacquer table. Each place setting had been done in black with accents of rust and pearl. Long black lacquer chopsticks replaced the usual knives and forks.

Satisfied that all was in readiness for the evening ahead, Jonathan heard the intercom announcing Devon's arrival at the security desk in the lobby below, but didn't bother to answer. He had already arranged for her to be sent up in his private elevator.

Under different circumstances, he would have been looking forward to the evening. As it was, after what Derek Preston, his chief investigator, had learned this morning about his guest—and considering what he was prepared to do with the information—he found little pleasure in the victory he was about to grasp.

Only the knowledge that the past would be laid to rest again and his son out of harm's way made the hours ahead somewhat palatable.

Jonathan brushed several grains of sticky white rice from the front of his gray cashmere sweater, brushed off his custom-tailored black slacks, and strode toward the foyer, arriving just as the elevator doors slid open.

Maria Delgado, his housekeeper, a plump, dark-haired woman in her late forties, had already arrived, to take

Devon's fox-trimmed beaver jacket with great efficiency, and hang it up in the entry closet.

"That'll be all for tonight, Maria."

She nodded and glided away as silently as possible—for a woman her size—toward her quarters in the rear of the spacious apartment. Considering the attraction Jonathan felt for the tall blond woman standing in front of him, it had crossed his mind to let Maria have the evening off, leaving him free for a try at seduction. He had discarded the notion as swiftly as it came.

In the first place it was out of character. He hadn't been with a woman other than his mistress for the past three years. In the second place, involving himself with Devon James could only mean disaster. Fate had already determined his course, there was little he could do to change things.

"Good evening, Devon."

"Hello . . . Jonathan."

She looked every bit as good as he expected, better maybe. Her mouth was the exact coral shade he remembered, raising with stirring force the question he had posed about the color of her nipples. Her hair was incredibly shiny and so pale at times that it looked silver. She had to be a natural blond, he thought, and felt himself harden as he considered finding out.

Damn. He forced himself under control. "I'm glad you could make it." Devon seemed a little more nervous than she had at their last meeting. As she took in his cashmere sweater and slacks, a tinge of pink worked its way up the hollows in her cheeks.

"I was sure you'd be the blue blazer type," she admitted with a trace of embarrassment. "I hope I'm not overdressed."

In fact, he'd damn near worn exactly that. Only the thought that his home was his last true refuge, a place where he left his armor behind, had kept him from it. If she was going to be there, she would have to accept him the way he was.

"You look lovely." Elegant but not overly so. He flashed her a reassuring smile. "A woman is never overdressed in basic black."

She relaxed a little at that. "Your apartment is beautiful. Do you entertain here often?"

"As a matter of fact, I don't. I'm still not certain why I asked you here." That was an understatement. *Damn, what had possessed him?* He should have taken her to the Four Seasons or Twenty-One, someplace where he could have kept his distance and continued to play the game. Now that he had seen her again, had felt his body's unwanted response, he realized even more strongly just how foolish the gesture had been.

Added to that was the confrontation he planned. Though he already knew the outcome, it was harder here. Somehow he felt disadvantaged. "Maybe I thought you would enjoy seeing my art collection."

Devon seemed to brighten, her smile warm if not a little bit wary. "Oh, yes . . . I'd like that very much."

"Why don't I fix us something to drink first? White wine still your preference, or would you rather have something else?"

"White wine would be perfect."

He led her into a corner of the living room and opened the bar hidden behind a cabinet on one wall. He had furnished the apartment with an emphasis on Asia: Japanese ink drawings in black lacquer frames, sixteenth-century Chinese vases, a pair of eighteenth-century illustrated folding screens. The effect was softened by traditional furniture in cream and black, accented with cloisonné platters and deep red cinnabar jugs.

"It looks like you, I think," Devon said, glancing around the room, "though it has a certain warmth I wouldn't have expected."

Jonathan poured two stemmed crystal glasses of Montrachet and handed one to Devon. "Somehow I don't think that's a compliment." Devon blushed again. He hadn't seen a woman do that in years. He found he rather liked it.

"I only meant that as beautifully designed as it is, it still feels kind of homey."

Jonathan smiled. "I like to think so. I've always loved the Orient. It's only natural to have my home reflect my interests. But I also have my son to consider. We have a game room, of course, where he can watch TV and I can relax, but I didn't want even this room to be so austere a small boy wouldn't feel comfortable."

"Will your son be joining us for supper?" Not a hint of surprise in those wide green eyes at the mention of a child, but then he had expected her to be thorough. He wondered exactly how much she knew about Alex.

"No, he won't be home until later." Not for another night, in fact. Alex spent four days a week at the clinic, but he wasn't about to tell her that. "I thought we'd be able to speak more freely without him."

Devon walked around the room admiring his collection, the indirect lighting giving her fair skin a soft peach glow. He couldn't help admiring her long shapely legs or the subtle curve of her breasts. Her hips were slender but well rounded, and unconsciously his hands itched to cup them. She stopped in front of a picture that happened to be one of his favorites, and he walked up beside her.

"That's an ink drawing of Hotei, one of the seven good-luck Gods of Japan. It was done in the sixteenth century by Miyamoto Musashi, the great Japanese swordsman and strategist."

"It's lovely."

He pointed to a narrow gilt-framed picture beside the first. "That's a nineteenth-century rendition of Musashi. He's practicing the art of fencing using two sticks. It's a Kuniyoshi."

Devon took a sip of wine. "I tutored drawing as a student in college, but I'm afraid I know almost nothing about Oriental art."

Jonathan smiled. "In that case, you should rely strictly on instinct—enjoy what pleases you." That's what he'd like to do. Right now he couldn't think of anything he'd like more than to please himself with Devon's slender body.

She glanced again at the artwork, the bold black strokes against the paper, the finely etched lines that in some subtle way suggested the emotions of the characters. "They're beautiful—even the ones that portray scenes of violence. I can see why you like them."

"Business takes me to Japan several times a year. I've come to appreciate the culture and customs. In some ways they're very different from us, in others not so different at all."

Devon started to say something then stopped. "Do I smell something burning?"

"Damn!" Jonathan ran back the way they had come, down the hall and into the kitchen. His teapot had just gone dry—he'd been meaning to buy one of the whistling kind for the past two years.

"Everything all right?" Devon walked through the kitchen door and came toward him.

Jonathan set the teapot off the gas burner and found himself staring in her direction. God, she looked lovely in her simple black knit dress, her blond hair gleaming above her shoulders. Sophisticated, yet somehow fresh. Maybe even a little bit vulnerable. He wondered what she would say if he told her he had thought about taking her to bed.

He wondered, too, what she would say to the discovery he had made and the way he intended to use it.

"It's only the water for our tea. I prepared most of the dinner ahead of time. Why don't we finish our wine and then we'll eat?"

"All right." But on their return to the living room, she stopped in the hall in an open doorway that led to his study. "Is that your son?" She pointed to a picture of Alex when he was just three.

"He's eight now," Jonathan said a bit more coldly than he had meant to. The picture was an enlarged color photo of the two of them. Alex was holding a small plastic baseball bat and wearing a Mets cap. He was whole then. He wouldn't play baseball again.

"I love children. I'd like to meet him sometime."

"You have no children of your own?" He knew she didn't.

"My husband . . . I mean my ex-husband, wasn't ready for that kind of commitment. He said he didn't want to be tied down. In the end, it turned out he was right."

"What about your plans for the future?" What about Michael Galveston? he wanted to ask, suddenly bothered by the idea that she was engaged to be married.

"For a while I was engaged, but things didn't work out. Someday I hope to find the right man and settle down. I know it isn't in vogue, but I'm really very old-fashioned."

He thought of the feminine way she had blushed. "I think I like that trait in a woman."

"I was raised that way. My mother and father have been happily married for thirty-five years. It may be old-fashioned, but that's the kind of marriage I want."

She smiled softly. "Paul and I didn't make it, but I'm optimistic. Who knows . . . maybe someday . . ."

In spite of himself, Jonathan found himself responding to her candor. She was guileless in a way he hadn't expected. He led her back to the living room, then sat down beside her on the cream and black moiré sofa. He wondered what had happened to end her relationship with Michael Galveston.

"How is your research on the Staffords coming along?" he asked, almost hating to broach the subject. "Turned up any skeletons in the family closet?"

She looked decidedly uncomfortable with his choice of words. "Actually, I haven't gotten all that far. I've worked up a genealogy starting with your great-great-grandfather, Sheridan Stafford, and coming forward to the present. So far most of my efforts have been concentrated on the Staffords who lived in Connecticut."

He took a sip of his wine. "But you plan on getting to me eventually."

Devon's eyes swung to his. "I suppose so . . . eventually."

No you won't, he thought but didn't say so. "You've finished your drink." She set her empty glass down on the glass-topped coffee table. A twelfth-century bronze bowl rested in the lighted case beneath it. "Why don't we go in to dinner?"

"I have to admit I'm starving. I'm not much of a cook myself. I've been looking forward to this meal all day."

"I hope I don't disappoint you." He helped her up, catching the scent of orange blossoms. Then he settled a hand at her waist to guide her into the dining room. She was quiet as they walked along, watching him with eyes that seemed to reach somewhere inside him. She had noticed his hesitation to talk about his son. In fact she seemed to notice almost everything.

"What's for dinner?" she asked, her tone purposely light.

Jonathan felt relieved. He skirted the long polished table, seated her in a high-backed black lacquer chair, then went into the kitchen, returning a few moments later with a tray of steaming covered dishes.

"It's the Oriental custom to serve all of the courses at once." He uncovered a platter of small delicately patterned cakes of rice and fish molded in a circle of seaweed, two each of two different kinds, then deftly lifted each portion onto a rectangular black lacquer plate using a pair of long black chopsticks. "I hope you like *sushi.*"

"I like sushi very much. Did you make it yourself?"

"Yes. This is made with smoked *shiro*—albacore. And this is *maguro*—yellow-fin tuna. I would have made *sashimi,* but I wasn't sure you would like it."

Devon smiled. "Actually, I'm fairly adventurous when it comes to food." She looked at the delicate maple branch that served as a centerpiece, the rust-colored leaves carefully arranged at the base. "Did you make this, too?"

"Yes. You gave me an excuse to come home early. I find this sort of thing relaxing. I'm usually far too busy to indulge myself."

"Then I'm flattered."

You won't be. "The pleasure is mine, Miss James." Unfortunately, that was the truth. At first it had been just her body, the subtle sexuality she seemed to exude. Now he found, just as he had before, that he was enjoying her company—far more than he should have been. She was intelligent and sincere, and warm in a way he wouldn't have expected.

"We're also having *agemono,* in this case, deep-fried *hirame* and *anego*—that's halibut and eel." He held up small wooden sticks, each with a batter-coated object on the end. "There's deep-fried squash, too. It's much like *tempura.*"

"It smells delicious."

"We're having a turnip, chrysanthemum, and carrot salad, and the main course is *Shabu Shabu.*" He set a crock of hot broth—kept warm by a small bright flame—on the table in front of them, along with a platter of chicken and fresh vegetables, cut in bite-sized cubes. "You get to cook your own."

Devon smiled brightly. "Sounds like fun."

And it was. They talked through dinner. Devon fumbled a bit with her chopsticks until he showed her the proper way to hold them, enjoying the excuse to get close to her.

"Like this," he said from behind her, gently encircling her shoulders with his arms, then carefully placing the long tapered sticks between her fingers. Her heart was pounding, he could feel it where her back pressed into his chest. Her hands felt delicate, fine-boned, the skin so smooth he wondered what it might feel like to touch her all over.

"Yes, now I see. I never could get the hang of it before."

Her breath fanned his cheek, and he felt a jolt of desire.

"It's really very simple," he said, his voice a little bit rougher than it was before, "once you get used to it. And the Japanese make their rice a little bit sticky, so it's easier to pick up." Reluctantly, he turned away from her to accomplish some obscure task in the kitchen, then returned once more to his seat.

They talked about her writing, discussing *Journeys,* her latest novel, but neither of them mentioned her current work. They talked about his business. Devon asked him about Stafford Enterprises, encouraging him to discuss some of the projects he was involved in, then laughing easily at some anecdote he told.

He liked her, he discovered—too much.

It was a shame that by the end of the evening, she would definitely not like him.

Six

As Jonathan served dessert, Devon watched the casual grace with which he moved and thought how perfectly it matched his easy confident manner. She had been watching him all evening, assessing him, trying to figure him out. Several times she had caught him watching her with that same sort of speculation, twice she had been sure she'd seen blatant masculine interest, but each time he had disguised the look so rapidly that she couldn't really be sure.

"I'm afraid I cheated a bit on this," he admitted, clearing away their empty dishes then returning with two small white plates, which he set on the table in front of them. "Coconut bananas—they're from Thailand."

"I have no idea where I'm going to put this," Devon said with soft laughter, "but it certainly looks too good to pass up." Small pieces of banana sautéed in some sort of brown sugar sauce and rolled in coconut. She took Jonathan's lead, picked up a bite with her chopsticks, and popped it into her mouth. "Ummm . . . this is delicious."

"Dessert is my weakness, though I don't indulge myself often."

"Neither do I. I'll have to skip lunch tomorrow, but this is so good it'll be worth it." She smiled at him warmly, unable to remember when she'd had a more pleasant evening. Jonathan had put her at ease from the moment of her arrival and though he spoke little about himself or his son, he had proved to be quite charming. She had expected to see more of his polished, slightly plastic, all-too-practiced facade, but found only a handsome, intelligent man who was very good company.

They continued the meal in easy conversation. Jonathan regaled her with Japanese superstitions that had them both smiling at their absurdity.

"The word *shi* means both four and death. Nine is *ku,* which means pain or worry. Japanese hospitals don't have rooms with the numbers four, nine, fourteen, nineteen, or forty-two. They think it's also bad luck to step on the cloth border of a *tatami*—a floor mat—or to stick your chopsticks upright in a full bowl of rice."

Devon smiled. "We're superstitious about the number thirteen or stepping on a crack in the sidewalk. I guess people really aren't so different."

"The Japanese also believe badgers can turn themselves into women. They lead their unwary victims into the forest never to be seen again." He grinned. "Where do you suppose that notion came from?"

Devon laughed. "And I thought all Japanese women were trained to be subservient! What about *good* luck?"

"Gambatte kudasai." He smiled warmly. "I think having you here has been my good fortune."

Devon returned the smile, but said nothing more. She kept thinking of his hands, how dark and strong they were, of the hardness of his chest when he had stood behind her, the incredible width of his shoulders. She didn't like the appeal he held for her. As the hour grew late, she grew more and more pensive. Jonathan's manner, too, became less relaxed, until his easy smile and good humor had faded away completely. Finally, he tossed his napkin down and shoved back his chair.

"Why don't we have an after-dinner drink in my study?" he suggested. "As much as I've enjoyed our conversation, I'm afraid I asked you here for more than just dinner. It's time we discussed your project."

Devon stood up and let him pull back her chair. "All right." Her wariness returned with a vengeance. This was the man whose voice she had heard on the phone. All business, determination, and an underlying note of displeasure. How much should she tell him about her work? She would have to wait and see.

They left the dining room, crossed the hall, and entered Jonathan's study. With its brown leather sofa and chairs, leather bound books, and family photographs, the room was more typically masculine than the rest of the house. A fire had been built in the hearth sometime earlier, but it had burned to glowing coals. While Devon sat down on the sofa, Jonathan knelt in front of the hearth, added a few small logs, then used a long black poker to stoke up the flames.

"Brandy all right?" He brushed off his hands as he came to his feet, his imposing height and build even more impressive in this very masculine room.

"Yes, that's fine."

Jonathan walked to a heavy walnut table in the corner behind his desk. He poured a dollop of brandy into each of two crystal snifters, handed her one, then took a seat in the overstuffed brown leather armchair across from her. As he swirled the amber liquid in his glass, his eyes grew more distant than they had been before. There was a tautness in his bearing and a grimness in his expression that sent a thread of uneasiness up Devon's spine.

Jonathan leaned forward in his chair. "I won't mince words, Devon. I want you to stop working on this project."

Devon fought to stay calm. She knew why he'd asked her to dinner, but the evening had been so pleasant, she had started to hope she might be wrong. "I'm afraid I can't do that."

Jonathan eyed her a moment through the sweep of heavy black lashes above the finely carved bones in his cheeks. "Why not?"

"Because this book is important to me. As an author, I feel obligated to pursue a subject that has come to me so strongly."

"You know my feelings about this. It involves my family, and anything that involves them involves me. I'm asking you, as a special favor to me, not to write this book."

"The book has very little to do with you. It's about people long dead, it's about—"

"It involves the Stafford name, does it not?"

"Yes."

Jonathan released a long slow breath. "I was hoping it wouldn't come to this, but it seems you leave me no choice." He shifted in his chair, tailored black slacks growing taut over hard-muscled thighs. "If my sources are correct—and I'm certain they are—you received in excess of half a million dollars in advance money for your latest book proposal."

He was right. Devon didn't bother to reply.

"I'm prepared to write you a check for one million dollars if you'll forgo any further work on this project."

Devon sucked in a breath. She'd expected some sort of move but certainly nothing like this. "I can understand your desire for privacy, Jonathan, but I find it difficult to believe you'd be willing to pay a million dollars for it."

"Obviously I would prefer not to, but if that is what it takes . . ."

Devon assessed him carefully but found no clue to what he was thinking. "I've done well with my books—far better than most of the writers I know—but I certainly never expected to make money by *not* writing something. What is it you're afraid I'll discover?"

Jonathan's look turned guarded, his gray-blue eyes became dark and unreadable. "I have nothing to hide, Devon. But I have a son to think of. The Stafford name has been respected for hundreds of years. From what Mrs. Meeks tells me, you're determined to write some sort of ghost story that involves my family and the Stafford Inn. It's the kind of thing the tabloids would love. I won't have it. If it costs me a million dollars to keep you from writing it, then I'm willing to pay it."

Devon smiled dryly. "I'm sorry to disappoint you, Mr. Stafford, but what I write is my business. I'm not interested in your money."

Jonathan's features turned hard, the skin growing taut across the finely carved bones in his face. "I don't believe that's quite true, Miss James. You see, the people who work for me are exceedingly efficient. I happen to know you need that money very badly. You own an expensive brownstone here on the Upper East Side, you pay for your parents' high-rise apartment, you wear expensive clothes, furs, jewelry . . . I also know you're a year and a half behind on your current writing project, and that even if you write this book, you won't be able to sell it—you haven't completed your contract on the last one."

Devon felt the heat creeping into her cheeks. It matched the anger that burned at the back of her neck. "You're very thorough, Mr. Stafford. But then I knew you would be. Unfortunately, none of what you've discovered makes a damn bit of difference—I'm still going to do what I set out to. I'm still going to write this book."

Jonathan got up from his chair, walked behind his massive walnut desk, and pulled open the top drawer. He drew out a leatherbound checkbook, sat down and took the top off his burgundy Mont Blanc pen.

"I know exactly how much your monthly expenses are, Devon. I also know you've got less than forty thousand dollars in your savings account. Besides your own expenses, you've got your parents to think of. How do you propose to make it through the next year?"

Devon's anger soared. *How dare he!* "You're so sure of yourself, aren't you? You think you've got all the answers—well, this time you haven't. In the first place, I'm behind on my new book because my divorce nearly killed me. I couldn't write, I couldn't think—if it hadn't been for Michael Galveston, I don't know what I would have done. But all that's behind me. *Traces* is nearly complete—a month, maybe two at the most, and I'll be finished. My publisher owes me a quarter of a million dollars on that book, which I'll receive the moment it's turned in." She came to her feet and stood facing him on the opposite side of the desk.

"But that really has nothing to do with this. The project I'm working on now is different than anything I've ever done. It's important. It isn't just a story I'm writing, it's something that happened to me, something that changed my whole life. I would write it if I had to sell my apartment, if I had to hock my furs and my jewelry. I would write it if I had to work two jobs and live in a cold-water flat! As for my parents . . . my father walked a beat on the Lower East Side for more than thirty years. He's a tough old bird and so is my mother. They would make whatever sacrifices

I asked of them—fortunately, I don't believe they'll have to."

For the first time Jonathan looked uncertain. "A million dollars is a lot of money."

"Yes it is. But it isn't everything." Devon felt a mixture of anger and bitter disappointment. "Whether you believe it or not, Mr. Stafford, there are things you can't always control. People you can't buy."

"Why?" he asked, coming to his feet. "Why is this book so important?"

"Because I have a chance to know something about myself few people ever have the opportunity to discover. Because I have a chance to learn things about life—and death. Because I have a chance to right something that's gone terribly, terribly wrong."

Jonathan stared at her as if seeing her for the very first time. "I'll stop you," he said softly.

"Did you ever hear of the First Amendment?"

"Have you ever heard of slander . . . or libel? I'll get an injunction and end this nonsense before it goes one step farther."

"You can try. But if I can prove my allegations—which I intend to—there is nothing you can do to stop me."

"Allegations? What are you talking about?"

Devon leaned across the desk, her hands pressing hard on the polished wood-grain surface. "You've tried to stop me without even knowing what my story is about. Well, I'll tell you. Something happened in that house of yours. Something monstrous. And I intend to prove it."

"This really *isn't* about money, is it? I thought you were trying to capitalize on the Stafford family name. A book linking my family to an uncertain past could earn you a fortune, even if it wasn't the truth."

"No, it isn't about money. It's about something far more important." She looked at him standing there, tall and incredibly handsome, and wondered what it might have been like to have had a chance to know him, to explore the attraction she felt without all the anger that lay between them.

She smiled tiredly. "I enjoyed the dinner, no matter what reasons you had for inviting me. I can see myself out. Thank you and good night." She started for the door, but his deep voice stopped her.

"I'll have Henry bring the car around, then I'll walk you down."

Devon said nothing. Just headed for the entry and waited for him to help her on with her coat. Jonathan spoke to Henry through the intercom into the garage, pushed the button on the elevator, and the doors slid wide.

"You really needn't bother." Devon stepped into the dark wood-paneled interior. Jonathan followed her in as though she hadn't spoken. He took her arm as they crossed the lobby, and Devon tried not to notice the strength that seemed to flow from his hand.

Henry held open the limousine door, and Devon slid onto the gray leather seat. Jonathan leaned into the open car door. "This isn't over, Devon. I'll call you later in the week."

"But I'm not—"

Jonathan's smile cut her off. He looked no less determined than he had before, but his eyes held a hint of respect. "I enjoyed the evening, too. You're very good company." He ducked out of the car and closed the door solidly behind him.

Devon leaned back against the seat. Her heart was still hammering against her ribs. She didn't know what to make of Jonathan Stafford. She was angry at his arrogance and audacity—his invasion of her privacy. Yet, in a way, she was doing the very same thing.

She thought about the way he had left her. He'd seemed almost pleased that she had turned the money down. How could that be?

She only knew for certain that she felt drawn to him in a way she hadn't expected. He was handsome, yes. Interesting and intelligent. But he hadn't played the usual sexual games, hadn't made the predictable male moves Paul or even Michael would have made. There was something about Jonathan Stafford that intrigued her, some depth of emotion he worked to hide. She seemed to sense a need in him that even he wasn't aware of.

On top of that, she felt a growing desire for him. He was tall and dark, lean and hard and indecently masculine. Just the brush of his hand on her arm made goosebumps race across her skin and her breasts grow taut. What would it be like to kiss him? To touch him and have him touch her? It was a heady thought, though she knew the danger of it.

She didn't trust him—couldn't afford to trust him—either with her business affairs or with her emotions. Would he call her again as he had said? Or would she be facing a summons in the morning?

Either way, she had meant what she told him. Once she found her proof, Bernard and Annie's story would be written, no matter the obstacles in her way. She would write it for them and for herself.

She really had no other choice.

Devon awoke later than she meant to. She hadn't slept well, had tossed and turned and worried about her clash with Jonathan Stafford and the path she had set for herself.

She had been attracted to him again last night, and for a while she'd been sure he had been attracted to her. Yet she had carefully suppressed those emotions and she would continue. The man was an enigma—inscrutable, distant and most of the time reserved. Though he had let his guard down several times during the course of the evening, she still wasn't certain which man was the real Jonathan Stafford—the charming, personable host, or the ruthless, demanding power-wielder determined to stop her no matter the cost.

And after what had happened in his study, she felt certain he was hiding something. Though Jonathan wasn't the object of her research, she would have to find out what it was. She almost smiled. He had nothing to fear from her, yet he'd offered her a small fortune to leave him alone. She wasn't interested in Jonathan's affairs—at least she hadn't been until he'd made his incredible offer. Now, sooner or later, she would have to find out why he'd made it.

Devon went into the kitchen to brew a pot of coffee, the "real thing" today instead of decaf. Inhaling the fragrant aroma of fresh-ground beans always made her look forward to the morning. Once the coffee was made, she poured herself a cup, then carried it into the living room. Still wearing her yellow terrycloth bathrobe, her blond hair fastened loosely atop her head, she sat down on the sofa with her notebook.

It took an effort of will to think of something besides her disastrous evening with Jonathan, but she was determined to get on with her work.

She looked down at the pad. *County Histories* were next on her list. A glance at the clock on her small French desk in the corner said that if she hurried, she could stop at the New York University library before her meeting with

Christy. The school allowed alumni great latitude in the use of their facilities and she needed an interlibrary loan.

A Bibliography of American County Histories by P. William Filby was a reference she had used before. County histories were books which began being published in the 1870s, though the majority were printed from 1880 to 1910. Each volume gave a history of the area and biographical sketches of residents. Florian Stafford was sure to be among them.

Unfortunately, the people who sponsored the books—members of the community who could afford it—were always pictured with a bit of a halo. She wondered what the book would have to say about Florian.

Also on the list was Nuck-Muck—the *National Union Catalog of Manuscript Collections,* published by the Library of Congress. Each year the NUCMC published a volume of old letters, diaries, journals, and research papers, indexed by both subject matter and the people involved. Maybe something of the Staffords had wound up there.

Devon set her notebook aside, showered and dressed, hailed a cab, and headed for NYU, on Washington Square. The library was crowded with students and teachers, but dressed as she was, in simple beige wool slacks, a beige silk blouse, and matching cardigan sweater, few of them paid her much notice. She found the reference section, then made arrangements for the volume she needed to be loaned from a neighboring library. Afterward, she scanned the Nuck-Muck indices, running her finger down the columns and spotting the Stafford name more than once.

She felt a thrill of triumph. There were half a dozen old documents, including correspondence between Florian and his brother, Captain William Lowell Stafford before his death in 1912. She read two items, but one was in another volume, which someone else was using. Since her time today was short, she would have to come back to read that one.

The most intriguing item, she found in a later volume—a letter written in 1925 from Anna Mae Stafford to her younger cousin, Estell—Jonathan Stafford's great aunt. It made no mention of Florian, but by that time Annie was twenty-six and had probably moved out of the house. Though Estell was ten years younger, it appeared they were friends of a sort. Since Estell Stafford Meredith was still alive, it was a lead she couldn't ignore.

Devon slid her notes and the copies she had taken of several different documents into her maroon leather briefcase, grabbed her camel-hair coat and cashmere scarf and left the library, heading down La Guardia Place toward the Insight Book Store on Macdougal Street, just a few blocks away.

As she walked along the crowded sidewalk, she thought again of the Staffords—and especially of Jonathan, recalling the enjoyable evening she had spent with him, and its abrupt and unpleasant end. When would he make his next move to stop her?

What did he have to hide?

Devon shoved her hands into the pocket of her coat against the cold. She passed a rusted-out barrel with a fire burning hotly in the bottom and smelled the burnt odor of roasting chestnuts. The vendor wore ragged pants, a frayed sweater that didn't quite cover his bulging stomach, and worn-out gloves with holes cut in the ends so his fingers could poke through. "Hot nuts!" he called out. "Get your hot roasted chestnuts!"

Devon just kept walking, but the smell made her stomach rumble, reminding her she'd forgotten to eat. A stiff November chill tinged the air; the hazy cloud of her breath moved with her as she hurried along the crowded street.

As always, Greenwich Village bustled with activity: students, tourists, hot-dog vendors, street people—a mixture of the odd and out of place.

Devon crossed the intersection onto Macdougal Street. Halfway down the block she spotted Christy, who waved a hand in her direction. Wearing tall black Cossack-style boots, a plum wool sweater, and a calf-length paisley wool skirt in mustard and plum, Christy waited in front of the bookstore. Her hair was tied back in Gypsy fashion. Big gold earrings dangled from her ears. She seemed oblivious to the cold wind gusting around her or the flat gray clouds overhead that boded storm.

"Devon! God, I'm glad to see you. It seems like it's been ages."

"A phone call just isn't the same, is it?" Christy Papaopolis hugged Devon, and she hugged her friend back. The busty, dark-haired, slightly off-beat Greek girl had been her best friend since college. In most ways they had little in common, yet it didn't seem to matter. Their friendship had endured through Devon's failed marriage to Paul, two of Christy's disastrous matrimonial attempts, and Devon's troubles with Michael.

"Let's go inside," Christy suggested, "get out of this godawful cold."

"I didn't think you noticed."

Christy laughed, a throaty, sensual sound. "I may be a ding-dong but I'm not completely numb to the world."

Devon laughed, too. "Impervious, but definitely not numb."

They stepped inside, ringing the bell as the door swung open then closed. The smell of incense invaded Devon's nostrils. "Just like being back in the dorms," she whispered, then wondered if kids still did that sort of thing. She had been a good deal more of a free spirit then, though never as far out as Christy. She realized how much her life had changed.

"Those were the days, weren't they?" Christy always thought of them with fonder memories than Devon did. She and Paul had gotten married in Devon's senior year. She'd worked two jobs to help him finish law school.

"They had their moments, I'll admit," Devon said, thinking of how much in love she had been—or at least she had thought so at the time.

"Remember that SAE fraternity party Paul took you to? I'll never forget that gorgeous Harvard football player I wound up with."

"Don't you dare start reminiscing about your love life," Devon warned, "neither of us is in much of a position to be fantasizing about men." Devon's look reminded her that both of them were once more unattached.

"True, but I just met the most delicious little Italian . . ." She grinned wickedly and Devon laughed, used to her friend's male entourage.

Christy was the only college friend she still felt close to. They lunched together often and made a point to stay in touch. Since Devon's terrifying experience in the yellow room, they had spoken on the phone at least once a day, talked about Michael—and Devon's unexpected relief that their relationship had ended—and briefly discussed Jonathan Stafford, though Devon had made no mention of the attraction she felt for him.

"Come on," Christy urged, taking her hand and starting off down one of the narrow aisles. "We've got work to do."

"Yes . . ." Devon agreed, beginning to take in her dark

and musty surroundings, the long, narrow, high-ceilinged room lit by a few ancient fluorescent lamps that managed little more than a dim purple glow. Then something brushed her arm, and Devon glanced up, into a pair of hideously glowing red eyes.

It was all she could do not to scream.

Seven

"Take it easy," Christy suggested, as Devon stopped dead in her tracks.

"What . . . what is that thing?" She pointed to the grotesque black-painted head that hung from the ceiling, its thick gaping lips, sharp white teeth, and red-rimmed eyes threatening them from above.

"It's only a mask. One of the customers makes them."

"What's it for?"

"All Hallows' Eve, I suppose. I don't really know. Witchcraft isn't my thing."

As they started walking again, Devon's heart still pounded. The building was old and dim and musty, but it was the dark menacing occult posters on the walls, and the ritualistic robes displayed beside them that bothered her. The narrow wooden slats of the floor creaked beneath their feet as Christy led them past a row of low-burning candles sputtering softly in their growing pools of wax.

"I hope you're prepared for this," Christy said, sensing her growing apprehension. "I know how much you hate this sort of thing."

That was an understatement. "This place is . . . is . . . whatever it is, it gives me the creeps." As if to prove her point, Devon shivered. Her chest felt tight and her palms had begun to sweat. Feelings of anxiety brought memories of her hellish night at the inn.

Black-art pentagrams were on the walls, together with charts listing various herbs, oils, and potions and their use in black magic. Shriveled-up plants hung in clusters from the ceilings along with several larger dried-up objects she determinedly ignored.

"You've always shied away from anything to do with the metaphysical," Christy said. "I can't believe you're actually going to write a book that deals with the subject."

"Neither can I." Like most of the people in the world, she was both intrigued and repulsed by the paranormal. Her parents, devout Protestant Irish, had taught her from childhood to shun anything that pertained to the supernatural, labeling all of it Satanic. From what she'd seen so far, she was tempted to agree.

"Look at this stuff, Christy. *The Meaning of Witchcraft, Witchcraft Today,* and the *Witches' Bible Compleat.*" Devon pulled out one of the volumes. "This one's called *The Magic Circle.* Looks like a step-by-step manual for starting your own witches' coven."

"How about this one? *The Prince of Darkness,* an examination of radical evil." Christy laughed, but Devon's insides churned.

"Are you sure this is the right place, Christy? I'm interested in ghosts and telepathy, not witches."

"Relax. We just haven't come to that section." They started walking again, turning the corner to pass such tomes as *The Voudown Gnostic Workbook* and *Tarot Shows the Path.* Another turn and Devon felt a wave of relief to see *The Encyclopedia of Parapsychology and Psychical Research* and other books like *The New Age Encyclopedia.*

"Here's a good one." Christy pulled out a paperback volume by Loyd Auerbach entitled *E.S.P., Hauntings, and Poltergeist.*

But Devon was looking at the row beneath. Robert Curran, *The Haunted: One Family's Nightmare.* Beside it, F. W. H. Myer, *Human Personality and its Survival at Bodily Death.* There was Raynor Johnson, *The Imprisoned Splendor,* Time-Life *Phantom Encounters,* and Gould and Cornell, *Poltergeists.* Book after book, and the shelves went the length of the room.

Devon's scalp began to tingle beneath a tight band of tension. Memories of her terror-filled night in the house on Church Street hovered at the edges of her mind but she forced them away.

"Are you all right?" Christy asked.

Devon nodded. "I can hardly believe it, Christy. Look how much has been written about this." The subject seemed endless.

"Did you think you were the first person to have this kind of experience? Honey, this is nothing new—people have been encountering strange phenomena and seeing ghosts for centuries. In case it's escaped you, millions of people believe Christ returned from the dead and walked the earth for thirty days. They say thousands of people saw him."

Devon's eyes swung to Christy's. "I never thought about it that way."

"Neither do most people. They're determined to believe ghost encounters are nothing but hoaxes. Thankfully, not everyone is so closed-minded."

"Are you ladies perchance discussing me?" A large, balding man with fringes of graying hair and thick gray eyebrows rounded a corner of the aisle. He smiled rather wolfishly when he spotted Christy. "Christina, my dear."

Taking her hands in his pawlike pair covered in freckles, he leaned over and kissed her cheek. "It's always good to see you."

"Devon, this is Nathaniel Talbot. He's the owner of the bookstore."

"Hello, Mr. Talbot."

"Please . . . Nathan will do." He took Devon's hand and brought it dramatically to his lips. "Welcome to the Insight Book Store."

"Thank you." *I think.* She eyed his black pants and long-sleeved black turtleneck, then glanced at the heavy silver talisman that hung from around his thick neck.

"Christina is one of our best customers," Nathan Talbot told her. "Since you two are friends, why don't you let me show you around?"

"Well, we really don't have that much time . . ." Devon hedged, but he had already taken her arm.

"I brought her here to meet Sara," Christy said from behind them. "Is she in her office?"

"Sara's not here. Some kind of problem with her daughter. She won't be back for a couple of weeks."

"Darn, I should have called before we came."

Devon stopped in the aisle and turned back to them. "It's all right. At least they've got some of the books I'll be needing."

"Perhaps if you told me your interests," Nathan said, "I might be able to help."

Devon glanced at Christy, who looked unhappy but resigned. "If Sara's gone, I don't see that we have any other choice."

Picking up on their subtle exchange, Nathan Talbot looked them over. "If you ladies have some sort of problem, why don't we go into my office and you can tell me about it? I've been in this business for sixteen years, surely there's some way I can help you."

"It's fairly involved." Devon wondered what Talbot would say to her story.

"Believe me, Nathan's heard it all," Christy put in.

An hour later, the tale had been told and Nathan had arranged an appointment with Zhadar, a channeler of some renown whom Christy recalled seeing something about on TV. Devon armed herself with half a dozen books on the subject of ghosts, hauntings, and telepathy, and a monthly magazine Nathan recommended entitled *Karma,* containing articles by people involved in the study of the metaphysical. She said good-bye to the oversized bookstore owner and walked outside with Christy to hail a cab.

"Well, what do you think?" Christy asked.

"I hate this whole eerie business, but I'm not daunted. I'm going to see it through."

"Not all New Age bookstores look like that one. I only brought you here so you could meet Sara Stone. Sara keeps regular hours at the Insight, since it's close to her apartment, and the customers she brings in help Nathan's business."

"What does Sara do?"

"She's a trance medium. She's able to contact the spirit world."

"A trance medium. It all sounds so unbelievable."

"To most people it is, but you've committed yourself to discovering the truth, so you've got to keep an open mind."

"I'm trying."

"I know you are."

"Is Zhadar a trance medium?"

"Zhadar's a spirit."

"What?"

"A woman named Patricia Solomon channels for Zhadar.

He's the spirit she connects with to find the answers to your questions."

"I see."

Christy laughed. "No you don't, but you will. I've never met Patricia, but hundreds of people go to her lectures or seek her out privately for her advice. By the way, an hour of her time won't come cheap."

"How much does she charge?"

"I'm not sure. Three hundred dollars might do it."

"Three hundred dollars! Is she really that good?"

"So they say."

"Well, the money doesn't matter. If she can help me, then the price will be worth it."

"That's what I figured you'd say."

As the first of two cabs pulled over, the women hugged each other good-bye. As Christy climbed in the bright yellow taxi, she promised to join Devon on Wednesday evening the following week for their scheduled appointment with Zhadar.

Devon hefted the heavy shopping bag filled with newly purchased books and climbed into the taxi behind. Between now and next week, she had a lot of reading to do.

Jonathan Stafford surprised himself by ordering Henry to make an unscheduled stop on their return trip back from New Jersey. Several hours earlier, he'd had a meeting with top-level Holidex management at the company's corporate headquarters in Franklin Lakes. The last-minute session had been called to discuss the threat being posed by Tri-Star Marine.

It hadn't gone well.

In fact it had run several hours longer than it should

have, with no new avenue of affirmative action. So far it looked as if Tri-Star's new Kelovar plastic could actually stand up to its revolutionary claims. Once the word was out that Kelovar was as tough and strong as metal, could be shaped into the thousands of odd sizes utilized as fittings by the small-boat industry, and was corrosion-resistant to salt, sun, water, and wind—then Holidex—and a dozen other casting and stamping companies across the country—would be in serious trouble.

Jonathan shifted on the gray leather seat in the back of the limo, then leaned forward to review once more the notes of his afternoon meeting. In his experience, nothing was ever quite the panacea Tri-Star claimed Kelovar was. There had to be something his people were overlooking, something that would even the gap between Holidex's tried and true products and Tri-Star's innovative new Kelovar line. All he had to do was find it—before it was too late.

Jonathan glanced out the tinted windows as the long black limousine made its way through the traffic on the George Washington Bridge. Below him, the Hudson River sparkled in the late afternoon sun, and the wakes of a bevy of small and large vessels formed patterns in the glistening blue water. For reasons only the traffic gods knew, the road was fairly uncongested as they turned onto Broadway and headed south toward the Woodland Memorial Children's Clinic, a colorless gray cement building on Columbus, just south and east of Columbia University, and across from Morningside Park.

Though he wasn't scheduled to pick Alex up until early in the morning, and the clinic frowned on his occasional unscheduled visits, he missed his son. After the pressures of a day like this one, he needed to see him. One reassuring hug from the small wonder who was the only thing good to come of his marriage could ease away the burdens of the day.

He'd thought about the boy for hours after Devon James had left his apartment. Her talk of children and home had left him in a melancholy mood. She'd surprised him again by refusing the money he had offered, and except for Alex and the threat she still posed, he'd surprised himself by being glad she did. His respect for her had grown, as well as his interest.

Unfortunately, his desire for her had mushroomed right along with it. A dozen times during the evening he had found himself wondering what it might be like to make love to her. He imagined her naked, and tried to guess how she might respond. Would she be wild and abandoned, or cautiously reserved? How much experience had she had? Would she eagerly accept the things he could teach her? Or would she be prudish and old-fashioned, as she had seemed?

Only his worry for his son, and his sheer determination to stop her from continuing her work, had enabled him to disguise the train of his thoughts.

Still, whatever his feelings for her—and even he wasn't sure what they were—he would have to put an end to her ridiculous speculations about his family. He couldn't afford the risk to his son.

Jonathan thought of him now, sitting in the clinic in his wheelchair instead of playing outside in the park with other children. He spent nights away from home, with doctors and nurses surrounding him instead of his family. There was no other choice and yet it still wasn't right.

Jonathan sighed into the emptiness inside the car. God, he missed him. Strangely enough, Alex handled his situation far better than his father. It was Alex who usually buoyed

Jonathan's spirits, not the other way around. He thought of his small son's resiliency and smiled. He'd be quite a man someday.

It didn't take long to reach the clinic, a highly praised and extremely expensive institution specializing in children's psychiatric medicine. He had chosen the place for its sterling reputation—and the fact that it wasn't too far from their home.

"You can wait right here, Henry," Jonathan said as the limousine pulled to the curb, "I'll only be gone a few minutes."

He got out of the car and crossed the sidewalk. Pushing through the heavy glass doors into the lobby, he found the place bustling with activity: children and parents coming and going, white-coated doctors and nurses striding purposefully down the halls. Jonathan didn't bother to stop at the reception desk, where a youthful dark-haired nurse bent over a stack of papers. He knew where his son's room was, and what he needed wouldn't take long.

When he got there, he found the gaily decorated semi-private room empty, though the bright-colored quilts on the two single beds had been mussed and the window beneath the sunny yellow curtains had been opened a crack to let in fresh air. Jonathan left and headed farther down the hall to the children's playroom. The spacious, airy enclosure had walls painted with murals of kids at the beach. And there were toys of every shape, size, and description.

The room hummed with activity: children huddled in groups playing jacks on the floor. Others were coloring. Several were playing Nintendo. Their eyes were fixed with unwavering interest on the images lighting the computer screen. A few children noticed Jonathan's entrance but soon dismissed it and returned to their play.

With a glance around the room, Jonathan spotted Alex in the corner, his small dark-haired head bent over the tray table of his wheelchair. The boy was drawing, using pastel chalks on a page in one of the many sketchbooks Jonathan constantly provided.

Moving closer, he looked over the small boy's shoulder and felt a surge of pride to see the intricate lines which captured so well the long shaggy golden hair of a small Pekinese puppy who'd been brought to the clinic for a visit. Animals were used by the staff for therapy. If Alex's enthusiastic conversations about the pets were any indication, the concept was reassuringly sound.

"Hello, son," Jonathan said gently, stepping around the stainless-steel spokes of the wheelchair into the line of his young son's vision.

"Dad!" Instinctively, Alex reached up, and Jonathan bent down to receive the small boy's welcoming hug. At the feel of the child's slender arms around his neck, Jonathan's chest went tight and a lump rose up in his throat.

It was always that way, though he never let his son know. And the moment of sadness passed quickly, leaving him with a warm tender smile.

"I thought you weren't coming to get me till tomorrow." Alex's narrow face brightened with the hope that he could leave early.

"I'm afraid you can't go till then, but I . . . *missed you* . . . was traveling this way and you were so close by, I couldn't resist stopping in."

At the news that he wasn't going home, disappointment flickered in Alex's blue eyes, then it was gone. Only pleasure shone in the face that was a smaller version of Jonathan's own dark features, strong cheekbones, black hair, and finely arched brows. But Alex had been blessed with a dimple Jonathan didn't have.

"I'm glad you did, Dad. I had kind of a tough day."

Having had that very same thought, Jonathan felt the pull of a smile. "What happened? Old Mrs. Livingston giving you trouble?"

"Nah, she's okay. Kinda grouchy sometimes, but I don't think she means it."

"Trouble with Raleigh?" Raleigh Johnson was Alex's roommate, a chubby little blond boy the kids called "Rollie" since he overate every time he got the chance. His family had brought him to the clinic to try to correct his eating disorder before it got any worse.

Alex shook his head. "I guess I was just wishing . . . you know . . . that things could be like they used to. That I could play baseball and stuff, like the other kids."

Jonathan's chest grew tight once more. "I know, son. But that's why you're here . . . so that someday you'll be able to."

"That's what Mrs. Livingston says. I just have to keep doing my therapy so my legs don't get too weak, but . . ."

"But what?"

"But sometimes I'm not sure I believe her."

Jonathan hugged him again. Most of the time, Alex's spirits stayed high and he rarely spoke of his paralysis—or the accident that had caused it. But once in awhile he was troubled by the presence of the other children, whole—at least physically, doing the things he wanted so badly to do but no longer could. Then again, that was part of the strategy. The doctors hoped to create a strong desire for normalcy, so that Alex would overcome the obstacles.

"I know it's hard, son. But the doctors know what's best. They believe you'll be well again—and so do I."

Alex looked at him, saw the apparent conviction behind his words, and grinned, bringing the dimple to his cheek. The tension seemed to drain from his slender young body, and in that moment Jonathan wished more than ever he could take his young son home.

"I'm glad you came, Dad."

"Me, too, son."

They talked about the sketch Alex had drawn. Jonathan praised him on the accuracy of his work and looked at several of his other sketches. Then—tall, formidable nurse Livingston barreled into the playroom.

"Good afternoon, Mr. Stafford. I didn't see you come in." Her disapproving frown said that if she had, his visit would have been even briefer—or maybe nonexistent. She knew exactly how to prey on his concern for his son to get him to do exactly what she wanted.

"I was just leaving, Mrs. Livingston." He squeezed Alex's small hand, the slender fine-boned fingers so much like his own. "I'll see you in the morning, son. I thought we'd go to the zoo. They're bringing in a rare white tiger and two of her cubs. I thought you might like to see them."

Alex brightened. "Could I draw them?"

"I don't see why not."

"That'd be swell, Dad." One last hug and Jonathan was gone. He'd been right to stop in, no matter what the damnable psychiatrists said.

Yet surely they knew more than he did. The hours Alex spent away from him, away from the private school for handicapped children where he spent another good portion of his time, would pay off, they promised. In the six months since Alex had come to the clinic, Jonathan had seen little evidence of the boy's improvement. But that was not unexpected, they said. This sort of therapy was bound to take a good deal of time. There was a very good chance—sooner or later—that Alex would return to normal.

As long as there were no setbacks.

He thought of Devon James and her determination to dig into his family business. Sooner or later, she was sure to discover that Alex's accident had happened in Stafford. His son would be dragged into her crazy speculations and the old outrageous rumors would all be dredged up again. He couldn't afford to let Devon continue, couldn't risk any harm that Alex might suffer from her interference.

He would find a way to stop her. If persuasion didn't work, he would discover something that would.

Jonathan was banking on it.

He wanted his son whole again.

And he wanted him to come home.

More fatigued from her unsettling experience at the bookstore than she had guessed, Devon unlocked her apartment door and stepped inside. Tossing her heavy bag of books on the sofa, she turned on the stereo, choosing an Andrés Segovia classical guitar disc in the hope of soothing her nerves.

She checked her phone messages, made a note of the calls she would need to return in the morning, then sank down wearily on the sofa. She had just begun to rummage through her newly purchased volumes when a familiar knock sounded at the door. Two short raps then another. Michael. He still had a key to the front door of the building. Wanting to let him down as gently as possible, she had postponed asking him to return it. Now she wished she had.

She opened the door to find him standing in the hall in a dark gray three-piece suit.

"Hello, Devon." His hazel eyes ran over her beige slacks and slightly rumpled beige silk blouse. "You haven't forgotten what day it is, have you?"

"I guess I must have. What day is it?"

"The opening at the gallery. Jaimendez. You've been planning this night for weeks."

"Oh, my God." She had wanted to go all right—but not with Michael. How could she have forgotten to call him? "I just assumed . . . under the circumstances . . . you'd consider the evening canceled."

"On the contrary, I've been looking forward to it. Things may be a bit cloudy between us, but we're still friends, aren't we?"

"Of course."

"I promised you weeks ago I would take you to the opening. I intend to keep my word."

"I . . . I don't know, Michael. It's already getting late, and I haven't even dressed."

"You've never let that stop you before. Come on. It'll be good for you to get out of the apartment."

She hadn't the heart to tell him she'd been out all day. Devon sighed. It wasn't fair to Michael not to go. He'd been looking forward to the Brazilian artist's opening as much as she had. They'd both found his work impressive. Devon had hoped to buy at least a piece or two at the show, though she couldn't really afford it. Then again, *Traces* was almost done, which meant the balance of her advance would be due, and if the artist was really as good as she thought he was, she couldn't afford not to.

She glanced in the mirror, took in her wind-blown hair and the worn look to her makeup. "Why don't you mix yourself a drink? I'll get ready as fast as I can."

She appeared half an hour later dressed in a backless

royal blue silk dress, her blond hair fashioned in a coil at the back of her neck, with wispy strands floating beside her ears.

"You look lovely," Michael said, repeating the same words Jonathan Stafford had said to her that night in his apartment. But when Michael said them, her pulse didn't pound and there was no warm tingling in her stomach.

"Thank you." She opened the closet door and took out her white mink coat. "We'd better get going." Michael nodded and helped her put it on.

Downstairs in front of the building, the doorman hailed a cab at Michael's instruction and it waited for them at the curb. They climbed in out of the cold and were on the way to *Intrepid,* the small but influential gallery on Fifty-third near Fifth where the show was being held. Michael told her how good it was to see her and how much he had missed her. Then he launched into a discussion of his new role as Vice President of Darnex Marketing and went into great detail about his "incredible new marketing plan."

"If I don't get another promotion out of it, my name's not Michael Galveston."

"I'm happy for you, Michael."

"There's just one thing, Devon, that would make it perfect."

"What's that?"

He took her hand and raised it to his lips, pressing his mouth against her fingers. "Having you to share it with."

Devon glanced out the window, amazed at how little Michael's touch affected her. An icy drizzle had started and the car slid precariously around a corner before the driver righted the wheels and sloshed on down the street. "We've talked about this, Michael. My career and yours just aren't compatible anymore."

Michael squeezed her hand. "Not necessarily. Adjustments could be made."

Like giving up my work.

"Just think about it. Christmas is coming. It wouldn't seem right if we weren't together."

Christmas. It had always meant so much to her and very little to Michael. "It's still a ways away." She was trying to evade him. They had a long evening ahead; she didn't intend to fight with him.

The taxi slid to a halt in the middle of the block, and the burly black-haired driver turned to speak to them through the hole in the plexiglass separating the passenger section. "That'll be three-sixty."

Michael slid out, helped Devon climb out, then leaned in and paid the bill. A chill wind whipped her hair and the icy drizzle stung her cheeks. She burrowed her face into the soft fur collar of her full-length mink, glad she had worn it instead of just her jacket.

Taking Michael's arm, she crossed the sidewalk and someone pulled open the beveled glass door to *Intrepid.* The Jaimendez opening was well under way by the time they stepped inside. For such a small gallery, the event was a lavish affair—huge bouquets of flowers, French champagne, Russian vodka and caviar. The men were dark-suited while the women wore cocktail dresses, most of them costlier than hers, but few of them prettier than the rich blue silk she had chosen.

"From the looks of the clientele," Michael said, "I'd say the word's already out. Your boy could be on his way to stardom."

"It certainly seems possible." A waiter carrying a tray of champagne walked by, and Devon and Michael each picked up a stemmed crystal glass. The gallery itself was simply designed: stark white walls, plush gray carpet, black track lighting beneath an exposed ceiling where air vents, pipes, and conductors had all been painted black. The effect was interesting, but subtle, taking nothing away from the paintings expertly hung on the walls.

Particularly not *these* paintings, Devon noted, enjoying the vivid yet modulated colors, the way the artist had captured the everyday life of Brazil, its artisans and peasants. The rounded figures, reminiscent of Botero, evoked the folk style of Thomas Hart Benton, yet in another way the work was totally different. The style was completely the artist's own.

"They're wonderful," Devon said, "the most incredible work I've seen in years."

"The program says he's already being exhibited in a number of museums in Brazil."

"Yes. And look how many of his paintings have already sold." There were tags on at least a half-dozen pieces and the show had just gotten started.

"Why don't we go meet him?" Michael suggested, surprising her. He had only developed an interest in art in the last few months they had been together. Initially, he had balked at attending the shows, and paying homage to the artist was his least favorite part.

"All right." They walked in that direction, waited until the crowd around the handsome dark fiftyish Brazilian had thinned, then stepped forward just as another couple did the same. Devon turned at the brush of a man's jacketed arm against her shoulder. Unusual gray-blue eyes locked on her face.

Jonathan Stafford smiled. "Good evening, Ms. James."

Devon started at the resonance in his voice, and the tingling began in her stomach. "Hello," she replied, bringing her surprise under control. "Michael, this is Jonathan Stafford. Jonathan, meet Michael Galveston." The men made appropriate responses and shook hands, sizing each other up as men do. Jonathan introduced the small well-dressed woman at his side as Akemi Kumato, and Devon recognized her instantly as the beautiful Asian woman she had seen pictured with him in several magazines.

The woman inclined her head in a slight bow, the gesture very Oriental, though for some reason it seemed artificial, done more to please Jonathan than herself.

"You are enjoying the show, Miss James?" she asked.

"Yes, very much," Devon said politely, but had to force herself to smile. The tiny woman was gorgeous, all smooth dark skin and big dark eyes. Her yards of glossy black hair had been swept up, very chic and extremely becoming. She seemed cool and self-assured, though somewhat remote and untouchable—until she looked at Jonathan. She wondered if the woman was in love with him.

"Quite a turnout for such a small gallery." Jonathan's deep voice drew her attention. "Looks as though it's going to be a very successful show." He glanced toward the Brazilian artist. He had already been besieged by another round of admirers.

"I think Jaimendez is incredibly talented, but I'm surprised to find you here. I thought your interest was chiefly in Oriental art." She had to work not to look at the woman. Just how much interest did Jonathan have in her?

"I'm also concerned with art as an investment. Jaimendez looks to be a very attractive prospect."

"I couldn't agree more." Michael slid a proprietary arm around Devon's waist. "Devon and I are considering several pieces."

Jonathan arched a fine black brow in her direction. "Is

that right, Ms. James? You and your *fiancé* are making the purchase together?"

Damn Michael Galveston! What on earth could she say? "I'm not certain what Michael intends. As for myself, yes. I've already seen several likely prospects."

Jonathan seemed to digest that bit of information. His eyes touched hers, searched, probed, then held and did not stray. "Then I wish you good luck—*gambatte kudasai,* the Japanese would say." Words he had spoken that night in his apartment. Was it meant as a gentle reminder?

"Enjoy the show." He urged the petite Asian woman back into the crowd with a hand at her waist.

Michael turned on Devon the moment they were gone. "Jonathan Stafford—Stafford Enterprises, right?"

"Yes."

"He's also the guy who owns the Stafford Inn."

"Yes, he is."

His mouth thinned into a disapproving line. "He certainly gave you the once over. Just exactly how well do you know him?"

Devon worked not to glance away. From now on, what she did was none of Michael's business. "He called me about my research on his family. We had lunch together."

"Lunch."

"Yes."

"And what does Mr. Stafford think of your project? Surely he can't be happy about you prying into his family affairs."

Devon bristled even more, knowing Michael had guessed the truth. "What Jonathan Stafford does or doesn't think is none of your concern. We're here to look at art, Michael. If you'd rather stand here and argue, I suggest you go on home."

"Damn you, Devon."

"I mean it, Michael."

"Is that what you want? Do you want me to leave?"

If Jonathan had been there alone, she might have said yes, and the truth of the thought surprised her. Devon shook her head. "I came with you, I'll leave with you. Whatever happens between us, I hope we'll always be friends."

"We're more than friends, Devon. Can't you see that?"

"Please, Michael."

He took a deep breath and slowly released it. "All right, have it your way. Look, I've got to make a couple of phone calls." He smiled. "Don't want good ol' Cliff Corbin getting the jump on me." Corbin was a long-standing rival, another Darnex VP. "I'll be back in a minute." After setting his drink on the edge of a gray marble pedestal beside a small bronze bust, Michael shouldered his way through the crowd toward an office in the rear of the gallery.

The moment he was gone, Devon sagged in relief. It had been a mistake to go out with Michael, but at least now she knew for sure that ending their relationship had been the right thing.

She walked a few more paces along a gallery wall until she came to a painting of laborers toiling on a Brazilian beach. The colors were bold yet muted, brick red against azure blue, evoking an ebb and flow like the beckoning surf in the background and posing a sharp contrast to the laborers' back-breaking work. The painting made her ache for a simpler time, a simpler way of life, yet it also spoke of the hardships those people endured.

"I like that one, too." A note of intimacy softened the deep voice beside her. She didn't have to look, to know who it was. She turned, and found him alone, watching her intently. In his double-breasted dark blue suit, he exuded power and wealth, yet the smile he gave her seemed to breach the distance between them almost as if he had touched her.

"What happened to your lady?" She hoped the question sounded casual, just pleasant conversation, nothing more.

"She's in the powder room. What about Galveston?"

"Making some phone calls."

"From our talk the other night, I got the impression it was over between the two of you."

Did it matter? She found herself hoping it did. "Michael and I are no longer dating. He's only a friend."

"I see."

"What about you? Not that it's any of my business."

"It might be . . . if you agreed to go out to dinner with me."

Devon's heartbeat quickened. Whether in warning or anticipation she couldn't be sure. "Your friend wouldn't mind?"

"My friend is just that—a friend."

"A long-time friend," Devon remarked dryly, and Jonathan arched a brow. *Touché,* his expression said.

"What about dinner?" Gray-blue eyes moved over the curves of her body, warmed with admiration at the fit of her blue silk dress, then returned to her face.

Devon's cheeks grew warm. "I'd love to but . . ." She had to say no. She knew why he was asking. He wanted another chance to convince her to stop her work.

"But?"

"Under the circumstances, it's probably not a good idea."

"The circumstances being that you're determined to write your book and I'm equally determined to stop you."

"Exactly."

He looked back at the painting. The movement was too

casual. A sure sign his efforts at persuasion were hardly at an end.

"How's your research coming?" Jonathan asked evenly.

"Slowly . . . painfully. Then again, this isn't an easy subject."

Jonathan's compelling eyes fixed on her face. "I wish I knew exactly what the subject was. You owe me that much, you know. If you're bound and determined to pry into my family affairs, you should at least be willing to tell me why."

He had a point. She couldn't deny it. "You won't like hearing what I have to say."

"I'd rather hear it from you than read about it in your book."

Score one for him. "All right, I'll accept your invitation to dinner on one condition—"

"What's that?"

Devon smiled. "You promise not to offer me money—it was hard enough to refuse the first time."

Jonathan laughed and so did Devon.

"No more money," he promised, "as long as you'll agree to tell me what this is all about. I want to know why you're so determined to write this damned book."

Devon's hand trembled slightly as she imagined Jonathan's reaction to her tale. Unconsciously her fingers tightened on the stem of her champagne glass. "You probably won't believe me, but I guess you deserve to hear it. I hope you'll try to keep an open mind."

"I'll try, Devon, I promise." He looked over her shoulder, saw Michael approaching, and took a sip of his champagne. "I'll call you the first of the week."

"All right."

With a last brief smile, he turned and walked away.

Devon watched him longer than she should have, drawn by the light reflecting off his wavy blue-black hair. He was taller than most of the men in the room, but she suspected that even if he hadn't been, he would seem so.

"I brought you another glass of champagne," Michael said, making her jump and her face flush with guilt. Dammit, Michael was out of her life—she intended to keep it that way. "Thank you."

"Have you decided which piece to buy?"

"Yes. I like this one." She pointed to the workers on the beach.

"Why don't you pay for it so we can get out of here? Cliff and Gladys expect us to stop by for a drink."

Devon groaned inwardly. She had met a few nice people in Michael's company, but at his level, the competition for promotion was fierce. Even the women took up the battle, and Cliff and Gladys Corbin were two of the worst. "Cliff and Gladys—Mr. and Mrs. Corporate America."

"Come on, they aren't that bad. Besides, they've missed seeing us."

With a sudden flash of insight, Devon turned on him. "You haven't told them about us, have you? They still think we're engaged."

"There's nothing to tell. You've still got my ring, haven't you? Just relax, Devon. Everything's going to work out. You'll see."

Devon eyed him warily. Michael was always confident, but not *this* confident. What did he have planned? She shuddered to think of it. He was always such a schemer. Why hadn't she seen it before?

Devon bought the painting and made arrangements with the gallery to have it delivered to her apartment the following morning. Once she and Michael left the gallery, she pleaded a headache and asked him to take her home.

"Dammit, Devon, Cliff and Gladys are going to get their feelings hurt."

Cliff and Gladys don't have any feelings, she thought but didn't say so. "I'm sorry, Michael, I'm just not up to it."

They rode in silence until the cab reached her brownstone apartment, then Michael walked her into the warmth of the softly lit lobby.

"Why don't I come up for a drink?"

"I told you, Michael, I'm not feeling very well."

His light brown brows drew together in an unhappy frown. "All right, I'll call you next week."

"Fine." *And I'll write you tomorrow, explain again exactly how things stand, and return your damned ring.*

"Good night, Devon." He tried to kiss her, but she turned away.

"Good night, Michael." All the way up in the elevator, she wondered what she had ever seen in him. And thought how different the evening might have been if Jonathan Stafford had been bringing her home.

Eight

Jonathan stood at the window in the living room of Akemi's high-rise apartment. Twenty stories below, miniature automobiles clogged the ribbon of a street and a million ant-sized people jostled and collided yet never really interacted, their lives as separate and remote as Jonathan tried to keep his. Across the way, a galaxy of lights brightened the inky blackness of the cold November evening.

"You are sure you do not wish a drink?" Akemi asked. "It would help you to relax." She still wore the off-the-shoulder, gold-trimmed black velvet dress she had worn to *Intrepid,* but she had taken the pins from her hair, letting the heavy black mass hang loose around her shoulders.

"No. I've already had more than I should have." He stared out into the vastness, his mind wandering, drifting, returning unbidden to the events of the evening. Still lost in thought, he made his way to the sofa and sank down wearily, stretching his long legs out in front of him.

"She is very pretty."

"Who?" Jonathan turned away from the mind swirls, knowing very well whom she meant.

Akemi just smiled. "Devon James. She is a writer, yes?"

He nodded. "Quite a well-known writer."

Akemi walked behind the sofa and began to massage his shoulders, her small fingers expert as they wrested the knots of tension from the muscular bands of flesh. "You are attracted to her. That has not happened in some time." She worked the buttons on his shirtfront, then slipped a hand inside the starched white fabric to splay across his chest. Her long hair teased his cheek as she leaned forward to nibble an ear. "Why don't you close your eyes and pretend I am she?"

"What?" Jonathan started, fresh tension seeping through his body.

"It might be exciting." Akemi shrugged in a gesture of nonchalance while her fingers teased the curly black hair on his chest. "Just think how tall and fair she is, how soft and pretty are her lips. Imagine her touching you as I am." Another hand slid down the front of his slacks, pressing intimately against his sex. "The way you looked at her, I should think it would be easy."

As she began to work the catch on his zipper, Jonathan came to his feet. "Don't."

Akemi straightened, studying him, eyeing him far too shrewdly. "What is the matter?"

He didn't answer.

"Jonathan?" The concern in her small voice made him pause, but only for a moment. Then he walked to the chair across from the sofa and reached for his dark blue suit coat.

"It was only a game," she said, coming up behind him. "We have played such games before."

"I know." There was little they hadn't done. Akemi knew dozens of ways to heighten the art of pleasure. "It isn't your fault, it's just . . ." He stuck his arm into the sleeve of his coat and pulled it across the width of his shoulders.

"Surely you are not leaving? It storms outside and the hour grows late."

He hadn't meant to. But he felt more restless than he

had when he came, and what Akemi had in mind wasn't the answer.

"This is not a good night for me." They had always been honest with each other, nothing less would do now. And yet what *was* the truth? That his encounter with Devon James had once more stirred emotions he wasn't ready to explore. That his blood ran hot for her though he knew he shouldn't let it?

"My mind's a thousand miles away, that's all. I need to get some sleep."

Akemi watched him a little longer, her almond eyes assessing him—maybe even a little bit hurt. "I will ring for you a cab."

Jonathan merely nodded. He picked up the tie he had carelessly tossed on the overstuffed chair, accepted the cashmere overcoat she handed him, and started for the door.

"Good night," he said a bit more abruptly than he'd meant to, then he stepped out into the hall and firmly closed the door.

By the time he'd reached the street, he felt better.

He was very much afraid he knew why.

Devon's phone had rung two other times by the time Jonathan called Monday morning.

"I know I asked you to dinner," he said to her, "but how would you feel about a night at the theater instead? A friend of mine phoned and asked if I wanted two Wednesday-night, third-row center seats to *Les Misérables*. Something's come up and he won't be able to use them. I know the play's been running for a while, but I've never had a chance to see it."

"Neither have I."

"We could have a late supper and talk things over then."

What was the note she heard in his voice? Business as usual, and yet there seemed something more, something close to anticipation.

"Are you sure this is a good idea?"

"Considering the circumstances?" he asked, repeating her words at the gallery.

"Yes."

"It might be interesting to mix a little pleasure with business for a change. I rarely get the chance."

She hesitated only a moment. "Wednesday, you said?" Her meeting with Zhadar wasn't until the following week.

"Yes."

"All right then, it sounds like fun. What time should I be ready?"

"I'll pick you up at seven."

"As I recall, you know where I live." It seemed he knew damned near everything about her, or at least thought he did.

Jonathan paused. "I know where you live," he quietly admitted.

"Then I'll see you Wednesday."

He arrived promptly, looking handsome in an expensively tailored black suit that appeared to be Italian. Devon invited him in while she went to get her coat.

"Very nice." He glanced at his surroundings, the paintings and sculptures, the tasteful blend of antique and modern. "Elegant but comfortable. I like it very much." The same sort of approval she had voiced about his apartment.

"Thank you. I did most of the design work myself."

He smiled. "Then it's too bad we haven't got more time.

I believe a person's inner feelings are very much reflected in his home." He looked around again. "Just imagine what I might learn about you, Devon James." Gray-blue eyes moved over her face then drifted to the curve of her breast. She felt them almost as if he had touched her, even through the layers of her clothes.

Devon smiled a bit nervously and took his arm, turning him toward the door. "As you said, we haven't much time and we certainly wouldn't want to be late."

On the way downstairs, Jonathan remarked approvingly on her white silk brocade blouse and full-legged trapeze-style black silk pants, but once they reached the solitude of the limo, they spoke very little, except for polite conversation about the icy weather, a foray here and there into events of the day.

It might have been just a casual evening out, if it hadn't been for the touch of his shoulders against hers, the way he entwined her fingers with his. Devon felt the power and strength of the man, his indisputable sexuality. It made her insides tremble and her mouth feel dry. She saw the way his eyes moved over her, saw the way he watched her, and wondered if the same sort of feelings were pressing in on him.

As clever as he was at masking his emotions, his expression betrayed only his excitement about seeing the show, and Devon found herself pleased that he had asked her.

Not that she should have been. She knew exactly why he had done it—the man had made it clear he'd do everything in his power to put an end to her work. This was just another avenue of persuasion. But she stood firm in her convictions, there was nothing he could do to convince her not to proceed.

Just say no, she thought, feeling the pull of a smile at the anti-drug slogan. It wasn't like he was out to do her bodily harm. Still, he was a man to be reckoned with, and her overpowering attraction to him put her at a distinct disadvantage. She had to keep things well in hand; she couldn't afford to let her personal feelings get in the way of this project.

"I haven't been to a Broadway show in years," he said, cutting into her thoughts. "I'm usually just too busy."

"I'm beginning to believe, Jonathan Stafford, that you work far too much."

He sighed with what sounded like resignation. "That's no secret. In fact, it's a problem I've been trying to solve for some time. Unfortunately, I've had little success in finding someone I feel is capable of taking over a major portion of the responsibilities. I'll know him when I meet him. At least that's what I keep telling myself, but I certainly haven't found him yet."

"Maybe you're too particular."

Jonathan smiled. "I'm extremely particular." He threw her a glance that was decidedly approving. The man was devastating, all hard muscle and bone, smooth dark skin, and finely etched male features. She found herself smiling and blushing as if she were fifteen instead of nearly thirty. With his easy smile and practiced charm, Jonathan played her like a well-tuned musical instrument.

She knew what he was doing and still couldn't stop herself from falling under his spell.

The show itself was the only thing that saved her from letting him charm her completely. It sucked her in, from the moment the orchestra struck up the overture; and it held her in thrall until the final curtain. With its brilliant costumes, lavish stage sets, incredibly talented cast, and wonderful musical score, *Les Miz* was as exciting a bit of showmanship as ever hit the Broadway stage.

Jonathan seemed even more taken with the performance than she was. "I'd forgotten what an incredible experience a Broadway show can be. I'll have to take Alex. I'm sure he would love it."

"He's never been to a Broadway play?"

"No, he's—" At the shift in conversation toward his son, something flashed in Jonathan's eyes, then it was gone. "No."

"The New York Ballet is doing the *Nutcracker* at Lincoln Center next month. Why don't you see if you can get tickets? I'm sure any little boy would love—"

"I'll do that," he said shortly. "That's a very good idea."

From that moment on, the evening went downhill. Dinner at Sardi's was a perfunctory finish to what should have been a memorable night. They ate rather quickly, mostly in silence, then left, Jonathan suggesting they go somewhere quiet where they might speak more privately.

"Why don't we go back to my apartment?" Devon offered. "I've a very good bottle of brandy that's hardly been touched."

"All right." But the tension that had settled over him at the end of the evening didn't seem to lessen. They took the slow-moving elevator, and once inside the apartment Jonathan helped her off with her coat, and hung it up along with his overcoat. While Devon walked to the small antique walnut sideboard that served as a bar, Jonathan prowled the room, looking at her paintings, admiring a small bronze sculpture, and an unusual hand-painted ceramic plate. Then he came to her antique French desk and stopped.

Brandy snifter in hand, Devon froze. A copy of Florian Stafford's will lay open on the dark green leather inset, along with a sheet of notes from family letters she had read at the library.

When Jonathan turned, his face was a study in anger barely suppressed. "I see you've been hard at work."

For a moment she couldn't think of anything to say. She just stared into his cold, disapproving features.

"I know you're unhappy about my research, Jonathan," she began softly, "but you promised to hear me out. I expect you to keep your word." When he said nothing, she crossed the room and handed him a snifter of brandy. "Please, won't you at least listen to what I have to say?"

His face remained hard, though at the brush of her fingers against his hand, his eyes swung to hers and some of his tension seemed to ease.

"I said I wanted to know, and I do, but . . ." He raked a hand through his wavy black hair, shoving it back from his forehead. "This is difficult for me, Devon. I'm a man of privacy. I don't approve for a moment your delving into my family affairs."

"No more than I approve of your delving into mine—but I believe I understand why you did it, and I'm trying my best to be fair."

Jonathan sat down on the sofa, tugging his trousers up as he stretched his long legs out in front of him. "All right, tell me what this is all about."

Devon sat down beside him, gathering her wits about her, praying she would speak the right words. "It started one night in October a little over a month ago. Michael and I were returning from a conference in Boston. On the way, we had—that is, I had—made arrangements to spend the night at the Stafford Inn. I thought it would be romantic, I thought . . . anyway, whatever I believed, I was hardly prepared to deal with a house full of ghosts."

"Ghosts!" Jonathan openly scoffed.

"I suppose that's a poor choice of words," she went on, "and yet I don't know any others that you would more readily accept."

"I'm sorry, Devon, but I just don't believe—"

"I know. And in the beginning, neither did I." Slightly embarrassed to be discussing such a subject, Devon told him the rest of her story. It was relatively easy—every minute detail seemed to have been burned into her brain.

Still, Jonathan's disbelief did not lessen. "The mind can be a powerful force, Devon."

"It wasn't just my imagination," she defended. "It was terrifying in that room, unlike anything I've ever experienced or hope to experience again. The malevolence was unspeakable, unbelievable. If you could have felt it, you would have known without doubt that I'm telling you the truth."

"I've been in that house, Devon. A number of times. I've never felt anything frightening."

"I'm not sure why it happened to me, but I hope to find out."

"What about Galveston? Does he believe all of this, too?"

"Michael would never admit it, even if he did believe it. He would be too concerned about what it might mean to his career."

"But he felt those same things you did? Some sort of terrifying presence?"

Devon sighed. "I don't know for sure. He acted very strangely . . . the whole night was strange." She glanced up at him. "It was worse than any nightmare I've ever had—and I was awake."

"There's a reasonable explanation for all of this. Surely you can see that."

Devon threw up her hands and came to her feet. "I knew you wouldn't believe me. I don't even know why I bothered."

"This whole thing is crazy, Devon. There is no such thing as ghosts."

She walked over to the desk and pulled out the notebook she had used that morning at the Stafford Inn. "Oh, no? Well, take a look at these—" She handed him the notebook. "I wrote these notes the morning after my night at the inn. I wrote them before I knew anything about that damned house—*before* I spoke to Mrs. Meeks."

Jonathan scanned the pages, his gray-blue gaze intent, his black brows drawing together here and there. "Just what, exactly, do you believe all this nonsense means?"

Devon came to a place in front of him, her feet planted apart as if she meant to do battle. "It means I somehow sensed the death of a small child, and Florian's son did die—rather mysteriously, or so rumor says."

"Anything that happened that long ago can seem mysterious. Records weren't well kept, files are missing or have somehow been destroyed."

"Did you know that other guests have experienced some of the same phenomena I did? One of them saw the ghost of an old woman, and another was disturbed by dreams about something locked in a trunk in the closet—Mrs. Meeks said so."

"Mrs. Meeks is melodramatic. Maybe she believes a ghost story here and there is good for business."

"I hardly think so. The woman is completely paranoid on the subject."

"The point is, Devon, this whole thing is circumstantial. A child is dead and you believe—"

"Did you know the house on Church Street is built over a cemetery?"

"No, but—"

"More specifically, did you know that the house is built over little Bernard Stafford's grave?"

"No."

"Why would a sane man do something so totally *in*sane?"

"How do you know for sure Bernard is buried there?"

"They found his tombstone down in the basement."

"God!"

"I know this all sounds crazy, Jonathan. If it hadn't happened to me, I wouldn't believe it, either. I hate even dabbling in this sort of thing. If you want to know the truth, it scares me to death."

"What about the girl?" he asked. "You've got no proof whatsoever that she was molested. That story is as far-fetched as the other one, maybe more so."

"I haven't been able to document anything yet, but I've only just started. I've got dozens of avenues I haven't explored. I want to speak to your aunt Estell—"

"No." Jonathan surged to his feet. "I won't have it. This has got to stop, Devon. Please, I'm asking you, begging you not to go on with this."

"Can't you understand, I have to? My writing is a gift. With it come certain obligations. Something's been asked of me. I can't just ignore it."

"What's been asked of you? For God's sake, what is it you're crusading for?"

Devon turned away from him, walked to the window, then absently moved to the desk. Toying nervously with the will, she silently scanned the lines she'd already read twice before. "I'd rather not tell you. You aren't going to believe it, and it will only make things worse."

"You owe it to me, Devon, and I want to know."

Devon lifted her chin and turned to face him. "Very well. I believe the souls of Bernard and Annie Stafford are trapped in that house and that they came to me to help free them. It may sound farfetched, but I've already read enough on the subject to know there's a way that might be done. The soul that's locked on the earth plane has to be shown the truth of its mortality. If Florian is somehow keeping them there, he's got to be made to face the fact of what he's done so that they can all be free. I've got to prove it, Jonathan, and I intend to."

Jonathan released a weary breath, stood up and crossed to the place beside her. She had to tip her face up to look at him. "Do you have any idea how insane this all sounds?"

"I know. Believe me, I know." Devon's throat began to close. She cared about Jonathan Stafford. She didn't want him looking at her the way he was now.

"Do you really believe all this?"

"If you want to know the truth, I'm not completely sure. I'm only certain I have to know, one way or the other."

"Damn you."

Tears stung Devon's eyes. "I wish I'd never gone to that house, but I did. I can't turn my back on this now. I can't . . . and I won't."

She looked into his handsome face, willing him to understand. Jonathan read her troubled emotions, saw the wetness on her cheeks, and some of the hardness seeped from his features.

"I don't believe for a moment that any of this is real. I hate the fact that what you're doing may wind up hurting my family." He moved closer and the force of his gaze held her still. There was something different in his eyes now, something dark and unreadable.

"I know I'm going to have to stop you, that I should stay as far from you as I possibly can . . ." A long-fingered, dark-skinned hand slipped through her hair, cupped her head and forced it back. "Then I look at you, watch the way you smile, listen to your laughter. In your eyes I see your worry, your concern, and all I can think of is how it might be to hold you . . . to kiss you." His thumb moved back and forth along her jaw and Devon trembled.

"I don't know how I'm going to stop you, but I *can* find the answer to this." He drew her close and settled his mouth over hers, fitting their lips together perfectly then softening the kiss and drawing her in. Devon made a small sound in her throat and swayed against him, her palms coming up to his chest, her fingers curling into the front of his coat. His tongue slid into her mouth, his breath tasted warm and male and hinted of brandy. Honeyed warmth seeped through her limbs.

Jonathan shifted, deepening the kiss, and Devon slid her arms around his neck. *Don't do this!* her mind warned. *You know what he's after!* But it made no difference. Heat swirled around her, melted her, drew her until she pressed against his tall hard length, felt the corded muscles in his neck, the silky strands of his thick black hair. Vaguely she noticed his hands running down her back, sliding over her white silk blouse, kneading her waist, moving lower, cupping her buttocks, massaging, warming, suggesting. Ripples of heat slid through her as his tongue tangled with hers, calling out his urgency, his need. Then she felt his hardened length pressing against her, incredibly male, incredibly seductive—incredibly insistent—and Devon broke away.

He was breathing hard, and Devon's hands were shaking. "We shouldn't have done that."

"No," he said softly, "considering our . . . circumstances . . . probably not."

"I'm sorry."

One corner of his mouth curved upward. "You're sorry? I'm not."

"I . . . I think you'd better go."

"Yes . . . that would be the wisest course." But he made no move to leave, just stood there, his eyes more blue than they usually were, traveling down her body, stirring her almost as if he still held her, then returning once more to her face.

"I wish things were different. I wish I didn't have to . . ."

What? she wanted desperately to know. Instead he turned away, walked to the door and pulled it open. "Thank you for another pleasant evening, Devon."

"Good night, Jonathan." Even as the taste of him lingered on her lips, Jonathan walked out the door.

Devon sank down on the sofa, her legs suddenly weak. Her heart still pounded and the blood seemed to sing through her veins. She had never felt such an overwhelming attraction for a man. Certainly not for Michael. Not even Paul.

Of all the men on earth, why did it have to be this one?

"Shall I bring in the Wilmot Ltd. file?" Jonathan's secretary, Delia Wills, asked over the intercom. He sat behind his wide teakwood desk, looking at a spreadsheet for Pacific American, one of the company's small boat-building firms.

"Is there a copy of the revised design on that seventy-five-foot offshore rig-tender included in the paperwork?" He heard her thumbing through the papers.

"Sure is."

"Bring it. And you might as well bring the list of invoices from the Bartlett Fiberglass Company. I think they're easing the prices up on us."

Neither of them mentioned that he had an entire floor of accountants to worry about those sorts of things. As long as the problem affected Stafford Enterprises, Jonathan considered dealing with them part of his job.

"I'll be right in," Dee said.

Just one more problem in what seemed a lengthy string. Then again, solving them was his job, and certainly it was not unusual for him. Maybe he was just getting tired. He hit the send button again. "And get me that schedule for the London sales conference. I want to make a couple of changes."

"Will do."

"Thanks, Dee."

In the space of several minutes, she opened the door to his office and walked in, her winter-white suit immaculate, gold buttons glistening up the front. Delia Wills was an attractive brunette in her mid-thirties, of medium height and build, a conservative dresser, intelligent, and incredibly good at her job—which was basically to keep Jonathan Stafford running smoothly so the company could do the same. She had been with him for the past five years—he couldn't imagine how he'd ever gotten along without her.

She set the paperwork in front of him. "Did you find the file Derek Preston put on your desk while you were in conference with Tony Hughes on Pacific American?"

"Unfortunately, I did." He glanced at it now, though he'd already read it. A legal-sized manila file, the index tab a bit dog-eared, the label handwritten and slightly faded. DEVON JAMES. It wasn't as neat as the carefully typed and labeled files in his office, but other than that it didn't look too much different.

Except that this file was stolen.

"Daniel McConnell is on the line from London. Shall I ring him through?"

Jonathan took the call, discussed a problem with Wilmot they'd been working on, then hung up and took a call from Garrett Browning on the Holidex staff in New Jersey. The intercom buzzed the moment he'd finished.

"There's a Michael Galveston here, Mr. Stafford," Dee addressed him formally, as she always did when someone else was around. "He doesn't have an appointment, but he seems to think you might be interested in what he has to say."

Galveston. What the hell's he doing here? "Send him in."

Jonathan came to his feet as the slightly shorter man walked in. Michael did his best imitation of a peer to peer greeting, determined not to be impressed by his surroundings, but Jonathan saw it in the way his hazel eyes swung directly over to the floor to ceiling windows with their sprawling view of the city, took in the size and opulence of the office, the custom Eames chair behind his huge teakwood desk. The subtle gray of the walls and draperies enhanced the deep burgundy hue of the thick wool carpet, the expensive original artwork on the walls—most of it Oriental.

Jonathan rounded his desk and extended a hand, which Galveston shook, and Jonathan indicated one of a pair of black leather chairs in front of his desk.

"What can I do for you?" he asked, taking his usual seat

behind the wide expanse of teak. If he'd liked the man better, he might have suggested a seat on the soft leather sofa in the comfortable grouping over in the corner, meant to put people at ease. As it was . . .

Michael took a moment to frame the words. "It isn't what you can do for me, Stafford, it's what I can do for you."

Jonathan cocked a brow. "Oh really?" Steepling his fingers together in front of his chest, he leaned back in his chair. "And just what exactly might that be?"

"Since you and Devon seem to know each other fairly well, I assume you also know about the story she's writing."

Jonathan merely nodded.

"My guess is, having Devon meddle in your family affairs is the last thing you want."

"You are safe in assuming that, yes."

"Well, I know a way to stop her."

"I see . . . And you're willing to tell me how to manage that? Why?"

Galveston crossed his legs and worked to look relaxed. He wore a yellow power tie, wing-tip shoes, and a black three-piece suit, obviously expensive and not a wrinkle anyplace. He must have changed clothes just before he came.

"Because I don't want her writing this book any more than you do. I've got my career to think of. Once Devon and I are married, everything she's involved in will reflect on me. If she writes this damnable ghost story, people are bound to think she's three bricks shy of a load. I can't afford for my wife to have that kind of image. I want this project stopped and the sooner the better."

"And you think you know a way to do that?" Jonathan asked, thinking he'd been right about the man from the moment of their first meeting. He didn't like him, and he couldn't imagine the man with Devon. They weren't remotely the same. And what was all this about them getting married? If Devon was still engaged to Galveston, why had she gone out with him? Why had she kissed him? Or at least let him kiss her? He shifted in the chair, growing hard just at the thought.

"I know the real reason Devon is so determined to write this," Michael was saying, "and it has nothing to do with ghosts."

"Go on."

"You know she's divorced?"

"Yes."

"Well, six months after Paul James left her, Devon started having a mental breakdown. At first she thought it was physical—she was feeling light-headed, experiencing dizzy spells, then she started having respiratory problems, heart palpitations, and difficulty sleeping. When the doctors told her there was nothing physically wrong with her, she got pretty scared."

Jonathan thought of Alex, of the weeks following his son's accident. He'd been mad with grief, unable to work, unable to sleep. He blamed himself for leaving the child with his aunt, blamed himself for working later than he should have. His mind had been in tatters—he knew exactly how scared she had been. "I can imagine," he said smoothly.

"She started seeing a doctor named Townsend, a psychiatrist. He told her she had a textbook case of anxiety brought on by stress. Devon had every possible symptom—including a tendency toward hallucination. She told me once that sometimes she felt like her mind was separating from her body. That she could be sitting in a room, listening to other people talk, but she felt like she was floating somewhere above them. She had tunnel vision, heat flashes—the whole bit."

"I see." But Jonathan didn't need to hear any more. The file on his desk had come from Dr. Townsend's office. When the doctor had refused to give Derek Preston information on his former patient, claiming client privilege, Derek had broken in, located the file in an out-of-date client drawer, and taken it.

Jonathan hadn't ordered the burglary. He had only told Preston he needed to know what the doctor was treating her for. Preston's job was to get the information—one way or another. It wasn't the first time the man had stepped on the law to get what he wanted and it wouldn't be the last. Yet, Jonathan trusted his judgment—and his methods—in most things. He did what he had to. In this case, Jonathan couldn't afford to fault him.

"So you see," Galveston was saying, "all this stuff about ghosts is nothing but bull. Devon's anxiety is coming back. She's under a lot of stress—a different kind to be sure—her work mostly and of course our marriage plans, but the result is apparently the same. She imagined all that hocus-pocus up at the Stafford Inn, now she's terrified she's having a relapse. Since she's unwilling to face the fact, she's determined to prove that her 'ghosts' are real."

Jonathan's jaw clenched imperceptibly. Anxiety attacks were hardly the same as a mental breakdown. Millions of people suffered varying degrees of stress every year—with myriad complications. But what kind of man would tell a total stranger all about it? And what about Devon? How would she feel if she knew what Michael had done? Jonathan felt a rush of protectiveness toward her, though he knew he could hardly afford it.

"Just exactly how do you suggest I use this information?"

"That's easy. Confront her with it. Devon's ashamed of what happened to her. She harbors a secret fear of going crazy. Even her parents don't know about the shrink. Tell her you know about Townsend and that you'll bring it all out in the open if she tries to go any further on her project."

Jonathan fixed him with a cold-eyed stare, disliking him more by the moment. "You aren't worried about what that kind of information might do to Devon? How it might affect her, or what it might do to *her* career?"

Michael looked taken aback, as if the possibility of Jonathan actually using the information had never really occurred to him. "I told you this in confidence . . . I mean, you only have to threaten her with it. I never intended for you to actually use it."

"Of course not, you wouldn't want that. Believing in ghosts is bad enough. It certainly wouldn't do your career any good to have people think your wife is an outright crazy." Galveston blanched. It appeared as though he hadn't realized the ramifications of what he'd just done until that very moment. Now that he did, his face looked decidedly pale.

"I told you this in confidence," he repeated. "I thought you'd understand I was trying to help us both."

"I do understand, Michael. And you may rest assured that I'll do everything in my power to put an end to Devon's project." *Without destroying her in the bargain.* Jonathan came to his feet, indicating an end to the interview.

"Then I can count on your discretion?"

"As long as we accomplish our ends. That's what we both want, isn't it?"

"I—I don't want Devon hurt."

Now you worry about it, you son of a bitch. "Neither do I." But someone was bound to get hurt, if things kept going as they were.

"I hope you'll take it easy on her. She probably won't need much persuasion, once she understands how much you know."

Probably not. He knew from reading Townsend's file that Devon was just as worried about her anxiety as Michael believed. In fact, he'd known he had the trump card he'd been after, the moment he'd started reading. Now, seeing the way Galveston was as ready to use it against her as he had been, made him feel slightly sick. He was just as big a bastard himself.

Galveston left, still looking somewhat nervous, and Jonathan sat down at his desk, his fingers unconsciously reaching for the file. He hadn't read it all, and he wasn't going to. But he had read discussions of her early years. Discussions of how out of place she had always felt, how lonely, even with parents who loved her. Being adopted, Townsend believed, was an underlying cause of her anxiety. Coupled with Paul James's desertion, it enhanced her feelings of isolation, of being unwanted.

Jonathan closed the file. Everything that had happened pointed to the fact that Devon's experience in the Stafford mansion had been nothing more than a bout of anxiety brought on by stress. The fact that it wasn't the first time something like this had happened in Stafford was only coincidence. Figments of people's imaginations—of his son's imagination. He knew it without doubt. He was a sane, reasonable, rational-thinking man. Devon was having the same kind of problems she'd had before.

Then he thought of the time he had spent with her, thought of her intelligence, her determination—her conviction. Except for her story about the night she had spent at the inn, Devon had shown no sign at all of undue stress or strain. In fact, she'd seemed more open, more down to earth and rational than any woman he had met in years.

It would be so easy to believe what was in the file, so simple an explanation. Why was it that no matter how hard he tried, Jonathan could not?

Nine

Wearing her yellow terry robe, her hair pinned carelessly up on her head, Devon sat on the sofa, long legs curled under her, a book gripped firmly in her hands. Though darkness had fallen and the fire burned low, she couldn't stop turning the pages. Eric Vandermuir, *Best True Ghost Stories.* Scattered around her on the floor were: Hans Holtzer, *Ghost Hunter;* Jean Anderson, *The Haunting of America;* Simon Marsden, *The Haunted Realm;* beside them *Realm of Ghosts, Haunted Houses,* and at least half a dozen others. All had been skimmed, many read from cover to cover.

She finished the chapter entitled "Lady of the Mists" and started reading "Phantom in Gray." When a gust of air rattled the windowpanes, Devon's head jerked up. As she glanced around the apartment, her heart was thudding painfully.

Only the wind.

All evening, she'd been jumpy, starting at the slightest sound, glancing constantly over her shoulder. A weight pressed on her chest and, off and on, her palms had been damp.

"God, I hate this stuff," she muttered aloud, setting the book aside. Not that it wasn't fascinating. For hours, she had been delving through one book after another, some written by the most prominent psychic investigators in the world. *They believe in ghosts,* she thought with a mild fit of pique.

The voluminous number of reported incidents made the likelihood of a spirit world seem highly probable. Then again, some of the stories were so farfetched that she continued to have her doubts.

Only one volume seemed to cast any real illumination on an otherwise dark and ominous subject. Dr. Francis Linderman, *The Imprisoned Spirit.* Linderman gave several case studies of dwellings inhabited not by just one ghost but by two or three or even as many as six. Linderman claimed, as Devon had read in some of her earlier research, that a malevolent spirit could hold other spirits hostage, keeping them imprisoned on the earth plane through the centuries.

She read that seventy percent of all reported hauntings were the simple, garden variety: transparent apparitions gliding through a bedroom in the dark, wispy figures disappearing in front of a number of witnesses, that sort of thing. Twenty-eight percent were poltergeists, those playful, mischievous spirits who pulled out drawers and moved furniture around. Only two percent were demons or malevolent spirits.

Only two percent—and I had to find one of them.

Linderman also gave examples of the most common sorts of phenomena reported by someone who'd had a phantom encounter: footsteps on the stairs, chains being rattled, a feeling of icy cold. Devon's pulse increased as one of the items on the list caught her eye: an odd, unusual and often offensive smell, sometimes likened to creosote. That was exactly the smell she had noticed in the yellow room. Even Michael should recall it.

The ghost descriptions themselves varied widely, but odd,

glowing, or even missing eyes were often mentioned, bringing to mind the old woman she had seen. A mention was also made of clothing that wasn't quite discernible, just dark and vaguely outlined, as the old woman's dress had been.

Linderman's book also proposed that ghosts could make contact with the human world—if they had a message to deliver. Often, he suggested, they imparted this information during sleep, but sometimes it was merely sensed by the subject being contacted.

It was all supposition, of course, and yet it gave her the first real seeds of hope.

Devon glanced at the clock. Nearly midnight. Before all this had happened, the last horror story she had read was William P. Blatty's *The Exorcist.* It had given her nightmares for a week. Thinking of some of the terrifying tales she had read tonight, she wondered if the same thing might happen again.

She thought especially about the tale entitled simply *Demon.* It was about an entity that viciously haunted its female victim to the point of brutality, leaving the woman's body bruised and battered by an unseen force. Worst of all, when the woman had finally moved away from the house, believing her terror would end, the force had followed, attacking her again with such violent menace that the woman was admitted several times to the hospital. Just the thought of it made Devon shiver. Could Florian Stafford do something like that? Could he know what she intended, and if he did find out, could he do something to stop her?

Surely not, but as impossible as it seemed, it worried her, just as it had in the mansion, the following morning, when she refused to write her address in the guest book.

Something clattered in the kitchen, and Devon whirled in that direction, her heart hammering hard once more.

She knew it was only her mind and yet she moved with elaborate caution. She breathed a sigh of relief to see that a slow-dripping faucet had filled up a soup bowl sitting in the sink, upsetting its precarious balance until it had tumbled over. The spoon inside had clattered loudly against the drain.

"Why did they have to pick me?" she grumbled, spouting more of her earlier sentiments. She couldn't even go to a scary movie, now here she was battling unseen demons and ghosts.

Or herself.

Not wanting to linger on that unwelcome thought, she poured herself a sherry to insure a night of sleep, and took herself off to bed.

Nightmares of a two-headed apparition with glowing eyes and blood on its clothes intruded on her dreams, and she awoke with a shot of terror. Closer to morning, she dreamed the same dream again, but this time the apparition vanished, replaced by the feel of a man's hard body pressing her into the mattress. Jonathan's mouth came down over hers, his touch at first gentle, just as she remembered. Then the kiss became heated and she opened to the plunder of his tongue. She was writhing beneath him, calling his name, but when she opened her eyes, it was Florian who drove himself inside her, Florian who rode her with such fierce determination. He was laughing at her, taunting her even as he took her.

She awakened with a second jolt of fear, heart pounding, but the images faded quickly, and she was able to go back to sleep. When she woke up the next morning, she couldn't quite recall it, just a vague recollection of jumbled images that reminded her of her terrifying night in the yellow room.

For one brief moment, she wished Jonathan *would* find a way to stop her. He had called several times since their evening together, but his schedule had been hectic and so had hers. Off and on for days, she had thought about him, remembering the kiss they had shared, surprised by the magnitude of it, amazed that she had responded so passionately, considering the threat he still posed.

Whatever he intended, she was determined to finish this project, with or without his cooperation, and even against his interference.

Devon sighed as she climbed from the bed. Looping a strand of sleep-tangled pale blond hair over an ear, she made her way toward the kitchen to brew a fresh pot of coffee. When she reached the living room, she heard the jangle of the phone and picked it up on the second ring.

"Devon?" The voice on the end of the line sounded vaguely familiar. But it was early Saturday morning. Even her mother didn't usually call quite so soon.

"Yes?"

"This is Ernie Townsend."

She smiled into the receiver. "Dr. Townsend! It's good to hear your voice. How are Beverly and the kids?" Townsend had to be the only doctor in the world who shared his personal life with his patients, just as they shared theirs with him. It made him human and reachable, and it was why Devon had trusted him almost from the instant of their first meeting.

"Fine, fine. Everyone's fine . . . how about you?"

Devon took a deep breath. "I've been working awfully hard, but I can't tell you how much I'm enjoying it. I've a new project, a new book I'm writing. The challenge is incredible, but I think I'm up to it—possibly more than I've ever been."

"That's wonderful, Devon. I'm proud of you. I'm glad things are going so well, but there's another reason I called."

They hadn't spoken in several years. She had wondered when she heard his voice what he could possibly want. "What is it?"

"Probably nothing, but I thought you should know. Several days ago, a man came to my office. A private investigator. Someone named Preston. He asked a lot of questions about you, wanted me to tell him the nature of your visits. I refused, of course."

"Yes . . . of course."

"He offered me money, Devon. Quite a lot of it. I thought you should know."

An investigator. Only Jonathan would go to such lengths—he had done it before. But how had he known about Townsend? "Thank you, Doctor . . . I appreciate your telling me."

"I'm afraid there's something else."

Her fingers tightened around the receiver. "Something else?"

"Your file's missing. It may be our fault, maybe it's just gotten misplaced, but . . . considering how determined that Preston man was . . . I just don't know."

Devon said nothing and the silence hung on the phone. "As you said . . . it's probably just misplaced." Her voice sounded reedy, a little bit far away, and even as she said the words, she knew it wasn't the truth.

"If it's been stolen, there's not much we can do. We have no proof; nothing else in the office was disturbed. I don't even know what made me look for it . . . just a hunch, I guess. He was just so determined."

"Thank you, Dr. Townsend." She fought to pull herself

together. "I'm sure it's nothing, but I certainly appreciate your concern."

"If something's wrong, Devon . . . if for any reason you need to see me . . . don't hesitate to call."

"I'm fine, Doctor. Thanks." She set the phone in the cradle and sat woodenly down on the straight-backed chair.

She didn't want to believe that Jonathan would do such a thing—not after the evening they had shared . . . not after the way he had kissed her. But what little she had read about him should have been a warning. He had a reputation for being ruthless in his business dealings—he had bankrupted more than one company that had dared to get in his way.

Now she had dared. She had bucked him at every turn, never once backing down, determined to uncover the facts about his family. If he was ruthless in business, imagine the lengths he might go to, in order to protect his family name.

She thought of the file he had paid to have stolen. What was in it? Notes of her interviews with Townsend, her bouts with anxiety—panic attacks, he had called them. Stories from her childhood, small, embarrassing moments, her feelings of loneliness even in the midst of her parents' love. The file would surely contain revelations about her disastrous marriage to Paul, her feelings of sexual inadequacy when he left her. Just thinking about it made the bile rise up in Devon's throat.

Dear God, what kind of a man was Jonathan Stafford to do such a thing? Vile, despicable—utterly without conscience. It didn't sound like the man she knew, and yet . . . Devon's stomach clenched as an image of Florian, cruel yet somehow compelling, rose unbidden in her mind. They looked so much alike—in some ways handsome, in others, forbidding. And the same Stafford blood ran through their veins. Down deep, were the two men really the same?

Devon's hands balled into fists. She wasn't as powerful as Jonathan, but she wasn't afraid. Not anymore. She had taken charge of her life, and she wasn't about to let go. Her mouth thinned in anger and she clamped her teeth together. Damn him! She wouldn't let him defeat her—she wouldn't! Monday morning she would confront him. Monday—two whole days away.

"Bastard." She spun and headed toward her bedroom. Now was the time; she wouldn't wait till Monday. She knew where he lived; she would make him let her in.

Showering quickly, she combed her hair and pulled on a pair of black slacks. She grabbed a pale blue turtleneck sweater, slid her stockinged feet into a pair of black penny loafers, jerked her camel-hair coat out of the closet, and headed for the door.

Outside, the wind whipped her pale blond hair; she hooked it over an ear, out of the way, and bent to get into the cab the doorman had halted. All the way to Jonathan's Fifth Avenue apartment her anger mounted. How dare he! There were limits to the lengths a civilized man should go. This was far outside the extremes.

She paid the cabby and crossed the sidewalk. Entering the lobby of his building, she headed straight for the central high-tech desk with its dozens of miniature television screens, monitors for every corridor and stairwell in the structure. Recognizing the security guard who'd been on duty the night she had come here to dinner, Devon walked in his direction. In the taxi, she had already decided that since Jonathan had invaded her privacy, she owed no consideration to his. If she could get into his apartment, she would. She wasn't about to be put off—not for any reason!

"Good morning, Gary." She smiled pleasantly. The blond man looked surprised, then pleased that she had remembered his name, not realizing that she had merely read the embroidered patch sewn onto his uniform pocket.

"Good morning, Miss James." So he remembered her, too. Good. Very good.

"I'm here to see Mr. Stafford. He said I could go right on up just like before."

Gary frowned, his blond brows drawing together over a pair of wide-set eyes. "That's funny. I don't remember him calling down. I'd better check the guest list."

"I'm sure you'll find my name." Devon started walking toward Jonathan's private elevator. "I'm awfully late, Gary, and you know how Jonathan is about that sort of thing." She must have said the right words because Gary grinned and started walking in her direction, the elevator key in his hand.

"He's pretty particular about everything." The security guard stuck the key in the lock and turned. In seconds, the elevator door slid open and Devon walked in.

She smiled warmly. "Thanks, Gary. You're a doll."

Upstairs, the door opened into the marble-floored foyer, and Devon glanced around. The housekeeper was nowhere to be seen and neither was anyone else. Devon searched the living room then the dining room. She glanced into the kitchen and saw the short, dark-haired housekeeper bent over the sink, her bulky frame jiggling in rhythm to the movements she made while scrubbing a heavy stainless-steel skillet. Devon marched down the hall to Jonathan's study. He wasn't there, but she could hear a man's voice farther down the corridor.

There were a dozen reasons she shouldn't be doing this—no, a hundred. But the blaze of her red-hot anger blotted all sensible thought. The voice grew louder, there were two of them now, and she realized the men were speaking Japanese. Devon stopped in the open doorway just as one of the men made a quick sharp movement with his arm, and his leg shot out. The other man landed with a grunt on the flat of his back, and Jonathan grinned down at his opponent.

He was standing in a large mirrored room complete with barbells, a NordicTrack machine, an electronic bicycle, and stair stepper, as well as several pieces of weightlifting equipment. The floor of the room was protected by a thick foam mat, which Jonathan and his opponent were making good use of.

Speechless, Devon stood there staring as the two men warily circled each other, totally unaware of her presence, completely absorbed in their combat. They were barefoot, each of them dressed in Oriental-style loose white cotton pants and a wrap-around tunic belted with a wide black sash. Jonathan's hung open to the waist, baring a wide dark chest roughened with coarse black hair. He was perspiring heavily. The wetness was reflecting off sleek bands of muscle and running in rivulets down the washboard ridges of his stomach.

Devon's mouth went dry. He was bronzed and hard and he moved with the grace of a panther. There was power there, too, lethal and brutal, though carefully held in check. She watched him with awe, unable to move if the house had been aflame.

She dragged her attention to Jonathan's opponent, an Asian man—smaller, darker, all pure sinew and bone. He made a quick movement, which Jonathan countered, then he turned and came at Jonathan from another direction. Jonathan's hand came up and so did his eyes, connecting with hers, widening imperceptibly, then he was sprawling on the mat, looking into the face of the man who stood over him grinning.

"Nani o shte imas ka, Jonathan-san?"

"I'm afraid I got distracted," he answered in English, coming easily to his feet and tipping his head toward the door where Devon stood watching.

More Japanese was spoken. Jonathan smiled, they faced each other and bowed from the waist, then Jonathan crossed the room in her direction. It took a full ten seconds for her to remember why she had come. She did so with a fresh rush of anger that overcame her embarrassment for being where she shouldn't have been.

"I'm sorry to interrupt your . . . performance . . . but I need to see you."

Jonathan arched a fine black brow. "Give me a moment to shower and change and I'll join you in the—"

"Now."

Jonathan's face closed up. "How did you get in?"

"I have my ways, just as you have yours."

A muscle twitched in his cheek. The Asian man said something that obviously pertained to her. Then he threw Jonathan a towel, which he used to blot the perspiration from his face and the back of his neck. "Come on." He gripped her arm a little too hard and propelled her down the hall to his study.

"Do you want a drink?" he asked, once they got inside and he had closed the door. "You look like you could use it."

Her hands were shaking, but it was from anger not fear. "It's a little early for me, but you're certainly welcome to indulge."

Jonathan looked annoyed. "Why don't you sit down?"

"I'd rather stand, thank you."

"All right, Devon, what's going on?"

"Damn you, you know very well what's going on. You broke into Dr. Townsend's office and stole my file."

"I didn't steal anything."

"Don't you dare deny it. I know it was you. Maybe not in the flesh, but you arranged it. There isn't anyone else who would want it."

"I didn't *arrange* for anything, either. My investigator took it upon himself to take the file."

At least he didn't deny it. Somehow that would have been worse. "But you've got it. You've read it. Now you know things about me no one knows . . . things about my childhood . . . about my marriage. Things I—" Her voice broke on the last, and Jonathan caught her arm. He tried to pull her close but she jerked free. "Don't! Don't even touch me."

"Listen to me, Devon. I didn't read it all. I didn't have to. I needed to know why you were seeing a psychiatrist. I didn't think your reasons for pursuing this were as selfless as you wanted me to believe. I knew there had to be more to it than what you told me. Now I know what it is."

"I'm doing this for Bernard and Annie," Devon said stubbornly.

"Don't lie to yourself, Devon. You're doing this to prove you aren't crazy. You're terrified that what went on in that room wasn't real. That you made it all up. You're afraid this is worse than anything you suffered before, that this time you might not be able to control it."

It was the truth, dear God, it was the truth! What if nothing she'd experienced were real? What if her mind had played some hideous, terrifying trick. If it had, what else was it capable of doing?

"It happened just the way I said. I didn't make it up. I

didn't imagine it. I know the difference. I remember how I felt before and this wasn't anything like it."

"Stress can be a terrible opponent, Devon."

"If you think this changes anything, you're wrong. I'm not quitting, no matter what you do."

Jonathan watched her a moment. His gray-blue eyes were probing, searching. "At least now I understand why this is so important."

She scoffed at that; it wasn't a pretty sound. "Do you? Then why don't you tell me why it's so important for you to stop me?"

"Devon . . ."

"You're hiding something, Jonathan. No one goes to this much trouble just to insure his privacy. The story isn't even about you, it's about some distant relative who happened to live in a house you own." Devon backed farther away. "Why is stopping me so important? What is it you're so determined to hide?"

A noise in the hall ended anything he might have said. "Hey, Dad, guess what?" Alex Stafford jerked open the study door and propped it against the rubber rim of his wheelchair. Surprise crossed his small dark face as he realized his father wasn't alone. "Sorry, Dad. I didn't know you had company."

Devon swayed on her feet, her mind, still reeling from the morning's confrontation, now staggered beneath this second heavy blow. Her eyes moved from the child's innocent features to the cold metal chair that overwhelmed his slender body. *Oh, Jonathan, why didn't you tell me?*

"It's all right, son." Jonathan held open the door and Alex wheeled himself in. "Ms. James's visit was a little unexpected."

With a will of iron, Devon forced a smile in the little

boy's direction. He was a smaller version of his father, inky black hair, wavy but not really curly, his features dark but a little bit softer. His eyes were bluer and far more trusting.

"This is Ms. James," Jonathan said. "Devon, my son Alexander."

She knelt beside the boy's chair and extended her hand. "Hello, Alex. I've been hoping to meet you."

"You have?" Alex accepted the handshake as if he had done it a thousand times.

"Yes. I love children. I'm afraid I haven't got any of my own."

"I was just coming in to show Dad my sketch."

She glanced at the tray table fixed to his chair. A sketch pad rested beside a box of pastel chalks. "A tiger. My, you're very talented."

"It's a special *white* tiger. They're very rare. We went to the zoo last weekend just to see it, but I only just got the picture done."

"You did a good job, son." Jonathan came up beside them, lifted the pad and admired the chalk drawing from several different angles. "We'll have to go again so you can sketch some of the other animals."

"That would be great, Dad."

"In the meantime, I need a minute or two with Ms. James, then we'll go get something to eat."

"Sure, Dad."

"It was nice meeting you, Alex," Devon said.

"Nice to meet you, too, Miss James." He stuck his small hand out and once more Devon shook it. Then he wheeled himself out of the room.

For a moment Devon said nothing. Just stared at the closed door, feeling all sorts of protective, motherly instincts she hadn't been sure she had. Her heart went out to the child for what he must endure. When she turned to face Jonathan, his face was a carefully emotionless mask.

"That's it, isn't it?" Devon said softly. "You've been trying to protect him. You're afraid of the bad publicity, afraid the children might give him trouble or maybe even the teachers. Is that it?"

Jonathan glanced away.

"Why didn't you tell me? We could have talked about it. I would have understood your fears."

"Would you?" His eyes swung back to hers. "How could you have any idea how terrified I am for him, how much I worry that he'll be hurt a second time."

"What happened?"

"There was an accident . . . a heavy wooden beam fell on him. He was five years old."

"Oh, Jonathan." She wished she could go to him, absorb some of his pain.

"He's an incredible kid. Intelligent, loving, generous. A man couldn't ask for more in a son."

Only that he had two good legs. "He's wonderful." Devon lifted a hand to Jonathan's cheek, cradled it against her palm. She could feel the stubble on his still unshaven jaw. "I'm sorry I came here. If I had a child, I'd do anything to protect him."

Jonathan caught her hand, clasping it gently with his long-boned fingers. There was such strength in that hand. "I'm sorry about the file. You can have it back anytime you like."

She smiled faintly. "Send it back to Dr. Townsend. The file is really his."

Jonathan nodded, and Devon started to walk away.

"You say you understand," he called after her. "Does that mean you'll stop working on this book?"

She turned to face him. "Let me think about it."

"I want to see you."

"Well, I . . . when?"

"If you don't mind getting a bit of a late start, we could get together this evening. Alex is in bed by nine. I could have Henry pick you up then come back for me. I know a charming little Italian restaurant down on Grand Street."

"I'd rather not talk about the book, if you don't mind. I need some time to decide what to do."

"Fair enough—as long as we don't talk about what happened to Alex. It isn't my favorite subject."

Devon nodded. She could imagine how painful it must be.

Jonathan brought her hand to his lips, turned it over, and kissed the palm. "I'll see you tonight."

The heat of his mouth sent goosebumps racing across her skin. She eased her fingers from his, smiled at him with a mixture of warmth and uncertainty, turned and left the room.

After she had gone, Jonathan sank down heavily in his chair. He felt rotten about the theft of her file, rotten for the hurt and betrayal he had seen in her lovely green eyes. Yet, he'd had very little choice.

Now, inadvertently, almost accidentally, Alex's arrival in his study might just have solved his problem. Devon believed his worry for Alex was the reason he had worked so hard to dissuade her, and of course that was the truth.

It just wasn't all the truth.

He rubbed his chin, his fingers rasping against the night's growth of beard, and wondered if maybe her concern for Alex—for obviously she had felt some—would end her determination to write her story. He didn't really think so. If he did, he might tell her the rest of it.

But she hardly knew the boy, and the tale of his accident would only make her more determined. Better to leave things as they were, let her believe what her eyes confirmed.

Maybe he'd get lucky. Maybe seeing Alex would protect him, the Stafford family name, and also keep Devon from getting hurt.

He hoped so.

God, he hoped so.

Leaning back against the chair, recalling the courage it had taken for her to come, the cleverness she had used to talk her way past the security guards, he almost smiled. He'd have a discussion with them about being more careful, he thought. Then he discarded the notion as soon as it came to mind. If he mentioned it, the guards would surely be upset with Devon for what she had done, and he didn't want her feeling uncomfortable whenever she came home with him.

Now there's an interesting thought. It occurred to him, not for the first time, he had exactly that notion in mind. Of course, not when Alex was there. But four nights a week, the house was empty. And Jonathan slept alone. For weeks now, he hadn't even been with Akemi. He hadn't wanted to be with her. Clearly, it was Devon he wanted in his bed.

How long has it been, old boy, since you've set out purposely to seduce a beautiful woman?

Years, certainly, and yet he hadn't forgotten how. How much wooing would it take? From what he knew of her, Devon's experience with men was fairly limited. Possibly only Galveston and her husband. No matter what Michael seemed to think, it appeared fairly clear that Devon meant to end their relationship.

Whatever her interest, she felt an attraction for him—

that, he did not doubt. He intended to capitalize on that attraction, build on it, and wind up with Devon in his bed.

It didn't escape his notice that in doing so, he might gain another hold over her. It wasn't his central purpose, but he couldn't deny the benefit. He could keep an eye on her, steer her away from areas of potential disaster while he continued to gently dissuade her.

Aside from that, he could satisfy the towering sexual desire he felt for her.

Jonathan shifted in his chair, already hard and uncomfortable just thinking about it. The kiss they had shared had been hot and far more arousing than he would have imagined. He could still recall the way her soft lips yielded to his, the slick moist warmth of her tongue, the way her nipples formed stiff little peaks as they pressed against his chest. She was warm and responsive, and her height and slender frame fit his tall build as if she'd been made for him.

What would she be like in bed? he wondered. How much persuasion would it take? Would he discover, as he had with so many others in the past, that once he'd had her, she would hold no special appeal for him? Or was there really something different about her, something that would fill the void that kept yawning wider in his heart?

Ten

Candlelight flickered in the small red glass holder on the table. White latticework woven with plastic ivy formed a canopy over their heads, and Mario Lanza sang softly against a background of violins. How many years had Valentino's been there? Devon wondered when they walked in, thinking what a charming Italian cliché the old place on Grand Street was.

Jonathan had chosen the restaurant for its casual comfort and especially for the food, which, he admitted with a charming white smile, was so sinfully rich he rarely indulged himself.

They talked about politics, discovering both were fairly conservative. Devon confessed that both her parents were exactly the opposite. They talked about their hobbies: the art they each collected. Jonathan admitted to a passion for skiing, which with his busy business interests he'd been forced to abandon years ago.

"I loved the sport," he said. "Skied since I was a boy. Every year as soon as it snows, I still miss being out on the slopes."

"I learned in college. I stopped going when I started dating Michael. He just couldn't seem to get the hang of it, and we always seemed to end up fighting."

"I'll bet you were good."

Devon smiled. "Not bad. I could have been better, if I'd been able to go more often."

"I know exactly what you mean."

They talked about sailing, another of Jonathan's abandoned hobbies, and she basked in the warmth of his smiles. "I've never been on a sailboat," Devon said, "but I think I'd like it. All that freedom . . . feeling the wind in your face. It has to be terrific."

"It is. It's a shame, really, that I ever sold my boat. Things always seem to come back to just not enough time."

In easy camaraderie, they enjoyed the meal: a big green leafy salad in an incredibly delicious wine and olive oil dressing, risotto with scallops for him, gnocchi sauced with Gorgonzola cheese for her. Dessert was tiramisu—a confection of spongecake soaked in espresso.

As pleasant as it was, neither of them could deny the underlying air of sexual tension. Jonathan's eyes seemed bluer, the curve of his lips a little more sensuous. Devon couldn't seem to keep her eyes from straying in that direction. She was remembering what that mouth had felt like on hers, the heat that it had enflamed.

"So tell me," she said with determined nonchalance, "what you were doing when I barged in on you this morning." Wanting to learn more about him, Devon smiled across the table where he sipped a glass of Chianti. His expression was warm and mildly amused.

"We were practicing *gojo-ryu* karate. It's another of my interests, one of the few I've had time to maintain."

"Tell me about it."

Jonathan set the wineglass down on the red and white checked tablecloth. As always, he was difficult to read, but tonight he seemed more indulgent, letting her glimpse his desire for her, making her feel feminine and womanly.

"Karate was invented by the Okinawans. It was used as a means of weaponless defense when their government was overrun and all of their arms confiscated."

"Karate," Devon repeated pronouncing it kar-at-teh, as he had. "Isn't that the one where you break bricks with the side of your hand?"

Jonathan smiled indulgently. "Hand blows dominate the form, but the elbows, knees, and feet are also used. I got interested in the martial arts when I was fifteen. My father was traveling extensively to Japan at the time, and I became fascinated with judo. That requires more flexibility, more body contact. It's much like wrestling. I enjoyed it, but my interest eventually moved on to karate."

Devon examined his hand, running her fingers along the hard ridge at the side, then looking up to see his eyes even bluer than before. The hand was callused more than she had previously noticed. It was firm and strong, but she couldn't imagine him breaking a brick with it.

"Only when I was younger," he said with amusement, reading her thoughts. "Now I use the sport as a means of exercise. Besides the home gym you saw in my apartment, I have one just like it at my office. I practice the solo form every morning, but only work out with my *karateka*—karate master—one day a week. The gentleman you saw was Sensei Tanaka Motobu. He's been my trainer as well as my friend for the past ten years."

"I thought the martial arts also involved some sort of meditation. Do you do that, too?"

"It requires a harmony between breath and action. Each breath must coincide with each movement. Mostly it teaches self-reliance and efficiency. It's said that if a man masters the art, neither physical danger from without nor rampant passion from within can dislodge him." He smiled wolfishly and his fingers tightened around her hand. "Looking at you assures me that I have not yet completely mastered the art."

Devon laughed, but her heartbeat quickened. "It sounds fascinating."

Jonathan shrugged. "As I said, mostly it's a matter of exercise, of loosening muscles and joints. Tanaka and I go as far as light physical contact, nothing more."

"And it was your father who got you started?"

"He took me with him to Japan. Once we got there, I rarely saw him."

"Tell me about him," Devon urged.

Jonathan let go of her hand and leaned back in his chair, studying her with interest, as he had for most of the evening. "Are you sure you want to know? I wouldn't want to shatter any illusions."

"Since I have none, I think we're safe."

He sighed. "Alexander Marshall Stafford. Tall, dark—I suppose I look a good deal like him."

"All you Stafford men seem to look alike."

"I hope that's where the similarity ends." Jonathan glanced away. He wasn't the kind of man who opened up to others. She wondered why he was doing it tonight, yet somehow sensed his need to.

"Go on," she gently urged.

"Marsh Stafford was cold and distant and calculating." He shifted uneasily, deciding how much to reveal. "Marsh hadn't the slightest idea how to be a father. For that matter, he wasn't much of a husband, either. My mother was always lonely and so was I. At least she had her country-club friends and all her charity work. I buried myself in my schooling." His voice had picked up speed, as if the faster he said the words, the quicker he could end his distressing revelations. "Even at that, I never pleased him. Neither did my mother. Yet under it all, we both loved him. I wanted his approval more than anything else in the world." Jonathan's face looked grim, and Devon's heart went out to him.

"He'd be proud of you now, Jonathan."

He smiled faintly and some of his tension seemed to ease. "Yes, I suppose he would. The closest I ever came while he was alive was when I graduated from Princeton and started in the family business. I began at the bottom, just like every Stafford male before me, working in the boat-building yard. I was determined to prove my worth, and I did, moving up the ladder, taking on job after job. I had just been promoted to a top-level management position when the corporate jet went down."

Devon's breath suddenly caught. She had read that somewhere, seen pictures of Jonathan and his sister, Madeline, dressed in black, standing in front of the coffin at the funeral.

"An hour after I got the news, corporate control passed to me."

"It must have been awful for you . . . so much responsibility on top of all your grief."

Jonathan swirled the wine in his glass, then raised it to his lips and took a drink. "It was a nightmare. I never realized how much I'd counted on him, in one way or another, until he was gone. On top of that, I had only just recently married. With my father gone, there was so much to learn I started working sixteen hours a day, seven days a week. There was never a moment for my wife, or later, very little time for Alex. I was making the same mistakes my father made, but at the time I couldn't see it. I wound up losing Rebecca. Then my mother died. Fortunately, I woke up to what I was doing. I spend as much of my time with Alex now as I possibly can."

Something moved across his face. A flash of guilt perhaps, because of what happened to his son?

Devon smiled softly, drawn to the pain she had seen. "I think he loves you very much."

Jonathan's tension faded, and his sensuous mouth curved up. "You do, do you?"

"Yes."

"And just how, exactly, have you made this grand assessment?"

"Woman's intuition," she said boldly. "I just know."

Jonathan's gaze swept over her pale peach cashmere dress with its gently rolled neckline. It rested softly on the peaks of her breasts, which at his frank assessment had begun to grow hard. His eyes looked dark and hungry in a way she hadn't seen them before.

He leaned forward in his chair and clasped her fingers, lacing them between his own. "Can your woman's intuition tell you what I'm thinking right now?"

Devon's mouth went dry.

"Do you have any idea how much I want you?"

Inside her, something heated, moved, slid restlessly through her body. Jonathan's thumb began a slow sensual rhythm across the back of her hand, and Devon trembled.

His eyes held hers; his voice sounded low and intimate. "I've wanted you since the first moment I saw you standing in that restaurant."

"B-But we hardly know each other."

"Do we? I've told you things about my family, about my life very few people know. Do you know why I did that?"

"Why?" So there had been a reason.

"Because I wanted to give back some of the honesty you've given me."

"I don't understand what you mean."

"I mean that I know things about *you* few people know."

Devon stiffened. "Because you read my file."

"Some of it, maybe. Most of it because you're open and sincere. I think I understand the kind of person you are but even if I didn't, I'd still want you. And if you're honest with yourself, I think you want me."

Devon wet her lips. In spite of herself, she couldn't stop a jolt of desire from sweeping through her. "There are o-other things to consider."

"Like Michael Galveston?"

"I told you, Michael and I are just friends."

"What then?"

"How about Akemi Kumato, for starters."

"It bothers you that I see her?" He seemed almost pleased.

"Well . . . it would if I were . . . if we were . . . involved."

"Miss Kumato and I have . . . an arrangement. Up until now, it has suited us both, but it involves little commitment. I'll speak to her."

"You will?" Did that mean he was ending his affair? And if he was, was that really what she wanted? "I don't know, Jonathan. I'm not interested in one-night stands."

"Neither am I."

Devon shook her head. "This is happening far too quickly. We don't know each other well enough . . . things might not work out. We have no way of knowing, and there's the problem of my story to consider."

"Life holds few guarantees, Devon. If you take no risk, you reap no reward."

"What about my project?"

"What about it? Have you decided to continue, knowing that Alex may suffer?"

"I'm not convinced that he would, but even at that, I've decided to compromise. I'm going to continue my research. I have to know the truth for myself. You made me face that fact when you took my file. I've got to know, one way or the other. But I'll keep my research quiet, and I won't decide what to do with the information until I'm finished."

He watched her a moment, weighing her words. His face became inscrutable. "All right. A compromise, it is."

Devon brightened. "You mean you won't try to stop me?"

"Not unless things get out of hand."

She couldn't resist a smile. "In that case, maybe you could help. Why don't you come with me on some of my appointments? If you did, we could discover the truth together."

"What if the truth isn't what you believe?"

Devon's chest grew tight. *What indeed?* "Then I guess you're entitled to know that, too."

"What about us, Devon? I'm a man used to getting what he wants. Now we both know what that is."

Devon swallowed and nervously took a sip of wine. "I need time, Jonathan."

"Do you?" His eyes pierced her, reading the desire she worked so hard to hide. "We'll see, Devon, just how much time you need." With that he turned away from her and hailed the waiter for the check. In minutes, the little aproned man rushed forward and Jonathan paid the bill. While Mario continued to croon, they swept beneath the ivy-laced latticework toward the door.

Out on the street, the wind blew sharply, but Henry was

waiting at the curb. As they approached, he started the ignition on the long black limo. Jonathan opened the door, and Devon slid onto the gray leather seat. On the crowded sidewalk, everyone was bundled against the weather as they hurried to their unknown destinations out of the cold. The car door thudded closed. Jonathan's tall hard frame was taking up the place beside her, filling the spacious interior with his overwhelming presence.

"Drive us around for a while, will you, Henry? We may want a drink someplace else." He sat closer to her than he ever had before. Devon could feel his body heat even through the layers of her thick fur coat.

"Another drink?" she teased, clucking in mock disapproval. "And you've already had pasta and wine and even dessert. My, but you are getting reckless. Maybe I'm a bad influence."

Jonathan's mouth curved up. "You, sweet Devon, are definitely a bad influence."

He pushed a button in the built-in console, and the panel that closed off the driver's section slid up, leaving them cocooned warmly in the back. The soft blue glow of tiny hidden lamps washed over them while the stereo played quietly in the background. They rode for a moment in silence, then Jonathan's hand came up to her chin, turning her face to his.

"I've been wanting to kiss you all evening."

Moth wings fluttered in her stomach as his mouth came down over hers, feather-light at first, merely brushing, then settling possessively across her own. Devon made a small sound in her throat and opened to him, allowing his tongue to invade the moist dark cavern, savoring the flood of warmth that seeped through her veins. She kissed him back, knowing she probably shouldn't, that succumbing too easily to a man like Jonathan Stafford could only bring disaster. Still, she allowed herself these few heated moments, feeling his arms around her, his fingers laced in her hair.

He deepened the kiss, using his tongue in an achingly sensuous manner, taking her mouth with all the power that was Jonathan Stafford, all the sensuous force. She wasn't sure she had ever experienced such an incredible strength of passion. Had she ever felt so entirely possessed by a man, so utterly consumed?

She didn't break away until she felt his hands beneath her breasts, easing upward, barely touching the place where the fullness began to swell. When she did end the kiss, Jonathan said nothing. He brushed his thumb along her jaw, but he didn't back away.

"I dreamed about you last night," he finally said, breaking into the silence.

"You did?"

"Yes. Shall I tell you about it?"

Devon's hands began to tremble so she steadied them against her soft cashmere skirt. She wondered if he could hear the pounding of her heart.

"I was kissing you," he said, "very long and very hard. We had come home to my apartment after dinner, and I carried you into my bedroom, over to my big king-sized bed. You had on a bright red sequined sweater but no bra. I could tell by the way your nipples grew stiff and tight and pressed against the fabric."

Devon sucked in a breath.

"I kissed you again and then I eased the sweater up until I had bared your breasts. They were lovely . . . perfectly shaped to fit my hand. I can remember exactly how they tasted, so warm and sweet, like lapping up rich thick cream."

Devon made a soft sound in her throat, feeling suddenly light-headed, dizzier with every word. She had to say something to stop him—anything—but she couldn't force a sound past her lips.

"You were wearing a black silk skirt," he went on, "short, but not too short. You had on a black lace garter belt and stockings, but you weren't wearing any panties. I knew because when I slid my hand along the inside of your thigh, I touched—"

"Jonathan!"

He smiled sensuously, wickedly, a hungry, determined look in his eyes like nothing she had seen. "Shall I wait to tell you the rest?"

"There's . . . there's more?"

"Quite a lot more. Of course, if you'd rather, I could show you." His hand cupped her breast through her sweater and he lightly massaged the peak, making it harden.

Devon stared at him as if she had never really seen him before and hastily slid away. "I think you had better take me home."

For a moment he said nothing, just watched her in that too-assessing way of his. "I will if that's what you want, but I don't think it is."

Devon sat up straighter, working hard to maintain control. "I-I didn't realize you were so . . . so . . ."

"Male?" he supplied. "If you find that disappointing, Devon, I'm sorry. I never set out to just be your friend."

Devon eyed him warily, embarrassed and aroused, acutely aware of the wetness between her legs. "It's just that you've always been such a gentleman, and I've never had anyone . . . I mean, I can't believe you said those things out loud."

"You didn't like it?"

Lie, damn you. "Well, I . . ." Devon glanced away.

Jonathan read her hesitation, the desire she tried to disguise. Passion warred with uncertainty and what might have been a trace of fear.

"If I've offended you, I apologize." He flashed a look of amusement. "I believe, Ms. James, in a way you're even more innocent than I imagined." Even in the dim light, Jonathan could see the pink that rose in her cheeks, a sight that pleased him inordinately.

"Don't be ridiculous." She drew herself up even straighter. "I've been married before . . . a-and of course there was Michael."

Jonathan smiled dryly. If he was any judge—and he was—saying she'd been with Galveston wasn't saying much. "It won't be the same, I promise you."

"But I—"

"I'll give you the time you need, Devon. But sooner or later, I intend to have you."

"But—"

"If that frightens you, I'm sorry." He leaned down and kissed her again, gently this time. "You can always stop seeing me, if that's what you really want."

It wasn't. He could tell by the look on her face. Inwardly, he sighed in relief.

"That would be the wisest course." She spoke the same words he had once chosen.

"Not from my vantage point."

"I like being with you, Jonathan. It's just that I've made mistakes in the past, and now I'm a little bit frightened."

So am I, he thought, suddenly jolted by the realization. For the first time, it occurred to him that Devon held the same unexplainable power over him he seemed to hold over her. He prayed she would never find out.

"We'll take things slow and easy. When the time is right, you won't be the least bit afraid." He smiled gently. "I promise."

He pressed the button on the driver's seat partition, bringing it partway down. "Ms. James has decided to go on home, Henry." He caught Devon's breath of relief, but it only made him more determined. She'd decided to go forward with her book, which meant he had to stop her.

And he wanted her. Now more than ever.

He'd had plenty of women jump into bed. This one wouldn't, and he was glad. Besides, when they finally did come together, it would only be the sweeter.

He shifted on the seat, his body still hard and throbbing from the kiss they had shared. Devon wanted time and he wanted Devon. He wondered just how long he would have to wait.

Devon tossed her purse down on the sofa and switched on the message machine. She felt nervous and excited, edgy and unsure, and certain she was in way over her head. She wouldn't be able to sleep for hours—but she wouldn't change a blessed thing.

She'd had a wonderful time with Jonathan again tonight—even with his blatant attempt at seduction. And he was right—she wanted him, too—not that she was anywhere ready to admit it.

The machine whirred, and she listened to a call from Christy, then one from Michael. The third message was from her mother. Devon rewound the tape and played that call back a second time.

There was nothing unusual in her mother's words, just something in her voice as she rattled on just a little too long. Devon wasn't quite sure what it was, and it was far too late to return the call tonight. She consoled herself by deciding in the morning she would stop by in person, check things out for herself.

After a night of sleep as restless as she had expected, Devon dressed in a calf-length brown wool skirt and a leather-trimmed bulky knit sweater. She was just about to leave the apartment when Christy hailed her through the intercom. Her throaty voice came from just downstairs.

Devon pressed the send button. "I'm on my way out the door, Christy, off to see my mother. Why don't you go with me?"

"All right. I was just prowling, anyway, looking for something to keep me entertained."

"Great, I'll be right down." Devon grabbed her camel-hair coat and muffler and raced out the door, taking the stairs instead of the slow-moving elevator. The girls hugged briefly.

"I'd love to see your mom," Christy said. "God, it must be years."

"Probably not since Paul and I got divorced. Michael hated to entertain. We never had my parents over, not even at Christmas. We always just went over there."

"Your mom's such a doll—the epitome of the world's perfect mother."

"Funny thing is, she's for real. Believe me, I know. No one appreciates her more than I do."

"Your dad's an all-right guy, too."

Devon laughed. "Dad's hardly perfect. He drinks too much, swears too much, and he can be incredibly demanding. My poor mother puts up with a lot."

"Oh, come on, Devon, you know you're crazy about him."

"What can I say? Saint or sinner, I love him dearly."

They climbed into a cab, and the driver ground the gears as he lurched out into the street. "Any special reason for the visit?" Christy asked once they'd settled themselves inside. "Your mom's not sick or anything?"

"No, it's nothing like that. She just sounded kind of strange on the phone, worried or something. I thought I'd drop by just to be sure she's all right."

Christy tossed back her thick dark hair, making the tiny white crystals dance in the center of her long gold earrings. "So what else is new and exciting?"

Thinking of the night before, of Jonathan's beautiful mouth and strong brown hands, Devon felt the heat creeping into her cheeks. She glanced out the window, hoping Christy wouldn't notice.

"My God, you're seeing someone!"

"Not exactly."

"Not exactly? Don't give me that. I know you too well."

"I've only seen him a couple of times."

"But you like him, don't you? You haven't been to bed with him, have you?"

"Christy!"

"Well, have you?"

"Of course not."

"Who is he? Anyone I know?"

It was no use. Christy would probe and probe until the truth came out. "Jonathan Stafford."

"Not *the* Jonathan Stafford? As in handsome, charming fabulously wealthy—owner of the Stafford Inn—Jonathan Stafford?"

"Yes."

"Oh, my God."

"We met through my research on his family. We're just friends, really."

"Oh, sure. A guy like Jonathan Stafford has lots of women friends. He's such a saint he hasn't even kissed you, right?"

Her cheeks burned again. "Well, he might have done that."

"Was it yummy? God, I'll bet it was."

"Please, Christy, I'd rather not discuss it."

Christy smiled with cunning. "That's a sure sign something's going on."

Devon started to deny it, but Christy stopped her. "All right, no more questions—at least for the time being. Which reminds me . . . I've got this little problem about making our Wednesday night appointment."

"What! You're not backing out, are you? You promised, Christy. You know how much I hate all this metaphysical stuff. You promised to go see Zhadar with me. You promised!"

"I've got a date, Devon. With that little Italian I'm so crazy about. He doesn't get to town that often. Please be a dear and say you'll let me off the hook."

"No."

"I've got an idea. Why don't you get Jonathan to go? He owns the inn, doesn't he? Maybe there's something he knows about it that might be of help."

Just thinking of him made a sweep of warmth rush into her stomach. "I don't think that's a very good idea. Besides, he's probably busy." But little Alex wouldn't be home that night. Jonathan had told her the boy spent four nights a week in therapy at the clinic. And she *had* broached the subject with him.

"The least you could do is ask . . . after all he's such a good *friend*."

Devon laughed. "All right, I'll ask. But if he says no, you're not getting out of this."

"Deal," Christy said. They shook on it as the taxi pulled over to the curb. A thick mat of clouds had gathered and a fine mist of rain began to fall. Devon paid the driver, and they crossed the sidewalk into the lobby, out of the wind that whipped Christy's long gray wool skirt and thick dark hair.

The apartment building was modern: simple clean lines, large comfortable rooms, modern fixtures. Her dad had been adamant: If they were going to move, he never wanted to see another drippy faucet. No steam heat for him, he said. Forced air, shiny new linoleum, and a brand-new kitchen for Eunice.

In truth, the move had been a necessity. In the old neighborhood many of the buildings were being torn down or converted to expensive condominiums. Her parents' apartment house was one of them. Devon had found the perfect place just on the perimeter of their old 86th Street neighborhood—her mother's single stipulation.

"All our friends are here," Eunice had said. "I'm not about to leave 'em." Having come to the city from Ireland as a girl, her mother spoke with an occasional hint of brogue. But Devon's grammar and speech were perfect.

"You'll not have a poor education holding you back, like your mother and me," her dad had said. From the time she was little, Devon had had private tutors. Her father had been determined to see that she would get every opportunity to improve her "fine mind." When she was twelve years old, she'd accidentally discovered why they thought it was so important.

That was the day she'd come home from school early with a sore throat and heard them arguing in the kitchen. Her mother wanted to tell her the truth about her birth, said they should have done it years ago. Her father said that if they kept their mouths shut, she would never find out and that would be far and away the best.

Her presence in the doorway ended that speculation.

They told her she had been left on their doorstep, a three-day-old unwanted bundle. Six months later, with the help of their local minister, she had been adopted. Though Devon had been crushed to discover the truth, she had never pursued the subject. Other adopted kids wanted to know who their real parents were, wanted to find them. Devon loved Eunice and Paddy so much she couldn't bear the thought of sharing that love with anyone else.

Especially with someone who didn't want her.

At least she finally understood why she was so different. Not only in looks, but in her likes and dislikes, her attitudes, goals and dreams, and just about everything else.

It really didn't matter. At least that's what she'd thought until Paul James divorced her and she'd started having panic attacks. The differences she had tried so hard to ignore contributed heavily to her stress, or at least that was what Dr. Townsend had said.

"Come in, come in." Eunice Fitzsimmons threw her thin brittle arms around her daughter's neck and hugged her close. She was a frail, small-boned woman in her mid-fifties—fragile, yet strong in a way Devon had always admired. "And Christy! Good Lord, y' don't look a day older than y' did the last time I saw y'. I'm so glad y' came."

They sat in the kitchen, which smelled of the rich beef stew her mother was cooking, talked about old times, about

Christy's current beau, "the little Italian," and her upcoming trip to Europe.

"I can certainly afford it," Christy said. Both her exes had been wealthy. "And Francisco is dying to show me Venice."

"Francisco," Devon repeated, "I wondered when you'd get around to telling me his name."

"You know I don't do that until things get serious."

"Yeah, at least two or three dates."

The girls laughed and so did Eunice, though she would have been horrified if Devon lived that way.

"Where's Daddy?" Devon asked.

"Down at Danny Boy's. A little celebration for Sean O'Reilly, one of the fellas he used to work with. Today's Sean's last day on the force."

"If I know Daddy, that means you'll have your hands full tonight."

Eunice rolled her eyes, crinkling the lines at the corners. "Y' can say that again."

Christy said something about men in general being a pain in the neck, and they laughed.

"What about Thanksgivin'?" her mother asked. "What time will you be comin'?"

"Early if you need help."

"Ten o'clock or so is plenty early. I know you aren't much of a mornin' person." She turned to Christy. "You're certainly welcome—bring your I-talian friend, if you want. We always cook more'n enough food."

"My parents will be in town for a change," Christy said, "but thanks for the invitation." They were usually off gadding about in some distant corner of the world. It was easy to see where their daughter got her wanderlust.

They talked a while longer, then Devon focused her attention on her mother. Her expression turned serious. "On the phone last night, you sounded upset about something, Mama. Is anything wrong?"

"Well, love, to tell y' the truth, your dad and me've been worried about you and Michael."

Devon sighed. She knew this was coming, she had already dodged the issue far too long. "I supposed I should have told you sooner, but . . ." She let the words trail off.

"Told us what, honey?"

"You're not going to like this, Mama, but Michael and I are not getting married."

"What?"

"I should have told you when it happened—almost a month ago—but I didn't want to worry you until I was sure."

"But why, for heaven's sake?"

Devon explained things as clearly and simply as she could, but her mother only seemed more distraught. "I'm beginnin' to think Michael's right. All this trouble is because of that crazy ghost story of yours. You said it was just a book you were thinkin' about writin', but he says you really believe it. He says—"

"Michael came here?"

Eunice nodded. "Last week. He's worried about you, love, and so are your daddy and me."

"Damn him!"

"Now, honey. Michael's just afraid you might be workin' too hard. He's afraid you might be havin' the kinda trouble you were havin' after Paul left."

"I'm going to kill him."

"Listen to me, Devon, y' work awful hard and sometimes life just gets a little too tough."

"That isn't it, Mama, I promise you. This ghost thing

is . . . is just what I said—a story, a book I'm working on. It's no different than any other book I've written. Michael's just angry because I broke off our engagement. He's hoping you'll side with him and convince me to marry him."

"Maybe y' should."

"Just because I slept with him, doesn't mean he's the man I should marry."

"Lord in heaven, if your father heard you talkin' like that, he'd likely keel over in his tracks."

"I know, Mama, but times are different than they used to be. I'm not going to marry Michael just because you and Daddy think it's the moral thing to do. I want to be happy—I'm not willing to settle for anything less. And it's damned unfair of Michael to drag you and Daddy into this."

They argued back and forth another half hour, until Devon had her mother calmed down and had won a promise that Eunice would work on Paddy. Devon played down the issue of the ghost story, knowing her parents would be certain that Michael was right.

"Damn him," she repeated to Christy, once they were back outside on the street.

"Personally, I think dumping Michael Galveston was the smartest thing you ever did."

"I didn't exactly dump him."

Christy just smiled. "I didn't think your parents were all that crazy about him."

"They aren't. It's just that they're so old-fashioned. Now Michael's got them all stirred up with this ghost business. They'll think I'm crazy, just like everyone else."

"I don't think you're crazy."

"You're about the only one."

"Don't get discouraged, Devon. Nothing's ever easy. Besides, if things get too hot, you can always come to Europe with Francisco and me."

Things were hot, all right, and they might just get hotter—but it was Jonathan Stafford not Michael Galveston who was turning up the heat.

Eleven

"We have known each other far too long to play games, *aijin.*" Wearing a short royal blue wool suit trimmed with black piping, chic and very American, Akemi rose from her place beside him on the white silk sofa and crossed the room to the window. Outside it looked bleak and stormy, dark angry clouds hanging low on the horizon.

"Yes, I guess we have." Jonathan shifted his position on the couch, uncomfortable with what must be done, but no less determined. "I suppose that's why I came to you now, instead of waiting."

Akemi looked down at the afternoon traffic. The muffled sound of a siren wailed somewhere in the distance. "I have always known the time would come when your grief for your son would lessen and you would go on." Her gaze remained locked on the throbbing beat of the city. She had always been drawn to it, the surging nameless throngs reminding her in some small way of the crowded Tokyo streets back home. "It appears that time has come."

Jonathan had chosen the afternoon instead of waiting till evening, setting the tone for their meeting without the necessity of words. "Yes, perhaps it has."

"How does she feel about you?"

There had been very little need for explanation. Akemi knew him too well. "I don't know."

"You have not known her long and yet you want her."

He smiled faintly. "Yes."

"You are not a man who takes his desires lightly."

"No, we both know that I am not."

She turned in his direction, walking with purpose, her old self-assurance returning. She stopped in front of where he sat, meeting his gray eyes squarely, certain once more of her course. "If you have such feelings, you must seek them out."

Jonathan came to his feet. There was moisture in her big dark eyes and sadness in the curve of her lips. He had expected little emotion, just a simple business farewell, or a parting between two old friends. That she would be truly upset had never occurred to him. Now he felt some of her pain, felt responsible somehow for letting things between them go too far.

"You are feeling pity for me," she said. "I beg you not to."

"It isn't pity . . . but I have no wish to hurt you."

"Some hurt cannot be helped. You will go to the woman, but what of me?"

She had changed in the last three years, he suddenly realized. She seemed more woman than girl, or was it just that she seemed more independent? Maybe it was her studies at the university, or just becoming more American. She had hidden it from him before.

"The lease on your apartment is paid for the next two years. I'll settle a reasonable amount on you. Money enough to see you well cared for until . . ."

"Until I can find another protector?"

"Yes."

"Now that I have known you, Jonathan, I can no longer do that. I have known love with you, Jonathan."

He felt her words like a blow to the stomach. There was truth in her face, and sadness, and heartbreak. How could he not have seen it before? Had he been that wrapped up in his problems, in his work? "Akemi—"

"I have always known it would not last, that what you felt for me was not the same, and I am ready to let you go. But I cannot return to the life I led before. In a few more months I will have my degree in business. The Japanese I speak, as well as my heritage, will provide the opportunities I need. As for men . . . this time I must follow my heart . . . just as you must now do."

Jonathan watched her a moment, then cupped her face between his hands. "You have been a great joy to me, a friend when I needed one badly. Part of me will always remember."

Akemi smiled forlornly. "As you have been a joy to me . . . I wish you great happiness, *aijin.* There is no man who deserves it more."

He cradled her against him for several long moments, absently stroking her hair. She thought it was love he was after. He didn't tell her it wasn't, that even he didn't know what he wanted for sure. Akemi clung to him, then pulled away.

"Good-bye, Jonathan, my love. If there is ever anything you need . . ."

It shouldn't have been such a difficult parting and yet in a way it was. *"Domo arigato,* Akemi-san. I wish you well." He turned and walked out the door.

"I'll pick you up at five-thirty."

"You're sure this isn't too much trouble?" Devon asked into the phone.

"I've a house on Long Island," Jonathan answered. "I haven't been out there since last year. This will give me a chance to check on the place. Besides, how could I possibly turn down a chance to meet the famous Zhadar?"

Devon laughed softly. She said her good-byes and hung up the phone, uncertain whether to be relieved or anxious. As she had promised, she'd phoned Jonathan yesterday, but he had been out, then she had been out when he'd returned the call that afternoon. Now that he had agreed to go with her, she phoned Christy and relayed the news, which meant Christy could spend the evening with Francisco.

Christy with her *little Italian.* Devon with Jonathan.

Devon's hand trembled slightly at the thought of the tall athletically built man and his darkly forbidding good looks. The last time they had been together he'd left a fire burning inside her she had yet to put out. Jonathan was intelligent and charming, sensuous and charismatic. That he should also be so virile, so totally male, she had known but had purposely ignored. He had told her he wanted her, and though in a way it frightened her, just thinking about the hunger in his eyes when he'd said it turned her insides liquid, and made her heart thump painfully in her breast.

She couldn't deny she found the idea of Jonathan making love to her exciting. But it was also incredibly dangerous. Even if he hadn't been opposed to her project, she'd be leaving herself open and vulnerable, accessible to more of the rejection she had experienced with Paul. Was she ready to deal with that sort of pain? She knew what she would be risking. No amount of will could ever erase those feelings of failure, of being unwanted, unloved. Of needing someone who didn't need or love her in return.

Giving herself to Jonathan would be putting herself at risk, there was no way around it. She wasn't the kind of woman who could sleep with a man without the emotional attachment that went along with it.

Not even Michael. Fortunately at the time she met Michael, she was still recovering from her disastrous marriage to Paul. She hadn't been ready to let her guard down again, let her emotions get out of control. The truth was, she had never really felt the kind of involvement with Michael she'd already begun to feel with Jonathan.

What manner of hurt might she suffer by exposing her innermost self to such a powerful, enigmatic, possibly ruthless man?

And yet, as he had said, if she never took the risk, she would certainly never reap the reward. Was she willing to let her extraordinary attraction to Jonathan go untested? If she did, would she wonder through the years what might have happened if she had only been strong enough to take the chance?

The solution lay in knowing where she stood with him before his potent male charm overwhelmed her completely. Whatever they felt for each other, there had to be a basis of respect, a feeling that whatever happened between them, even if things didn't work out, she'd be able to face him in the morning. That came only as a result of trust.

Devon sighed a bit wearily, considering that it was only a little past noon. She sat down at her small French writing desk. She had better things to do than spend the day worrying about Jonathan. Knowing him as she was beginning to, she was certain he was far too busy to spend time worrying about her.

Determined to forget him at least for the next several hours, she picked up her pencil and began to review her extensive notes on ghost encounters—notes that had been taken from the books she had been reading. At four o'clock, content with the progress she had made, she set her notes aside and went in to shower and change.

What to wear? she thought as her weariness washed away with the warm cleansing spray of water. Already her uncertainties had begun to recede, replaced by a growing anticipation. After all, as wealthy and commanding as Jonathan Stafford was, he was—unlike his uncle Florian—only a flesh and blood man. In the past few weeks, Devon's confidence had been slowly increasing. Maybe she was ready for just such a man.

Buoyed by the thought, she wound up choosing a bright red wool jersey jumpsuit that accented her long-legged figure and subtly showed off her curves.

Now that the ground rules had been set down, Devon felt safe in revealing a few of her assets. After all, they both knew what Jonathan wanted, what both of them ultimately wanted if things worked out, and the jumpsuit made her feel feminine and sexy. She wore it with a gold Hermès scarf, red pumps, and big gold earrings. Two could play Jonathan's game.

She was standing in her living room, listening for Henry's summons over the intercom, when Jonathan's deep voice boomed into the room instead.

"I'll be right down." She grabbed a long red wool coat that matched her outfit and a big red leather bag. As she pushed through the etched glass lobby door, Jonathan grabbed her hand and hustled her off toward the street.

"We've got to hurry; I'm double-parked." He had dressed as casually as she—a white cotton turtleneck beneath a dark gray cable knit sweater and a pair of black wool slacks. He looked as handsome as ever, and his hand felt warm and strong gripping hers. Devon's pulse increased and a tendril of heat uncoiled in her stomach.

Resigned to the effect he always had, Devon searched among the cars until she spotted not the long black limo, but a low sleek navy blue Lamborghini. "This is yours?" she asked as he opened the door and she slid into one of the deep red leather bucket seats. Jonathan shut the door and strode around to the opposite side, ducking his tall frame into the driver's seat.

"I haven't driven it in ages, but yes, it's very definitely mine."

Devon ran her fingers over the wood dashboard, and listened to the throaty purr of the powerful engine. "It's fabulous. I love it!"

Jonathan laughed softly. "Then as soon as we're out of the city, I'll let you drive it."

"Oh, but I couldn't."

"You do know how to drive, don't you?"

"Yes, but I've never driven anything like this. Usually just rental cars."

"This isn't that much different. Just a lot more fun."

True to his word, when they reached the expressway, he pulled over and they changed places. Devon slid nervously behind the leather-wrapped steering wheel. It didn't take long to get the feel of the powerful, low-slung auto, and when she did, the exhilaration of speed and control charged her with excitement.

"God, this is heaven!" Already driving too fast, it was all she could do not to punch the gas pedal down even more.

"I think I've unleashed a demon," Jonathan teased and Devon laughed, but recalling his words, she slowed the car back down to the speed limit and grew a little bit pensive.

"Don't look so serious," he said. "I was only teasing."

"I know, I was just wondering about our appointment with Zhadar. I wish I knew what to expect."

"Relax, Devon. Whatever happens, there's nothing to worry about. Besides, the way you've been driving, we haven't got much farther to go. We'll know soon enough."

The house near Eastport sat across the street from the beach, a two-story gray wooden structure with white-painted trim.

"Channeling must pay pretty well," Jonathan said. "This is a damned expensive piece of real estate."

"Three hundred dollars an hour. Sometimes a whole lot more, depending on what you want Zhadar to do."

Jonathan whistled. "I hope you get your money's worth."

So do I, she thought, but she wasn't sure exactly what that was.

Devon parked the car and they headed up the sidewalk to the house. Stiff salt grass bent into the wind, and sand covered much of what passed for a lawn, but the landscape was open and lovely and Devon thought she could have moved right in.

"Like it, do you?" he said, responding to the approval on her face.

"I love the ocean. It's beautiful out here."

"Good, then you'll like the Stafford family cottage in Southampton. And showing it to you gives me a good excuse for getting back out there." When they reached the front door, Jonathan pressed the bell, ringing clear bright chimes. In less than a minute the big front door swung wide.

"Good evening, Ms. James," said a small blond woman in a stiff gray uniform. "Mrs. Solomon is expecting you. She's waiting in the study." The small woman pointed down the hall.

"Thank you."

Jonathan took Devon's hand, and they walked in that direction. The house was elegantly furnished, very traditional, European antiques mixed with contemporary sofas and chairs, a designer's touch throughout. Only in the study was there evidence of the business Patricia Solomon engaged in.

That dark wood-paneled room was dimly lit and shrouded in heavy burgundy velvet draperies. Candles flickered in small glass holders on the tables. Incense burned in small brass dishes and gave off a sandalwood scent. Oriental carpets covered the floors. Several large books sat on the coffee table, all with metaphysical titles. A small fire burned in the oak-manteled hearth.

Patricia Solomon entered the room through a side curtain in the far wall. Her slender hands extended in greeting. A lady's gold and diamond Rolex was strapped to her wrist.

"Good evening, Ms. James."

"Good evening." Devon accepted the woman's handshake, little more than the brush of cool fingers. "Mrs. Solomon this is Jonathan Stafford. I suppose you could say he's here for moral support."

Patricia Solomon smiled. She was slender and attractive, early forties, her wavy short brown hair just beginning to gray at the temples.

"Welcome, Mr. Stafford. Zhadar is always pleased to make new acquaintances." Devon got the distinct impression she could have added, "Especially those of immense power and fortune." Obviously, Patricia Solomon was not a stranger to the *Wall Street Journal*.

"Thank you." Jonathan also accepted her welcoming hand. "Ms. James and I both look forward to meeting him."

"Why don't we sit down and you can tell me the reason for your visit."

At Christy's advice, Devon had said very little to the woman on the phone, just confirmed the time and date of their meeting and the charges she would incur. If the encounter were to be given any credence, the less Patricia Solomon knew about Florian Stafford and what Devon believed had happened at the house on Church Street, the better. They followed the woman to a place in front of the low-burning fire. Patricia lifted her long-flowing forest green dress up out of the way as she moved. Jonathan and Devon sat down on a burgundy sofa.

"Now, what is it you hope to learn from his Most Imperial Being?" Patricia sat down in a large high-backed chair across from them.

"You mean Zhadar?" Devon asked.

"Of course."

"I was told that he might be able to contact members of the spirit world."

"Yes, he is often called upon to contact loved ones who have journeyed beyond the veil."

"These particular spirits are still earthbound," Devon said with an uneasy glance at Jonathan. Whatever he was thinking, he kept very carefully concealed.

"I see . . ." Patricia Solomon shifted, straightening her skirts out around her. "You realize it may take several visits before Zhadar can make contact with the spirits you seek."

At three hundred dollars an hour. "I thought he'd be able to do that this evening."

Mrs. Solomon laughed softly, her voice ringing with a clear, bell-like sound. "If only it were that simple . . . No, my dear, I'm afraid these things take time."

"So where, exactly, do we start?"

"We start by having you meet Zhadar. Once you've come

to know him, you will understand his incredible powers. From there we shall see."

Devon was feeling less certain about this whole idea, yet she wasn't about to back down. "All right, let's get on with it."

Patricia made a motion with her hand, and theatrically the lights went down. "I'll need your help in this. In a moment, I'll begin my deep breathing. When I've gone far enough inside myself, Zhadar will take over my body. The process will go much faster if you will help me."

"I'm afraid I don't understand," Devon said.

"When I breathe, you breathe. Count to five and let your breath out slowly. When you've done this six times, silently chant the word Zhadar over and over until he appears."

In spite of herself, Devon flushed. What in God's name was Jonathan thinking about all of this? "I don't know, Mrs. Solomon, this seems just a bit—"

"I assure you, this is necessary. Why don't we just get started?"

Six very deep, very long breaths later, Patricia Solomon slumped softly against her chair, her eyes closed, her breathing little more than light puffs of air. Devon watched her carefully, hearing the hiss of the fire behind her, nothing more. Then the woman's body went rigid, neck straight, shoulders squared. Though neither Devon nor Jonathan had repeated Zhadar's name as the woman instructed, her eyes flew open and she gripped the arms of her chair.

Devon hadn't paid much attention to the high-backed antique before. Now she noticed that carved gilt scrolls formed a backdrop above the woman's head and each arm of the chair curved into the head of a falcon, its sharp beak open, its neck ringed in long gilt feathers.

"I am Zhadar!" the woman proclaimed in the husky

voice of a man. She gripped the falcons' heads beneath her fingers. "Why have you called me?"

Devon just stared, saying nothing. Not for a moment did she believe Patricia Solomon's spirit was real. It was all too prearranged, too theatrical, too much of a show.

"Why have you disturbed my sleep?" The thronelike chair lent just the right mystical aura to Zhadar's performance.

"We need to reach someone," Jonathan answered, "someone in the spirit world." There wasn't an ounce of mockery in his voice, and yet it was there in his face, if one knew where to look.

"Why?" Zhadar surged to his feet, his entire posture altered from that of the woman. Somehow he even seemed taller. He strode back and forth in front of the sofa and except for Patricia Solomon's female features, which also seemed altered, it might have truly been a man who spoke.

"We need to know if the spirit we seek still lives on the earth plane," Devon said, figuring if Jonathan were willing to play the game so was she.

"Which spirit is it?" Zhadar asked. "A mother? A father? Tell me of them so that I may know where to search."

"It's a child," Devon said impulsively. "A young boy who was murdered."

"Murdered?" Something flashed in Zhadar's eyes—the glitter of anticipation—and future reward. "Who has done this foul deed? The guilty one must be punished for such a heinous crime. It is the law of Allah!"

Devon grimaced, wondering how in the world she'd be able to face Jonathan when they were through. Zhadar went on to spout a twenty-minute philosophy lecture on life's injustice, pledging to contact the dead child and learn the guilt of the person who had committed the evil deed. His loud and emphatic discourse was punctuated with questions about the child's family, subtle probings for information that could later be explored, or so Zhadar explained.

Devon felt Jonathan's grip on her arm grow tight with warning, but he needn't have bothered. There was no way on earth she would have given up a single clue. Sidestepping each of Zhadar's questions, Devon checked her watch and was surprised to discover more than an hour had already passed.

At least the show was entertaining.

Zhadar reluctantly acknowledged her withdrawal. He made a grand show of being called away, and Patricia Solomon slumped forward, exhausted, against her gilt-backed chair. Her forehead was covered by a fine sheen of perspiration. Her breathing was labored, but eventually, her eyes fluttered open.

"Well?" She sat up to face them, looking as if she hadn't the slightest idea what had occurred.

"I'm afraid your friend wasn't much help," Jonathan said.

"You mustn't get discouraged. Next time things will be different. Zhadar will gather information from other spirit guides and when you return—"

"I'll call you," Devon broke in, "just as soon as I get a moment's free time." The good news was, the Solomon woman didn't even have her phone number, and Devon intended to pay her in cash—no check, no address, no account number. She opened her purse to extract the money, but Jonathan pulled his wallet from the pocket of his overcoat and spread out three one-hundred-dollar bills.

Devon felt the warmth creeping into her cheeks, but said nothing. Not until they had reached the car and settled themselves inside.

When Jonathan inserted the key in the ignition and started the engine, Devon pressed three hundred-dollar bills into his hand. "This was my idea, Jonathan, I hardly meant for you to pay for it."

He watched her a moment, awaiting her reaction to Zhadar's performance, and Devon flushed once more, and added, "I'm not a fool, Jonathan. The woman is obviously a charlatan. I can't imagine anyone falling for that incredible garbage she spouts, but obviously they do."

Jonathan grinned, his expression relieved. He handed back the money. "It was worth three hundred dollars just to see the look on your face when she told you we had to breathe in unison and chant Zhadar's name."

Devon laughed, feeling a sweep of relief at his light teasing, but she pushed the money away. "This is my project; it's my responsibility. You have no idea how embarrassed I am about this. You took time away from your work to bring me out here—God, I'd like to strangle that woman, and my friend Christy Papaopolis for talking me into this crazy idea in the first place."

"I'm glad you didn't believe her, but I'm not the least bit sorry I came."

"You aren't?"

"No."

She smiled at him warmly. "Then neither am I."

Jonathan's hand slid behind the nape of her neck, and he drew her toward him, his mouth coming down over hers. It was a gentle lightly probing kiss, but it jolted her like a white-hot brand. Her heart leaped hard against the wall of her chest, and her breathing instantly quickened. When Jonathan ended the kiss, Devon glanced away, embarrassed at her fiery reaction. He shifted into gear and pulled the car out onto the road, but when he turned east on the expressway instead of west, back toward the city, Devon's eyes swung to his face.

"Where are we going?"

"My house in Southampton. I told you I needed to check on the place."

"Now?"

"Can you think of a better time? There's no one there but a caretaker. I called ahead and had the heat turned on."

Devon's guard came up with the force of a snowstorm. "I think you've turned the heat up enough already."

Jonathan merely chuckled. "I think you'll enjoy seeing the house, and I really do need to see that it's being well cared for. It won't take long . . . you don't mind, do you?"

Devon shook her head. It didn't seem much to ask after the trouble he had gone to. "You took time off from work to drive me out here, and it isn't really all that late."

They drove in companionable silence along Route 27 to the Southampton exit, then Jonathan wound his way through the town, passing narrow streets with quaint old-fashioned names like Ox Pasture and Meeting House Lane. They drove past pleasant colonial houses with cedar-shake roofs and others with Victorian gingerbread trim. On Meadow Lane down by the water, Jonathan drove up in front of a two-story white stucco building, contemporary in design, with walls of tinted blue glass that looked out over the ocean.

"This is your idea of a family cottage?" Devon's lips curved up with amusement as Jonathan helped her out of the car.

"You expected New England quaint, I suppose."

She smiled. "Yes, I guess I did."

"My father had the house built just before he died. My

late wife and my sister are the only ones who've ever gotten much use out of it."

A brass and glass chandelier burned in the entry, lighting the foyer when Jonathan used his key to open the door. Black marble floors contrasted the high vaulted ceilings, white overstuffed sofas and chairs, and stark white walls, where huge contemporary art pieces provided the only bit of color.

"Well, what do you think?" Jonathan took her hand and led her into the massive open living room. Sea and sand sprawled just outside the tinted glass and the spacious airy room seemed to beckon them in.

"I like it. I like it very much." A fire had been started in the oversized hearth, whose sweeping lines reached the ceiling, as clean and straightforward as the rest of the house.

"I hoped you would." He helped her off with her red wool coat and seated her at a sofa grouping in front of the fire. "I'll just tell the caretaker we're here, and take a quick look around. I'll be right back."

He returned a few moments later, carrying a silver tray loaded with cheese and crackers, a small container of caviar, a bottle of Montrachet and two chilled stemmed crystal glasses.

"I thought we weren't staying that long," Devon said with a hint of accusation, her nervousness suddenly returning.

"We don't have to stay . . . not if you don't want to." He set the tray on the long low white stone coffee table in front of the sofa but stood waiting for her decision, making no move to sit down.

"I don't suppose one glass of wine would hurt."

Jonathan smiled that devastating white-toothed smile of his and took a seat beside her. He made a grand show of opening and pouring the wine, but the sound of the water lapping at the sand outside the window drew her attention instead. When she didn't accept the glass he handed her, just kept staring out at the blackness, Jonathan gently nudged her hand.

"You're a thousand miles away. What are you thinking?"

Devon accepted the glass. Some of the moisture fell on her fingers. "Sorry." She took a sip of the slightly amber liquid, sat back, and began to relax. "I was thinking about Zhadar." And how disappointed she was that tonight was, like most of the books she'd been reading, another dead end. "I was wondering how many people there are who want to believe in life after death so badly that they're willing to accept a fraud like Patricia Solomon."

Jonathan sipped his wine. "A good many, I suppose." Over the rim of the glass, his eyes fixed on her face. "What about you, Devon? Are you so determined to believe what you think happened at the inn that you're willing to deceive yourself?"

Devon felt no anger, for she had asked herself that question a hundred times. "I hope not, Jonathan. I don't want to fool myself, even for a moment. But neither am I willing to ignore the possibility that what I experienced was real."

Jonathan leaned back against the sofa, his shoulders just brushing hers. He seemed reasonably satisfied with her answer, saying nothing as he drank his wine, merely watching her, his eyes turning bluer as they moved from her face, down her throat, to the curve of her breast. Beneath that look, her heart set up an uneven rhythm in her chest.

Jonathan put his wineglass down on the table, reached for hers and set it next to his. "I think I like your honesty best of all." He leaned closer, his fingers coming up to her chin, cupping it, tilting her head back so he could settle his mouth over hers.

Devon stiffened under his touch, but only for a moment. His lips felt warm and firm, his breath tasted of the wine he'd been drinking, and he smelled of lime cologne and salty sea air. When his finger strummed the pulse beneath her ear, Devon opened her mouth to receive his tongue, and the slick hot feel sent a jolt of desire through her body. Making a small sound in her throat, she slid her arms around his neck and laced her fingers through his wavy black hair.

What are you doing? an inner voice cautioned, but the blood roared through her veins, drowning out the sound. Her breasts had begun to swell where they pressed against the muscles across his chest.

Devon heard him groan. It was warm in the house. The room was lit mostly by the flickering light of the fire. One of Jonathan's long-fingered hands splayed over her back while the other rode at her waist, easing upward, slowly, deliciously, until his palm cupped her breast.

Dear God, Devon thought, knowing their surroundings were far too seductive, the feel of him far too arousing. It wouldn't be long before she gave herself over to the exquisite sensations he was stirring. That, she could not allow.

"Jonathan . . ." she whispered when he began to trail kisses along her throat to her ear. With slow erotic strokes, his thumb and forefinger pebbled the peak of her nipple until it pressed with aching awareness against her white lace bra.

Just a few moments more, she told herself. Jonathan kissed her again, his tongue sweeping into her mouth, probing deeper, making the hot wet dampness seep between her legs. She heard the buzz of her zipper sliding down to her waist, felt his hands stroking her flesh. A soft click marked the release of her bra; then he was lifting a breast, cradling it, working it gently but remorselessly until her back arched and she pressed herself farther into his palm.

"Jonathan . . ." she whispered again, knowing the time to stop this reckless game had long since passed.

"Easy, love," came the husky softness, as his tongue was laving the inner shell of an ear. His hands moved with gentle sureness and her jumpsuit slid off her shoulders as he urged her down on the sofa. Instinctively her hands came up to his chest to hold him off, but he gently pushed them away. "It's all right, I'm not going to hurt you."

One more deep hot kiss and Jonathan lowered his head to her breast, taking it into his mouth, laving it with his tongue, suckling it gently.

Devon moaned at the heat erupting inside her. *Dear God, what am I doing?* But she knew without doubt, and instead of pulling away, she clutched his shoulders, feeling the muscles bunch beneath her hands. There was power in that sinewy frame, and hard male strength. All Devon could think of was what it must be like to touch his naked flesh, to feel all that sleek smooth muscle she had only glimpsed before.

"We've got to stop," she finally told him, forcing the words past lips that were sweetly bruised with his kisses, soft and pliant and aching for more. "I can't do this. I—"

"Hush." He nipped the side of her neck. "This was bound to happen, sooner or later. It might as well be now."

Devon tried to sit up, but Jonathan lowered his head once more to her breast. His tongue slid out and around her nipple, making it ache and harden. Then he opened his mouth and drew in the soft white swell.

"Oh, God," Devon moaned, her head falling back. Jonathan's powerful frame was covering her, pressing her into the sofa.

Passion and heat swirled around her, desire and yearning, but with them came desperate warnings. What would happen tomorrow? What if making love meant nothing more to him than a moment of satisfaction? What if *she* meant nothing? Was she ready to accept that?

"Jonathan, no . . . please . . . we can't . . . I can't do this." She wedged her hands between them and pushed against his chest. He was breathing hard, his unusual eyes a deep grayish blue and glazed with passion. It occurred to her that he might not stop. After the way she had responded she would have no one to blame but herself.

Instead he paused, pulling just slightly away. "I told you I wouldn't force you, but I won't let you pretend this isn't what you want."

Devon nervously wet her lips, her mouth suddenly dry. "It's what I want. I won't deny it. But . . ." She sat up, pulling her jumpsuit back over her shoulders with hands that had started to tremble.

"But?" Jonathan's gaze turned dark as it clashed with hers. "I don't like playing games, Devon." He caught her wrist and forced her hand against the front of his slacks. He was rock hard and hot, so full and pulsing she could feel every beat of his heart.

"I . . . I'm sorry. I knew we shouldn't have come here. I was afraid this would happen. I didn't mean for things to go this far."

"Bullshit," he said, surprising her. She had never heard him swear like that before. "You wanted me to kiss you. You wanted a helluva lot more than that."

Devon swallowed hard. Outside the window the night encroached, suddenly dark and ominous. "If you weren't who you are and I wasn't who I am, maybe I wouldn't have stopped you. As it is, I'm just not ready to hop in your bed."

Jonathan's mouth thinned into a hard disapproving line. "You think not? I ought to push you back down on this couch and show you exactly how ready you are."

Devon's bottom lip trembled. Her breasts still ached and so did the place between her legs. "Please, Jonathan, I already feel bad enough."

His gray eyes pinned her. "Shall I tell you the rest of my dream?"

"No! I mean . . . I'd rather you didn't." But just the memory of it, the way his voice had taken on that husky purr, sent a fresh jolt of heat through her body.

"Why not? You liked it the last time, even if you won't admit it."

Dear God, it was the truth! And if he kept on talking, used that deep sexy voice to describe what he'd dreamed of doing, she'd be finished for sure.

"Jonathan, I . . ." She felt like the worst kind of tease, the kind of woman who gets her kicks out of leading a man on, then saying no to him. Tears formed in her eyes and she had to glance away. "I'm sorry. When I'm with you . . . sometimes I don't . . . I can't seem to think straight."

Jonathan went silent for a moment, then swore softly beneath his breath. His fingers cupped her chin, turning her to face him.

"I'm sorry, too. Sorry I pressed you so hard. It isn't like me, really. In fact, I can't believe half the things I do when I'm with you."

Something warm uncurled inside her. Devon gave him a soft, slightly tentative smile. "You mean like ordering wine and pasta and even dessert?"

"And going to the theater and driving my sports car. But more than that, it's the things I think when I'm with you, the way I feel when I touch you." Jonathan turned her back to him, and zipped up her red wool jumpsuit. "The truth is, I can't remember wanting a woman the way I want you."

Devon leaned over and gently kissed his lips. "Just a little longer, I promise. I have to be sure."

Jonathan nodded, then sighed with resignation. "As much as I enjoyed the drive out here, I suddenly wish we were sitting in the back of the limo, letting Henry take us home. Even if we didn't make love, there are at least a dozen things I'd enjoy doing to your beautiful breasts."

"Jonathan!"

He laughed. "You inspire me to the outrageous, sweet Devon. No one else makes it so much fun."

"I'll drive back, if you want, but you may be taking your life in your hands."

"I'll drive. Besides, with my hands on the wheel, you're probably safer."

Safer, yes, but she was rapidly learning that being safe from Jonathan was the last thing she wanted.

"By the way, are you busy tomorrow night?"

"No, why?"

"I've got a business meeting in New Jersey, but it shouldn't take long. There's a wonderful restaurant I know in an eighteenth-century mill near Franklin Lakes. We'd still be home early."

"I'll go on one condition."

"Which is?"

"We leave the chauffeur's partition open."

Jonathan shook his head, a strand of jet black hair falling softly across his forehead. "I'm beginning to believe that it's you, love, who's mistress of the black arts. I think torture is your specialty."

Devon only smiled. She wondered if she were really torturing him—or if she were torturing herself.

Twelve

"You'd better wind things up, Jonathan." Dee Wills stood in the doorway between their two offices. "You're going to be late for your Holidex meeting. Even Henry can't make all that rush-hour traffic disappear."

Jonathan nodded. "I suppose you're right. I wanted to read the updated file on Wilmot Ltd., but I guess it can wait till tomorrow."

He shoved back his high-backed leather Eames chair, grabbed his black pin-striped suit coat from where it hung on the wooden valet beside the teakwood credenza that matched his desk. He shrugged the jacket on over his shoulders. Walking over to the closet, he retrieved his black cashmere overcoat.

He had chosen these clothes especially for this meeting. He wanted to present an image of authority—though his name alone was enough. He wanted the staff at Holidex to grasp exactly how serious their problem with Tri-Star was, and he wanted all of them to be involved in finding a solution.

Jonathan pulled open the heavy walnut door and followed Dee back into her office. "I'll see you in the morning," he said as he passed by her work-laden but neatly organized desk.

"Don't forget this is a short week. Thanksgiving's this Thursday."

"Damn. That's right, it is. Sometimes I think I'd forget whether it was night or day if it weren't for you."

"You might forget something as trivial as that, Jonathan, but ask you about a ten-year-old file and you'd be able to remember every little detail."

He grinned. "All too true. Which just goes to show you how screwed up my priorities are. One of these days, I'm going to turn things around and make business come second in my life."

"It already does." Dee smiled. "Right behind Alex."

That was true enough, and knowing that it was so, made him feel a little bit better. "What are you doing for Thanksgiving? Did you get the turkey I sent to your apartment?"

"You bet I did. The damned thing's big enough to feed half the office, but it won't go to waste. Not at our house. Those kids of mine will annihilate that bird the way you did Burton Production in your takeover last year."

He laughed. "Promise to save me some leftovers? You know how Alex loves your stuffing."

"I always do, don't I?" She closed one of the files on her desk and picked up another. "You know you two are invited." She always invited them and he always turned her down. Thanksgiving was for family.

"Believe it or not, my sister and her brood are coming to town." Usually it was just he and Alex. "They'll be staying out at our cottage in the Hamptons. Alex's going to spend the weekend. He hasn't seen his cousins in a couple of years." Maddie and Stephen and their three kids. The rare family gathering would be noisy, but he found himself looking forward to it.

"That's wonderful, Jonathan. I know Alex will love it."

"He's really looking forward to it. He's always loved his aunt and his cousins."

"Alex loves everyone."

Jonathan acknowledged that truth with a smile and pushed the button on the private elevator leading down to the main office lobby. His sister was an unpredictable whirlwind, but she was great with the kids. Madeline was tall and dark, like all of the Staffords, with striking blue eyes and a slightly wicked smile that made men go crazy. Six years younger than Jonathan, she had married an English baron by the name of St. Giles five years ago and moved to his estate outside London. She had settled down—some—but she was still Maddie, glamorous, fun-loving, and though they hadn't been close since childhood, he looked forward to seeing her again.

Jonathan rode down in the elevator and crossed the lobby, his mind swinging back to his meeting with Holidex, then to Devon and the evening ahead. Outside on the street, he found his limousine waiting at the curb. Henry held open the door, and Jonathan bent to climb in. He smiled when his shoulders collided with Devon's as she slid gracefully over to make room for him.

"Hi," he said a bit inadequately.

"Hi." She glanced at his alligator briefcase. "Ready to launch the attack, I see." On the way back from Long Island, he had told her about the problems he'd been having with Holidex Industries and Tri-Star Marine. Except for his one-sided conversations with Akemi, it was slightly out of character for him to discuss his business dealings with someone outside the office, yet he'd discovered it felt good to unburden himself. And Devon had seemed interested.

"I'm afraid I don't know much about business," she'd

said, "but it's certainly a fascinating subject, and I'd love to learn."

"You keep writing books as good as *Journeys* and you're going to need to know a whole lot about business. You'll be making investments, and if you think Patricia Solomon was a charlatan, you won't believe the number of frauds who come out of the woodwork in the guise of investment brokers, ready and willing to relieve you of your hard-earned money."

A funny thing had happened as he'd said those words—he'd known then and there he wasn't about to let that happen. Devon was on her own in the world and in many ways naive. Somehow he'd make certain that no one took advantage.

He glanced at her now. Beneath her fox-trimmed jacket, she'd worn a short black wool skirt and an emerald green sweater trimmed with leather and sequins. She had on black hose and black pumps. It wasn't the conservative wool suit he would have expected, far bolder, less subtle. There was something seductive in the outfit, or the way she wore it, but he shoved that notion away.

He'd spent the better part of the day convincing himself—no easy task—that tonight would be just a casual evening out. He wanted Devon and he intended to have her, but there were other things he wanted as well, and he wouldn't get them by pushing her until she did something she might regret later.

Tonight there'd be no attempts at seduction, no passionate fondling of her beautiful breasts—and they were indeed that, he recalled from the night before—apricot-tipped, small and firm, yet as lush as a freshly ripened peach. He groaned just to think of the way they had nestled in his hand.

Not tonight, he reminded himself sharply. Tonight there'd be nothing between them but a kiss good night when he walked her to the door.

"How was your day?" she asked sweetly, and he had to force his eyes away from the shiny coral lipstick that moistened her lips. Damn, the woman had the most powerful effect on him. Already his pants fit a little too snug—not an auspicious start to the evening.

"Busy, as always. This meeting, of course, is of utmost importance. I've got to make the staff at Holidex understand how serious Tri-Star's threat really is."

"If Kelovar's as good as you say, what can you do to stop them from succeeding?"

"I said it looked good—so far. What we have to do is uncover the flaw. There's bound to be one—there always is. It's up to the boys in the Holidex lab to discover Kelovar's weakness. Once we know what it is, we'll be able to stop them—or at least slow them down."

"What if there isn't one?"

He released an unhappy sigh. "There'd better be. Or a bunch of those guys will be pounding the pavement looking for work."

Devon studied him from beneath her dark gold lashes. "That's important to you, isn't it? The welfare of the people who work for you."

"I feel responsible for them, yes. It's been a family tradition to support the loyalty of our employees. During the depression, my great-grandfather nearly lost everything by making drastic cuts in profit rather than laying off his workers. Everyone shared equally in the company's problems, but most of the men kept their jobs and that kept food on the table and a roof over their families' heads."

"My grandfather was a longshoreman," Devon said. "He

died when I was five years old, but I guess he was a tough old Irishman, just like my dad."

"You love your family very much."

She glanced away for a moment. "They aren't my real parents . . . I'm sure you know that."

"I know."

"But no one could have had a better family than I did. My mom was a great mother and my dad . . . well, he got drunk and rowdy once in awhile, but most of the time he was terrific. I love them both very much."

"You're lucky. I was never very close to either of my parents. My mother was involved with her charity work and my father with his business."

"I love them," Devon said, "but we're not at all the same. It always bothered me being so different. I used to wish I was short and freckled and that I had brown hair. My mom and dad are outgoing, fun-loving people. I'm more of an introvert. They never understood why I didn't have more dates, why I'd go to the dances and wind up standing in a corner."

Jonathan arched a brow, his eyes sweeping over her high cheekbones, well-formed lips, and silky pale blond hair. "That's a little bit hard to believe."

"I'm sorry to say it's the truth. Which is probably why my divorce was so rough. I didn't have a lot of self-confidence to begin with."

He ran his finger gently across her bottom lip, testing the rounded softness. "Is that one of the reasons you stopped me last night?"

Twin spots of color rose in Devon's cheeks. She tried to turn away, but Jonathan caught her chin and wouldn't let go. "Tell me."

"I wanted to be sure I meant more to you than just a one-night stand. I was afraid of getting hurt."

"Was?"

She smiled at him softly. "As you said, no risk, no reward. Some things are worth the risk."

Jonathan said nothing else, more certain than ever that in giving her time, he was doing the right thing.

He glanced out the car window and though it was almost dark, this stretch of winding tree-lined road with its scattering of large two-story colonial houses looked familiar.

"We're almost there. You can wait for me inside if you like, or there's a wonderful little pond in a park not far away. It's kept well-lit even in the evening. The big Canada geese often stop there on their journey south for the winter. By the time you get back, I should be finished."

"That sounds perfect." The car pulled into the parking lot of the four-story brick building that was the home office of Holidex Industries. "And don't worry about the time. I brought something along to read."

Jonathan took the small magazine from her hand. "*Karma.* That ought to be interesting." She caught the sarcastic note in his voice and grinned.

"That's what I thought. Nathan Talbot, the owner of the Insight Bookstore recommended it as a supplement to my research."

He felt a twinge of unease at that, but forced it away. Leaning forward, he started to brush her lips with a kiss, caught himself, and opened the car door instead. "I won't be long."

And he wasn't.

He met with Garrett Browning, the president of the company, Debra Dutton and Wayne Cummings, both VPs, and Carl Mills, head of the research division. There were half-a-dozen male and female underlings present he could also call by name, but the rest of the workers had finished their shifts and gone home. Jonathan was hoping these top-level employees could convey the importance of this work.

"What all of this really comes down to," he told them from where he stood behind the podium in the conference room, "is survival. If Kelovar plastic proves to be all it claims, it's only a matter of time before Holidex is out of business. Even if the reality turns out to be less than perfect, but the flaw in the product isn't discovered for several more years, it will still be too late. This company will already have gone down in flames."

Barbara Murphy raised her hand. She was the assistant lab director, a buxom, dark-haired, dark-eyed woman who wore mostly business suits and went out of her way to play down her feminine charms. "I'd like to know what kind of flaw you expect us to look for? We can't perform the right tests unless we know the questions we're trying to answer."

"If I knew the solution to that, we wouldn't be having this meeting. The truth is, it's you and Carl and your research staff who are under the gun here. But the rest of you can help by outlining scenarios of possible problem areas. How does the product respond to the elements that are predominant in the boat-building industry? for example. How long will it hold up in comparison to our cast-metal products? No possibility is too farfetched to overlook."

"You want us to come up with the questions," Debra Dutton said, "and the lab to come up with the answers." Sharp and aggressive, Debra had risen steadily through the ranks of the company.

"Exactly. And remember to keep an open mind. Listen to your colleagues' ideas and thoughts and those of your subordinates. See what you can come up with."

"We'll do our best, Mr. Stafford." Carl Mills leaned forward in his chair.

"That's as much as any man can ask."

The meeting ended on a positive note, and Jonathan made his way through the throng to the waiting limousine. Devon surprised him by greeting him with a soft kiss of welcome. Though it lasted only a moment, it was one kiss more than he'd planned on this evening, and the fact that she had initiated it made it all the sweeter.

Dinner at Ye Olde Mill was nothing particularly special, just fresh grilled halibut for him and lemon chicken for her. But the interior of the place, built in Washington's day—with its uneven flooring, hand-cut beams, and rough-hewn walls—was so quaint that neither of them minded.

Though Jonathan tried his best to be casually charming, to keep his mind on Devon's pretty face but off what had almost happened between them the night before, it seemed she had none of the same compunctions. All through the meal, she watched him. Her lovely green eyes returned to his mouth again and again. He found his own attentions drifting lower, down to the peaks of her breasts. He didn't realize he was staring until he noticed the stiff twin peaks that had formed beneath her sweater.

My God, she's not wearing a bra. "If you're finished," he said, his voice a little rough, "I think it's time to go."

"Yes . . ." She met his eyes boldly. "I believe it is." Taking his arm, she let him guide her out the door. Once they were back inside the limo, she settled herself next to him, their coats abandoned in the warm interior, her black wool skirt riding up on her thighs as it hadn't before, showing him more leg than he wanted to see, considering the decision he had made not to touch her.

"Jonathan?"

"Yes . . ." He dragged his eyes up to her face.

"Why don't you kiss me?"

The breath hissed out of his lungs. "I'd like that more than anything I can think of, but I wanted to give you some time. I wanted . . ."

"I know what you want, Jonathan. You told me once, and last night you tried to show me."

His heart slammed hard against the wall of his chest. When Devon pulled his head down for a kiss, urged his mouth open, and slid her tongue inside, hot blood rushed to his loins. Her arms went around his neck and she laced her fingers in his hair. Jonathan hauled her against him and deepened the kiss, using his tongue against hers, plunging it inside with the same deep thrusts he wanted to use on her body.

"I think you'd better put up the partition, don't you?" she whispered against his ear. "Henry might have a wreck if he keeps looking in the mirror."

One corner of his mouth curved up. "As I recall, you made me promise I wouldn't."

Devon shrugged her slender shoulders. In the soft blue light of the car, her blond hair gleamed against the curve of her throat. "Promises are made to be broken."

Jonathan pushed the button and the panel slid closed with a quiet buzz, sealing them warmly inside.

"Do you like what I'm wearing?" she asked with a throaty purr.

"I like the way you look in just about everything. Or better yet, I'd like you in nothing at all."

The hand she rested on his chest began to tremble, but she didn't back away. Instead she started unbuttoning his shirt, her fingers a little unsure but obviously determined. "Why don't you tell me the rest of your dream?"

Jonathan's brow shot up. Already aroused, his body hardened and the heaviness in his groin grew hot and throbbing. "If you're teasing me, sweet Devon, you may find yourself across my knee. I told you once, I don't like playing games."

She smiled seductively. "I'm willing to take the risk if you are."

His heartbeat quickened at the image, his palms almost itching to cup her firm little bottom. He smiled faintly, took her hand and slid it inside his now open shirt. It felt slender and warm, her touch a bit tentative as her fingers tested the tightness of the curly black hair on his chest.

"My dream . . ." he said softly. "How well I remember . . . You were wearing a short black skirt . . ." He glanced down at the portion of thigh her skirt exposed. "Much like the one you're wearing now."

Devon leaned back against the seat and kicked off her shoes, then ran her slender foot up his leg. Her ankle was trim, the arch of her foot high and feminine. "Go on," she gently urged.

"And a sequined sweater but no bra. I could tell by the way the peaks of your nipples grew hard and pressed against the fabric."

"The way they are now?" she asked, so softly he almost didn't hear.

He reached out and cupped one, feeling the stiff bud pressing against his palm. "Yes . . . just like now. You had on a black lace garter belt but no panties."

"How did you know?" she whispered.

"I knew because when I ran my hand up your thigh—" He followed the words with the softest of gestures, his palm skimming over her flesh. "I felt . . ." His hand stilled. He felt nothing but the flowered roughness of a black lace garter belt, nothing but the smooth warm skin beneath. Devon sucked in a breath when he reached the downy hair and soft moist folds of flesh between her legs, then she trembled and started to pull away.

"Easy, baby. You've come this far, don't stop now."

"Jonathan . . ." she whispered with the first real hint of uncertainty, and he realized how much it had taken for her to go this far.

"It's all right, love. Everything's going to be fine." He kissed her then, long and deep, pressing her down on the seat. "God, you're beautiful." Her skirt rode up even higher. He lifted the sweater, baring her breasts and lowered his head to take one into his mouth. He ringed her nipple with his tongue, laved it, and suckled it gently. Devon trembled beneath him and tried to tug free his shirt.

"I've got to touch you," she said, "I swear I'll die if I don't." Knowing exactly the way she felt, he finished unbuttoning his shirt and yanked it free of his slacks.

Devon's hands splayed over his chest, testing the bands of muscle, digging into his shoulders. Soft slim fingers teased his flat copper nipples. God, it was agony of the most exquisite sort. He wanted to take her right there, to drive into her and pound out the frustrations of the days and nights he'd spent thinking about her.

His hands slid down to her waist, then lower, parting the soft warm flesh of her sex, sliding his fingers inside. Devon arched her back, pressing against his hand. She was wet, and more ready than he ever would have guessed. He kissed her again, aroused by her musky scent, letting his fingers probe the fiery sweetness between her legs.

"I wanted things to be perfect," he said, his voice rough and husky. "I wanted to take you in my big soft bed, spend hours just kissing and caressing your breasts, but if you don't stop me now, it's going to be too late."

Devon touched his cheek with trembling fingers. Her eyes said this had already gone farther than she'd planned. "It's already too late." Her hands worked the zipper at the front of his breeches and his hardened length sprang free.

"Damn." Her small hand surrounded him, making him ache and swell even more, turning his mind from thoughts of a perfectly planned seduction to a reckless, impassioned mating in the back seat of his car.

"You were right about what you said." Devon slid her arms around his neck. "This was bound to happen sooner or later. I want you, Jonathan. It doesn't matter where."

The seat was wide and roomy. Jonathan kissed her, roughly, thoroughly, then he parted her legs with his knee and settled himself between her shapely legs. He could feel her trembling, more fearful than she let on but also wildly aroused.

"Easy, love. There's nothing to be afraid of." Jonathan eased himself in and drove hard into her hot damp flesh.

Devon sucked in a breath at the feel of him, not prepared for the thickness, the overwhelming length. He was so big! The men in her life hadn't been anywhere nearly his size and she felt filled by him and in awe.

"All right?" he asked, one brow arched, apparently surprised at the tightness. But she was slick and hot and ready, and in seconds her body stretched to accommodate his thick length.

Devon wet her lips. "I . . . yes . . . you feel wonderful."

"So do you." Then he began to move.

Dear Lord in heaven. Nothing had ever felt like this. As Jonathan kissed her, his tongue made passionate sweeping probes in rhythm to the movements of his body. His hard-muscled chest pressed erotically against her nipples. When his hands slid under her bottom to bring her even closer, Devon lost herself in a storm of passion, soaring to the heavens, then plunging back toward the earth. She bent her knees to draw him closer, and he thrust deeper and harder, driving into her again and again.

"Hang on, love," he said softly and she did, clinging to his muscular shoulders, her head thrown back letting wave after wave of sensation wash over her.

"Don't fight it. Just let it come."

It hit like a tidal wave, lifting her to the brink of a fiery red vortex then sucking her back into the sweet black depths of bliss. She was swirling among the stars, reaching for the moon and for a moment she touched it, all silver swirls and blinding white light. Jonathan followed in her wake, grinding out her name with the last hard thrusts of his body. His muscles tensed, then relaxed as he spiraled back down.

They lay quietly entwined, legs and arms, her cheek next to his, a sheen of perspiration covering their half-naked bodies. All too soon, Jonathan eased away. Reaching beneath the seat, he pulled out a black canvas bag, unzipped it, and took out a small white towel, handing it to Devon, who felt her cheeks grow warm.

"I play racquetball sometimes. I always carry a gym bag just in case."

"Handy for all sorts of things," she said a bit dryly. She used the towel discreetly and adjusted her clothes, but refused to think of him being that prepared for anything else.

Devon swung her eyes to his. "Oh, my God, we forgot all about safe sex."

Jonathan looked mildly amused. He drew on his shirt, tucked it in, and zipped up his pants. "Neither of us uses drugs. I'm not promiscuous, Devon, and from what I've learned, neither are you." He grinned. "Besides, I just gave blood."

She glanced out the window, her embarrassment growing by leaps and bounds. She had planned a night of seduction, *beginning* in his car, not ending there. This was without a doubt the wildest, craziest, most reckless thing she had ever done, and though she had never experienced anything more exciting, she was beginning to wonder if she'd done the right thing.

"Where are we?" she asked, realizing they'd had more than enough time to reach the city. She bent down to pick up her shoes and slid them on.

"Henry's nobody's fool. He figured we were . . . enjoying the scenery . . . so he kept on driving." Jonathan pressed the button on the intercom. "Time to go home, Henry."

"Aye, sir."

"God, how will I ever face him." Jonathan's soft chuckle told her she'd unconsciously said the words out loud.

"I take it your grand seduction was just supposed to begin in the car."

"I didn't think you would get so . . . that we would get so—"

"Henry is well paid for his discretion. He won't say a word."

Devon said nothing more. She rested her head against the seat, worrying again if making love to Jonathan had been the right thing to do—or if the hours she had spent convincing herself to fulfill his fantasy and working up the courage to carry it through had been her greatest folly. She felt warm fingers beneath her chin, turning her face to him.

"Regrets?"

Devon shook her head. "Not unless you do."

"You gave me a very precious gift. Thank you."

For the first time Devon smiled. "I hoped you would like it."

Jonathan pulled her into his arms. "I loved it." He held her gently until they reached her brownstone apartment. Henry pulled to the curb, got out and held open the door.

"Good night, Jonathan," she said a bit shyly. She felt awkward and embarrassed, but she smiled bravely and swung her legs out the door. She couldn't help wondering if she would ever hear from him again.

"Good night, Jonathan?" he repeated, sliding out after her. "That's all you have to say?"

"Well, I—"

"Either I'm staying here, or you're coming to my house. Which is it?"

"But I—"

"You heard me. Don't you think I know what's going on in that pretty little head of yours? This isn't a high-school dance and I'm not going to leave you standing alone in the corner."

The words touched a chord deep inside her and something tugged at her heart. "Would you like to come up for a nightcap?" She gave him a tenuous smile.

"I thought you'd never ask." Jonathan turned his attention to Henry. "I'll need you here by six. I've got a busy schedule tomorrow and I'll have to go home first and change."

Devon flushed again, but said nothing more. Jonathan's arm went around her, then he swept her up and carried her across the sidewalk to the heavy wooden doors of the lobby.

Once they reached her apartment, she nervously poured two snifters of brandy and handed him one. Jonathan watched her every movement. His eyes once more were blue instead of gray, and definitely hungry.

"Why don't we take these into your bedroom?" he said, his voice a little rough.

Devon's mouth went dry. This was what she had wanted and yet . . . "All right." She nervously wet her lips, and Jonathan eyed her with curious speculation.

"We've already made love, Devon. What's left to be afraid of?"

Not coming up to your standards. Revealing my insecurities. Letting you interfere in my work. Falling in love with you. This last was by far the most frightening. She knew what happened when a powerful man like Jonathan gained that particular hold over a woman.

"I guess I'm just not used to you," she said instead. "We haven't known each other very long."

Jonathan took the brandy glass from her hand and disappeared down the hall. In minutes, he returned, slid an arm beneath her legs, and lifted her up.

"After tonight, love, I promise you we'll know each other very well."

Ignoring the heat that unfurled in her stomach, Devon clung to Jonathan's neck as he carried her into the bedroom. He had already pulled back the covers on her queen-sized bed and turned on a lamp, the light no more than a soft yellow glow. As he let go of her legs, she slid the length of his body. Her eyes grew wide at the feel of his hardened arousal.

Jonathan kissed her, long and deep, then began to strip off her clothes. "I want to see you," he said. "All of you."

Devon swallowed hard. She was far more nervous this time than she had been before. All afternoon she had prepared herself to seduce him. Putting on the garter belt, going braless, she had felt seductive, worldly. Now she was just Devon James, a woman who knew very little about pleasing a sophisticated man like Jonathan.

He must have sensed what she was feeling because he pulled off her sweater, baring her breasts. But he stopped before he slid off her skirt.

"You're trembling."

"It was different before. In a way I was playing a part. Now I'm just me and I don't quite know what to do with myself."

"I know what to do," he said. Softly, expertly, he began to kiss her. His hands came up to cradle her breasts, his thumb and forefinger making her nipple tighten and pout. Devon moaned softly and swayed against him.

"Why don't you undress me?" he asked. "Do you think that might help?"

Devon's eyes met his. "Yes." In fact, it helped a lot. She was so busy stripping off his coat, undoing the buttons on his shirt and tugging it free of his pants, she didn't notice that he had removed her skirt until he stooped to roll down her stockings. She was standing there naked, and all she could think of was how incredibly beautiful his chest was, with dark and springy hair that curled between his flat copper nipples. Her eyes caught the puckered remains of a scar that ran from his wrist up his forearm to his elbow, but when she touched it, he pulled away.

Jonathan sat down on the edge of the bed and took off his shiny black loafers then stood up and unzipped his pants, letting them slide down a pair of hard, muscled legs. His small navy blue briefs joined the growing pile of clothes on the floor.

"You'll have to wear them in the morning," Devon said for lack of something better, picked them up and draped them over a chair.

"Come here." Jonathan caught her arm and the movement forced her eyes in his direction, down his body to where his shaft rode thick and hard against his belly. He pulled her against him and kissed her until her knees went weak. "I like this about you, that you're shy one moment and passionate the next. Whatever you're feeling, Devon, don't be afraid to let it show."

Lifting her up, he carried her over to the bed, but instead of joining her, he stood there beside her, letting his eyes move down her body.

"You're beautiful. As lovely as I imagined."

She came up on an elbow. "You're more than I imagined." Taller, more solid. "Bigger . . . everywhere."

One corner of his mouth slanted upward and he joined her on the bed. "This time we'll go slowly. Just take our time and get to know each other's bodies."

That's what he promised, but the reality turned out to be different. Kissing and exploration turned to urgent breathing and heated stroking, which turned to a furious joining, pounding fevered thrusting, and an incredibly fiery release.

"Damn," he grumbled, "that wasn't supposed to happen." With a dark look shaping his features, Jonathan pulled her into the curve of his arms. "I can't remember when a woman has been able to make me lose control."

Devon just smiled, sweetly sated, stretching lazily, then curling softly against his body. "Good for me," she thought, not realizing she spoke the words out loud just as she fell asleep.

Jonathan only smiled. Next time *she* would be the one out of control, he vowed silently into the darkness, reaching over to switch off the lamp.

But he held her close and smoothed her hair and thought how lucky he was to have found her.

He also thought how much easier it would be to keep her from uncovering his small son's secret and that even if she did find out, it might not matter. Not if he kept her busy and content and well satisfied in his bed.

Thirteen

Devon snuggled close to the solid warmth beside her. Her breasts tingled pleasantly and something nuzzled her ear. An instant later, her eyes flew open as she pushed the cobwebs of sleep aside and remembered who slept in her bed.

"Good morning," Jonathan said, though it was still dark outside and even the traffic had not yet begun in earnest. "Sleep well?" There was lazy satisfaction in that deep male voice and a long brown finger drew circles around the peak of a breast, making it pucker and tighten.

Devon smiled up at him softly. "Very well, thank you."

Jonathan stole a quick glance at the digits on the clock beside the bed, pulled her beneath him, and made love to her again, more gently this time but with no less passion. Then he swung his long legs to the side of the bed and walked naked into the bathroom.

"There's a brand-new toothbrush in the cabinet behind the mirror," Devon called out to him, admiring his taut round buttocks, remembering with a delicious rush of warmth how they had felt beneath her hands. Hearing his heavy male movements filled her with lazy contentment. She thought how few times Michael had used that room.

On the rare occasions they had made love at her house instead of his, he had always showered and dressed and gone home, unwilling to put up with the inconvenience of waking up somewhere else in the morning.

Jonathan pulled open the bathroom door, crossed the room and began to put on his slightly disheveled clothes.

"How about some coffee?" she offered. "It won't take a minute."

"Next time," he said, the words comforting in their implication. "Maria will have a pot going when I get home."

"Maria?"

He smiled. "My housekeeper. She takes very good care of me. You just stay in bed."

How could she argue with that? She stretched lazily, enjoying the damp reminder of their lovemaking that moistened the place between her legs. He was pulling on his shirt when she remembered the scar she had seen.

"What happened to your arm? I noticed it last night."

"I burned it."

"How?"

"A fire."

"Where did it happen? Does it still bother you?"

"What is this, Devon, twenty questions?" His voice had taken on a hard biting edge and Devon retreated under the threat of it.

"I'm sorry," she said, a little bit hurt. "I didn't mean to pry."

Jonathan crossed to the bed, leaned over and kissed her. "I'm sorry, too. I didn't intend to snap at you. I guess I should have accepted that coffee after all."

She smiled at that. "It's all right, I'm not much of a morning person, either."

Jonathan finished dressing. Once more wearing his pinstriped suit, he combed his fingers through his tousled black hair and returned to the side of the bed. "How about dinner?" Lifting her hair up out of the way, he kissed the nape of her neck.

Devon's smile widened. "How's eight o'clock? I'll cook you something right here."

Jonathan's eyes took on that bluish hue she was beginning to recognize as desire. "Even if you haven't the faintest idea how to cook, there is nothing I'd like better."

"I'll admit my cooking skills are minimal, but I think I can manage to keep us from starving."

"That you could do staying right where you are." He kissed her again, this time on the mouth, started toward the door, then stopped and turned. "I suppose you'll be busy Thanksgiving."

"Yes. My parents are cooking a turkey." She propped her elbows behind her, a tangle of pale blond hair brushing her shoulder. "Would you and Alex like to come? You could meet my mother and father and we could—"

"My sister and her family are flying in from London. I was going to ask you to join us."

"I guess we're at an impasse."

"Looks that way." He smiled. "Alex is spending the weekend with my sister and his cousins out at the cottage in the Hamptons. I'd been dreading my lonely apartment, but now you can keep me company. We can spend the whole time together—that is if you're free."

Her heart speeded up at the thought. "That sounds wonderful."

Jonathan pulled open the bedroom door. "See you tonight. If you need anything, just call my office and leave a message with my secretary. Her name is Dee."

Not a bad way to start the morning, Devon thought, once he had gone. She slept an hour longer, indulging herself, recalling the intimate moments of the evening, recalling every minute detail of their lovemaking until she was thinking about the night ahead with a rush of desire she had to fight down. Dammit, she had work to do. She shouldn't let thoughts of Jonathan keep her away from her research.

But her heart wasn't in it as much as it had been.

She kept thinking of Alex and the way Jonathan felt about him. Until last night, working on this book had seemed all important. But making love to Jonathan seemed to have changed things.

Devon showered and dressed in a simple dark green corduroy jumpsuit and went into her office. She hadn't worked in there for over a month, not since her frightening experience at the Stafford Inn. The computer screen stared back at her accusingly. The disks that held *Traces* were still sitting where she'd left them, the novel all but written, awaiting the last few unfinished chapters.

You've got to get back to it, she chided. *You need the money.* But instead, she gathered her burgeoning stack of research on ghosts and the paranormal, and the magazine, *Karma,* that she had begun to read in the limo last night in New Jersey.

One glance at the small magazine and she grimaced, recalling all too clearly the thoughts she'd had as she'd leafed through the pages. She thumbed back through them now and the same thoughts returned.

This is nothing but a bunch of bull!

Sitting down on the couch, she propped her notebook on her lap, grabbed the pencil she had stuck behind an ear, and started making notes. It wasn't fair to ignore those things that disproved her theory simply because she didn't want to believe them.

And if there was ever a case against the paranormal, ever an indictment that the entire metaphysical realm was nothing but a trumped-up scheme to fleece people foolish enough to believe, it was *Karma* magazine.

She turned to the first page.

Self-Hypnosis, the ad said, the key to your inner being. All you need is the astounding Astro Wave Synchronizer, model VC 5. The complete package can be yours for the cost of the instrument alone! Not a thousand dollars, not eight hundred. For a mere four-hundred-forty-nine dollars and ninety-nine cents, you can own this revolutionary electrical phenomenon and change the course of your life!

The photo showed a small metal box with a light inside, something like a projector. The subject was supposed to stare into the beam until he sank into a deep hypnotic trance. Devon figured the poor fool who tried it would probably wind up with nothing but a colossal headache—or worse.

Page two.

Atlantean Crystals. Guaranteed to come from the Lost Continent. These crystals can help you discover missing treasures, find lost pets, attract love into your life, direct healing energy, help you locate your spirit guides, and find the answers to your most troublesome questions. Send your money today!

Page three.

Do you have the courage to be lucky, loved, and rich? For two thousand years, people have used the power of talismans to bring them health, wealth, and happiness. Replicas of these same magical magnets can be yours for under ten dollars apiece! Protect yourself against evil. Attract good fortune. Garner peace and good health. Send for yours today!

Next came an article entitled "Snakeman, Creature from the Dark World," followed by an ad for the famous Psychic

Turbo Brain Generator, an astounding revolutionary device which "magnifies your telepathic abilities and allows for astral projection from the body."

At the bottom of the page, there was "Past Life Regression, an unsurpassed program that will guide you to the life you lived before. All you need is an hour of time and someone to read you the guidelines. Hurry and make this astounding purchase today!"

Devon shuddered to think of the hundreds of people duped into sending their hard-earned money. People like Zhadar were ready, willing, and able to prey upon those in the world who were desperate for answers, in whatever guise they might come.

With a sigh of despair, she closed the magazine, still unfinished, and set it aside. Another dead end. Aside from Dr. Linderman's book on ghosts, so far she had found almost nothing to validate what she believed had happened at the inn. It was more discouraging than she could have imagined.

Her mind strayed to Jonathan. She could just imagine what he would say if he had read the magazine. He hadn't said much about it lately, but she knew he still wanted her to quit. Sometimes, she wondered why she didn't. It would make so many people happy.

Deciding that a fresh cup of coffee might boost her spirits, Devon got up from the sofa and started toward the kitchen. When she was halfway there, her father's voice boomed through the intercom coming from outside the lobby. She answered, buzzed him in, and waited while he rode the slow-moving elevator up to her floor. It was rare for him to drop by, especially without a phone call. He carefully respected her privacy, and she wondered with a frown of worry what had prompted his unexpected visit today.

"Hi, Daddy." She hugged his thick neck and he hugged her back. He was a short, stout man, portly, some would say. He'd always been brawny but since his retirement from the police department, he'd grown a paunch. His thinning reddish brown hair had begun to recede.

"Hello, little girl."

She didn't bother to correct him. To Paddy that's what she would always be and in a way it pleased her. "How about a cup of coffee?" she asked him, knowing he'd accept and already heading into the kitchen.

"Sounds good, but I can't stay long."

"What's up?" she called back through the swinging door. She returned before he could answer and handed him a heavy china mug.

Paddy shrugged his thick shoulders, sat down on the sofa and toyed with the buttons on the front of his slightly rumpled beige cardigan sweater. "Nothin' much. I just happened t' be in the neighborhood. Thought I might as well drop in."

Devon rolled her eyes. "Come on, Daddy, that line's as old as the hills. What's going on?"

"Your mother says you'll be comin' for Thanksgivin' dinner."

"Of course. When have I ever missed?"

He nodded. "That's good. She's already started cookin'. She'll fix too much, as usual."

"I'm sure she will."

"That bein' the case, when Michael called I invited him to join us."

Devon sat down with a sigh on the arm of the sofa. "Oh, Daddy, you didn't."

"Now listen, honey. Whatever's gone wrong between you two, it can't be all that bad."

"Nothing's gone wrong between us. The truth is I just don't love him. I never have and I never will."

"Michael loves you. Maybe that's enough. He's a good provider—you said so yourself. He could take away some of the strain you've been under."

Here it comes, Devon thought as the truth began to come out.

"You could take time off from your work," he continued, "relax a little."

"Stop writing my ghost story, right Dad?"

"Well . . . yeah. You know how your mama and me feel about it. We don't like the idea of your gettin' involved in all that occult stuff. It's ungodly, Devon. Nothin' but the work of the devil. Pastor Colby says so."

"Pastor Colby. That old goat is forty years behind the times and you know it. He still believes in the rhythm method and he isn't even Catholic."

"Well, Michael says you're workin' too hard. You know what happened the last time . . . how sick you were feelin'. Your mother and me don't want to see that happen again, and Michael says if you marry him it won't."

Thanks a lot, Michael. "I know you don't believe in ghosts, Dad, and I don't really blame you. Unfortunately, after what happened in Stafford, I do. Can you really be all that certain I'm wrong?"

Paddy took her hand. Worry lines creased his lightly freckled forehead. "It's all a buncha bunk, honey. People been spoutin' that same kinda malarkey for as long as I can remember. It wasn't true then any more'n it is now."

Devon sighed. First Michael, then Jonathan, now her mother and father. She had expected this, been determined to ignore it, and yet a part of her couldn't help but wonder if some of what he said might not be true.

Devon's stomach knotted. She thought of the magazine she had been reading, page after page designed to deceive believers. She thought of Zhadar and the way Patricia Solomon had been fleecing the public for years. So far, Devon had read about poltergeists, reincarnation, past life regression, ESP, spirit guides, psychic healing, automatic writing, psychokinesis, telekinesis, psychometry, out-of-body experiences, telepathy, and clairvoyance. She'd been sifting through the voluminous stacks of information, working to find some small particle of truth that would verify her experience.

Much of what she read seemed believable, some of it well-researched, but could she honestly say she had found even a single absolutely verifiable fact?

She looked into her father's worried face. He had high blood pressure and an over three-hundred cholesterol count. Her mother worried about him endlessly and so did Devon. At his age, he didn't need problems, especially ones she created.

"I don't know, Dad." She felt a surge of defeat that rolled over her like a wave. "I suppose part of what Michael said could be true. Maybe I could have been feeling the strain of the last few months. Before it happened, I'd been working hard on *Traces*. Michael had been pressing me about getting married. At the time, I was certain I didn't make it up, that it wasn't just coincidence, but the more I read . . . I just don't know." Devon forced a smile, the concern in her father's deep brown eyes infusing her with guilt.

"Tell you what." She took his hand, noticing how many more liver spots appeared there over the past few months. "I'll do some very serious soul-searching, okay?"

Paddy brightened. "Promise?"

"I promise."

"That's my girl." He hugged her tightly.

"As for Michael . . . isn't there any way you can *uninvite* him?"

Her father chuckled softly, the relief on his face more than clear. "He probably won't stay long. He's got his own parents to see to."

That was true enough. For the last several years, she and Michael had eaten two Thanksgiving dinners, one at her parents', one at his. "I guess I can stand it if you can. You two never were all that chummy."

Her father grinned. "Good girl. And you never know. You may just find out you care for him after all."

But all she could think of was the tall dark man who had left her house that morning. One more person who was certain that what she was doing was wrong.

Devon walked her father to the door, more aware than usual that she stood as tall as he. "Thanks for caring, Daddy. Tell Mom not to worry, everything's going to be fine."

He stepped into the hall and his shoulders seemed a little straighter. Was writing this book really worth it? Was hurting her parents, maybe even hurting little Alex, worth the cost of a story that might be nothing more than the residue of an overworked mind? Nothing more than a resurgence of her painful anxieties?

She thought of Nathan Talbot and his damp and musty Insight Book Store. Did she really want to deal with the dark and forbidding side of human nature? Did she want to dabble with the occult?

She shivered just to think of it, remembering with far too much clarity the feeling of terror—real or imagined—she had experienced that night in the yellow room.

Why not face the truth? She was a writer, a dreamer, a person who created works of fiction. She was also a victim of anxiety, a woman who'd been forced to seek psychiatric help in order to avoid a nervous breakdown. She was a woman under a great deal of stress and strain.

And there was Jonathan to consider. She was attracted to him. No, more than attracted. She had high hopes for their burgeoning relationship and she didn't want to damage that relationship by posing a threat to his son.

Tonight she would see him. Why not discuss some of her thoughts with him? Maybe he could help her see things more clearly, put things in their proper perspective. She would listen to what he had to say and then decide.

Devon gathered her research books and carried them back into her office. Her eyes moved automatically to the dead computer screen. If she set the Stafford project aside for a while, she could resume her work on *Traces*. Finishing the book would give her even more time to think things through, and the money would lessen the stress that might have caused all this trouble in the first place.

Feeling tired in a way she hadn't in weeks, Devon returned to the living room and sank down heavily on the sofa. So what if she'd imagined the whole damned thing? So what if her mind had been playing some hideous trick? What did it matter, as long as she protected the people she loved?

Yes, tonight she would speak to Jonathan and decide once and for all what she should do.

Paddy Fitzsimmons opened the door to his apartment to find his wife Eunice standing at the sink, with a wooden spatula in her hand. She set it down beside the stove where a pot of broth simmered, scenting the air with corned beef and cabbage. She wiped her hands on her calico apron, and hurried in his direction.

"Well, what'd she say?"

He glanced up at her absently, his mind lost in thought. "What? Oh, Devon, you mean?"

"Yes, o' course, Devon. That's who y' went ta see, wasn't it?"

Paddy sighed, sauntered across the room, and sat down in his favorite overstuffed chair, a leather recliner Devon had given him for Christmas two years ago. "She said maybe Michael was right. That she'd had a lot on her mind lately, just like he said. Coulda been the strain after all. I think she may just give it up."

Eunice threw up her hands. "Thank the Lord."

"Yeah, well, that's what I thought at first. Now I'm not so sure."

Eunice crossed to his side and hovered over him, fluttering her thin veined hands in an unconscious, birdlike gesture that was habitual with her. "What do y' mean?"

"I mean, I didn't like the way she looked when she said it. Kinda defeated like. That was the way she looked after that damnable husband of hers walked out on her."

"But I thought that was what y' wanted. I thought we both agreed Michael was right, and gettin' Devon to stop workin' so hard was the best thing for her. Besides y' know what Pastor Colby says."

Paddy shook his head. "I don't know, Mother. I don't like seein' our little girl like that. Maybe she was better off before, finding things out for herself."

"And maybe y' just don't like Michael Galveston all that much, and y' especially don't like sidin' with him against your little girl, even if he's got the right of it."

"Maybe."

"Well, it's too late ta worry about it now. You've done what y' set out to and that's that. Devon'll have to make up her own mind."

"I suppose." But he was thinking about Devon's face when she'd told him that Michael might be right. Sort of reminded him of the day he'd discovered the ad in the paper offering a reward for the little lost puppy she'd brought home. She'd looked up at him with those big green eyes and his stomach had tied itself in knots. In the two weeks after she'd found that little brown and white cocker, she had fallen in love with it. So much so, he'd damned near ignored the ad, but in the end he'd told her about it.

Devon had sobbed for hours, but the following day, she'd given the dog back to the little boy who'd lost it. Paddy had offered to get her another, but she wouldn't have it. She didn't want to love it and then lose it. She said it hurt too much.

Had she really imagined all that ghost stuff up in Connecticut? And if she had, how would she feel knowing her mind was playin' tricks on her again?

Damn, just like with the puppy, he wished he'd kept his mouth shut and left her alone.

"You seem a little distracted." Propped against the pillows at the head of the bed, the white flowered sheet bunched at his hips, Jonathan ran a finger along Devon's jaw, drawing her attention. "Except for the hours we've spent in bed, you've been that way all evening. Why don't you tell me what's wrong?"

Devon toyed with the sheet that covered her breasts. She looked relaxed, a woman pleasantly sated, and yet at the same time she didn't. "My father came to see me today.

He and my mother are pressing me to give up working on my book."

That was good news. "Why?" he asked.

"Because they don't like my getting involved with anything that has to do with the occult. Apparently Michael has been filling them in on the subject and giving them a blow-by-blow on the strain he thinks I've been under. To top it off, Franklin Colby, the pastor at my parents' church, has been convincing them I'm practically in league with the devil."

He smiled faintly. "How do you feel about it?" Devon looked away. There was something in her eyes, a sort of bleakness he hadn't seen there before.

"I don't know. Everyone thinks I'm wrong about what happened in Stafford. Michael, my parents . . . you. The farther I get from it, the more I'm beginning to think that all of you are right and I'm wrong. That I just made everything up. Maybe it was just some overblown coincidence."

"Would it be so terrible if that were the case? You're only human, Devon. Sometimes those things happen."

"It gnaws at me, Jonathan. I think about it night and day. It's like a wound that won't heal. In my heart, I don't believe I made it up. I believe what I felt was real, that Annie and Bernard were real, and yet . . ."

"And yet, you're not certain."

"No, I'm not certain."

"Maybe if you took some time, finished your other project."

She smiled, but looked a little forlorn. "That's what I was thinking. Maybe if I went back to work on *Traces,* took a little more time to think things through, I'd be able to see things more clearly."

"That sounds like a good idea." *Liar.* If anyone else had approached him with as much conviction as Devon had—no matter the subject, whether he believed in it or not—he would have encouraged that person to continue his search until he uncovered the truth. Devon needed that encouragement now. She desperately hoped he would give it to her, and yet he could not.

"So you think stopping my work for a while is the right thing to do?" she asked. Big green eyes fixed on his face. He forced himself to ignore the entreaty he read. She had been so wary of him in the beginning. Now she trusted him. He wanted to shake her, to warn her that she shouldn't.

"Considering that you could use the money from *Traces,* I suppose it is." Of course, she could work on her book in the mornings, meet her contract deadline, and still go on with her research, but he didn't dare suggest it.

"Then I guess that's what I'll do."

Something tightened inside his chest. A few weeks ago, she wouldn't accept a million dollars to stop working on this project. Now, because of her parents, because of her growing uncertainties, because of her feelings for him, she was willing to give it up.

"Come here." Sliding an arm around her waist, he pulled her on top of him, drew her head down and captured her lips. In minutes, he felt the tension ease from her body. He couldn't give her the encouragement, the support she so desperately needed, but he could give her this. He parted her legs and settled her astride him.

She gasped softly, feeling his hardness pressing for entrance, then she was lifting herself up, taking him inside her. He would make it good for her, he silently vowed. He would take her mind off her worries and soon she would forget all about what had or hadn't happened that night at the inn.

He would make her forget everything but the feel of him inside her.

And he would protect his son.

"Are you sure it's all right, Dad?"

"Of course, I'm sure. Just don't let those cousins of yours get you into trouble."

Alex whooped with joy, and his three small cousins joined in, pushing his wheelchair off with a burst of speed back toward the rear of the house. Warmed by the sight of his happily laughing son, Jonathan watched them go. It felt good to see Alex like this, no white-uniformed nurses, no cold linoleum floors.

Except for his stainless-steel chair, he seemed no different from the other three boys. They all liked bugs and snakes and Nintendo, and they all hated girls. They all forgot to wear their mufflers when they went out, and managed to get their feet wet and muddy. They all laughed a little too loud, and scuffled when they should have been sitting still. They all loved the out-of-doors and especially the ocean.

Alex was just like any other little boy, except when the other three kids went out to play, they could walk and run, shoot basketball hoops, or play baseball. Alex was bound to his chair.

Jonathan tamped down the dismal thought. Today was Thanksgiving. He and Alex had driven out to the family cottage in the Hamptons. They had spent the day surrounded by the warmth of family. Aunt Stell hadn't felt well enough to come, and Jonathan worried about her declining health, but he had called her this morning, and she had assured him she'd be able to join them for Christmas.

Madeline Stafford St. Giles and her husband Stephen sat across from him on the white sofa grouping in front of the fire. They had finished Thanksgiving dinner over an hour ago and been in comfortable conversation ever since.

All but the children. Alex, Thomas, Frederick, and Winifred—a name Jonathan still hadn't forgiven his sister for—had been pleading for the past fifteen minutes to drive into town to the show.

"Why don't you go with us?" Not surprisingly, his sister had been the first to cave in. Maddie was a goer. Anytime, anyplace, anywhere. Staying in one spot for more than a few hours was beyond his sister's comprehension.

"I don't think so. Alex is having a great time with his cousins, and I've a friend I'd like to see."

Something in the way he said it must have tipped her off. "A friend?" She had a way of reading people. He had always found it a bit annoying. "Female, I imagine."

He smiled dryly. "I imagine."

"What happened to your little Japanese mistress?"

Jonathan shrugged his shoulders in a gesture of nonchalance. "Akemi and I decided to part company for a while."

A wide white Stafford smile crossed Maddie's elegant features. "That's interesting." She looked a good deal like him, with her glossy black hair and olive skin. She was tall and thin, as leggy as any New York model, with big blue eyes and thick black lashes. "As I recall, the girl was almost a fixture. I take it your *friend* doesn't believe in sharing."

"You might say that."

"Very intriguing." She glanced at her husband. "What do you think, Stephen?"

"I believe this sounds serious."

Maddie grinned at Jonathan. "I should have known something was up. You've been avoiding the subject of women all day. What's her name?"

"Who?"

"Don't give me that, Jonnie. If you don't tell me, I'll find out on my own. But we both know I'll find out."

That she would. They had stubbornness in common, too. "Devon James."

"The writer?"

"Yes."

"I've seen her on the telly. She's lovely."

She's more than that, he thought, but didn't say so.

"You should have brought her with you, old boy." That from Stephen, whose interest had stirred at the first hint of gossip. Jonathan thought when it came to being in the know, the Englishman was worse than any woman.

"She's spending Thanksgiving with her parents. I thought I'd drop by on my way home." He knew where her parents lived though she'd never told him. Unfortunately, their phone wasn't listed and the number was in a file at the office. He hoped they wouldn't mind the intrusion.

"A trip to Mum and Da's." Stephen grinned beneath his pencil-thin moustache. "This does sound promising, doesn't it, Migs?"

Stephen's pet name for Maddie, whom he wildly adored. Stephen St. Giles, Baron Havengham, was a tall man, whipcord lean, with dark brown hair and eyes. He dressed G.Q.—loose, pleated pants and oversized jackets with the sleeves rolled up. When he smoked, which wasn't that often, he used a long black cigarette holder. He was without doubt the last man Jonathan could have ever imagined his sister choosing. But, ironically, he was the perfect mate for her.

"When do we get to meet her?" Maddie asked.

"Do you two honestly think I'd subject her to this madhouse?" Jonathan grinned at his sister's outraged expression. "Actually, I invited her here today, but as I said, she had plans."

Maddie laughed. "We'll plan a party. Something in the city . . . nothing elaborate . . . maybe a suite at the Waldorf Towers. I've been dying to find an excuse—Jonathan's new lady friend is as good as any."

Jonathan sighed. "She isn't my new lady friend." *At least not yet.* "We enjoy each other's company." *We enjoy each other in bed.* "That's all there is to it."

Maddie looked disappointed. "Oh, well, what can you expect from a dedicated bachelor like Jonnie?"

"You haven't changed a bit, have you, little sister?" Still matchmaking, hoping he would find the right woman and settle down.

Stephen slid an arm around his wife's narrow waist. "No, thank God, she hasn't. Migs is the same passionate creature I met and fell in love with seven years ago."

"Lucky for you," Maddie teased, turning into her husband's arms.

Just then Alex wheeled into the room, pushed by his eager-to-be-off-to-the-show pack of cousins. "We're going to be late, Father, if we don't get started," said Frederick.

"You won't be late," Stephen promised. "Get your coats on, and I'll have James bring round the Bentley." One of Marsh Stafford's toys. It stayed with the house in the Hamptons.

While the other three boys raced off to collect the necessary items, Jonathan approached his son. "I'll call you every day, make sure everything's all right." But he knew it would be. Alex got along with everyone. He had four more days before his return to the clinic, and he loved his cousins and his aunt and uncle.

"You won't get lonely, will you?" Alex asked.

"Of course, I will. I always miss you when you're gone, but Miss James is coming to visit, so I'll have someone for company."

Alex seemed to approve, his grin wide and white in his small dark Stafford face. "She's really pretty, Dad."

"Yes, she is."

"Thanks for letting me stay, Dad."

"Henry will be here to pick you up at noon." Jonathan leaned down and hugged him. "Have a good time, son." No matter how many times they parted, no matter for how short a time, the feel of the cold metal chair in contrast to the warmth of his son's small arms around his neck always brought a lump to Jonathan's throat.

And a shot of guilt.

If only he hadn't been working so hard. If only he'd been a better father . . . He forced the guilt away.

Promising to lunch with Maddie the first of the week, Jonathan said his good-byes and left the house. As always, he knew a moment of uncertainty in leaving Alex behind. The fear was there, the worry that something else might happen and he wouldn't be there to stop it. But he wanted the boy to lead as normal a life as possible. Jonathan would do what he had to to make sure that happened.

Even with the Thanksgiving traffic, Jonathan made respectable time driving the Lamborghini back to Manhattan. Careful to avoid the big parade on West Seventy-seventh, he drove to his apartment, left the car in the underground garage, since parking was always a problem, and caught a cab to Devon's parents' home near Eighty-sixth.

It wasn't like him to arrive without calling. Then again,

Devon inspired him to things that weren't like him. He wanted to see her, not tomorrow, as they had planned, but tonight. And he wanted to meet her parents. Since they were important to Devon, he wanted to know them. Maybe in a way, he wanted their approval.

Devon isn't the only one taking risks. He had almost told his sister the truth about their relationship, that Devon was coming to mean a good deal more to him than he had intended.

Still, he wasn't completely certain of his feelings for her, as she wasn't certain of hers for him. Besides that, there were factors which could end the relationship before it ever really got started. He had responsibilities to consider. Namely, his son.

He thought of the deceit he had practiced on Devon. He wished he could tell her the truth of what had happened that night in Stafford. And if he believed for a moment that Devon wouldn't latch onto the ridiculous tale like a drowning man clutching at straws, he would. But he knew without doubt that the stories that had blazed across the tabloids three years ago would only fuel her determination and renew her efforts to write her book. Alex would be involved, and God only knew what harm that might cause.

What if he appealed to her love of children? Told her his fears for Alex's recovery? Maybe that would work.

The truth was it might slow her down as it had before, but once he had added fresh fuel to her fire, she would definitely continue her research. And if she did, sooner or later, word of her work would leak out. The coincidence—and he truly believed it was one—of what happened that night and the involvement of the Stafford name would make all too juicy a story. He just couldn't afford to take the chance.

Jonathan raked a hand through his thick black hair and leaned back against the worn rear seat of the cab. Notes of "I'll Take Manhattan" blared over the cabby's tin-can radio, and finally penetrated his senses. He glanced out the window. A dog walker, in a Knicks basketball sweat shirt, gripped a tangle of leashes attached to a pack of dogs that pulled him along at a reluctant jog. As they rounded a corner, Jonathan glimpsed the top of a giant balloon doggedly making its way along the Thanksgiving Day Parade route.

The cabby honked his horn at a car stalled in the street and pulled to the curb just past the bus stop. "This is it, mac."

Missing Henry's impeccable service and the comfort of his limo, Jonathan opened the door, paid the driver, and stepped out onto the sidewalk. Glancing up at the lofty modern high-rise where Devon's parents' lived, he thought of her, thought of her project, and felt certain once more of his course. In minutes he'd arrived at her family's twenty-fourth-floor apartment and pushed the buzzer announcing his arrival.

Unfortunately, it was Michael Galveston who opened the door.

Fourteen

Jonathan bristled, then forced himself to relax. He'd be damned if he'd give Galveston the satisfaction of knowing how angry he was. "I was hoping to see Ms. James."

Michael Galveston smiled, though it looked more like a sneer. "Come on in."

"Who is it, Michael?" This from a small, frail, brittle little woman who had to be Devon's mother. She stepped up beside Galveston and gave Jonathan an uncertain glance.

"I'm sorry to intrude," he said, which was infinitely mild compared to what he was thinking. He wasn't sure whether he was more furious with Devon for continuing her relationship with Galveston, or with himself for being such a fool. "I'm Jonathan Stafford. I stopped by to see Devon. She mentioned she would be here."

Devon stepped into the entry. Her gasp of surprise at seeing him standing next to Michael gave Jonathan an inward shot of satisfaction.

"Jonathan! W-What are you doing here?"

He turned a hard look on her that did nothing to disguise his displeasure. "I believe I was invited to dinner. I didn't think you'd mind if I stopped by."

"No . . . no, of course not. Why don't you come in?"

"I am in."

Her eyes flashed a plea for understanding—which he had no intention of giving her. She turned to her mother while her father, a short, balding ruddy-faced man walked up beside them.

Devon's smile looked forced. "Mom, Dad, this is a friend of mine, Jonathan Stafford. Michael, you remember Jonathan? The two of you met at the gallery."

"How could I forget?" Michael said dryly.

Paddy Fitzsimmons extended a thick callused hand. "Nice to meet you." But he sized Jonathan up from head to foot and it was obvious he was withholding his judgment.

Mrs. Fitzsimmons gave her daughter a shrewd assessing glance, then smiled at Jonathan. "Well, we're mighty happy ta have y'. Come on in."

What other choice did he have? "I'm afraid I can only stay a moment."

"Nonsense." She took his arm. Her eyes scanned the perfect fit of his navy blue blazer, and she drew him into the living room, a warm friendly place filled with knickknacks and years of family clutter. The comfortable furniture was covered with small white hand-made doilies. "We were just gettin' ready for dessert and coffee. Y' haven't tasted pie till you've tried a slice of m' homemade pun'kin topped with real whipped cream."

Despite his anger, Jonathan smiled, liking Eunice Fitzsimmons more by the moment. "I love pumpkin pie," he said, though he'd never really been a fan. Anything to charm the gracious little woman. To Devon he was as far from charming as he could be, and still be civil.

Devon eyed Jonathan with a mixture of apology and regret. *Damn,* if there was a chance of something going wrong, it always did. She tried to meet his eyes, but the accusation she saw forced her to glance away.

"So Devon invited you to dinner," her father said, as if it were a criminal offense.

She moved between the two men. "Unfortunately, Jonathan had already made other plans. He spent the day with his sister and her family."

Her father eyed him warily. "No family of your own?" The way he said it, the question seemed far too personal.

"I have an eight-year-old son. He's spending the weekend with his cousins."

Surely her father hadn't thought Jonathan was married! But the look of relief that swept his face said he had. Devon might have smiled if she hadn't caught Jonathan's dark expression, unleashed on her though it was carefully shielded from her parents.

"You missed a mighty fine meal," her father said, his voice a little lighter. "Twenty-four-pound bird. Oyster stuffing. Devon brought the hot rolls and salad. Too bad you couldn't make it."

"Maybe next time." But his pointed glance said there might not be a next time.

"Yes, it would have been nice," Devon said lamely. She tried to think of a polite way to let him know it was her parents who had invited Michael, or a way to get him off by himself, but the opportunity never came up.

Her parents were too busy grilling him, under which he held up mightily, while Michael was busy trying to get in his subtle jibes. Jonathan finally set his empty pie plate down on the coffee table in front of the sofa.

"That was delicious, Mrs. Fitzsimmons. The best pumpkin pie I've ever eaten." She beamed and tried to convince him he should try another piece. Jonathan graciously declined with a shake of his head. "I'm afraid I've got to go." He unwound his tall frame and came to his feet.

"So soon?" Her mother stood up, too.

"Why don't I walk you down?" Devon offered, grasping the chance to redeem herself at last.

"I don't think that will be necessary." Jonathan accepted the overcoat her mother handed him, but gave her only the briefest glance.

Devon just smiled. "Well, I think it is." Grabbing his arm and turning him toward the door, she waited until her father had said his farewells, had firmly declined Michael's attempt to join them, then walked him out in the hall.

"I'm sorry, Jonathan, I—"

"What you do is your business, Devon." He pushed the elevator button. "I shouldn't have come without calling."

"I didn't invite Michael—my parents did."

He digested that for a moment. "But you knew he would be here."

"Yes, but—"

"You could have told me. I don't particularly enjoy making a fool of myself."

Devon colored beet red. He was right, of course. "I didn't think you'd stop by—not in a million years."

"That was obvious." He stepped into the elevator. "As I said, what you do is your business."

Devon stepped in beside him. "Dammit, Jonathan. Michael and I are just friends. Beyond that, I haven't the slightest interest in him. I . . ."

"You what?" he asked as the doors rolled closed.

"I . . . wanted to be with you."

He pondered that, weighed it for the truth. They rode down in silence but when the door slid open in the lobby, neither of them moved. Jonathan turned to face her. "If you wanted to be with me, you've still got the chance. Come home with me. Now."

"But my parents . . . it's Thanksgiving and—"

"And there's Michael to consider?"

She started to deny it, took one look at the hardness in his features, the angry set to his mouth, and knew words would not be enough. "I'll get my coat."

Gray-blue eyes raked her—sensuous, compelling eyes that turned a smoky blue at the choice she'd just made. "I'll wait for you here."

Devon wet her lips, thinking of the hours ahead, fighting down the butterflies that brushed the walls of her stomach. "I won't be long, I promise."

And she wasn't.

Surprisingly, when she told her parents she was leaving, they seemed almost pleased. "Don't worry about the dishes," her father said. "I'll give your mother a hand."

"Thanks, Daddy."

"Your Mr. Stafford is sure a handsome man," her mother whispered, hugging her tightly, so much shorter than Devon she had to stretch to reach her daughter's shoulders. "Seems real pleasant, too."

Michael of course was furious. "You leave with that guy, you and I are finished."

"We've been finished for weeks. I sent back your ring, remember?"

"Don't do it, Devon. You're making a mistake. Jonathan Stafford is out of your league. He'll chew you up and spit you out in little bitty pieces—just like Paul did—and this time, I won't be around to help put you back together."

Devon felt a chill of apprehension. It was possible. All too possible. And yet her decision was made. "We're friends, Michael. The truth is that's all we ever were."

"Devon—"

She left him standing in the entry and joined Jonathan

down in the lobby. They caught a cab and went straight to his apartment. With Mrs. Delgado, his housekeeper, off visiting her children for the long holiday weekend, they had the whole place to themselves.

"Let me take your coat." Jonathan helped her take it off then hung it up in the closet. "Now your dress."

"What?"

"You heard me."

She had. She just couldn't quite believe it. "But—"

"Turn around."

She complied a bit stiffly, felt the zipper slide down with a buzz. Within several short minutes, Jonathan had collected every stitch of her clothing.

"I intend to hold these for ransom," he teased, leaving her standing in the foyer, naked and more than a little embarrassed while he strode off down the hall.

"Jonathan—"

He returned before she could finish her protest, scooping her into his arms, carrying her into his bedroom. At the foot of his bed, he let go of her knees and she slid the length of his body. Jonathan kissed her, slowly, thoroughly, running his tongue into her mouth, while his hands were cupping her breasts, and his thumb was rubbing up and down across her nipple until it puckered. Warm heat slid through her body. Her pulse throbbed a sensual rhythm and her limbs felt weak and pliable. With trembling fingers, she worked the buttons on his shirt and tried to tug it free of his pants, but he caught her wrists and forced her to still.

"Not this time. Every time we've been together, you've driven me half out of my mind. I intend to have you, but not until I've given as good as I've received."

Devon wet her lips. "But I don't think—"

"Good idea—don't think. Don't do anything but feel."

Jonathan kissed her again. His tongue was hot and probing, as he eased her back on the bed. He joined her there, with his hard-muscled body pressing against her, his shaft thick and rigid against her thigh. Long-fingered hands stroked down her body, massaging her breasts, dipping into the curve of her waist, moving lower, across the flat plane below her navel.

His mouth followed his hands, drawing her breast in, suckling it gently, then lower. A hot warm pull reached the place between her legs, the ache there growing until she moaned. Jonathan's dark head came up at the sound, but only for an instant. Then he returned to his task, and Devon arched beneath him. It wasn't until he parted her legs and settled himself between her thighs that she stiffened.

"Jonathan?" She started to sit up, but he urged her back down.

"Easy, love. If you don't like this, I won't force you."

"I-I don't know. I've never . . ."

He came up over her body and kissed her mouth—hard. "God, you're sweet. So incredibly sweet."

Right now she felt anything but. She wanted Jonathan, ached for him. If he didn't take her soon, she would surely disgrace herself by begging. "Please, Jonathan, I need . . ."

"I know what you need. Trust me just a little while longer."

He turned away from her long enough to strip off his clothes, then he was kissing her breasts again, moving lower, spreading her legs and easing down between them.

Devon gripped the soft feather comforter at the feel of his mouth over her sensitive flesh. He was stroking her, laving gently, sucking, forcing her mind into swirls of sensuous pleasure. He knew exactly where to touch her, how to touch her, how much pressure to use, how fast to go and then how slow. She was writhing beneath him, her fingers laced in his hair.

He didn't stop until she climaxed, bursting with white-hot pleasure, soaring and soaring, yet still needing to feel him inside her.

"Please . . ." But she needn't have said the words. Already he was lifting her hips, driving himself inside, thick and hot and hard. Jonathan withdrew almost full length then thrust home, filling her with his powerful presence as well as his hard male body. His need for her grew with every movement, every heartbeat, arousing her as nothing else could have.

She arched her back and welcomed him, needing him just as badly, gripping his muscular shoulders, arching her hips, taking him farther inside. Again the waves of pleasure began, the incredible soaring sweetness. Dimly she heard herself calling his name, heard him groan, felt his hard muscles bunch and the warm pulsing wetness of his seed.

Dear God in heaven. Nothing she'd experienced had ever felt like this. They lay quiet for a while, holding each other, spiraling down. Jonathan traced a finger along her jaw and down her throat to her shoulders. "You were wonderful."

Devon smiled softly. "So were you."

"It's funny . . . I know a hundred erotic tricks, a hundred ways to heighten a man and woman's pleasure." He drew a lazy circle around her nipple. "But when I'm with you, they all seem to fly out the window."

"What you did to me, wasn't that an erotic trick?"

He smiled wickedly into the soft golden glow of the lamp. "That, sweet Devon, was pure male lust. I just had to taste some of that sweetness you've been hiding for so long." He kissed her mouth and she breathed in her own musky scent. "See what I mean?"

"I've always wondered what it would be like."

"Well, now you know."

"Yes." She grinned. "A fact you may one day regret."

Jonathan laughed and rolled her beneath him. "I doubt that, love. I doubt that very much."

That appeared to be true. Jonathan was already hard and ready for her again. They made love the rest of the afternoon and evening, fell asleep, then woke up and started all over again.

It was that way all weekend. Neither of them was able, it seemed, to get quite enough. But they did other things, too. Like walk along Fifth Avenue in the late evening chill, watching the animated window displays at Saks and Lord and Taylor's. One day they went to the new exhibit at the Met and afterward to a deli for pastrami on rye, garlic pickles, and an egg cream, which Jonathan confessed he hadn't tasted in years.

"I'm beginning to think I really am a bad influence," Devon teased him.

"Oh, I don't know. I've been trying to slow down a little, learn to relax. Maybe you're a very good influence."

Devon smiled up at him warmly, hoping it was the truth. To make up for their extravagance, she suggested they eat sushi for dinner. Jonathan chose a small Japanese restaurant just around the corner from his apartment. They enjoyed the meal and went home, hoping to get to bed early, which they did. Only to stay up half the night making love.

On Saturday morning, they were roused from their sleep by the forgotten arrival of Tanaka Motobu, who came for Jonathan's weekly karate practice.

"Damn, I meant to call and cancel. Maybe you *are* a bad influence." He flashed her a scowl but his lips twitched.

A little embarrassed at being discovered in Jonathan's

house, Devon forced the feeling away. "Why don't you go ahead with your practice? I'll indulge myself, spend some time in the Jacuzzi before I shower, then read until you finish working out."

He nodded. "All right, if you're sure you don't mind."

She didn't. And for the last fifteen minutes of the session, she watched them, noting with pleasure the incredible grace of both men. Jonathan moved with a swift solid sureness that gave credit to the years he'd spent with his teacher. Though he was speaking Japanese, several times he seemed to refer to her.

"He kept looking over here," she said after he had left. "I could have sworn he was talking about me."

"He thinks you're exquisite. He calls you *tenshi*—angel. Except in your case, he remembers the way you burst in on us that very first day. Tanaka calls you my fire-breathing angel."

"No!"

"Yes."

Devon started to laugh and so did Jonathan. "I suppose he's right," she finally agreed. "At least about that day. I was pretty upset."

"You were incredible. So beautiful, so full of passion. I wanted to tear off your clothes and make love to you there on the floor."

"You did?" They stood in that very same room, Jonathan still wearing his belted white cotton shirt and loose-fitting pants. He glanced at their reflection in the mirrored walls of the gym and flashed a wicked smile. With the same sureness and speed he had demonstrated with Tanaka, he nudged her legs out from under her, twisted and took the weight off their fall with his elbows. Devon found herself beneath him on the thick foam mat that covered the floor.

"Yes, I did." He lowered his mouth and kissed her, and just as he'd wanted, they made love right there on the floor.

Later that day, while Jonathan was wearing a sweat suit, and Devon had on her yellow terry robe—part of the clothes she'd retrieved from her apartment on Friday—they sat curled up on the brown leather sofa in front of the fire in his study. Devon couldn't remember when she'd felt more relaxed.

"What was he like?" Jonathan asked, breaking into the comfortable silence.

"Michael?"

"Paul."

Devon leaned her head back against Jonathan's shoulder, and he brushed strands of pale blond hair from her face.

"Nothing like you. Paul never seemed to be completely in control. On the surface he appeared to be, but actually it was the world around him that controlled Paul. Do you know what I mean?"

"I think so."

"Everything we did was for Paul—getting him through law school, meeting the right sort of people, attending social events that would help his career. He kept saying things would be different, once he'd really made it, but they never were. That was why I started writing. I was alone a lot and I got bored. I worried that Paul might object, since he demanded nearly constant attention, but the truth was he didn't seem to notice. As long as I was there when he needed me and the rest of the time stayed out of his way, he was happy. Later on I found out why."

"Because he was cheating?" Jonathan asked, knowing at least that much about her divorce.

"Chasing everything in skirts. Paul was an intelligent, good-looking man, but he was insecure. He constantly needed his ego stroked, and the women he took to bed did that for him."

"How did you find out?"

"I came home early one afternoon and found him in bed with a redhead. I was supposed to go shopping and then out to dinner with Christy, but I got a headache. Believe me, it got a whole lot worse."

"What did you do?"

"Packed my bags and left. As soon as I did, people began to tell me about his other women. It seems there were legions of them. I couldn't work, couldn't eat, couldn't sleep. That's when I started having anxiety, but at the time I didn't know what it was."

Jonathan kissed the side of her neck. "Do you mind talking about it? I'd really like to know."

Devon sighed. "It was the oddest thing I've ever experienced. The first time it happened, I woke up in the middle of the night and couldn't breathe. I lay there for hours, forcing the air in and out of my lungs, my heartbeat abnormally rapid, my body bathed in perspiration. I honestly thought I was going to die. When morning came, I intended to go to the doctor, but by then I felt better. I thought maybe it was an allergy, or an insect bite, or something I'd eaten. It didn't happen again for several weeks, but other things started to occur."

"Like what?"

"My chest would close up. Something like an asthma attack. It was hard to get even enough air to talk sometimes. Then I started feeling light-headed. I'd be standing at the counter in Saks or in line at the post office and the room would start to spin. I'd have to brace myself to keep from falling."

"Why didn't you go to the doctor?"

"Eventually, I did. They ran tests, of course, but didn't find anything. When Dr. Dannon called me into his office and suggested the whole thing might be mental, I was terrified. I couldn't go to my parents; I didn't want them to worry. Besides, my father thinks psychiatrists are nothing but expensive entertainment for bored rich people too weak to solve their own problems."

"What changed your mind?"

Devon shivered, suddenly cold. Jonathan sensed her withdrawal and shifted to enfold her in his arms. "You don't have to talk about this if you don't want to."

"I *don't* want to. I never want to think about it again. But denying it isn't healthy. Besides, I don't want secrets between us."

Jonathan said nothing, but his hold imperceptibly tightened.

"It was late one evening when it happened. Paul had called earlier—he kept telling me he had changed and that all I had to do was give him another chance. I knew it wasn't true—Christy had told me only the day before that he was still seeing the redhead. My savings had just about run out, and I was worried about the contracts I was supposed to sign with my publisher for another two books. My editor and my agent had called and been pressing me about it, but I couldn't seem to concentrate enough to go over them."

"No wonder you were having problems."

Devon nodded. "I suppose that's true enough. I remember I was standing in front of the sink, listening to the whir of the garbage disposal. All of a sudden, I felt an overwhelming urge to stick my hand inside. It was incredible, almost as if my fingers were attached to an appendage separate from my body. God, it scared me, Jonathan. That I would actually consider doing something like that."

"Is that when you called Dr. Townsend?"

"Yes. Christy was off on a jaunt around the country. I found Townsend's name in the phone book. If there was ever divine intervention, that was it."

"And Townsend diagnosed your problem as anxiety."

"Yes. He told me I was a textbook case. Once I understood what had brought my symptoms on, I began to get better. But I was still afraid to go out of the apartment, afraid I'd faint or hyperventilate or something. Little by little the problems lessened, and I stopped seeing Townsend. I'd had only an occasional mild recurrence . . . until that night at the Stafford Inn."

Jonathan shifted. His muscles tensed against her. "That night the symptoms recurred."

"Some of them. The heart palpitations, the difficulty breathing. But they're also the symptoms of fear—and I've never been more afraid in my life."

Jonathan grew quiet, mulling over her words, but he said nothing more on the subject. It was an intimate evening, conducive to exploration. Jonathan was more relaxed and open than she had ever seen him. When she asked him about his divorce, he told her he blamed much of what happened on himself.

"I've always been a workaholic. I was young, aggressive. I never realized what that kind of a lifestyle can do to a family. With me, it wasn't other women, it was my work."

"Surely it wasn't all your fault."

"No, it wasn't. Becky wasn't ready for marriage, certainly not for children. She didn't want the responsibility of a husband and son."

"But she married you. She must have loved you."

"I don't think either of us really knew what love was. We were wrapped up in the glamour of it. Our families were pressing us. It just seemed the right thing to do."

"What about Alex? She must have loved her son."

"Becky hated being pregnant. She resented my part in it and to make matters worse, she had a tough delivery. Things were never really the same between us after Alex was born. But yes, she loved our son. She didn't really spend as much time with him as she should have, but she was crazy about him. When we divorced, I fought her for custody because I didn't really believe he would get enough of her attention. After Becky died, I was damned near as bad, until Alex's accident. I learned then the most important thing in the world is the people you love."

Devon smiled softly. Jonathan had suffered a bitter lesson, but he had learned from it. Some people never did.

She started to ask him about the accident, but he always closed up. He had given her enough of himself for one night. She didn't want to spoil the intimacy that was growing between them.

As the hour grew late, the talk changed again to subjects less serious and eventually Jonathan pressed her down on the sofa.

"All this conversation has worn me out. I think I need something to revive my flagging spirit." He dipped his head to nuzzle her neck, and his hardened arousal pressed against her.

"I have a feeling your 'flagging spirit' isn't flagging anymore." Jonathan laughed and kissed her, opened her robe and began to fondle her breasts.

"So lovely," he whispered, taking one of them into his mouth. They made love with abandon, and afterward he tossed her over his shoulder, carried her into the bathroom, and dumped her into the Jacuzzi with a splash. He made love to her again before they wound up in his bed.

All in all, Devon's time with Jonathan was more wonderful than she ever would have dreamed. Off and on, she thought about her project and the decision she had made to give it up. But she found the thought depressing, and she wasn't about to spoil the time they had together.

In the end, the sensuous lazy days and passion-filled nights were overshadowed only by the arrival of Sunday morning and Jonathan's not-so-subtle assumption she'd be leaving before his son got home. It hurt a little, this line that had clearly been drawn between his lover and his son. She had hoped that she and little Alex could get to know each other, in time become friends.

Clearly, Jonathan wasn't ready for that kind of involvement. He had no intention of letting her insinuate herself into his son's affections—just in case she wasn't around that long.

Give him time, she told herself. *He just doesn't want Alex hurt.* The boy had already lost his mother. He had suffered an accident that had left him paralyzed. Jonathan was protective of him and Devon could hardly blame him.

Still, she wondered at Jonathan's intentions toward her, wondered if her growing feelings for him were truly being returned.

She tried not to think about it Sunday evening when she sat in her apartment alone. She started to do some mending, but she'd always hated to sew. She tried to watch TV, but at the first commercial grew bored and turned it off. She had even less interest in resuming her work on *Traces,* though she knew very well how badly she needed to finish the book.

She finally picked up a novel written by an author friend

she usually enjoyed. Unfortunately, the story of a powerful corporate executive who seduced one trusting young woman after another came far too close to her own uncertain circumstances. She finally gave up, turned the lights out, and went to bed.

In the morning she called Christy and set up lunch at Akbar's on Park Avenue near Fifty-eighth, a favorite of theirs that served food from Northern India. She had called Christy several times after her fiasco with Zhadar, and Christy had warned her not to let one or two "false starts" be too discouraging.

Now, as they sat across from each other, eating Tandoori roast chicken, curried rice, and the flat, brick-oven baked bread Devon loved to distraction, it was time she told Christy the decision she had come to last week.

"I don't believe it, Devon. You can't mean to quit."

"I've thought this thing over, Christy. This isn't a rash decision." Devon toyed with the food on her plate, shoving it from one side to the other. "In a way, I don't want to, and in another way, I feel relieved."

Christy reached for her glass of white wine, jangling the thin gold bracelets at her wrist. She had pulled her long dark hair to the side and tied it at her shoulder with a scarf.

"You feel relieved because you can run away from a subject you feel uncomfortable with." Christy took a sip of wine and set the glass back down on the table. "You can't afford to run away, Devon. You'll always wonder if what happened that night was the truth or if you made it up. I don't believe you did—not for a moment. But you aren't sure—at least you aren't anymore. This will eat at you, Devon. I know how scared you were when you were going to see Dr. Townsend. This time he can't help you—you've got to help yourself."

Devon straightened in her chair. "There are other factors involved here, Christy. I've got my parents to consider . . . and Jonathan."

"I know all about Jonathan. He's the guy who offered you a million bucks not to write this, remember?"

"His son is in a wheelchair. He's bound to be concerned."

"Assuming his son is his real motivation, has it occurred to you he might be sleeping with you in the hope you'll do exactly what you're doing now—giving up."

Devon absently twirled her fork, then set it aside, suddenly unable to eat. "It's occurred to me."

"But you're still going to quit."

"Yes."

Christy sighed. "I wish there was something I could say to talk you out of this. I know how important this story is to you. I know it isn't something that's going to just go away."

"How can you be sure? Maybe I'm better off not knowing. Maybe the truth would be harder to face than never really finding out for sure."

"And maybe it wouldn't."

Devon started to argue, but Christy cut her off with a wave of her ring-bejeweled hand. "All right, all right. I won't say another word." She covered Devon's fingers where they had curled into a nervous ball on the table. "You know whatever decision you make, I'll support you. We've been friends through a lot worse than this."

Devon smiled forlornly. "I suppose that's true." But she wasn't really so sure. What if Jonathan *was* only using her, as Michael—and even Christy—had suggested? Worse yet, what if her mind *had* been playing some hideous trick on her that terrible night in Stafford? If it were, it was conceivable that somewhere in the depths of her unconscious might lurk an enemy far greater than any she would ever have to face at the Stafford Inn.

"Now that that's settled—" Devon flashed a determined smile. "Why don't we go shopping?"

Though Christy wasn't fooled for a moment, she made all the appropriate responses to Devon's change of subject. "Good idea. Maybe we can get a jump on the Christmas hordes this year."

"That'd be a change."

Christy laughed. They were usually making last-minute purchases on Christmas Eve. Devon called for the check, and paid the bill, since it was her turn, and they left the restaurant.

Outside on the street, she pulled her cashmere coat more closely around her. She should have felt better, knowing how pleased Jonathan was that she had decided to end this crazy project—and how pleased her parents were. She should have been thrilled to know she wouldn't have to deal with a subject she abhorred. She should have been delighted that the decision was behind her, yet she couldn't shake the feeling she was letting someone down.

Maybe it was the souls she had once believed were locked inside the house.

Or maybe that someone was herself.

Fifteen

Since Devon's talk with Christy, her decision seemed even more firmly set. Early the following morning, she left her apartment for the New York University library to return the books she had checked out. Students clutching textbooks, or talking softly to friends, filed by as she dumped the stack into the big metal return book bin and dusted off her hands, as if the gesture would put an end to the subject. Still, as she passed the NUCMC records, her pace unconsciously slowed.

She had forgotten to search out the volume containing the letter from Florian's father to his mother, or the one from Florian to his brother. There was probably nothing there, and yet . . . what could it hurt to take just one last look?

Ignoring a feeling of uneasy warning, she located the letter from Florian's father, Edward Ephram Stafford to his wife, Eloise, written in 1878. Florian would have been nine years old. Devon saw his name in the body of the letter, where he was mentioned in reference to some sort of indiscretion he had made.

I will not countenance such blatant misbehavior, his father's letter read. *You may tell my son that upon my return, he may expect a very sound thrashing at the least. He may also expect to spend time reflecting upon his misdeeds in the sanctity of the closet.*

A chill swept down Devon's spine. Hadn't she read somewhere that child abuse was often a response passed on from parent to child? Wouldn't it be logical for Florian to discipline his own son using the same harsh principles instilled by his father?

She swallowed hard and the hand holding the volume began to shake. *Do you really want to start this whole distasteful business all over again?* Devon found the idea so utterly distasteful she soundly closed the book. Instead of reaching for the second volume, the one with the letter from Florian to his brother William, Devon turned and walked resolutely toward the door.

She almost made it. She wanted to—dear God, at that moment there was nothing on this earth that she wanted more. Still, she stopped and turned. Just this one last document, she promised, returning to the bookshelves, pulling out the volume she needed, then thumbing through the pages.

It didn't take much effort; almost of its own accord, the book fell open to the page containing Florian's letter to William. It was dated the tenth of June, 1897, just two weeks after the death of his son. She should have noticed that date in the indices, should have read this document in the very beginning.

Of course, it might be nothing.

It started with a typical salutation, *My Dearest Brother,* but the tone of Florian's words made his heartbreak all too clear.

I cannot abide this feeling of hopelessness and despair. He was my only son, the blood of my loins, the child upon whom I placed my hopes and dreams. The days ahead loom bleak and barren. My wife weeps incessantly; she will not allow me to comfort her, nor give succor to my needs. In truth, I cannot give succor to myself.

The thought of the lonely days without him are unbearable. If it weren't a sin of the greatest magnitude, I believe I should follow him to the grave. As it is, I have scourged myself daily, until my back is raw and bleeding and yet it is not enough.

Almighty God, what have I done?

Devon swayed against the table, gripping the edge for support. Around her the room spun crazily. She steadied herself, fought to calm her pounding heart. Her palms had begun to sweat, and her chest felt so tight she could barely breathe.

It was true! All of it. It had to be.

She sank down into a chair, her arms leaden, her legs still unsteady. She would take a copy of this letter to Jonathan, better yet, bring him here and make him read his uncle's words. Surely then he would believe her—

Or would he say it was merely another coincidence? That Florian's ominous words could mean at least a dozen different things?

She thought of how pleased he had been that she had given up her project. But she had also sensed an underlying tension in his manner, a guardedness in his expression. At the time she'd paid little attention, certain it had only been her imagination. Now she wondered. Did Jonathan know about this letter? Had he suspected the truth all along? And if he had, why was something that happened so long ago so important?

Devon reread the letter, then made copies of both documents for her file. Still shaken from what she had read, she started once more for the door.

A second time she didn't make it. Instead, something stirred in the back of her mind, conversations she'd had with Jonathan, his incredible offer of money, the tension he'd displayed whenever they'd discussed the subject of her work. Crossing the library, she headed toward the newspaper section.

What was it Jonathan had said? Something about the papers having a field day if they found out about her project? Hadn't Mrs. Meeks also made reference to the papers? *You're not a newspaper reporter, are you?*

Thinking of the discovery she'd just made, and wondering once more if Jonathan might have known about the letter and been trying to cover it up—or if he was hiding something else—she sat down at one of the lighted viewers and began to search the microfiche records for articles that referenced Jonathan Stafford or the Stafford family name.

She would begin with his marriage eleven years ago and work forward. If that turned up nothing, she would go back even farther.

She found little of interest until she reached the year of his divorce. Stories of the breakup of his marriage confirmed what he had said about his dedication to work being the primary cause. There was also mention of Rebecca's style of living, her jet-set friends, and her heavy involvement in Society. The battle for custody of little Alex came as no surprise, but it was surprising that Rebecca had been killed in an automobile accident before the divorce was final.

Alex was left in Jonathan's care, which he desperately wanted, and the Stafford fortune remained intact. *Very convenient for Jonathan,* Devon couldn't help thinking. Still, she had spent enough time with him to believe his wife's death couldn't have been anything other than an accident. Jonathan would never be a party to a crime like that.

Which meant she was searching for something else.

Devon pressed the forward button, spinning the reel. She concentrated on the print rushing past on the lighted screen. If it took the rest of the day—the rest of the week—she intended to know all there was about Jonathan Barrett Stafford.

She prayed to God, he had been truthful—and that he had nothing to hide.

Devon stood up and stretched. The muscles in her shoulders ached as well as those in her arms and back. The glare of the harsh overhead lights burned her eyes, and the hard oak chair had numbed her bottom. All day yesterday and most of the morning, she had spent in front of the metal viewer here in the library, straining her eyes to read the pages of newsprint. Articles about the Stafford family seemed to go on forever.

She'd said nothing to Jonathan, who had phoned several times but been swept up in problems at work. Holidex Industries was suffering its first serious loss of business to Tri-Star Marine, fortunately just a few of their smaller accounts, he had said, but an indicator of what was to come.

Devon was glad for the respite, which gave her a chance to continue her search without explanation. Though she had turned up nothing that would account for Jonathan's original determination to stop her, she had gained a tremendous insight into the man himself.

And she had begun to see a pattern.

In a dozen different interviews over the years, Jonathan's pride in his family and its accomplishments had surfaced, along with his deep sense of responsibility to see Stafford Enterprises grow and prosper as it had throughout the years.

"The Stafford name has remained an icon of integrity in the world of business," one article said. Another quoted Jonathan as saying, "The proud Stafford name remains untarnished, a respected leader of the business community."

Which is not to say the Stafford men weren't often referred to as ruthless. When a London-based company by the name of Wilmot Ltd. had been foolish enough to start false rumors about the quality of fiberglass hulls produced by Pacific American, a Stafford-owned corporation, Jonathan had begun to quietly buy up their stock. By the end of the year, the majority of Wilmot shares belonged to Stafford Enterprises, and the president and top-level management found themselves on the outside looking for work.

Another company by the name of Burton Production had been taken over only last year.

The articles were only two among half a dozen that Devon uncovered, each of them pointing to Jonathan's almost fanatical insistence on retribution for wrongs his company suffered at the hands of his competitors.

As she read page after page, her mind recalled an image of the man Jonathan had been that night in his study when he had made his incredible offer of money. Cold, hard, and utterly determined. Unfeeling, she would have described him. She remembered the file he'd obtained from Ernie Townsend's office. *Ruthless,* the papers said.

And obsessed with his family's heretofore untarnished name.

Then she thought of the hours she had spent with him, the way he had held her after they'd made love. There was a gentleness there, too. She was sure of it. And a sensitivity lacking in most men. She had seen it in the beautiful paintings he kept around him, in the way he had looked at his son. There she had also encountered his protectiveness. He guarded his son with the same burning intensity that he felt toward his company and his proud family name.

If he loved, it would be with just as much passion. And believing these things about him drew her like a moth to a flame. It made her want to be included in that incredible aura that surrounded him. She didn't want to discover anything bad about Jonathan. She cared about him. More than cared.

And yet she also cared about herself.

Devon stretched again then got up and took a walk down the long narrow aisle, trying to get the blood flowing back into her cramped muscles and joints. When she returned to the viewer, she sat down wearily and started working again.

As tired as she was, she accidentally hit the power button, moving the roll of film backward. Damn, it was difficult enough keeping track of where she was without this. She started forward again, went too far, and worked to rewind the reel. She was plowing through five years' worth of the weekly tabloid *National Inquisitor* when one of the headlines jumped out at her.

STAFFORD SON PARALYZED IN FIRE. SAW GHOST, BOY SAYS. Devon's heart began to pound. The article was dated April 15, three years ago. Her untimely button-pushing had skipped ahead, bringing her to the date of little Alex's accident. She quickly scanned the article, her blood pumping faster with every word.

The first line told her that Alex had been injured in Connecticut—in the old original Stafford mansion just down the street from the house at 25 Church Street. She had noticed the burned-out shell of the mansion, but never dreamed the house had remained standing until only three short years ago. She hadn't thought to ask about it, and of course no one in Stafford had dared to bring it up.

Devon read on. *Heroic arrival of multimillionaire father, Jonathan Stafford, said to have saved young son's life.* The article told how Jonathan had also been injured in the fire, receiving second-degree burns on his arm.

No wonder he hadn't wanted to talk about the scar she had seen!

Alex had been pinned beneath a fallen beam, just as Jonathan had said. Jonathan had lifted the beam off the child and carried him out of the burning house to safety, then returned to save his aunt, Estell Stafford Meredith.

"I saw something in the flames," badly injured and nearly hysterical five-year-old Alex Stafford told reporters on the scene. "It talked to me. It tried to make me stay."

Devon's fingers tightened on the edge of the table. *Dear God in heaven. This is what he's trying to hide!* It wasn't Florian's letter—it was his own son's experience in the old Stafford house!

The article continued.

Elwood Dobbs, a long time resident of Stafford, claims the house had long been haunted. "Everybody 'round here knows it. We tried to tell Mrs. Meredith she shouldn't move back in, but she wouldn't listen. Said there weren't no such thing as ghosts. Bet she'll listen now."

So this was his secret. But was it worth a million dollars? Jonathan had said he wanted to protect his son. No—*she* had said that. She had assumed that was his reason the moment she had seen the boy sitting in the doorway in his wheelchair. But what exactly had Jonathan said? *I have a son to think of. The Stafford name has been respected for hundreds of years.*

It wasn't Alex he was protecting—it was Alex's family name!

Article after article had proclaimed Jonathan's obsession with his spotless family tree. Florian Stafford's crimes might reflect on that untarnished image. Florian was a Stafford. To Jonathan that was all that mattered.

Devon finished reading the article, then leaned wearily back in her chair trying to digest the words. Her chest felt tight and her palms were damp.

For long moments she just sat there. Then little by little, the ramifications of her discovery began to sink in. Jonathan had lied to her. By omission, she allowed, but the result was the same. Jonathan had done exactly what he'd set out to do. Knowing how much it meant to her, knowing what she had been through far more intimately than any other person except Dr. Townsend, he had stopped her from discovering the truth about what happened.

As he had intended from their very first meeting, Jonathan Stafford had succeeded in his goal—he had stopped her from writing her book.

And she had made it easy.

Oh, my God. Devon's throat closed up as she thought about the days they'd spent together, the intimate conversations, the feverish way they'd made love. She had wanted to believe in him so badly, been so attracted to his dark good looks and overwhelming presence that she had ignored the words of warning her mind kept shouting. She had given in to her needs, to all her feminine yearnings. Jonathan had played his part with magnificence. She had really believed he felt something for her, that when he made love to her, it was more than a moment of passion.

The ache in her throat matched the knot that had formed in her stomach.

It was more, all right. It was Jonathan's way of controlling her. Why hadn't she seen it? How could she have been so easily duped? How could she have believed he cared for her at all when she knew—knew—what he was after. For God's sake, the man had told her his intentions from the start.

I'm going to have to stop you.

And he had. He had smiled at her and charmed her and won enough of her heart to end up in her bed. His skillful manipulations had actually convinced her that giving up her project was her own idea.

"I'm such a fool," she said, speaking her thoughts aloud. "And you're a bastard, Jonathan." She gripped the pencil she'd been using, and her thumb pressed so hard against the wood it nearly snapped in two.

She would return to the library tomorrow, when she was clear-headed, and read every article she could find on Alex's accident. Obviously there was a link between what happened to her at the inn and what happened to Alex. Jonathan knew it, and he also knew she would recognize it immediately. To stop her, he had worked his way into her confidence, gently fostered her uncertainties, and reinforced her anxieties until she'd convinced herself that what she'd experienced was just her imagination.

Now she knew it was real. Both the letters she had read and the fire in Stafford pointed toward the truth of her encounter at the inn. Though it still wasn't enough, it was more than enough to renew her determination to seek out the facts. And this time *nothing* would interfere.

She pushed the PRINT button on the viewer, making a copy of the article. She pulled the strap of her heavy leather bag over her shoulder, picked up the yellow legal pad she had been using to take notes, and headed toward the door.

Angry tears blurred the stacks of books as she walked by, until all she could see was Jonathan lying beside her in his big king-sized bed as she revealed her innermost thoughts and fears.

How he must have laughed when she'd told him she decided not to continue. How satisfied he must have been that, as usual, he had won.

Devon shoved open the library door and a blast of icy air sent a chill through her bones. She hardly felt it for the white-hot rage that pumped through her veins. An image of Jonathan in his limo, of her in her slinky black skirt and sequined sweater came to mind, and a wave of nausea swept over her. Devon leaned against the side of the building for support.

Never in her life had she felt so used, so betrayed. She had given herself to him like a Bowery whore. She had played into his hands and given him exactly what he wanted.

Given him more than he wanted.

For the truth Devon now had to face was that she had also given him her love.

A sob of despair rose in her throat while scalding tears slipped down her cheeks. She wanted to cry, wanted to moan and rage and sob out the agony that felt like a burning brand inside her.

She stumbled toward the curb, tripped and fell against a student hurrying past carrying a scarred leather briefcase. He dropped the case, but stopped her from falling to the pavement.

"You okay, lady?"

"I-I'm sorry. I must have tripped. Th-Thank you."

"Here, you dropped your notebook." He handed her the notebook she had been carrying, then bent and retrieved his briefcase. "You sure you're all right?"

She certainly didn't look it, not with tears streaking her cheeks and her mascara running. But his words gave her the impetus she needed, and Devon lifted her chin. "I'm fine. Thank you again."

As the lanky youth continued on his way, she braced herself, walked to the curb and hailed a cab.

"Three-eighty-five Park Avenue," she told the driver as she slid into the back seat. "Next to the Seagram's Building at Fifty-third."

He grunted some sort of guttural Arabic understanding and nodded his shaggy black-haired head. Devon felt the quick momentum of the cab lurching forward, then carefully blanked her mind until the taxi reached its destination and the driver asked for his fare.

She fumbled through her purse for her wallet, paid him with unsteady hands, and got out of the cab. Crossing to the front of the towering glass and steel building, she shoved open the heavy glass doors into the impressive four-story lobby of Stafford Enterprises. Great metal sculptures loomed above her. A huge Benton-like mural of workmen building ships covered one wall.

Devon took a deep breath for control, a moment to straighten the skirt of her plum wool suit and smooth her wind-tossed hair. Then she read the office roster posted in the brass-framed enclosure next to the elevator. The long ride up to the forty-fifth floor gave her a second to compose herself, but inside, her rage continued to build. More than likely this would be the last time she would ever see Jonathan Stafford. It would be a time he would never forget.

The elevator doors slid open, and Devon walked out. The forty-fifth floor reeked of power and money—thick gray carpet and raw silk sofas, original Oriental art on the walls.

Jonathan Stafford through and through. It made Devon's stomach churn.

"I'm here to see Mr. Stafford." She prayed her smile looked more real, her skin less pasty than it felt. "My name is Devon James."

A blond receptionist in her twenties used the intercom on her black lacquer desk, and an instant later an attractive, thirtyish woman dressed immaculately in a navy blue three-piece suit appeared.

"Hello, Ms. James, I'm Delia Wills. Jonathan has mentioned you on several occasions."

"Has he?" There was an edge to her words she had hoped to avoid.

"Yes." Dee Wills eyed her strangely, apparently noticing her tight smile, the hands that clutched her bag a little too tightly. "He's in the middle of a conference call, but if it's important, I can certainly interrupt him."

"That won't be necessary." Another forced smile. "I believe I can handle that myself." The woman's eyes went wide as Devon marched past her, opened one of the huge double doors that led to Jonathan's office, and walked in. She closed it firmly behind her. The sound drew Jonathan's attention, from the speaker phone on his impressive teakwood desk, to where she stood rigidly in front of the door.

One brief glance must have been enough. "I'm sorry, Hastings, something's come up. We'll have to finish this call a little later. Monty, I'll get back to you sometime this afternoon."

The intercom buzzed the moment the line went dead. "Jonathan, Ms. James was rather insistent. I wasn't quite sure—"

"It's all right, Dee. I'll take care of it."

He rounded his desk at Devon's approach, meeting her

halfway there. "What is it? What's happened? You're as pale as a ghost."

Devon bit her trembling lip. Hysteria threatened to bubble over any minute. Half of her wanted to laugh at his absurdity. The other half wanted to scream out her rage and pain. She started to tremble all over, felt the sting of tears but forced them away.

Jonathan gripped her arms. "Devon you're scaring me. What in God's name has happened?"

"What's happened?" She flashed him a shaky, pain-filled smile. "I'll tell you what's happened. For the past two days I've been at the library."

His face went rigid; his grip grew tight on her arms.

"I know everything, Jonathan. I know about the fire in Stafford. I know about Alex's accident—I know about his *ghost.* I know you lied to me, used me, purposely misled me. I know you manipulated me until I gave up something I believed in, something that gave me hope and strength. Something important, Jonathan. Maybe the most important thing I would ever do in my life."

Jonathan's face looked paler than her own. "Listen to me, Devon."

She laughed at that, a bitter heartbreaking sound. "Listen to you? I've already listened to you, Jonathan. And I believed you. I don't anymore."

He shook her gently, as if he were trying to reach her. "I never meant to hurt you. You've got to believe that. I did it for Alex. I was trying to protect him."

"How could you do it?" she asked, ignoring his words. "But then I made it easy, didn't I? I believed every word you said."

"I didn't lie to you."

"No? Why didn't you tell me what happened? How could you hide the truth when you knew how important it was?"

Jonathan bristled. "The truth? What truth? That there was a fire in the house and Alex was injured? That he was nearly hysterical and out of his mind with pain. That for three long years he's been tied to a wheelchair? It had nothing to do with you then—it has nothing to do with you now. Alex is my concern not yours!"

That she meant so little to him made her heart wrench harder, though as numb as she felt, it surprised her she could feel any pain at all. "No wonder you wouldn't let me near him. You were afraid he might say something, that I might find out what happened and see the connection. You were trying to stop me all along, and I was too taken with you to see it."

"I don't want him hurt. I'll do whatever it takes to keep that from happening."

"You'll do whatever it takes to protect your spotless family name. After all, 'It's an icon of integrity'—isn't that what you said?"

"It's Alex I'm worried about, can't you see that?"

"I don't believe you, Jonathan. I don't believe what I'm doing could possibly hurt him. I think you're using your son just like you used me. You'll do anything to protect your precious family name."

"That isn't true."

She grabbed his wrist and turned it over, exposing the trailing seam of the scar that ran up his forearm. "You got that in the fire, didn't you?"

"Yes . . ."

"But when I asked you about it, you wouldn't answer."

"I told you, I was trying to protect my son. I'll do whatever it takes to keep him from being hurt."

Devon's eyes fixed on his face. "And that includes conning me into your bed."

Jonathan flinched but didn't look away. "If I thought it would stop you—yes."

Tears pooled in her eyes and no amount of will could hold them at bay. "Good-bye, Jonathan." She turned to leave but he caught her arm.

"Devon," he said softly, his hand coming up to her cheek, gently brushing away the wetness. "I never really believed making love to you would keep you from writing your book. I wanted you. It's that simple. I still want you."

The ache in her throat grew more painful, but Devon lifted her chin. "You played your game to win, Jonathan. I came here to tell you that you're going to lose."

She turned and walked out the door.

Jonathan stared after her, knowing there was nothing he could do, nothing he could say to change her mind. It was too late for that. Maybe it had been too late from the start.

"Jonathan, are you all right?" That from Dee, who stood in the doorway looking at him with concern.

"No. But there's nothing you can do about it."

"Are you sure?"

Jonathan shook his head. "Not this time."

Dee's expression changed to one of sympathy, and she quietly closed the door. She had been with him long enough to know this was a problem he would have to solve on his own. Except there *was* no solution. He released a weary sigh and went back to his desk, but sat there unable to concentrate, staring straight ahead, his mind in turmoil.

He spent the next two days that way, trying to work, but accomplishing little, thinking about Devon, hating himself for the way he had hurt her. At home, he was little better, moving restlessly around the apartment, thinking of the hours they had spent there together, missing her more than he ever would have dreamed. Still he made no effort to call her. Thursday morning he made up his mind the only way to end this torture was to throw himself into his work.

And so he tried. By God, he tried. He went over files that needed his attention, though he had to read them several times, returned the stack of phone calls he had ignored, then hung up and tried to remember what he had said.

It was nearly one o'clock when his private phone line buzzed. Only Alex, Maddie, Stephen, Aunt Stell, and the Stafford family retainer had that number. Funny, he had been meaning to give it to Devon. She had gotten that close to him.

He picked up the receiver.

"You haven't forgotten our lunch date, have you, Jonnie?" Maddie's crystalline voice rang into the phone.

"Actually, I did. How did you know? It's still only fifteen minutes till."

"I know you too well. If it's anything but business, your mind goes into second gear."

Jonathan sighed. "I'm afraid something's come up. I'm going to have to cancel."

"Wrong," she said sweetly. "If you don't show up, I'll arrive at your office, make my usual scene, you'll be embarrassed and lose all that precious work time anyway. Get down here, Jonnie. Belle Monde is only two blocks away."

"I'm really not up to it, Maddie."

She was quiet for a moment. "Yes . . . I can hear that in your voice. Please come, Jonnie. Maybe I can help."

Maybe she could. They'd been close once, years ago when they were children. He'd been six years older, protective of her, but oddly enough, young as she was, she'd been equally protective of him. Then he'd gone away to school and after graduation, into the family business. He'd gotten married and so had she, they each started a family. They lived thousands of miles apart now, rarely spent time together, yet if it weren't for their busy schedules . . .

"All right. I'll be there at one." Maddie couldn't change what had happened any more than he could, but maybe telling her about it would somehow make him feel better. God, he hoped so. He couldn't remember the last time he'd felt this low. Besides, he'd gotten used to confiding in a woman. *Devon.*

His stomach clenched. He was back where he had started the first day he'd met her: she determined to dredge up family skeletons and endanger Alex's recovery, he just as determined to stop her.

If only things could have been different.

Jonathan raked a hand through his wavy black hair then pulled his suit coat off the wooden valet behind his desk. Tonight he would have taken Devon to dinner, maybe caught a movie after. He hadn't been to the show in years. Instead he faced another lonely night in his empty apartment. In his empty bed.

God, he missed her.

Sixteen

"Hello, Jonnie—you look terrible." Madeline Stafford St. Giles watched her tall, handsome, usually imposing brother sink down wearily into the chair across the table. Around them, Belle Monde waiters scurried past carrying trays of exquisitely arranged creations of French cuisine, and silver ice buckets heavy with expensive wines. But her brother didn't seem to notice.

"Thanks a lot."

His skin looked oddly pale, considering how dark he was, and his glossy black hair needed combing. There were smudges beneath his gray-blue eyes and a tightness around his mouth. She hadn't seen him looking this ravaged since those dismal days at the hospital after the fire.

"It isn't Alex, is it?" She sat up straighter in her chair, suddenly jolted by the thought that it might be. "His condition hasn't worsened?"

"No, no. It's nothing like that."

"If business has you looking this grim, I think I'd better prepare for a major cut in my spending."

"No more Christian Dior suits?" he teased, taking in her bold black and white hound's-tooth checked jacket piped in red, which zipped up over the front of a matching skirt. Very sixties, very stylish. She'd worn her sleek black hair pulled back from her face in a tight chignon and used heavy black liner to give her eyes the modish tilted effect that was in vogue.

"Ungaro," she corrected.

Jonathan smiled faintly. "It isn't business."

"So . . . if it isn't Alex and it isn't business, where does that leave us?" She tapped her water goblet with a long red manicured nail making the lemon wedge dance. "Ah . . . the lovely Ms. James."

"Not bad. Third guess. You haven't lost your touch."

Madeline reached out a hand and covered one of his that rested on the table. "Why don't you tell me about it, Jonnie? I know you're an expert on the feminine gender but not all females fit into typical male molds. I have a feeling your Devon might be one of them."

He sighed heavily. "I'm afraid that's all too true. Why don't we order and I'll fill you in while we eat . . . though I'm not sure I'll be able to taste it."

"That bad, is it?"

"Worse."

Feeling no such compunction herself, Maddie ordered the duck with Armagnac and Burgundy along with a radicchio salad while Jonathan ordered a bowl of scallop bisque soup.

"That's all you're going to have?" she asked when his food arrived.

"It's more than I've eaten for the last two days."

"Oh, Jonnie." With only a gentle nudge here and there to keep him going, Maddie quietly sipped a glass of Pouilly Fumé while Jonathan told her what Devon believed had happened to her on a night last October at the Stafford Inn. He told her about Paul James and the divorce that had driven her close to a nervous breakdown. He told her about Devon's insecurity and her feelings of isolation as an adopted child, about Devon's anxiety and why writing this book was so important. He mentioned Michael Galveston, and how Devon had let him pull the strings of their relationship for over two years.

Knowing that Devon's secrets were as safe with her as if he'd never spoken them, he told her far more than she ever believed he would have, which only showed her how important Devon James was.

"You feel protective of her. You never felt that way about Becky."

"Becky never needed anyone."

"But Devon does."

"Maybe."

"And so do you."

"Me? I'm hardly a charity case."

"Everybody needs someone, Jonnie."

He said nothing in answer to that. Instead he talked about his role in what had happened between them, admitting his decision to keep silent about Alex's accident and about the stories about the old estate being haunted. He also admitted that much of what Devon had accused him of was true.

"I was damned near as bad as Galveston. I figured I could control her, that once I took her to bed, she'd be easier to handle."

"And she was," Maddie put in a bit darkly.

"Yes. She's too damned trusting for her own good. She usually stays out of situations like these so she won't get hurt."

"Situations like these meaning a virile, sexually attractive man's bed?"

"When it comes to men, Devon's naive. I knew she wasn't just a one-night stand, but I wanted her . . . and it served my purpose. I used her, just like she said. And I manipulated her by subtly convincing her to quit when I knew how important this was. Worst of all, under the same set of circumstances, I'd probably do it again."

Maddie's sleek black brow went up. "I see . . ."

"I'm glad someone does."

"What I see, Jonnie, is that you did exactly what you felt you had to—all except taking her to bed. That you did for yourself."

Jonathan said nothing, just reached for his glass of Perrier and took a drink.

"You didn't really use her, you know. At least not that way. You cared about Devon . . . you still do."

Jonathan said nothing.

"The problem isn't what's already happened, it's what you're going to do about it."

"There's nothing I can do."

"Not as long as you're convinced that Devon's wrong. As long as you believe that you've got to protect your family—our family. You can't have some woman—no matter how attractive she may be—running around writing books that dredge up lies about our family. On the other hand, what if she's right? What if Florian Stafford is the villain Devon says? What if he really is keeping the souls of Annie and Bernard locked up in that house? Could you live with that, Jonnie? Knowing how they must be suffering?"

"That's insane. Surely you can't believe something like that."

"You forget I live in England. Everyone in Britain believes in ghosts. Besides, I'm not nearly as pragmatic as you are. I believe in God and the devil, in life after death, heaven and hell, good and evil. If you accept those concepts, then something like what Devon and Alex encountered might be possible."

"Alex? Surely you can't mean to consider the tale of a hysterical five-year-old boy."

Madeline shrugged. "I don't know. Seems a rather odd coincidence."

"They didn't even happen in the same house."

"True enough, but there still may be some link."

"I don't believe it."

"You meditate, don't you? Isn't it part of your martial arts training?"

"Yes, but what does that have to do with any of this?"

"Explain the concept to me."

"We meditate to enhance our *Chi'I*, to get in touch with the intrinsic energies within us. It's the untapped power each of us carries inside of us."

"Some people call that force the soul."

Jonathan looked at her strangely.

"A number of people believe the soul is indestructible. That it's like wood, which burns and changes into smoke, but doesn't entirely go away. If that is the case, then . . . well . . ." She smiled at him and gently squeezed his hand. "Are you beginning to see what I mean?"

"You're saying the same thing Devon did—that I should keep an open mind."

"At the very least, Jonnie."

"But what about the newspapers? Sooner or later, they'll discover what Devon is up to. Alex's accident will be dredged up, and they'll be hounding him again. I can't afford the risk of upsetting him, of undoing all of the doctors' hard work."

"How much progress has he made?"

"Almost none that I can see, but that doesn't matter. At least these people say he has a chance."

"And what about you, Jonnie? Don't you deserve a

chance, too? This woman means a great deal to you. You've nearly destroyed whatever it is the two of you were building, but if you want her back badly enough, you'll find a way—without endangering Alex."

"I don't know . . ." He stared off in the distance, his eyes fixed on a point above her head.

"Just think about it. Give it some time. If she feels as strongly as you do, eventually she'll be ready to listen. When that time comes, you'd better know what it is you're going to say."

Jonathan leaned back in his chair. "I'll think about it, Maddie. Believe me. I'll be hard-pressed to think of anything else."

Madeline only smiled. Jonathan knew women, but Maddie knew her brother—even after all these years. Jonathan was in deeper than he had ever intended. At this point he could use Devon's anger as a means of ending the closeness he felt to her, or he could look inside himself and see what it was he really wanted.

She was pulling for the James woman. She sounded like a fighter. Maddie just prayed her brother was wrong about the papers getting involved and what it might do to Alex.

She hoped she had given him the right advice, but the truth was she couldn't really be sure.

Devon heard the clock strike 2:00 A.M. An hour later, she heard it strike three. It was quiet outside, except for the occasional blare of a car horn, but Devon still couldn't fall asleep. Instead, she stared up at the ceiling above her bed, mulling over the events of the past few days and all that had happened.

Thank God for Christy, she thought. Devon had gone to

her the moment she had left Jonathan's office, cried for at least two hours, been cosseted and pampered, and commiserated with. Yes, Jonathan was indeed a bastard, Christy of course was adding, "all men are." But there were no I-told-you-sos, nothing but comforting words and protective support.

In the days that followed, Devon's rage kept her working. The fires of her anger and pain fueled her determination, blocking out thoughts of Jonathan and allowing her to go on with her work.

She returned to the library and read every article in every tabloid, newspaper, and magazine that dealt with the fire and little Alex's accident. If she hadn't been embroiled in her problems with Paul at the time, she might have read something about it at the time the accident had happened.

Then again, most of the "ghost" stories had been printed in the tabloids, which Devon never bought. Alex's ghost story was always mentioned, but the references to what had actually happened were hazy. Devon needed to talk to the child, needed to know exactly what he had experienced.

That Jonathan would stop her if he found out, did not matter. She wasn't about to let him defeat her again.

Unfortunately, during the lonely December evenings he came very close to stopping her. Christmas decorations glittered all over the city, and people were well on their way into the spirit of the season. Before this had happened, Devon had secretly dreamed of spending the holidays with Jonathan. They would go Christmas shopping for their families and of course for little Alex. She imagined he would take her to see the lighting of the giant Christmas tree at Rockefeller Center and afterward they would stay to watch the skaters gliding around the rink.

At night, as she did now, she stared up at the ceiling

trying not to remember the time they'd made love in her bed. But the images were there—fierce, passionate images of Jonathan kissing her, his fine dark hands caressing her breasts. Thoughts of his body moving inside her kept her tossing and turning while her body ached and burned.

As much as she hated him, she wanted him. Jonathan had aroused her as no man had, carried her to heights of passion. She moaned into the pillow at the terrible loss she felt and hot tears rolled down her cheeks.

In the morning, she awoke feeling tired and out of sorts. It was only her driving determination to discover the truth about what happened at the inn that kept her going.

Finishing the last cold dregs of her coffee in an effort to fortify herself, Devon pulled on her heavy camel-hair coat, picked up her purse, and walked to the door. A car and driver waited downstairs to carry her the long miles to Stafford. She had found Elwood Dobbs through the long-distance information operator, phoned him, and he had agreed to see her at ten o'clock that morning. She had gotten up early to make the three-hour drive, and she was anxious to be off.

Reviewing her notes along the way made the trip in the icy weather pass swiftly, but Devon's nerves began to build the moment they turned onto the narrow road leading into Stafford. The driver of the dark blue executive town car had no trouble finding Dobbs's small unimposing house on Pearl Street, not far from the burned-out ruins of the original Stafford mansion. Ignoring the uncomfortable weight she felt in her chest, she made a mental note to stop and examine the remains of the old estate before she left.

"We're here, Ms. James."

The car pulled up to the curb, and Devon stepped out before the tall brown-haired young man who had driven could turn off the key. "I shouldn't be long." When he nodded his understanding, she turned and made her way up the brick path to the small white wood-frame house. A narrow, weathered, unobtrusive sign hung from a chain on the overhanging porch: "Elwood Dobbs Handyman—You break 'em, I fix 'em."

She smiled. It seemed fitting for a man with a name like his. Devon crossed the porch to knock on the tattered screen door. One of the shudders at the window tilted at an odd angle and banged lightly against the house in the wind. *Like the cobbler whose son has no shoes,* she thought wryly as the heavy wooden door behind the screen swung wide.

"Hello, there. You Miz James?"

"Yes, may I come in?"

"Why, sure." He pushed the screen door wide and stepped back so Devon could walk past him into the living room. With its old-fashioned built-in mahogany bookshelves filled with stacks of old magazines, the place was a little bit dark and a little bit musty. But Dobbs made several adjustments in the yellowed white lace curtains at the window, and a few weak rays of sunshine pushed their way in.

"Hope you'll forgive the clutter. Used to be a real nice place before my wife Betsy passed on. Kinda hard to keep things up now that she's gone over." Elwood Dobbs was a tall man, though slightly stoop-shouldered, with thinning gray hair and a day's growth of bristly gray beard. His face was wrinkled but it was a pleasant face, and his dark brown eyes were warm. He shoved a week's worth of newspapers out of the way, pointed to the spot he had cleared on the worn brown sofa, and Devon sat down, still wearing her coat.

"Gone over?" It seemed an odd way to phrase the death of a loved one.

"Sure. Death's just passin' from one side to the other. Least ways that's what I believe." Tugging up the knees of his faded coveralls, Dobbs sat down in the overstuffed chair across from her and Devon smiled in his direction.

"In a way, that's what I came here to talk to you about. I'd like to ask you some questions about what happened the night the old Stafford mansion burned down."

"That's what you said on the phone . . . you sure you ain't no reporter?"

"No."

"Personally, I don't give a fiddler's damn, but after I spoke up before, nobody 'round here'd talk to me. A man gets kinda lonesome, you know?"

She knew a lot about being lonely. "I know."

"You said you read about it in the papers. How come you want to know?"

The weight returned to her chest. "Because of something that happened to me at the Stafford Inn. I had a very strange experience—a terrifying experience. As crazy as it sounds, I believe the ghost of Florian Stafford is in that house, and I want to find out if it's true."

Elwood bent forward, his thin arms resting on his knees. "He built that place over his dead son's grave, ya know. I'm the fella who found the boy's tombstone down in the basement."

"You were the one?"

He nodded. "I was workin' on remodelin' the bathrooms. Eerie, it was, I gotta tell ya. Man'd have to be crazy to build a house over a damnable cemetery."

"That's exactly what I thought. Have you heard of anyone else who's had an experience in the house?"

"Hell, there's been stories goin' 'round about that place since I was a kid. Funny noises, lights goin' on by themselves, footsteps on the stairs, all the usual stuff. After Ada and Edgar Meeks moved in, things seemed to settle down. My guess is them two is just keepin' things quiet. They love that old place. Couldn't pay me enough to live there."

Me either, Devon thought. "What about the other house, the old original Stafford estate?"

"Before the fire, it stood vacant for years. Couldn't rent it out, couldn't sell it. Sometimes a family would move in for a while, but they never stayed long. House got real rundown. Weren't for Estell Stafford Meredith decidin' to move back in, place probably wouldn't have lasted another couple years. Roof was nearly gone, whole damned floor was eaten up with termites. Miz Meredith spent a fortune bringing it back to its former glory. She was real proud of it and so was her nephew, Jonathan."

"Jonathan?" Devon's mouth went dry just at the sound of his name.

"Yes, ma'am. Nice fella. Come out to visit several times while I was workin' on the house—I did some odd jobs for Miz Meredith. Sometimes Jonathan left his son with his aunt for a visit. That's what he'd done that weekend. Said he had some catchin' up to do at work, so he left the boy with his aunt that Friday night, then come back to pick him up on Sunday. Only some kinda meetin' kept him workin' late. By the time he got to Stafford, the house was in flames."

"God, Jonathan must have been terrified."

"He was a real hero. Ran into that fire and brought out his boy, then went back for his aunt and brought her out, too."

"Were you there?"

"No. House went up so fast, it was pretty far gone by the time the fire trucks got there—we only got a voluntary department, ya know."

"Alex said he saw something in the flames. There wasn't much else in the papers. Is there anything you can tell me?"

"I believe he seen somethin' pretty frightenin'. He was near hysterical when the ambulance came. Kept talkin' about seein' someone his aunt couldn't see."

"How did the newspaper tabloids get the story?"

"One of 'em got past the security guard at the hospital. Went in to see the boy, and I guess he told 'em. Leastwise that's what Miz Meredith said."

"What happened to her afterward? I mean where is she now?"

"Miz Meredith spent the night in the hospital . . . smoke inhalation . . . but otherwise she was okay . . . not like poor little Alex. As to where she is, she's livin' right here in Stafford. House on Front Street. Kind of an old folks' home, but there's only two other women who live there. They got someone who tends 'em 'round the clock, but it's more like a home than a hospital. Real nice place, and Stell . . . I mean Miz Meredith's real happy there."

"I take it you two are friends."

"Yes, ma'am, we are. I stop by to see her whenever I get the chance."

Devon saw the opportunity Dobbs presented and felt a surge of excitement. "Do you think you could get me in to see her?"

"Sure. Miz Meredith loves visitors. I'm sure she'd be real pleased."

"When?"

"If you got time for me to shave and put on my Sunday clothes, I'll take you over there right now."

"I'll make time, Mr. Dobbs, and thank you."

He smiled warmly. "Just El will do, ma'am. That's what everybody calls me." He stood up from the chair. His tall thin frame unwound like a rusty lever, and he stalked off down the hall.

By the time they reached the car, they were on a first-name basis, and Devon felt better than she had in days. Elwood Dobbs believed her story. She couldn't wait to see what Estell Stafford Meredith would have to say.

"Stell? It's me, Elwood."

She was sitting in a cane-backed rocker in the parlor, watching the branches of a leafless tree that scraped against the windowpanes in the wind. She lived in a lovely old Victorian house, painted yellow with bright white trim. One of the other two ladies who lived there had shown them in, but quietly retired to her room upstairs using a small hidden elevator behind one wall.

Devon focused her attention on the small but robust woman sitting in her rocker. A bright red crocheted afghan covered her lap. At first she made no sign that she knew her friend was there, just kept staring out the window, then she turned and smiled in his direction.

"It's good to see you, El. And I see you've brought a friend." Estell Stafford Meredith was one of the loveliest elderly women Devon had ever seen. Her hair was a rich lustrous silver curling softly around her face, and her eyes were an indigo blue. Skin that had probably once been dark, as with the rest of the Stafford clan, now appeared veined and translucent, but it took nothing away from her gentle expression or her soft warm welcoming smile.

"Stell, this here is Miz James."

"Hello, Ms. James."

"It's a pleasure to meet you, Mrs. Meredith."

"Lord, I'm just Aunt Stell to most folks."

"My friends call me Devon."

"She wants to talk to you about the fire, Stell."

Estell made a clucking sound and shook her silver-haired head. "Terrible thing, terrible. I don't really like to remember."

"I'm sure it's very painful," Devon said gently. "Mr. Dobbs told me most of it. Unless there's something else you could add."

"Don't remember much. My nephew got us out, you know."

"Yes . . ." Devon shifted nervously. "Is there anything you can remember before the fire? Someone there who shouldn't have been? Something out of the ordinary?"

"It all happened so quickly . . . I never really understood what happened."

Devon stepped closer and knelt by the old woman's chair. "There's something else, Aunt Stell. I was hoping I could talk to you about your cousin, Annie."

"Annie? Whatever for?" There was something in those deep blue eyes . . . a shrewdness Devon hadn't expected.

"Why don't you ladies go on and talk," El said, "I'll just wander into the kitchen, make myself a cup of tea."

He left the room and Devon returned her attention to Stell, whose look had turned a little bit wary.

"I'm doing some research on the Stafford family." Deciding honesty might be her only chance for success, Devon took a breath for courage. "Annie's only part of it. I want to know about her because of something that happened to me when I stayed at the Stafford Inn. It was a very frightening experience, Aunt Stell. No one believes it really happened, and I have to know whether or not what I believe is the truth."

"How did you know about the fire?"

"I ran across it in the papers. Jonathan said something—" Devon broke off as she realized the slip she had made.

"Jonathan? Are you a friend of my nephew's?"

Pain squeezed the area around her heart and some of it must have flickered across her face. She tried to school her features, but she felt certain the older woman had noticed. "In a manner of speaking, yes."

Aunt Stell patted the chair across from her. The shrewdness came back in her eyes. "Why don't you sit down, dear, and start from the beginning."

Devon found herself confiding in Estell Stafford Meredith, telling her much of what she believed had happened in the house on Church Street, but purposely leaving off any mention of Annie. When she finished, Aunt Stell shook her head.

"Anything you have to say about Florian doesn't surprise me. He was a very cruel man."

"Annie told you?"

She nodded.

"I know you two were friends. I saw a letter she once wrote to you."

Stell sighed wearily, her former vitality beginning to fade. "She was ten years older than I, but she was family . . . and yes, we were friends. She was only thirteen when she moved in with Florian and Mary. I was just a child then. It wasn't until years later that she told me about the time she spent there."

Devon's heartbeat quickened. "She told you about it?"

Aunt Stell nodded. "They treated her badly. Mary was jealous of Florian's interest in her, I think. Made her work from dawn till dusk . . . made her sleep upstairs in the servants' quarters."

"Yes, Mrs. Meeks mentioned that." *But I already knew.*

"He was brutal in his treatment of her. Used to take his belt to her every chance he got. Guess he got some kind of pleasure out of bringing the poor child pain. Lord, how she hated him."

Devon's chest went tight and the room seemed suddenly airless. She could almost feel the agony Annie must have suffered. "From what I know, Florian was a strict disciplinarian, just like his father."

"That's what Annie said. She said she'd heard stories about him even before she moved in. People said that after his little boy Bernie died, he went a little bit crazy. I guess he took out on her his anger at losing the boy."

Devon could only nod. The images were returning inside her head, images of suffering and pain. "What else did he do?" she asked, her voice suddenly shaky and barely above a whisper.

Indigo eyes swung to her face. For a moment Stell said nothing, just looked at her with that same awareness Devon had seen before. "You know, don't you?"

Devon wet her dry lips. "Yes . . ."

"How? How could you know?"

Tears welled in her eyes and slid down her cheeks. "Annie told me."

"But that's impossible. You couldn't have known her, you're too young."

Devon leaned forward in her chair. "It happened at the inn. The night I was there . . . she told me . . ."

Stell's hand fluttered up to her chest. "Lord protect us."

"You probably don't believe me, but it's the truth. The night I stayed at the inn . . . somehow she told me."

Aunt Stell looked back out the window. Her expression was bleak and somewhat distant. When she spoke, her voice sounded brittle. The words were spoken with an underlying pain that made Devon's throat close up.

"She told me about the first time he came to her. She was only a child, just turned thirteen. She was afraid of him . . . so terribly afraid. He had punished her that morning, beaten her for some small infraction of his rules. But she sensed this time it was more than a beating he was after." Aunt Stell toyed nervously with the crocheted robe that covered her lap. "He tried to get her to be quiet, threatened to beat her again if she didn't give him what he wanted. She fought him, fought him hard, but he forced her down on the bed. She told me he tore off her nightgown. It had been a present from her father before he died, long and white, embroidered especially for her."

The ache in Devon's throat grew more painful. "Dear God."

"She said she remembered the sound of the rending fabric for years . . ."

Tears welled in Devon's eyes and slid down her cheeks, streaking them with wetness as her mind continued to replay the terrible images she had seen that night in the yellow room. She felt caught up in Annie's nightmare. Consumed with it. "There was blood on the sheets," she whispered.

"She was so small," Stell said softly. "He tore her badly when he entered her."

A sob escaped the muscles in Devon's throat. "Don't . . . please. I can't stand to hear anymore."

Aunt Stell sighed and leaned back in her chair. "It's all right, dear," she finally said. "It's all in the past. Annie finally escaped him and later she was happy."

"Happy? How could she have been. From what I've

learned, she lived alone all her life. She never married or had children. How could she have been happy?"

Aunt Stell smiled faintly. "She was happy, that much I can promise you."

Devon didn't really believe it. How could a woman possibly be happy living a lonely existence in a house where she had suffered so much? Devon pulled a tissue from her purse and wiped the tears from her cheeks. "God, he was a monster."

"I think his mind was gone. Annie said he was often irrational, flying into rages, unable to control himself. She left the house as soon as she was old enough, went away to boarding school and didn't return until both of them were dead and the house was empty. I saw her again when she came to my family's home for a visit. It didn't take long for us to grow close."

"I can't stand to think of what he did to her."

"As I said, dear, all that is over. He can't hurt her now."

Can't he? Devon wondered. She started to say so, but the serenity had returned to the old woman's face and she didn't want to destroy it. "I don't understand any of this or why it has happened to me," she said instead. "I'm not even sure what I'm supposed to do."

Aunt Stell leaned forward and patted her hand. "I'm sure you'll know when the time is right. The Lord works his miracles in very strange ways. You do whatever it is you need to and don't let anyone stop you."

"Not even Jonathan? He doesn't want me involved in this. He wants to protect the Stafford name."

"Poppycock. Florian Stafford wasn't the first black sheep in the family and he won't be the last. You do what you have to." Stell squeezed her hand. "And if my nephew has a lick of sense, he'll help you."

Devon shook her head. "He'll never do that. He's used every means he can think of to stop me." *Including taking me to bed.*

"That must have involved a good bit of his time."

"We were together a lot these past few weeks."

"I gather Jonathan got angry and ended the relationship."

Devon's head came up. "*I* got angry when I found out he'd been hiding things from me. *I* ended the relationship."

Aunt Stell smiled. "I see. . . ."

"I wish none of this had ever happened, but it did. I can't just ignore it."

"No and you shouldn't. Just remember, dear, if God's will is involved, he'll show you the way."

Devon pondered that, thinking maybe he'd been doing that all along. She started to say something more, but Aunt Stell was once again staring out the window, rocking back and forth in her chair.

Devon reached over and squeezed the old woman's hand. "I guess I'd better be going," she said softly. Aunt Stell said nothing. "It was really nice to meet you."

Aunt Stell just smiled and kept on rocking in her chair.

Seventeen

Devon left Aunt Stell feeling sad for what Annie Stafford had suffered. But Devon felt somewhat unburdened, knowing now for certain that what she had sensed that night in the yellow room had been real. Now more than ever, she was determined to expose the truth about Florian and—if there was such a thing—free little Bernard and Annie.

She dropped Elwood Dobbs at his house on Pearl, thanking him for his help with Aunt Stell, intent on prowling the shadowy remains of the old Stafford mansion. Unfortunately, by the time she got there, a heavy rain had started to fall, a bitter reminder of the first time she had come to Stafford.

"I guess I'll have to make another trip," she said absently to her driver. "It's been a long day anyway; I'm more than ready to go home."

Along the way, she made notes of everything that had transpired with Aunt Stell and Elwood Dobbs, and got back to her apartment late that afternoon. The phone was ringing when she stuck the key in the door. She raced across the room and grabbed the receiver just seconds before the message machine would have clicked on.

"There you are, Devon. I've left half a dozen messages on that awful machine." Her literary agent, Marcia Winters. "Were you ever going to call me back?"

"I'm sorry, Marcia, this week has been hectic."

"I hope you've been busy finishing *Traces.*" Devon didn't miss the accusation in her tone.

"I'm working on it every morning." That was a bit of an exaggeration, but the words renewed her pledge to finish the book. As she had vowed before, from now on she would work on *Traces* every day until noon, then start on her Stafford project.

"When do you think you'll be through? The publisher is having a conniption fit. The company will do a far better job for you if you stay on their good side."

Devon thought for a moment, mentally arranging her schedule and how much work she still had to do on the novel before it was finished. "Give me till January thirty-first. I promise the completed manuscript will be sitting on your desk by five o'clock."

"Good girl." Satisfied, Marcia hung up, but the phone rang again almost immediately. This time it was Evelyn Frankie, her editor. The conversation went much the same, and Devon's resolve strengthened. Once *Traces* was finished, her money problems would be over and her conscience clear; she could work on the story she wanted to write more than anything else in the world.

The Silent Rose.

The name had come to her as stealthily and as forcefully as everything else about the project. She wasn't certain why she had chosen it, she only knew it felt right somehow. Just as everything else was beginning to have a rightness to it.

Devon rewound the answering machine, listened to her messages, ignored the unwanted flicker of hope that Jonathan might have called, and headed into her office. She would review her notes on *Traces* and start working on it again tomorrow. She'd walked only several feet when the phone rang a third time. Determined to get to work, Devon let the machine pick it up and continued on down the hall. She stopped at the sound of the deep male voice.

"Devon, it's Jonathan. I want to talk to you. Please call me."

She stood there a moment, until the receiver clicked and the line went dead. She found with irritation that her hands were trembling and her pulse had increased.

"Damn you." She knew what he wanted. This was just another attempt to stop her from working on the book. It was infuriating that just the sound of his voice could upset her so. She unplugged the phone in her office, just in case he called again. And she went to work with an iron resolve, with Jonathan firmly blocked from her mind. Or at least as firmly as possible.

Over the weekend, she immersed herself in *Traces,* better able to concentrate than she had expected, accomplishing a good deal more than she had hoped. Jonathan phoned twice each day, but she never answered the phone or returned the calls. Still, it kept him in the forefront of her mind. His image was so compelling that by Sunday she was tempted to speak to him just to tell him to stop calling.

Thank God she was working so hard. At least while she was writing, she was free of the intense longings that thoughts of Jonathan stirred.

On Monday, she started back on her research, returning to the library for a fresh stack of books on ghosts and the paranormal. For a change of pace, she picked up the issue of *Karma* she had started but never finished. She was surprised to discover that she hadn't really given the publication enough of a chance. As she had discovered before, the advertisements often pointed up the commercial side of the metaphysical. But the magazine also contained fairly well-documented articles on ghost encounters, ESP, clairvoyance, and even UFOs. Some of the items seemed outrageous and yet there was much food for thought, if she set aside her prejudices.

She read and made notes until the intercom buzzed, announcing Christy's arrival at the door downstairs. Devon had phoned her before the weekend to tell her about Aunt Stell and her recent visit to Stafford. They'd arranged to have coffee at Devon's apartment Monday morning.

"Sara Stone is back," Christy said even before Devon had taken her coat.

"Who's she?"

"You remember—the trance medium at the Insight Book Store."

"Oh, no you don't. I've been down that rosy path and I'm not going again."

Christy caught her hand, gold bracelets jangling. Today she wore a cream-colored blouse and a calf-length red-plaid skirt over a pair of soft camel boots. "This is different. Sara isn't like Zhadar. She's a true medium. She isn't rich and she isn't famous. Her fee is minimal; she just helps people out when they need her."

"Christy—"

"Trust me. This time it'll work."

"Trust me," Devon repeated. "That's what Eve said to Adam."

Christy laughed. "Come on, I'm not that bad."

Devon sighed. "I'll think about it."

Christy seemed satisfied with that for the moment, but her grin said she wasn't about to give up. They went into the kitchen, and Devon poured them each a steaming cup of coffee.

"How's Francisco?" Devon asked, opting for a change

of subject as she mopped at a drop of spilt liquid on her freshly donned gray wool pants.

"Adorable as always."

"I thought all men were bastards."

"All right, so he's an adorable bastard . . . speaking of which . . . have you heard anything from Jonathan?"

Devon's stomach tightened. Her coffee suddenly tasted tepid and muddy. "He's called . . . left messages on my machine. I haven't talked to him. I don't ever want to see him again."

"I thought maybe . . . I don't know . . . you're a little naive when it comes to men, but you've got a way of sensing goodness in people. I thought maybe this time . . . with Jonathan, I mean . . ."

"So did I." Devon smiled weakly. "You can't imagine how much I miss him. At night I remember what it was like being with him. I don't think I'll ever feel quite that way about another man."

"Maybe the next time he phones, you should see what he has to say."

Devon shook her head. "You don't know him like I do. Once he starts talking, he's nearly irresistible. I can't risk getting involved with him again."

Christy didn't argue. "Love always seems to hurt, honey."

"I trusted him, Christy. I hate being used like that. It makes me feel so cheap."

"Like I said—all men are bastards."

That night Devon had a hot, wet dream about him. She awoke in the throes of climax, astounded that just the image of him thrusting inside her could have such a potent effect.

"Damn you to hell, Jonathan Stafford," she whispered into the darkness. For the balance of the night, she tossed and turned, then woke up feeling tired and lethargic. When the phone beside her bed began to ring, she listened for the click of the message machine, then realized she'd forgotten to turn it on.

"Damn." She reached across her pillow to her nightstand, lifted the receiver and pressed it against her ear.

"Hello."

"Hello, Devon."

"Jonathan . . ." The word came out on a soft breath of air.

"I've been calling . . . I want to see you."

Devon's stomach clenched. She could almost see him, almost feel him reaching out to touch her. "I don't want to see you."

Silence. "I'm sorry about what happened. We need to talk."

"I have nothing to say to you."

"I'll do the talking for both of us."

You can't trust him! her mind screamed. *Don't let him do this to you again!* "I don't think it's a good idea. We both know where we stand."

"Not necessarily. As I said, we need to talk."

Oh, God, he was doing it to her again. Devon fought against the hope that was rising. Hope and a flicker of the overwhelming emotions she had felt for him. "I can't, Jonathan." A hard ache swelled in her throat. "I just can't." She started to hang up, she wanted to—desperately—and yet she could not.

"Devon, please. Just give me an hour. Half an hour. If afterward you still feel the same, I promise I'll leave you alone."

Devon said nothing, but her eyes slid closed and her grip on the phone grew tighter.

"Devon . . . ?"

"All right," she said softly. "When?"

"Tonight. I'll come to your apartment, or you can come to mine."

"No!" she nearly shouted, remembering that in each place they had made love. "How about someplace neutral? A restaurant or something?"

He took a while to answer. "All right. I'll send Henry for you at eight . . . if that's convenient." So formal, so businesslike.

She nodded, though he couldn't see her. "Fine." What did he want? Would he try to make another deal? Or did he think that if he enticed her back into his bed, he could charm her into giving up her work as she had before? Her anger began to stir.

"Devon?"

"Yes?" she answered with a bit more control.

"I've missed you."

Devon hung up the phone.

Jonathan set the receiver back in its cradle. *I've missed you.* That was an understatement if ever he had made one. Damn, he'd been lost without her. He had tried to forget her, worked himself until he dropped, then dragged himself home and collapsed on the couch, unwilling to sleep in his bed. When he had tried, she'd been there with him, laughing softly, snuggling against him. Looking at him with those big green eyes.

Trusting him when she shouldn't have.

Maddie was right. He should have kept an open mind, tried to see her side of the problem. Now she might not let him.

Jonathan's stomach twisted. He had hurt her—badly. He could hear it in her voice. It would take patience on his part to mend the damage he had done, but he intended to try. Part of him demanded to know how he could have let her become so important. Another part assured him it was only the intense physical attraction he felt for her and, of course, a certain bond of friendship. That part said even a friend deserved better treatment than he'd given her.

Whatever the truth of his feelings, just knowing he would be seeing her made him feel a whole lot better. He worked the balance of the day, concentrating on the Holidex problem, which continued to mushroom. As he kept on working into the evening, he accomplished more than he had in days. By seven-thirty, he was dressed in a light blue turtleneck sweater and navy wool slacks, clothes he had carefully chosen to appear casual and non-threatening, and was anxious to be on his way. If he hadn't been thinking of the evening ahead, he might have smiled. He'd learned a few helpful tricks in the years he'd been in business.

At Devon's apartment, he sent Henry in to get her. He didn't want her any more wary than she already was. As it was, all he noticed as she slid onto the seat beside him was the slightest flaring of her pretty green eyes.

"I-I assumed you would be meeting me at the restaurant."

"I changed my mind." He'd wanted to see her; he had waited long enough. Now, as he sat there beside her, inhaling her orange blossom scent, it was all he could do not to gather her into his arms and bury his face in her hair.

"Where are we going?" She shifted nervously, drawing a little farther away.

"Valentino's. Tino will see that we get a quiet table in the back."

Devon wet her lips, making them glisten. He could see she was remembering the last time they had been there. The night he had told her about his dream. His groin tightened. Devon glanced away from him out into the darkness.

"Would you rather have gone someplace else?"

"No, no. Valentino's is fine."

They were ushered in and taken to the same intimate table, with its red checkered cloth, where they'd been seated at before. A single small candle in a red glass holder flickered in the middle.

"You're awfully quiet," Jonathan said gently, after they had ordered.

"You said you'd do the talking. I'm here to listen, nothing more."

Jonathan took a deep breath. She wasn't going to make this easy. "Let me start by saying I'm sorry. I should have told you about the fire. You were honest with me, I should have been honest with you. I didn't tell you because I hoped your interest would wane and this would all go away."

"You hoped my interest would wane?" she said, her chin coming up. "I'll just bet you did—especially after you took me to bed."

Jonathan's jaw tensed. "I told you before—I wanted you. I'll admit the idea that you might be easier to deal with crossed my mind, but—"

Devon shoved back her chair and stood up. "I want to go home."

Jonathan stood up, too. "Dammit, Devon, you promised me you'd listen."

"I've already heard enough."

"No you haven't. Not nearly enough." A good six inches taller than Devon, Jonathan glared down at her until she sank back into her chair. He smiled faintly. He could be damned intimidating when he wanted.

The waiter brought their salads, but neither of them lifted a fork.

"As I was saying," he began again once they were alone, "I hoped you would give up your project, but I went to bed with you because it's been years since I've wanted a woman as badly as I wanted you."

"I don't see where all this is leading. Whatever happened between us is over. You've got a duty to your family, I've got a duty to myself."

"That's exactly why I'm here." *Among a dozen other reasons even I don't understand.*

"What do you mean?"

"I spent the weekend with Alex just as I always do. We went back to the zoo." He smiled softly, thinking of the new set of drawings his son had made. "I kept looking at the animals in those cages, and I kept thinking about what you said." *And what Maddie said.* "I kept thinking, what if you were right? What if souls could really be trapped here on earth? What if Annie and Bernard *were* trapped in that house, enduring their imprisonment through the ages."

She eyed him warily. It was obvious she didn't believe him.

"I can't tell you I really think it's true . . . but I'm willing to concede the possibility."

"Why?"

"Because you believe it . . . and I believe in you."

For the first time her tight control slipped. "Don't do this to me, Jonathan. Don't play your hurtful games."

He covered her hand with his. "I'm playing a different game this time, Devon. And this time we're both going to win."

"What are you saying?"

"I'm going to help you . . . any way I can."

Her eyes fixed on his face. He could read the anger, the hurt—and the wariness. "If that's the case, prove it. Let me talk to Alex."

He shook his head. "My family is out. Alex is undergoing treatment, and Aunt Stell isn't all that well."

"I've already spoken to her."

Jonathan clamped his jaw. "Dammit, Devon. She's eighty years old! The fire was a tragedy she's tried to forget for years. That's exactly the kind of thing I'm trying to prevent."

"You underestimate her, Jonathan. Your aunt is a lovely, intelligent woman. I'll be happy to show you the notes I made from our interview. You might be interested to know they confirm what I believed—that Annie Stafford was sexually molested by her uncle, Florian Stafford, when she was thirteen years old."

The air hissed from Jonathan's lungs. "Aunt Stell told you that?"

"I'll be happy to show you my notes . . . or you can speak to her about it yourself."

Jonathan just sat there.

"I don't know why this has happened to me . . . I don't know why I was chosen. I only know I have to see it through."

"Then let me help you."

"No. I don't trust you, Jonathan. You've been trying to stop me all along. You've lied to me, tricked me, taken advantage . . ."

"I won't take the blame for what happened between us. You wanted me just as much as I wanted you."

Devon had the grace to blush. "All right, I admit I had some part in it."

"A very big part, as I recall." He couldn't help thinking about the night she had seduced him, and a fresh surge of blood filled his loins. Devon's cheeks turned a brighter shade of pink, a look he found enchanting. He wanted to hold her in his arms, but he knew he didn't dare.

"All right, a very large part. But all that is past."

"Let me help you, work with you, find out the truth for myself."

"I know the truth. I just need to find out what to do about it."

"Then show me, dammit. I'm involved in this as much as you are."

"I told you, I don't trust you."

"Think of Alex. If what you say is true, maybe there's some connection to the fire that crippled him. I owe it to him to find out."

For the first time Devon seemed uncertain. Her head came up and her pretty green eyes searched his face. "Is that the duty you were talking about?"

"Part of it. But Annie and Bernie are Staffords, too."

"So was Florian," she reminded him darkly. "And so are you."

He didn't miss the connection and a tightness squeezed his chest. "If he's the man you say, I'm nothing like him. Surely you know that much about me."

"I know you're ruthless and calculating. That you'll do or say anything to get what you want."

"Maybe. If I am, then consider this: I want you now, this minute, just as badly as I did the last time we sat at this table. But I won't press you. I've lost your trust and until I have it back, I won't touch you."

"I need to get into that house," she said, pointedly ignoring his words. "I want to see the guest list. I want to interview some of the other people who have stayed at the inn."

Ada Meeks had told him about Devon's phone calls. Once Devon had stopped by the house, but Ada wouldn't let her in. "I'll take you there myself. Whenever you like."

"I'll let you know." She slid back her chair as the short, aproned waiter arrived with their dinner. "I'm afraid I'm not hungry after all. If you'll excuse me, Jonathan, I'd like to go home."

Jonathan said nothing but his insides started to churn. What had he expected? "All right. Let me get the check."

"I've got a better idea. I'll go on with Henry while you finish eating. I wouldn't want you to miss your dinner."

He didn't try to stop her, just watched her walk away and wondered how long it would take her to forgive him. He didn't doubt she would; it was only a matter of time.

Devon had been right about one thing: He'd do whatever it took to get what he wanted. As hard as he'd fought it, the truth was he wanted her.

Devon came home feeling shaky and very near to tears. Jonathan always had the most amazing effect on her. Just the short time she had spent with him had left her heart racing and her stomach tied in knots. She shouldn't have agreed to see him, yet much of what he'd said made sense.

Alex was somehow involved in all of this, even if Jonathan didn't believe it. She felt an obligation to the boy, just as she did to herself. And to Annie and little Bernard. Besides, she needed Jonathan. Or at least his permission to get back into the house. As much as she hated the idea, in the back of her mind she was afraid she would have to return. If she did, it would be a lot easier with Jonathan's assistance.

He phoned early the following day. When he asked if she wanted to drive up to Stafford to look over the guest books, Devon told him that she spent her mornings now working on *Traces*.

"I think that's a good idea," he said, sounding surprisingly pleased. "I only wish I'd been the one to suggest it." He wasn't pleased at all when she put off their trip, but he would have been furious if he had known the reason.

"I'll call you later," he finished with a note of irritation when she wouldn't bend to his wishes.

Instead, she finished the chapter she'd been working on, turned off the computer, and grabbed her coat and purse. At the corner outside her apartment, she caught a taxi to the Woodland Children's Memorial Clinic, where Jonathan had told her Alex spent four days each week. Since Jonathan had always been hesitant to talk about him, Devon had purposely avoided the subject. She knew very little of Alex, but she did know he had several different tutors who worked with him at the clinic so that he could keep up with his studies.

What she planned wouldn't be easy, but seeing Alex seemed crucial in putting together the pieces of her puzzle. She needed him to confide in her, and the only way she knew to accomplish that was to win his confidence.

Devon braced herself as she pushed through the heavy glass doors of the clinic. Ignoring the slight wave of nausea brought on by the astringent hospital smells, she confronted her first obstacle, the dark-haired receptionist sitting at the front desk.

"May I help you?" the young woman asked.

"Yes. My name is Lynn James." She was afraid someone might recognize her real name. Lynn was her middle name, so it wasn't exactly a fabrication. "I'm here to see Alexander Stafford. His father sent me to tutor him in his drawing." Jonathan had only used her last name in his brief introduction to his son, and the boy might not remember.

"I'll have to let you speak to Mrs. Livingston. She's the head nurse on his ward." The receptionist made the proper phone calls, and the nurse appeared a few moments later—a tank of a woman whose starched white uniform stretched across her broad hips as though it should have burst its seams.

"You're Ms. James?"

"Yes."

"Mr. Stafford said nothing about a new tutor. Do you have papers, references, some sort of authorization? If not, I'll have to call him."

"I have the information right here." She was prepared for this. She handed over a sheaf of papers nearly half an inch thick, showing her degree from New York University, as well as several certificates dealing with the student teaching she had done in the field of art, and finally, letters of recommendation from professors and associates all the way up to the dean. The letters were old and outdated, but the names on them were impressive. She prayed the tactic would work.

"I'll only be coming for the next few weeks. Mr. Stafford just wanted someone to encourage his son in his drawing. He said to call if you weren't satisfied with my credentials." Devon could just imagine how much the woman wanted to tackle that task. Interrupting Jonathan Stafford in the middle of his work day couldn't be a pleasant experience.

"It says your first name's Devon."

"Yes, but I seldom use it."

"There's nothing very recent here."

"I was married for a while. I just started working again. As I said, Mr. Stafford said to call if there was a problem. I know how busy he is—conference calls all over the world, staff meetings, flying here and there—but I know his son comes first. I'm sure he won't mind the interruption."

Mrs. Livingston shoved the papers back into the envelope. "I suppose these will do. Alexander's schedule is extremely full, but he does love his drawing. I think we can squeeze in an hour or so right after lunch."

"That'll be fine."

"Since you're already here, why don't you go in and meet him?"

"Thank you. Mr. Stafford briefly introduced us, but we haven't gotten a chance to really get acquainted."

Mrs. Livingston relaxed at that, the last of her doubts appearing to fade. She led Devon down the hall and into a therapy room filled with all sorts of metal machinery. A pudgy little boy wearing steel braces stood between parallel upright bars, trying to pull himself forward one agonizing step at a time. A bearded young doctor at the opposite end spoke words of encouragement.

Alex lay on a table across the room, where a blond-haired nurse was working over him, massaging his thin legs, lifting and moving them so that they wouldn't atrophy. Devon's heart went out to him.

For a moment, she felt guilty for coming. What if Jonathan was right and her questions somehow hurt him? Then she thought of the fire, thought of the connection there might be to Florian, and worried that something like that could happen again.

"Andy," Mrs. Livingston said, calling him a name Devon

hadn't heard, "do you remember Ms. James?" Though she said the words blandly, Devon knew it was the final test. She held her breath.

He nodded his small dark-haired head. "She's a friend of my dad's."

Devon smiled. "Hello, Alex. Or did I hear Mrs. Livingston call you Andy?" He smiled, and Devon caught a glimpse of what Jonathan must have looked like at that same young age. Her heart turned over.

"It's short for Alexander. All the kids here call me that."

"I like it. Mind if I call you that, too?"

Alex nodded his head, to say it was okay.

The head nurse spoke to the young blond therapist. "Come along, Doris. Let's give them a moment alone."

The women walked off, and Devon turned back to Alex. "I came to help you with your drawings. I used to teach, a few years back."

Alex's face lit up, a row of small even teeth flashing white against his dark face. "You're gonna help me learn how to draw?"

"Yes. If you're willing to work, I think you could be very good."

"Did my dad ask you to come?"

"Not exactly. In fact, I thought maybe you could draw him a picture for Christmas and surprise him." She wasn't sure how long she'd be able to keep coming before Jonathan found out. He'd be furious, but she didn't care. In the meantime, she would do her best to discover what had happened to Alex and at the same time keep her word and help him with his drawing.

"That sounds like a great idea," he said. "What shall I draw?"

"That's the very first rule of being an artist, Andy. You

draw whatever you like. Whatever's inside you. In fact, that's your first assignment. Draw anything you feel like, and when I come back tomorrow, we can work on ways you can improve what you've done."

"Anything I want?"

"Anything. Just let your mind go and see what you can come up with."

"This is gonna be great, Miss James. I can hardly wait to start."

"You know what, Andy?" She smiled at him softly. "Neither can I." Surprisingly, she meant it. She had always loved children, would love to have a family of her own. Alex Stafford was bright and talented. He was the image of his handsome father and just as charming. Already she felt protective toward him. She would do anything she could to help him. As the therapy nurse walked back into the room, Devon reached over and squeezed Alex's hand. "See you tomorrow, okay?"

"Okay."

"And don't forget to keep our secret."

"I won't. Good-bye, Miss James."

"Good-bye, Andy."

The phone was ringing when Devon got home.

"Hello, Devon." It was Jonathan. "I need to see you."

She felt a mixture of anger and pain. "I told you, I'm busy."

"Remember that guest list you wanted? Well, I've got it. I called Ada Meeks and had her send it to me by courier."

"You always were resourceful."

He paused but ignored her biting tone. "The inn has been open two years. Ada has quite a collection of names, but some of the people live right here in the city. I thought we'd start with them, get on the phone, maybe go over and see some of them. I'll be at your place by five-thirty."

"The guests at the inn left their numbers?"

"Some of them." Another brief pause. "I was able to get hold of the others."

"How clever of you."

"Devon, please . . ."

"All right, damn you, I'm sorry. I just can't seem to help it."

She could almost see him smile. "I'll be there at five-thirty, my lovely little *Tenshi.* Maybe I can find a way to turn that fire of yours in another direction."

Devon gasped softly. "Don't even think about it!"

But he had hung up the phone.

Eighteen

Jonathan arrived at Devon's apartment at five-thirty sharp, surprising, since she knew how busy he was. The moment he walked through the door, she braced herself for the assault he always had on her senses.

Dressed in black wool slacks, black Italian loafers, a white shirt open at the throat beneath a black leather-trimmed V-necked sweater, Jonathan flashed a bright white disarming smile, and Devon's breath caught somewhere in her throat. With his dark good looks, tall, hard-muscled frame, and casual air of confidence, Jonathan seemed to dominate the very air around him.

"Hello, Devon." Gray-blue eyes swept over her, warming her wherever they touched.

"Jonathan." She tried to sound cool and distant, but God, it was hard. He had never looked better, and Devon felt even more vulnerable to his charm than she had the first time she met him.

"I brought the guest list." His words implied *strictly business,* but the husky note in his voice said something more.

"Thank you."

"Actually there are three books full of names." He held out a manila envelope, but his eyes remained fixed on her face. "Six rooms a night, at least four of them filled most of the year. That's a lot of people."

Devon glanced away from the force of his gaze. "Yes, it is. I never really thought how many there might be." Unconsciously, she stepped backwards, protecting herself from the pull of him. Jonathan must have noticed, for his posture altered slightly.

"I had one of the secretaries type up the names, addresses, and phone numbers," he said with renewed control, "then sort them by the areas in which each person lives. I thought it would make things easier."

"Yes . . . I'm sure it will." She forced herself to smile. "I wonder . . . if there are as many people as you say, maybe instead of calling, we should send out a questionnaire, see if any of them respond. It would be a considerable job, but—"

"That sounds like a good idea. It would certainly be less work for us, and probably a lot less threatening for them. You write the letter; I'll have Dee assign someone to see it gets mailed."

"All right."

"In the meantime, why don't you show me the information you've gathered so far? If I don't finish reading it before I leave, I can take it home and finish it there."

Devon eyed him warily, then stubbornly shook her head. "Those notes represent weeks of hard work. They stay here with me. I can have copies made if you like." She expected his anger, braced for it, and instead caught a flicker of pain.

"I came here to help you, Devon, not to sabotage your project. I'm not nearly as despicable as you're determined to believe." There was sadness in his fine dark features, and regret, and a yearning she hadn't expected.

She wanted to go to him, to slip her arms around his neck, rest her head against his shoulder. She wanted to tell him she missed him, that she trusted him as she had before.

She wanted to confide in him again and have him confide in her.

"That remains to be seen," she said instead, but there wasn't much bite in her words.

A bland look smoothed his features. "Then why don't I get to work?"

Devon brought in the files she had made, which included the letters she had copied from the NUCMC records—the one from Florian's father and the incriminating one he had sent to his brother. One file contained her original notes, made that morning at the Stafford Inn, while another contained interviews with Elwood Dobbs and Jonathan's aunt, Estell Stafford Meredith.

Devon set a stack of books beside Jonathan's chair, some of them purchased at the Insight Book Store, others checked out from the library. She placed the volume written by Francis Linderman, *The Imprisoned Spirit,* on the bottom, since it posed, she felt, the strongest case for the existence of ghosts on the physical plane, as well as in-depth examinations of telepathy, clairvoyance, and other extrasensory phenomena.

While Jonathan pored through the accumulation of her research, Devon worked on the questionnaire to be mailed to former guests of the Stafford Inn. Knowing how he felt about publicity, she carefully left out any reference to ghosts or the paranormal. Instead, she asked about the sort of experience the guest might have had at the inn—specifically, if he or she had been comfortable, or if there had been anything unpleasant or out of the ordinary. A stamped envelope for the response would be included and anything promising investigated further.

Satisfied with the letter, Devon went to work on some preliminary outlines for the book. It was several hours later that she glanced in Jonathan's direction—something she'd worked very hard not to do—and found him no longer reading. Instead he was looking at her oddly. His finely arched brows were drawn together in a frown.

The stack of books beside him had shifted. Many had been haphazardly tossed on the floor. She realized that he had already finished reading them—all of them. In the back of her mind, she recalled an article she'd once seen that had mentioned his speed reading. Every morning before he started work, he scanned newspapers from all over the world.

He closed *The Imprisoned Spirit,* which sat open in his lap, and came to his feet. Crossing the short space between them, he took her hands and drew her to her feet.

"You're finished?" she asked, trying to ignore how close he stood. The scent of his lime aftershave rose up from his jaw.

"Yes . . . And as hard as it is for me to admit this, I'm beginning to believe I may have done you a grave disservice."

Devon said nothing, just kept staring into those fathomless gray-blue eyes and feeling the warmth of the big dark hands that held hers so gently.

"I'm not sure I know what you mean."

"I mean that you've accumulated an impressive amount of evidence to support your case. There seems to be a very good chance this whole incredible phenomenon really happened. The notes you made that morning, what Ada Meeks confirmed, the letters Florian wrote, his background, what my aunt told you about poor little Annie. Linderman, and a number of highly respected authorities in the field, believe people can sense such things. That's what you must have done, somehow sensed the truth about Florian the night you spent at the inn."

"Yes," she said softly. "I believe it really happened."

"I'm still not convinced that Florian's ghost is involved . . . or Bernie's or Annie's. But something's going on."

"I wasn't sure at first, either."

"I still don't see how the fire at the old Stafford mansion fits in, but maybe I can find out something that will link the two events together."

She could feel his interest, his excitement, and it began to kindle her own. "Speaking of the fire, do you have any idea what Alex might have seen that night?" Of course, even if Jonathan told her, she wasn't sure she could believe him.

Jonathan shook his head. "All he talked about was seeing something in the flames. Maybe his psychologist can be of some help. Unfortunately, Dr. Meyers, the one he worked with for the first two years after the accident didn't seem to do him any good, so I got rid of him. The last I heard, he had moved out of Manhattan. Dr. Raymond's philosophy is to leave the matter in the past, try to move forward in a different direction. Tomorrow I'll start trying to track Dr. Meyers down."

It was a possibility, but not enough of a certainty to end Devon's visits to the clinic. "Then you're really going to help me?"

"That's what I said, isn't it? The first thing I want to do is go back through old Stafford newspaper accounts, see if Bernard Stafford was the only victim of scarlet fever at the time he died. The disease is extremely infectious. If he really died from that, there should be other cases."

"That's what I thought. It was on my list of things to

do, but I started seeing you, and I got . . . sidetracked." She thought of the nights they had spent making love and felt the heat creeping into her cheeks.

Jonathan's hand came up to her face. His thumb brushed lightly against her jaw. "I can't say I'm sorry. I enjoyed making love to you. But this time we won't let it stop us from finding out the truth."

Devon turned her face away from the warmth of his touch, though it was the last thing she wanted. "There isn't going to be a next time."

"Isn't there?" His eyes caught hers, held, dared her to disagree.

She eased away from him, hoping he hadn't felt her tremble. "If you're suddenly so intrigued by all of this," she said a bit defensively, "maybe you should hire your famous investigator. See what he can come up with."

"This sort of research isn't his area of expertise. Besides, you've captured my interest." His look said, in more ways than one. "I want to know what happened as much as you do."

"Not *that* much."

"But you *are* going to let me help you?"

Devon recognized the determined set to his jaw and sighed with defeat. "If you're certain that's what you want."

Jonathan's smile was so bright Devon's knees went a little bit weak. "What I want, lovely *Tenshi,* is to carry you into that bedroom and spend the rest of the night making slow passionate love."

Devon backed farther away. "That isn't going to happen, Jonathan. I have no intention of getting involved with you in that way again."

Jonathan's smile grew broader. "That, sweet Devon, remains to be seen."

* * *

The following afternoon, Jonathan stepped into the entry of Devon's apartment, careful to stand on the towel she'd spread out to catch the rain that trailed in rivulets down his trenchcoat. He set his umbrella in the corner beneath a gilt-framed impressionist painting of blooming pink flowers that made him grimace as he thought of the weather outside. And he tossed his gloves on top of the small marble-topped table.

He had worked all morning at the office, but spent the rest of the day on Devon's project, which he now considered his own.

"So what did you find out?" Devon asked from a few feet away.

Jonathan shrugged out of his trenchcoat and hung it up to dry on the coatrack beside the entry closet. "What kind of a greeting is that?" He turned in her direction. "Whatever happened to 'Hello, Jonathan. How was your day?' Or better yet, 'Hello, Jonathan. I've missed you. I've been thinking about you since morning.' "

Devon laughed at that. Her pretty face flooded with color. "All right," she conceded. "Hello, Jonathan—so what did you find out?" She swept a tendril of pale blond hair off her face and her soft coral lips curved invitingly.

Jonathan smiled, too. He wanted to cross the room and haul her into his arms, to feel her soft mouth tremble under his, to tangle his fingers in her hair. He wanted her to smile at him the way she used to. He wanted to hear the clear sweet sound of her laughter.

It wasn't going to happen. At least not today.

"I suppose that's a little bit better," he said grudgingly, "not very much."

"I guess I'll have to work on it."

Jonathan caught her arm and drew her closer. "Promise?"

Devon's soft smile faded. "I'm not promising anything, Jonathan."

Funny thing was, he didn't really blame her. If the situation had been reversed, if she had purposely deceived him, he would have walked away from her and never looked back. He wasn't very forgiving when it came to honesty and trust.

But Devon was. Maybe she understood his fears for Alex, maybe she just wasn't as tough as he was. Whatever the reason, every time he saw her, he felt a little of her wariness slip away. And she wanted him—every bit as much as he wanted her. He could see it in the way she wet her lips when he watched her mouth, the way her nipples grew hard when he brushed against her.

"What did I find out?" he repeated, keeping his voice purposely light, and Devon relaxed once more. "Well, I went through the *Stafford Sentinel,* and even some of the papers from surrounding towns, but I didn't find any more deaths from scarlet fever. Not around the time Bernie died. By itself, it means very little, but coupled with everything else . . ."

"Did your secretary get out our letters?"

Our letters. It had a very nice ring. "Yes. But don't be disappointed if nothing comes of it. I can't imagine anyone writing to tell us they saw a ghost."

"I really don't expect them to. I'm just hoping someone saw or felt something that made him uncomfortable, something upsetting enough to put it down on paper."

"Maybe. Oh, by the way, we've got an appointment with Francis Linderman next Thursday morning at ten o'clock."

"Linderman?"

"I located him through his publisher. Marty Goldberg, the C.E.O. at Gibralter Press, is a friend of mine. Believe it or not, Linderman is teaching psychology at Princeton. His interest in parapsychology is more or less a hobby. Kind of a shame since his work is so impressive."

"I thought so, too," Devon said. "Unfortunately, from what I've read, it's difficult to make a career in the field."

"So I gather. Most people are skeptics. Schools can't get funding and the professors get discouraged with the length of time it takes to get results. Very few colleges offer courses on the subject and almost none of them offers a degree."

"One of the books I read mentioned that the Institute for Parapsychology in Durham, North Carolina, has a laboratory. Apparently they run tests for ESP."

"Trying to catch the illusive *psi* can't be easy."

A dark golden brow went up. "Amazing. You're beginning to sound like an expert."

Jonathan smiled. "*Psi*—any psychic phenomenon; the exchange of information which occurs without the use of what are normally considered the senses and isn't explicable by the known laws of nature." His smile grew broader. "I forgot to mention that when I get interested in something, I tend to go a little bit overboard—which reminds me . . ."

He walked back to the coatrack and fished a small hardback book out of the pocket of his trenchcoat. "Goldberg gave me this. It's Linderman's newest book. It hasn't even hit the shelves yet." He walked to Devon's side. "I read it this afternoon. I knew you'd want to see it."

"*Parapsychology: The Study of Psychic Phenomena, Its Sources and Applications.*" Devon started to browse the pages, but Jonathan took it from her hands.

"This is the chapter I found particularly intriguing."

He flipped to page sixty-eight, and Devon read the chapter heading. "A Scientific Examination of ESP in Relation to Anxiety." She glanced up at him, her face suddenly pale. "Anxiety—oh, my God."

"Exactly. Linderman proposes that since stress and anxiety are often paramount in poltergeist cases—which involve the use of PK, psychokinesis, the ability to move objects with the mind—it might also be a factor in telepathy, clairvoyance, or precognition. Up until recently, it was believed that the alpha state of deep relaxation was the key to heightened awareness, but apparently during testing that didn't always hold true. Some people actually scored better in a highly nervous state. They got the best results when their heart rate accelerated and their skin became damp—a state very similar to anxiety. From what you've told me about your night at the inn, that may very well have been what happened to you."

For a moment Devon just stared at him. Then her hand started to tremble so badly that she almost dropped the book. He took it from her fingers and set it on the table.

"Do you know what this means?" she said.

"I know what it means to you."

She only shook her head. "You can't know. There's no way you can imagine how I've worried, wondered, prayed . . . The night it happened, I knew I was feeling some of the symptoms. During the weeks I was seeing Dr. Townsend, there were times I saw things I didn't believe were real, felt things I couldn't explain. I was so afraid I'd imagined all of this. That something was wrong with me." Tears brimmed in Devon's eyes, she closed them, and the wetness trickled down her cheeks.

Jonathan eased her into his arms, slowly, gently, so she wouldn't pull away. "It's all right, love."

Devon pressed her cheek against the front of his shirt, the dampness of her tears seeping through the fabric onto his chest. She looked up at him from beneath her lashes, spiky now with their wetness. "I-I'm sorry. I know I shouldn't be crying, but I can't help it."

Jonathan tightened his hold. "After what you've been through—what I've put you through—you deserve to shed a few tears." She always made him feel so damned protective. He wondered how he ever could have hurt her.

Devon brushed away her tears with the tips of her fingers, then her eyes swung up to his. "My anxiety must have made me susceptible, been a sort of conductor that allowed me to communicate with Annie and Bernard . . . to know what really happened in the house."

"It's possible. It may have somehow heightened your psychic awareness, but remember this only shows us *how* you might have known. We still aren't certain Annie and Bernard are really there."

Devon straightened, pulling a little away. "I know they're there. Just as I knew the rest of it. And I'm going to help them."

"We're going to help them," Jonathan corrected.

Devon turned to look at him. Then she smiled. *"We're* going to help them."

Alex Stafford shifted restlessly in his chair. Outside the window of his room, the wind blew papers across the lawn. One of the nurses walking along the sidewalk stepped in a puddle of water and cursed.

"Andy?"

He turned at the sound of his nickname. Miss James stepped through the doorway and he smiled. "I hoped you wouldn't forget."

"Are you kidding? I've been waiting all morning for this."

"Really?"

The tall blond woman nodded. "Uh-huh." She was pretty. Real pretty. He wondered if his father had noticed. And she had the nicest smile.

"Did you get a chance to work on your drawing?"

"I worked on it last night and a little bit this morning."

"Well, let's take a look at what you've done." She walked toward him as he wheeled himself over to his desk.

"I worked on this last night. I thought my dad might like a picture of a sailboat. He used to have one, you know. He told me he loved to go sailing." Alex couldn't imagine anything that might be more fun. He wished his dad still had the boat . . . but Alex guessed he probably couldn't go even if he did. He wouldn't be able to take his wheelchair on a sailboat. "I drew it from a picture Dr. Raymond had on the wall in his office. He said I could borrow it till I got finished."

Miss James examined the paper, holding it up to the light, looking at the lines he had drawn, checking the angles.

"That's very good, Andy." She pursed her mouth in concentration as she glanced again at the work, and Alex held his breath. "I think you might need a little bit of help with your perspective."

"Pre-spective? What's that?"

"Perspective is the way someone views the position of an object—the rightness we see with our eyes when we look at something. Here, let me show you." She reached for the pad of paper, turned to a clean page and drew a picture of a sidewalk disappearing into the horizon. She drew a row of houses along each side, then drew lines showing how they grew smaller as they moved farther and farther away. "See what I mean? It's an illusion, but it somehow looks right."

"I think I see what you mean."

"All right, now let's redraw the dock where your boat is moored."

She sketched a few quick lines, nothing nearly as fancy as he had drawn. Now he could see that the dock was closer in one spot, farther away in another, just as it should have been.

"See how it works?"

"Gosh, that's terrific!"

"Think you can do it?"

He chewed his lip. "I'm not sure."

"It will help if you draw lines like I did on the first sketch. Use a very light pencil and you can erase them later."

"That's a good idea." He looked at the sketch she had made. Yes, it made sense in some odd way. He wasn't quite sure why it worked, but it did. He could see that right off.

"Let's see what else you've got in here." She started flipping back through the pages, and Alex shifted nervously.

There were things in there he hadn't really meant for her to see. Things he'd drawn that had just sort of popped into his head. "Some of 'em aren't any good. I was just drawing whatever I felt like. You said that's what an artist should do."

Miss James had stopped turning the pages. "What's this, Andy?" She showed him the picture he had finished just this morning.

"My aunt's house. That's the way it looked before the fire."

"I see." Her voice sounded softer.

He wondered if she knew about the fire in Stafford and what had happened to him there. He kind of hoped she didn't. People always wanted him to talk about it, and that was the last thing he wanted to do.

"I think you've got a very good start," she said, still looking at the picture. "Maybe you should work on it a little."

"Maybe I will." The thought did intrigue him. If he closed his eyes, he could still see the brilliant orange-red flames burning up into the blackness of the sky. If it didn't make him feel so bad to think about it, it would make a very good picture. He would have to give it some thought.

"You have a nice sense of color," Miss James was saying. "Pastel drawings aren't easy, but they're a good place to start. You can go on to watercolors later."

They talked some more about perspective, and he thought he might just be able to handle it. He hoped so. Over the weekend, he would work on it, and on Tuesday when she returned, he hoped to have something to show her he could be proud of.

"I'd better be going," she said a little while later with a glance at the clock. "It looks like our time's already up."

"It sure went by fast."

She smiled that nice smile of hers. "Yes, it did."

"Thank you for coming."

"My pleasure. I hope you have a good weekend—anything special planned?"

"Dad's taking me to the *Nutcracker*. I've never been to a ballet before."

She knelt beside his chair, so he didn't have to look up

to see her face. "That's wonderful, Andy. I used to love the *Nutcracker.* I wish I were going along."

"Maybe my dad could get an extra ticket."

She only shook her head. "I don't think that would be a good idea—not while we're trying to surprise him. We might slip up and give ourselves away."

Alex grinned. "You really think he'll like the sailboat?"

"I think he'll love it. And when you get it just the way you want it, I'll have it framed. Would you like that?"

"Oh, yes."

She stood up, reached over and squeezed his hand. "I'll see you Tuesday."

He watched her walk away and wondered if she was anyone's mom. If she was, her kids sure were lucky. She was nice and she knew how to draw.

Nineteen

Devon returned to her apartment late that afternoon to find a message from Jonathan on her answering machine asking her, ironically, if she would accompany him and Alex to the *Nutcracker*. She didn't think Alex had suggested it, since he rarely saw his father before he went home from the clinic on Saturday mornings.

Devon sighed wistfully, thinking how much, just a few short weeks ago, she had wanted to be included in the time Jonathan spent with his son. Now she couldn't afford to take the chance of his discovering her deception at the clinic. She didn't want him stopping her before she found out what had really happened to Alex. Besides, she still didn't trust Jonathan—or more truthfully, she didn't trust herself.

When she returned his call, making the appropriate excuses, Jonathan tried his best to change her mind, which pleased her on the one hand but also made her wary. Was he just trying to use her again?

Over the weekend, she busied herself working on *Traces* and doing the first of her Christmas shopping. She bought a lovely cashmere shawl for her mother and a meerschaum pipe for her dad, who enjoyed one occasionally, since he had stopped smoking cigarettes.

In the department stores she visited, the pre-holiday crush

was less than she expected, much to the chagrin of the merchants. But the colorful decorations, and the Christmas music already being piped through the shops, made her wistful and more than a little depressed.

The truth was she missed Jonathan. Working with him wasn't the same as touching him, holding him, waking up beside him in the mornings. If anything, seeing him again only made her feel worse than she had before.

So far, he had been much more help than she had expected, and they had been getting along very well. Too well. It made her yearn for things to be the way they were and she knew that could not happen. Not when, sooner or later, he would discover her deception involving his son. That was a crime he would neither forget nor forgive. It made her heart feel leaden just to think about it, and yet there was nothing she could do. She had to know the truth, and on this issue, Jonathan wasn't about to give in.

Neither was she.

On Tuesday afternoon, after deftly avoiding her nemesis for yet another day, she returned to the clinic for her scheduled hour with Alex. He was as happy to see her as he had been the first time, and she wondered fleetingly if it was because he missed his mother.

"How was the *Nutcracker?*" she asked as they moved toward his desk to look over his last several days' worth of drawings.

"Terrific. Dad said it was the best one he'd ever seen. You should have been there." Alex launched into an expansive ten-minute discourse on marching tin soldiers and sugarplum fairies, giving her a scene by scene account of the ballet.

"Hold it, hold it!" Devon said, laughing softly. "With all

those lovely descriptions, maybe you ought to be a writer instead of an artist."

"I'm gonna be a businessman, just like my dad."

"Are you?" Devon arched a brow.

"Sure. But I'll still keep up my drawing. I'll do that just for fun."

"That's good, Andy. Some people forget to set aside time to play. It's important, no matter how old you are." She was thinking of Jonathan and how hard he had worked in the early years of his career. How much he still missed out on. "Speaking of drawing," she said, zeroing in on the subject, "what have you worked on over the weekend?"

"I drew a lot while I was home, but I saved the picture for my dad to work on here." He showed her the latest version of the sailboat he had drawn before. This one was moored in the harbor, with pale blue water lapping at the long sleek hull.

"This is much better. The lines are crisp, clean, the perspective is right." She smiled. "This is very good, Andy."

He grinned broadly, and she noticed the dimple in his cheek. How wonderful it would be to have a little boy like Alex. Devon felt a pang of regret that she and Paul never had a child. At twenty-nine, she was getting well into the child-bearing years. With Michael gone from her life, and her involvement with Jonathan no longer heading in that direction, chances were good she would never have a family. It made her sad to think what she would be missing. She sighed, beginning to understand how a woman might decide to have a child on her own.

Unfortunately, having known the kind of love that two parents could give, Devon would want nothing less for her own child.

She felt Alex's eyes on her and turned her attention to

his drawings. She leafed through the pages as she had done before. It didn't go unnoticed that Alex shifted nervously when she reached the drawing he had made of the old Stafford mansion. He had sketched the picture again, this time adding dark green shutters to the windows and an old-fashioned iron fence around the yard. She remembered seeing that fence, now nearly obscured by weeds, on her last trip to Stafford.

When Devon turned the page, the paper crackled noisily in the stillness of the room. Her hand stopped mid-motion. On the following page of the book, the old house had been drawn again, but this time it was engulfed in flames, wicked tongues of orange and red that leaped with menace into the black night sky.

"The fire," she said, almost unaware she had spoken the words out loud.

"Did my dad tell you about it?" Alex asked softly.

"Some of it. I've been to Stafford. I've seen what's left of the house."

"You have?"

"Yes . . . I spent a night at the inn." She worked to sound casual, but inside her stomach churned.

Alex nervously wet his lips. "It was awful."

Devon pretended to study the page, lifting it up to the light, looking at it from different angles. "I imagine it was." Then she noticed another drawing behind the one she studied. When she turned the page, her chest closed up until she could barely breathe. It was almost the same drawing as the one on the page before, but in this picture, a portion of the roof had caved in. The flames blazed furiously, but there was something different about them—there was the face of a man in the flames.

"What's this, Andy?" She pointed to the hazy, but unmistakable outline.

"Just something . . ." He chewed his bottom lip.

"Just something you felt like drawing?"

He nodded. "Yes . . ."

"That's good. An artist is supposed to express himself."

"He is?"

"Yes. He's supposed to let the feelings inside him come out on the canvas, or in this case your sketchbook." She looked down at him from over the edge of the pad. "That's what you did here, isn't it?"

"Yes."

"So the night of the fire, you saw a man in the flames?"

"I just thought I did."

"Why do you say that?" Devon eased down on the chair in front of his wheelchair. "Maybe you really did see something."

He shook his head, his expression suddenly guarded. "I just imagined it . . . when I got hit with the beam."

"Did your father tell you that?"

"No, but that's what he thinks. Dr. Meyers said so, and now Dr. Raymond. The nurses think so . . . lots of people."

"Dr. Meyers?" That was the name Jonathan had mentioned.

"Yeah. Dad took me to see him after the fire. He's a child psychol—psychol—"

"A child psychologist?" Devon supplied.

"Yeah, just like Dr. Raymond."

"I see. And Dr. Meyers and Dr. Raymond both told you the man in the flames was just a dream?"

He nodded.

"Did the man talk to you?"

Alex gnawed his lip. Devon's heart went out to him. She

wanted to comfort him, to tell him he didn't have to remember. But she needed to know—and something, some hidden feminine instinct, told her he wanted her to know.

"I only dreamed it."

"In the dream . . . did he talk to you?"

He nodded.

"What did he say?"

"I don't remember."

She spoke to him gently as she reached over and took his hand. "Are you sure, Andy? Or is it just that you don't like to remember?"

"I'm supposed to forget about it. It was only a dream."

She didn't want to push him and yet she might not get a second chance. "I had a dream like that once." His fingers felt cold where they laced with her own. "People said the same sort of things to me. They told me to forget it, but I couldn't. I tried . . . I tried very hard, but I just couldn't. I still can't."

Tears welled in Alex's blue eyes and slid down his thin pale cheeks. She could feel the tension in the hand she held onto. "Neither can I," he said.

"Oh, Alex." When Devon reached out and hugged him, his slim arms went around her neck and he clung to her, crying softly, trying very hard not to, his small body shaking with the effort. "It's all right. Maybe neither of us has to forget. Maybe it wasn't a dream at all, maybe it was real."

She felt the shake of his head. "It was a dream," he said against her shoulder.

"They can't know that for sure, Alex. They weren't there. Only you and I can know."

Alex drew a little bit away. "Do you really think so?"

"It's possible. I believe what I saw was real."

"The man in the flames . . . he told me to stay." There was raw pain in his voice, and a note of desperation. "The fire was all around me, but he told me to stay. I was crying . . . I was so afraid. The smoke was thick and black and i-it made me choke."

"Was your aunt Stell there?"

"She was on the floor crawling toward me. Then she stopped . . . I guess she couldn't breathe." Alex looked up at her. "The man in the flames . . . he kept begging me to stay. I didn't want to, but I couldn't leave. I tried, but I couldn't. Then the beam fell down a-and . . . that's all I remember till I woke up in the ambulance. My dad was there . . . He was crying. He never cries—never—but he was crying then."

Tears burned Devon's eyes, but she blinked them away. She hugged the little boy again. "It's all right, Alex. Sometimes grown-ups make mistakes. Sometimes they don't believe in people when they should."

He wiped the tears from his cheeks with the backs of his hands. "You believe it? You really believe it?"

"Yes. I believe it."

"But why couldn't Aunt Stell see him? If I could see him, why couldn't she?"

"I don't know, not for sure anyway. The important thing is that you believe in yourself and not what other people tell you, okay?"

He nodded. The tension was gone from his body. "Don't tell my dad I told you."

Devon smiled softly, ignoring the ache in her throat. "I won't."

"Are you coming again tomorrow?" He sounded as if, now that he'd told her what happened, somehow it might affect her feelings toward him.

"Of course, I am. We've got to get that picture of yours just right so we can get it framed and ready for Christmas."

"Do you think my dad would ever take me sailing?" His swift change of subject reminded her just how young he was.

She thought of how much Jonathan had once loved to sail, thought of Alex bound to his wheelchair, and wondered if Jonathan would be willing to risk taking the child out on the water. She forced a lightness into her voice as she answered, and hoped Jonathan would realize that it would be worth the risk.

"I think he might, if you told him how much you wanted to go."

Alex pondered that. "Maybe I'll ask him . . . after I give him the picture." But he didn't look like he believed it would happen, any more than she did.

"That's a good idea." Devon glanced around the room at the bright-colored quilts that covered the two narrow beds, at the ruffled curtains at the windows, and the airplane posters Alex had pinned up on the walls. It didn't matter how cheery the doctors had tried to make the room, Alex's family wasn't there to share it with him. His mother was dead, and his father wasn't even allowed to visit. That he liked the boy he roomed with, that the nurses were friendly, and the staff considerate didn't make it any better—nothing could take the place of home.

"You know, Andy, I think it's time you called me Devon, what do you think?"

He smiled shyly. "That would be great . . . Devon."

"Promise you'll work on your drawings?"

"I promise."

"Good, then I'll see you tomorrow." She wasn't sure she should hug him again, but he looked so forlorn in his oversized wheelchair, she couldn't resist. Surprisingly, Alex hugged her back.

"Bye," he said.

Fresh tears sprung to her eyes, so she turned away quickly, so he wouldn't see.

All the way home she fumed to think of what the child had been through. Why did adults always have to be so logical, so damned rational? Then again, up until lately she had been that way herself. Besides, most children probably would have been comforted to know that the man in the flames was nothing more than a terrible dream. Considering the trauma Alex had suffered, it wasn't surprising the doctors considered his story just a hallucination. What else could they think?

Devon caught a taxi back to her apartment, and a few moments after she arrived, the phone began to ring. It was Jonathan. He wanted to see her, and this time he wouldn't take no for an answer.

"I thought we agreed to work on this together."

"We did, but I've been busy."

"I thought we might discuss our interview with Linderman, be sure we get all our questions down on paper. I'll pick you up at seven."

"But I—"

"Wear something dressy."

"Dressy? But I thought you were coming over to work?"

-2"We'll have time to work before and after dinner. We're going out with Debra Dutton and Wayne Cummings. They're both VPs at Holidex. I want an update on the Kelovar problem, and I prefer to get it in person. Besides, it's Debra's birthday. She's been working overtime on this for weeks; taking her somewhere expensive for dinner is kind of a bonus."

"But we aren't—"

"I'll see you at seven."

He hung up before she could lodge any sort of a protest—and the truth was, she wanted to go. Maybe now that she had talked to Alex about the fire, she could tell Jonathan what she had done. If the truth were out in the open, maybe he would accept it. He'd be angry, no doubt, but it would be after the fact and a lot easier for him to deal with. Maybe she could go on with Alex's lessons as she had promised, at least until Christmas. She would give it some serious thought.

In the meantime, she would do as Jonathan asked and *wear something dressy.* Almost perversely, as she rummaged through her closet to pull out the smart black pearl-trimmed dinner suit she would wear, she also decided to wear her black lace garter belt and stockings. After that first night, she had started to wear them in the evenings whenever she dressed up. They made her feel feminine and sexy, and she wanted to feel that way tonight. Though, she assured herself, the result would not be to let Jonathan back into her bed.

Jonathan dressed in a low-vamped Bijan black worsted suit that emphasized his broad-shouldered build. He wore a white shirt, and gold-trimmed black onyx cuff links with a single diamond set in the center. He felt good in this particular suit and he wanted to look good tonight.

Reaching into the closet in the foyer, he pulled out his black cashmere overcoat with the sheared beaver collar. Then he turned and hit the elevator button. As the door slid open and he walked in, he thought of the evening ahead. It was still too soon to press Devon for a return of her affections, but he wasn't blind to the appeal he held for her and he intended to use that appeal every time he got the chance. If the way she'd been looking at him lately was any indication of the desire that was building inside her—inside both of them—he wouldn't have much longer to wait. But wait he would. And this time when it happened, he wasn't going to blow it.

"Evenin', sir." Henry stood beside the open door to the long black limousine.

"Good evening, Henry. Your back any better today?"

"Yes, sir, much better. I dare say, that grandson of mine is a 'andful, 'e is. Big like 'is daddy. I should of known better than to go liftin' 'im up that way."

Jonathan smiled. "I know what you mean. Alex is growing like a weed. It won't be long before lifting him in and out of that wheelchair is going to take a helluva lot of muscle."

Henry chuckled good-naturedly, but as the image lingered, Jonathan frowned. He would never get used to the idea of his son being handicapped, bound forever to a wheelchair. Never. Which reminded him of the errand he needed to run.

He tossed the small bag of clothes he was carrying into the back seat of the limo and climbed in. "I need to swing by the clinic, Henry. Alex forgot his clean underwear this morning."

"Right, guv'nor."

Of course he could have had them delivered this afternoon, but any excuse to look in on Alex was welcome. The car lurched away from the curb—dodging a dented white Cadillac whose driver was busy ogling a pretty little miniskirted redhead—and pulled out onto the street.

It wasn't long before they arrived at the clinic. Dodging the nurse at the front desk, Jonathan went straight to Alex's room to find him engaged with his roommate, Raleigh

Johnson, in a serious game of strategy between their two opposing plastic armies. G.I. Joe, it seemed, would never go out of vogue with little boys.

"Hi, Dad!" Alex pushed away from the desk where he sat playing and wheeled himself over toward the door. Though the two of them had been together just that morning, there was always something poignant in the greeting Jonathan received from Alex at the clinic, as if his staying there without Jonathan made their brief encounter somehow special.

"You forgot your underwear." Jonathan gave him a quick manly hug and handed him the small bag of clothes.

"Thanks."

He spent a few minutes listening to Alex's recount of the day's events, then the door to the room swung open, as he had expected it would.

"Good evening, Mr. Stafford." The usual note of disapproval rang in the stout woman's voice. His fatherly visits were not a part of his son's therapeutical curriculum, which Mrs. Livingston never failed to remind him.

"Alex forgot his clean clothes. I was just dropping them by."

"So I see." She glanced at the bag of laundry he had brought in but made no further comment.

"I'd better go, son. You guys have fun." He hugged Alex once more and crossed the room to the door. "Good night, Mrs. Livingston."

"Good night, Mr. Stafford."

Jonathan strode past her out into the hall, headed toward the clear glass doors in the lobby. He had almost made it when Mrs. Livingston's voice rang out just a few feet behind him.

"Mr. Stafford—"

"Yes?" His steps slowed, but he didn't turn around. Just glanced at her over his shoulder.

"I thought you might like to know how much Alex is enjoying his tutoring hour with Ms. James. I wasn't quite certain about it at first, but he does so like his drawing."

Jonathan slowly turned, coming to face her more squarely. "Ms. James?" he said softly. His jaw felt so tight he could hardly speak.

"Yes. Lynn James, the woman you sent to help Alex with his drawing."

"Devon Lynn James?"

"Yes."

"How"—he forced himself under control—"how did you know I was the one who sent her?"

"Why, she said so . . . and she showed me her credentials. Very impressive. And of course there was Alex. He recognized her right away."

"I see . . ."

Mrs. Livingston's thick gray brows drew together. "There isn't a problem, is there? I mean, everything seemed to be in order. I would have called if anything had looked out of place, but I didn't want to disturb you . . . not without cause. I-I mean, I know how busy you are."

It was the first time he had ever seen her on the defensive, and if he hadn't been so damned mad he might have enjoyed it. He took a deep breath and relaxed the hands he had balled into fists. "Everything's fine, Mrs. Livingston, at least for the moment. Don't be surprised, however, if Ms. James is unexpectedly forced to resign her position."

"But I don't understand."

"Neither do I." He clenched his teeth. "But I very soon will."

Jonathan climbed into the limo and slammed the door.

Grabbing the telephone hidden behind a panel on the wall, he dialed information for the number of Le Bernardin, pressed the appropriate buttons, and waited impatiently for his call to be answered.

"Hello, this is Jonathan Stafford. I'm afraid I won't be able to make my dinner reservation this evening. Yes, well, I appreciate that, however Ms. Dutton and Mr. Cummings should be arriving within the next half hour. I'd like you to convey my regrets, send them a bottle of Dom Perignon, wish Ms. Dutton a happy birthday, and put their dinner on my account. Tell them I expect to see one or both of them in my office at ten o'clock tomorrow morning."

A voice on the opposite end made sounds of efficient compliance. Jonathan rang off, and returned the receiver to its cradle, setting it down a little harder than he had intended. Damn her! Damn her to hell!

In front of her brownstone on Seventy-eighth, he climbed out of the car, crossed the sidewalk, and pressed the button on the intercom to her apartment.

"I'll be right there," she answered, her voice sounding tinny through the distortion of the speaker.

"I'd like to come up for a moment." He worked to keep his tone even and it was no easy task.

"All right, I'll buzz you in."

Jonathan listened for the sound, shoved open the heavy wooden door, and took the stairs two at a time up to her second floor apartment. He raised his fist to hammer out his arrival, caught himself, and instead knocked firmly but politely. He wanted to be sure he got in. Then again, that was never in question, just whether or not he would have to break down the door.

Devon smiled at him as she stood in the entry. "I'm almost ready. Just let me grab my coat."

She looked beautiful, and sexy as hell in her well-above-the knee pearl-trimmed black dinner suit. He remembered those long shapely legs wrapped around him, the feel of her small firm breasts in his hands as she moved beneath him on the bed. He remembered how it felt to be inside her, her lips ripe from his kisses. Jonathan's loins clenched, and the fact that he still wanted her—now, this very minute, knowing what she had done—made the anger seethe inside him and his fury turn to rage.

"You won't need a coat," he said harshly, stopping her midway to the closet. "We aren't going to dinner."

"We aren't?"

"No."

"Why not?" Her look turned uncertain. She approached him almost warily.

"Because I made the mistake of stopping by the clinic on my way over here. I had a brief but highly informative chat with Mrs. Livingston. I believe you two know each other rather well."

Devon froze. She had known this moment would come, sooner or later, and yet absurdly she'd prayed it would not. She lifted her chin and met the blazing silver glitter in his eyes. "Not at all well, really." She studied his face, feature by feature and read condemnation in every line. His jaw was set, his mouth hard, yet she still felt drawn to him as she never had another man.

"How could you do it?" he asked, moving toward her, almost stalking her.

She had never seen him quite this way, so dark and angry, so totally unreachable. For the first time she felt a little afraid.

"How could you look at him sitting there in his wheelchair, all the time planning some sort of inquisition?"

"I-It wasn't like that," she argued, backing away.

"Wasn't it?" Jonathan stepped closer, edging nearer, forcing her backwards until her shoulders came up against the wall and his breath fanned hotly against her cheek.

"I never meant to hurt him. I wouldn't do something like that."

He scoffed at that. "I think you'd do whatever it took to dig up the dirt you need for your seedy little story."

"That isn't true."

"I think it is. I think you'd take on anything or anyone who tried to keep you silent. You called me ruthless." His mouth curved up in a bitter half smile. "Sweetheart, I can't hold a candle to you."

Seeing the cold relentless fury in his eyes, Devon felt a surge of desperation. "I tell you it wasn't like that. I just wanted to talk to him. I knew you wouldn't let me. I-I had to do something."

Strong dark hands came up to her shoulders, pressing her harder against the wall. "If you were a man, I'd beat you within an inch of your life."

Devon swallowed hard. "Well, I'm not a man. I'm a woman."

Jonathan's hard gray eyes swept over her. There was contempt in that icy gaze. Contempt . . . and something more. "Yes . . . that you most certainly are. Which is why I've been such a fool."

Devon gasped as Jonathan's mouth came down hard over hers, brutal in its force. He wanted to hurt her, punish her. She tried to twist free, but he caught her face between his palms and tipped her head back, plunging his tongue into her mouth as he pressed his body against her. She could feel the tension in every muscle, every sinew, and yet the hands that gripped her didn't really hurt her. In fact they gentled even as she formed the thought. The lips that plundered didn't just take but began to give back.

Jonathan's hold remained firm, but there was something different about it now, something urgent yet almost possessive. She felt the soft moist heat of his lips, the hot demanding sweep of his tongue, and hers responded with the same sweet urgency. Her blood was pumping, her heart beating so fast she thought it must surely burst while the fiery heat of passion slid hotly through her veins.

Jonathan's hands left her face to cradle the back of her head and sift through her hair. He kissed her with tender determination, nibbling her lips, using his tongue in the most achingly sensuous manner. There was an urgency in his touch and a quiet desperation. Devon responded to it as to nothing else he could have done. For this brief moment, it didn't matter what lay between them; there was only this battering assault on her senses, this incredible driving need.

Jonathan deepened the kiss and Devon opened to him, sliding her arms around his neck, pressing herself against his muscular chest and the thick throbbing length that spoke its rigid promise from between them.

"Jonathan," she whispered when he broke away to trail kisses down her throat to the pulse fluttering wildly in the hollow. His hands worked the buttons on her jacket, he opened it, and unfastened the hook on her black pushup bra. Then his fingers were delving into the lacy cups, lifting her breasts, kneading them, rubbing the stiff little peaks until she moaned.

"I want you," he whispered gruffly. "God, how I want you."

In answer, Devon pulled his head down to hers and kissed him long and deep. She could feel his hands moving down her body, sliding her skirt up to caress her hips. They stilled for a moment when he felt her garter belt and stockings and only a tiny pair of black bikini panties. He made a husky sound in his throat as he eased the small bit of fabric over her hips and down her thighs. They slid to the floor, and she stepped out of them. Then he was parting her legs, running his hands along the insides of her thighs, cupping her sex then sliding his finger inside.

"So hot. So tight and wet."

Devon moaned.

"You like this, don't you?"

"Yes," she whispered, unable to stop herself, not really wanting to.

"And this?" He ran a second finger inside her, stroked the fleshy bud between her legs.

"Yes, oh, yes."

She heard the hiss of his zipper sliding down, then he was lifting her up, wrapping her legs around his hips, thrusting himself deep inside her.

"Oh, God." White heat surged through her body. Jonathan's big hands cupped the cheeks of her bottom, lifting her up then plunging her down on his rigid shaft again and again. Devon's head fell back. Her hair spilled over her shoulders as Jonathan drove into her, both of them nearly in frenzy. Just when she was certain he would climax, when she was sure she would, too, he stopped, holding himself carefully still.

"Hang onto my neck," he commanded, and when she complied, he carried her over to her small antique desk and sat her down on top of it. Still locked tightly inside her, her legs spread wide around him, he removed her suit coat and lacy pushup bra. Strong dark hands cupped her breasts. His tall hard body moved in rhythm to the pressure of his fingers on her nipples. Devon nearly sobbed at the feel of it. She arched her back and dug her nails into his shoulders, but he only pounded harder.

"This is what we could have had," he softly taunted. "This and so much more."

Devon heard the words and felt a sharp stab of pain. It was buried in the onslaught of passion and splendor and her towering need for him. "Jonathan, oh God, Jonathan." She came with a rush so explosive she thought she must certainly die of it. Liquid flames broke over her, a blaze of fiery orange heat and white-hot stars that spun out of control behind her eyes. And a tremor of pleasure so warm it made her body quake all over.

Jonathan came, too, long and hard, his tall frame shaking with the impact of his release. They stood there, still locked together, until Jonathan freed himself and zipped up his pants. Then he was pulling off her black high heels and tossing them away, lifting her into his arms, and carrying her into the bedroom. At the side of the bed, he stripped off his clothes with shift jerky movements while she slipped out of her skirt, unfastened and took off her stockings.

Jonathan whipped back the covers, lowered her to the mattress and came down on top of her, using his elbows to catch the balance of his weight.

With a flash of clarity, she realized that his anger had fueled his passion and he was once more hard and throbbing. He settled himself between her legs and with a single hard thrust, drove himself inside. Devon's hands came up to his shoulders, she felt the muscles bunch, felt the movement of sinew and bone. A melting heat slid through her body.

Though part of her wanted to stop him, to keep her heart safe from the feelings he evoked and the pain that waited beyond this fleeting moment of passion, another wilder, freer part wanted nothing more than to be swept up in the flames of his desire, to be joined with him and to stay that way forever.

It was that part that took over now, responding to his driving thrusts, the pounding deep rhythm he set up between them. It was that deeply feminine, hotly sensuous part that entwined her legs with his and arched her back to meet his demanding movements. It was that fiery reckless part that pulled his mouth down to hers, whose tongue slid inside, whose hands stroked the lean hard flesh over his ribs, traced the line of his flat copper nipple.

But when they had finished, it was the other, caring, trusting, loving part of her that knew by the tension in Jonathan's body that what he'd been working so hard to rebuild was at last at an end. It was that same yearning part of her that sobbed when he rolled away.

Jonathan swung his long legs to the side of the bed as if he didn't hear her and began to pull on his clothes.

"I can't let you go back," he said, his voice sounding flat and deceptively calm.

Devon wiped away her tears, wishing he hadn't seen them. "I don't really have to. I already found out what I needed to know."

His hand stilled on a button of his shirt. "He told you about the fire?"

"Yes."

He turned in her direction, his face an emotionless mask. "What did he say?"

Devon worked to keep her voice as even as his. "Mostly what the papers said . . . that he saw something terrible in the flames . . . he said it was a man."

"What else did he say?"

"He said no one believed him . . . and then he cried."

Jonathan leaned over her, bracing his hands against the headboard on either side of her face. "He cried? Are you sure?"

"Yes, but that really isn't so terrible, is it? I think he wanted to tell me about it. I think he needed to."

"Goddamn you! How could you force him to talk about something that has bound him to a wheelchair—possibly for the rest of his life?"

Devon sat up in the bed, pulling the sheet up to cover her breasts. She felt raw, exposed. "I didn't believe it would hurt him—I still don't. I think you underestimate him, just as you did your aunt. Alex is an intelligent little boy. His handicap doesn't make him any less so. Being in a wheelchair has nothing to do with it."

He turned on her, angrier by the moment. "He's my son, for God's sake. He means everything to me. You knew that, and yet you went behind my back and endangered his welfare. You betrayed me, Devon. Do you know how bad that hurts?"

"I didn't betray you." *I love you.* She knew that now with a certainty matched only by the knowledge that she had lost him. A hard lump swelled in her throat. "I didn't do anything that would hurt him. All we did was talk. How could that possibly hurt him?"

Jonathan's eyes searched her face, his expression changing from anger to uneasy suspicion. "How can it hurt him? Are you trying to make me believe you don't know?"

"Don't know what?" she asked, suddenly uneasy.

"That his paralysis is the result of his trauma. We're bound to have talked about it. You must have known."

"What are you talking about?"

"I'm talking about hysterical paralysis. Surely you knew. I don't believe we never discussed it."

"Explain it to me. I don't know exactly what that means."

For a moment he stood there staring. He raked a hand through his wavy black hair, but his eyes remained fixed on her face. "It means the falling beam did some damage to his vertebrae which in the beginning was assessed as the cause of his paralysis. Six months ago, the doctors re-evaluated their position. They unanimously agreed that Alex's condition was emotional, not physical. That's why he's staying at the clinic. You were there. You must have known."

Devon's mind began to whirl, fitting together the facts he had just revealed. "We never talked about Alex. I went out of my way to avoid the subject, since it obviously displeased you so much. Are you telling me that what he saw the night of the fire is what's keeping Alex in that chair?"

"I'm telling you it's mental not physical." Jonathan's face looked suddenly haggard. "Post-traumatic shock. I thought you knew . . . I thought you understood why I was so opposed to your talking to him."

Devon's stomach lurched with the ramifications of what she had done. "My God, Jonathan, do you really believe I would have gone to the clinic if I had known?" Fresh tears threatened and the ache in her throat began to swell. "What kind of a woman do you think I am? I want to write this story, but I wouldn't do anything—anything—I thought might harm that little boy."

Jonathan stood at the side of the bed, his hands clenching and unclenching, the expression on his face changing from harsh accusation to disbelief, and finally to acceptance. He assessed her a long moment more, then he sat down on the edge of the bed.

"I'm sorry. God, I'm so sorry. I knew it wasn't like you

to do something so reckless. I should have known you didn't understand. I should have realized I hadn't told you."

Devon leaned toward him and Jonathan swept her into his arms. Devon clung to him, the tears she'd been fighting sliding down her cheeks. "Jonathan, I . . . ," *love you so much.* But she couldn't bring herself to say it. It was too new, too raw. She had only recently discovered the truth herself. "If I had known, I never would have gone to the clinic. I would have found some other way to discover what happened or forgotten about it completely."

"It's all right. I'm the one who's to blame." He eased her away from him and wiped the tears from her cheeks with the edge of his thumb. He looked down at the rumpled bed then back to her, his eyes moving over her face and down her body. "But I'm not sorry for this." He reached out and cupped a breast, caressing it through the thin white cotton sheet. "I've wanted you every moment we've been apart. I've wanted you so much it hurt, and I almost walked away. I want you again right now."

"Then you're not angry with me anymore?"

He scowled but a faint smile curved his lips. "Of course, I'm angry. You did exactly what I told you not to. You're stubborn, and headstrong, and nothing but trouble. And I've missed you like hell."

Devon cupped his face with her hands, leaned over and kissed him. "I've missed you, too." More than he would ever know. "What about Alex? Is he all right?"

He nodded. "I saw him tonight. He was fine. I don't think your talk did any damage."

"Thank God." Devon closed her eyes and leaned against him. "I planned to go back tomorrow, but only to help him with his drawing. I promised him that, and I didn't want to break my word."

"Mrs. Livingston says Alex is really enjoying his lessons. Now that you understand the circumstances, it would be a shame if you didn't return, at least a few more times." Jonathan set her away from him, stood up and removed the cufflinks on the shirt he had just put on. He unbuttoned the front and drew it off his shoulders, leaving him once more naked.

"You're staying?" Short black hair curled appealingly across the width of his chest then arrowed down to surround his formidable sex.

"The only way you'll get me out of here tonight is to call the police."

Devon smiled. Her heart was swelling once more with the love she felt for him. "Maybe I should consider it—unless of course, you're willing to make some sort of . . . concession . . . for barging in here like an angry bull."

His heavy weight settled once more on the edge of the bed. He spread her legs, eased himself between her thighs, and kissed the flat spot below her navel.

"I think I know just the thing." His tongue slid across her skin into the tiny circular indentation, making Devon shiver. Jonathan moved lower and went to work in earnest. Devon forgot about calling the police. She only hoped the neighbors wouldn't hear her gasping moans, think she was being tortured, and wind up calling them for her.

Twenty

It was dawn when Devon awoke from a contented sleep. Jonathan shifted in the bed beside her, and she could hear his deep even breathing. She didn't move for a while, just lay there thinking about the events of the night before, of Jonathan, and of her conversation with Alex. His finger moved along her cheek. Devon turned her head on the pillow to look into his eyes, decidedly blue this morning in the dim early light, his features relaxed with contentment.

"What's going on in that devious mind of yours this morning, lovely *Tenshi?* I can almost see the gears turning behind those pretty green eyes."

Devon smiled softly. "To tell you the truth, I was thinking about Alex."

Jonathan sighed with false drama. "And here I was, sure you were thinking of me."

Devon poked him playfully in the ribs, then her look turned serious. "I was thinking about the talk I had with Alex at the clinic. I know this isn't a very good subject . . . I know you don't like to talk about the fire, but I was wondering if you would . . . just this once. I promise I won't ask again."

Jonathan released a lengthy breath. Adjusting his position on the mattress, he shoved his hands behind his head. "It's all right. We should have talked about him long ago. If we had, last night never would have happened."

Devon rolled to her side and propped herself up on an elbow. "Actually, some of last night was extremely pleasant. In fact I would say that most of it was extremely pleasant."

Jonathan chuckled, making a heavy rumbling in his chest. "I'm glad to hear it, since I've got an appetite for more of the same. As for my son, what would you like to know?"

"You said that six months ago the doctors ruled out the possibility of his injury being physical."

"That's right. They said what he had was called hysterical paralysis caused by post-traumatic shock. At the time, I wasn't sure if that was good news or bad."

"And now?"

"I'm still not sure."

"Why does he spend so much time at the clinic? I should think he'd be better off at home with his family."

"Sometimes I wonder about the wisdom of that myself. I agreed to try it, but only for a year. Dr. Raymond thinks the isolation, particularly from me, since we're so close, will increase Alex's desire to return to the life he had before. Given enough time and the right sort of therapy, they believe his wish to live a normal life and his desire to go home will eventually override the block that keeps him from moving his legs. That combined with the hours he spends in therapy with Dr. Raymond, trying to uncover the reason for his paralysis in the first place, should eventually enable him to walk. Of course during the time he's there, he also undergoes physical therapy, so his muscles will remain strong enough to support him."

"You said once that Dr. Raymond doesn't believe the fire is the cause of the problem."

"On the surface, of course, it is. The beam that fell on

Alex caused an injury to his spine that affected his legs, setting the stage for his hysterical paralysis. Except when his body recovered, his mind did not. Raymond thinks the true problem may have something to do with the death of Alex's mother. Some sort of anger for her abandonment, even though the accident that killed her was no fault of her own."

"Is that what you believe?"

"Maybe. It's as good an explanation as any."

"Well, I don't. I think Florian had something to do with it."

"Florian? You mean the man in the flames? I don't believe it."

"Why not? Alex said the man tried to make him stay. That he begged him to stay."

"So?"

"So Alex is a Stafford, black-haired, blue-eyed, dark complected. We know Bernard had black hair and blue eyes. He probably looked much the same. If Florian thought Alex was his son, he might have wanted him to stay. Alex said he tried to leave but he couldn't."

"He couldn't because a beam had fallen across his legs."

"I think he meant, before that. I'm telling you, Jonathan, when I was in that house, I felt the most incredible compulsion to stay there. I'm a full-grown, rational adult and yet I had to tear myself away. What might happen to a frightened child in a terrifying situation, facing a man engulfed in flames?"

"Need I remind you the house you were in was different from the one that burned down?"

"I know, but the actual murder took place in the old Stafford mansion. Maybe ghosts can move around."

"That's hardly likely, but even if they could, what does

any of this have to do with Alex's situation as it is today? The fire happened three years ago. The doctors believe he's put it behind him."

-2"What if he hasn't? What if it haunts him just like it's haunted me? Do you realize that for three long years that child has been told that what he saw was only a dream. He told his story to his father, inadvertently to the newspapers, to doctors and nurses—none of whom have ever believed him. What if he's bottled it all up inside him? What if he's wondering why, if it's only a dream, he can't forget it?"

Jonathan sat up on the bed. The sheet fell, settling low on his narrow hips. "He told you that? He told you he can't forget?"

"Yes."

"And then he cried."

"Yes."

"He never cries. Not since the fire."

"God, Jonathan, maybe that's important."

"And maybe it isn't. Look, Devon, I don't want you involved in this—I've told you that from the start. I've given Dr. Raymond a year, half of which is over. He's one of the country's most prominent child psychologists while you, on the other hand, have never even had a baby."

"Neither has he," Devon said stubbornly, and Jonathan's mouth curved up.

"I'm not going to fight with you. Not when we've finally decided we're both on the same side. But I want your promise that you won't do anything more to interfere with Alex's treatment."

"Couldn't we at least tell Dr. Raymond what happened?"

"You'll be there tomorrow. If you want to tell him, be my guest. But don't expect him to be overjoyed with what you've done. Or expect him to believe in any of this. I hardly think he'll be willing to include a session on ghosts in Alex's therapy."

Devon sighed. "You're probably right, but I still think it might be important."

Jonathan leaned over and kissed the side of her neck. "Promise me you won't interfere." He continued down her throat and along her shoulder, kissing her until she finally agreed.

"All right, I promise."

"Good." Jonathan tugged her beneath him. "Now let's talk about something more pleasant." His hand found her breast and he began to tease her nipple. "Better yet, let's don't talk at all."

Jonathan silenced her laughter with a kiss. Reaching beneath the covers, she guided his thick shaft inside her. Jonathan was right—she didn't feel like talking anymore.

Dee Wills looked up from the paperwork on her desk just in time to see Jonathan walk in.

"Were you able to hold the fort?" he asked, flashing a charming white smile, the kind Dee hadn't seen in days.

"As usual, the Indians are on a rampage," she countered. "Tri-Star would like nothing better than to stage a raid, and Bartlett Fiberglass is still trying to scalp us, but the good news is Pacific American approved the design of the new canoes." They hadn't played word games in ages, not like they used to, but the smile on Jonathan's face, and his jocular attitude were a good sign things were getting back to normal.

He chuckled at her quick repartee, sat down at his desk, and began to shuffle through the stack of messages that had already piled up that morning. "I'm expecting Debra Dutton or Wayne Cummings for a meeting at ten o'clock."

"They've already called to confirm. I told them you were in conference but that odds were you'd be available for your scheduled appointment." In fact, she couldn't believe he had walked in only now. Jonathan hadn't been late to the office in the past two years. Usually, he was several hours early.

"They're both coming?" he asked.

"That's what Ms. Dutton said."

"Must be bad news. If they had something positive to report, they wouldn't need each other to bolster their courage."

"You're probably right." He usually was. "Coffee?" He looked like he could use it. Though his skin was robust, his expression relaxed, it was obvious by the slight purple smudges beneath his eyes that he had gotten very little sleep.

"Sounds great. Thanks."

She brought him a cup while he poured over the paperwork on his desk. When Dutton and Cummings arrived, Jonathan asked Dee to sit in and take notes on their meeting.

It didn't last very long.

The two Holidex VPs gave their summation of the progress they had made in their campaign against Tri-Star Marine, then shifted nervously in their chairs at the end of the long teakwood conference table, awaiting Jonathan's reply.

"That's it?" He sounded deceptively calm. "That's all you've got to report?"

"I'm afraid so, Mr. Stafford." Wayne Cummings nervously cleared his throat. He stood about five-foot-ten, had thinning brown hair and light blue eyes. He was oddly shy for a corporate executive. But he was extremely efficient, which was why he'd advanced through the company.

"We've tested for wind damage, water deterioration, the effects of brine, erosion by ice and sand, even tested for possible negative effects of human body oils, thinking maybe some of the fittings that get a lot of hand contact might show signs of wear."

He shook his head. "Nothing. The truth is, Kelovar appears to be exactly what Tri-Star claims it is—the best damned substance ever invented for boat fittings—and probably a lot of other things. On top of that, Tri-Star has incredibly good management. They're making the most of this breakthrough, and our customers are beginning to abandon us like a sinking ship."

"If Tri-Star is such a formidable opponent," Jonathan said dryly, "maybe I should buy stock in the company." He cast Wayne Cummings a sidelong glance. "Listening to your enthusiasm for your competitor's product isn't exactly what I had in mind when I called this meeting." He shoved back his chair and came to his feet. "I'm well aware that a good deal of what you're saying is true. But my instincts say there's something we've overlooked. There's a flaw in that product—there has to be. Nothing's as good as Tri-Star says Kelovar is."

"I don't know," Debra Dutton put in, candid and forthright as always. "Fiberglass certainly changed the boating industry."

"Fiberglass has its drawbacks and Kelovar has them, too. We've got to expand our thinking. We can't afford to leave any stone unturned." He paused to search their faces. "Let's go through those files one more time."

So they did. Still to no avail. The meeting progressed along that dismal vein until the two VPs rather sheepishly left the office.

"At least they enjoyed the champagne," Dee said, remembering the thanks Jonathan had received for sending it to them the night before. "Too bad you couldn't make it."

Jonathan smiled. "Not really. As a matter of fact, I imagine my evening was far more pleasant than theirs."

Dee smiled, too. "I'm glad to hear it."

Jonathan's smile grew wider. "Not nearly as happy as I am."

It had to be the James woman. Dee knew he was seeing her again. For Alex's sake as well as any company emergency that might come up, Jonathan kept her carefully posted on his whereabouts. She also knew, though he hadn't said so, that things hadn't been progressing quite the way he had planned. Apparently they were now, and Dee was glad. Jonathan needed a woman in his life, a woman he could care for. He deserved to be happy. More than any man she knew.

She glanced at him sitting behind his desk, with his dark head bent diligently over his work. For the first time in years, he was letting down his guard with a woman. He seemed happy, contented. And yet she knew enough about the situation—about Jonathan—to know there could still be problems. Possibly some very big ones.

She just hoped Jonathan wasn't too involved to see things clearly. Or that if a problem did come up, he wouldn't use it as an excuse to run away from his feelings.

Because if either of those things happened, the odds were very good that one of them would wind up getting hurt.

Dee would go one step further. Odds were better than average one of them would end up with a broken heart.

"Tough day?" Devon eyed Jonathan, who stood in the hall outside her door. Worry lines etched his forehead. A shoulder was propped wearily against the jamb.

"Let's just say, I hope yours was better."

"Too tired to go shopping?" Henry was waiting with the limo.

Jonathan straightened his tall frame and stepped inside the door. "I was, a few minutes ago." He reached for her, circled her waist with an arm, and drew her against him. "Now that I've seen you, I'm feeling a fresh burst of energy." He smiled roguishly and began to nibble her neck.

Devon smiled back. "If you've got that much energy, we'd better get going. The sooner we get finished, the sooner we can come home."

"Right. To tell you the truth, I'm looking forward to our little excursion. Dee usually does my Christmas shopping—all but Alex's presents. This year, Maddie and the kids are in town. Aunt Stell's feeling well enough to join us. We're all going to celebrate Christmas together."

"That's wonderful, Jonathan."

"I was hoping you'd be able to join us."

Devon smiled, warmed that he had invited her. "I wish I could. Unfortunately, my parents would be crushed if I abandoned them."

"I'm not asking you to. There's Christmas Eve and Christmas Day. I'll go to your house; you can come to mine. We'll work it out somehow."

It sounded wonderful. "All right." He kissed her to seal the bargain.

In the limo, Devon told Jonathan about her day, the hour she had spent with Alex, which had gone smoothly, and of her brief conversation with Dr. Raymond, which hadn't.

"He did exactly what you predicted. Chewed me out for bringing up the subject to Alex, said it was no longer relevant at this point in his treatment. And he threatened to get me fired if I ever brought the subject up again."

"Fired?" Jonathan repeated, his smooth black brow arching upward. "Now that might take some doing . . . considering the benefits I'm receiving from Alex's tutor on the side."

Devon poked him playfully in the ribs and he grunted. They talked for a while. Jonathan told her about his meeting with the VPs from Holidex and their continuing Tri-Star problem, and Devon told him how hard she had been working on *Traces,* that the book was really progressing, and that she felt sure she'd be able to meet her deadline. Then she mentioned the call she'd received from Christy, wanting her to meet with Sara Stone, the trance medium from the Insight Book Store.

"I'm not going to tell you whether you should see her or not," Jonathan said. "So far your instincts have been right. Listen to them. If you want to go, I'll go with you."

"Even after Zhadar?"

One corner of his mouth curved up. "Especially after Zhadar. As I recall, that's the first time I saw your beautiful breasts."

"Jonathan!"

His merciless teasing continued throughout the evening, and Devon enjoyed every delicious moment of it. They shopped until the stores closed, mostly at Saks and Bonwit Teller, but a number of gifts were purchased at small intimate boutiques along the crowded sidewalk. Jonathan dropped money into the pots of every Salvation Army Santa on the street and gave to a few other charities just for good measure.

"You know what they say," he teased, "he knows if you've been bad or good . . . In your case you've been very good, but in mine . . . ?" He shrugged his wide shoulders, and Devon laughed.

"You're good, all right. Extremely good. But it's better to be safe than sorry. We'll see how good you are when we get home."

The hours that followed were some of the best they had ever shared. They made love twice and then fell asleep, since they had been up so late the night before. Jonathan held her in his arms while they slept, and she had never felt more secure.

In the morning, they showered together and she watched him shave, her heart swelling with love at the oh-so-masculine sight of him. He stood naked in front of the sink, his long sinewy legs slightly splayed, muscle moving over bone, his taut round buttocks flexing with every movement. It was amazing how just watching him could make her body feel warm all over.

"Ready?" he called to her from the living room, half an hour later.

Devon nodded. Wearing a red wool suit, she accompanied him down to the limo and they set off. Today was the day of their scheduled appointment with Francis Linderman. Stopping only once, at Jonathan's apartment so he could change into fresh clothes, the long black Lincoln rolled off down the street.

Dressed in a pair of gray wool slacks and a navy blue sport coat, a pin-striped shirt and burgundy tie, Jonathan settled himself back against the butter-soft tufted gray leather seat.

"This is getting to be a habit," he said, referring to his early morning return to his apartment. "I think maybe I'll leave a few things over at your place . . . that is, if you don't mind." He looked at her with a mixture of uncertainty and expectation.

"I don't mind," she said softly, and he smiled.

They took the Lincoln Tunnel onto the Jersey Turnpike then went south on U.S. 1, finally arriving in Princeton. Since Devon claimed she was starving, and they had left in plenty of time to make their ten o'clock appointment, Jonathan told Henry to stop at the Nassau Inn in Palmer Square. The coffee shop was open, but by the time they sat down, Devon discovered that her stomach was too jittery to eat very much. Instead of the robust breakfast she'd envisioned, they wound up with coffee and sweet rolls.

"Why so nervous?" Jonathan asked, sensing her growing uneasiness. He took a sip from the steaming white china mug he cradled between his hands.

"I don't know. I'm a little surprised myself." Devon glanced away. "Maybe I'm afraid he'll laugh at me."

Jonathan reached over and covered her fingers. "He isn't going to laugh, I promise you. If he does, I'll belt him one."

Devon smiled. "Black belt or brown?"

Jonathan laughed. "Black, as a matter of fact." They paid the check, left the restaurant, and drove on to the Princeton campus, arriving there in time for Jonathan to give her a brief tour of his alma mater.

"That's Nassau Hall." He pointed toward one of the buildings they passed. "It was built in 1756. During the Revolutionary War it served as a hospital. For a while it was home to the Continental Congress."

"I didn't realize this place was that old."

"It's definitely been here awhile."

"Did you like going to school here?" Devon asked.

"I liked it, but I was edgy, anxious to graduate and get out in the business world. I finished in three years."

Not really surprising, considering his intelligence. "Is this where you got interested in art? I read somewhere that they have sculptures from the Putnam Collection displayed right on campus."

"Nevelson, Calder, Lipschitz, Moore, and Picasso that I can think of offhand. The art museum has some beautiful Chinese paintings and bronzes. I used to go there often, and yes, in a way I suppose that was what got me started. After my father died and I took over the company, I was so busy I needed something to help me relax. I remembered how peaceful it was in the gallery, how much I enjoyed the Oriental paintings. I thought collecting might be a diversion, and it was."

Though Jonathan did his best to put Devon at ease, she had trouble concentrating on his words. Her state of nerves was increasing by the moment. By the time they reached Linderman's office and she had climbed out of the car, she was so jittery she tripped and nearly went sprawling. Only Jonathan's quick hands on her waist kept her from embarrassment, for which he received a nervous smile of thanks.

"Take it easy," he soothed. "Everything's going to be fine."

"I know, I'm just . . . I'll be glad when this is over."

Jonathan seemed a little surprised at her reaction. With Zhadar she hadn't been this nervous. Not when she had told him her story, either. But this was different. Linderman was an expert. According to his books, he had interviewed hundreds of people. His studies involved the total spectrum of psychic phenomena. He would know what she had been through—but would he really understand?

"All right?" Concern lined Jonathan's features as they stood outside Linderman's door.

Devon just nodded. Her chest felt tight, and her palms were damp. She hoped Jonathan hadn't noticed.

"Let's go on in." Linderman had already been informed of their arrival.

Jonathan turned the knob and led Devon into his office, which was small and high-ceilinged, with bookshelves all the way to the top and every space filled with hardbound volumes. Stacks of paper three feet deep sat on the corner of Linderman's scarred walnut desk, and files were heaped haphazardly around the floor. There was a general sense of disarray, and yet the pipe in the ashtray, the slightly crooked gold-framed awards and diplomas on the wall, the pictures of Linderman's wife and children sitting among the debris on his desk gave the room an air of comfortable warmth.

"Good morning, Ms. James, Mr. Stafford. It's a pleasure to meet you." Francis Linderman was a graying, thin-boned, skeletal image of a man. He stood taller than Jonathan, with slightly opaque pale blue eyes and veined translucent skin. On the surface he looked forbidding, but when he smiled, his stark features softened, and a gentleness came into his face.

"Thank you for seeing us." Devon forced the words past the dryness in her throat, which refused to ease even at Linderman's look of compassion. Jonathan reached over and shook the thin man's outstretched hand.

"Why don't we sit down?" Linderman suggested, eyeing her with a bit of speculation.

Devon merely nodded. She'd begun to feel a little light-headed.

Gesturing with a long-boned finger, Linderman urged them toward a grouping of worn leather chairs in one corner, and all of them sat down.

"Now, Ms. James, why don't you tell me a little bit about what brought you here."

Devon wet her lips and tried to smile. "I read your books.

I thought they were . . . your research . . . you seemed to know a lot about this sort of thing."

Kindly pale blue eyes moved over her face. "That isn't exactly what I meant." He noticed the way she toyed with a fold in her red wool skirt. "There's nothing to be nervous about. We're only going to talk. When Mr. Stafford arranged our meeting, he told me a bit of your circumstances and sent me a copy of your notes. I gather you had a very unpleasant experience."

She smiled tremulously. "Very unpleasant."

"You aren't the first person, you know. Lots of people have experienced psychic phenomena."

"I know. I've been reading a lot about it. But reading about it and actually having it happen are two different things."

Again that look of concern. "You seem abnormally upset, Ms. James. Let me be blunt with you. Did you have a sexual encounter? Were you raped?"

Devon's gasp filled the room. "R-raped? No, no, of course not. Could something like that really happen?"

"As a matter of fact, I've interviewed quite a number of women who claim it has. It isn't always rape, however. About eighty percent of widowed women report a sexual experience with their dead husbands. Apparently it can be very pleasant."

Devon felt a blush that began at the roots of her pale blond hair and went all the way to her toes. Secretly, she had wondered about the hands she had felt that night in the yellow room. The large, blunt, incredibly gentle hands she had wildly thought belonged so some dark foreigner.

"Ms. James? Are you still with us, my dear?"

"I-I'm sorry, Dr. Linderman. Something like that did happen to me that night. Up until now, I never really gave it much credence. Nothing has come up in my investigation to support it, so I simply ignored it. I . . ." Devon stared down at her hands.

"We needn't discuss it, if you don't wish to. Let me just tell you that apparitions—ghosts if you will—are often quite amorous. Some of them seem to have a very strong sexual nature. Given the fact that they have difficulty distinguishing past from present—a physical being from a nonphysical one—if they encounter someone receptive, they often take advantage."

Devon's face flamed even redder. She had gone farther than that—she had actually encouraged him! She couldn't bear to look at Jonathan, so she didn't.

"Since you seem to be having a problem with this topic, why don't we leave it for the moment? Tell me about your experience, what happened in Stafford and exactly how you felt."

With careful detachment, Devon relayed the story of her night at the inn. She told him about Florian and that she believed he had accidentally murdered his son. She mentioned his abuse of Annie, referred to the notes she had taken that Jonathan had sent ahead, and the research she had done confirming her theory. She told Linderman about Alex and her belief that the incidents were connected, at which time Jonathan broke in to disagree.

"I'm willing to admit that on the surface it looks as though Alex's 'man in the flames' may somehow be related to what happened to you that night at the inn, but the occurrences took place in two separate locations. Surely the same entity couldn't be involved in both incidents."

"Quite the contrary," Linderman said. "You see, a ghost is merely an ectoplasmic manifestation. It has no past, no present, no future. It knows no such thing as space and time. A true apparition can materialize anywhere it wishes. In any form it wishes. It can be the person it was as a child or an adult, or something bearing little resemblance to a human being."

"A *true* apparition?" Devon repeated. "Do you mean as opposed to a fake or fraud?"

"No. I mean some apparitions have no substance. They are merely part of a haunting. Over the past few years, those of us in the field have come to believe that certain traumatic events may leave an impression much like a tape recording. Intensity of the event seems to affect it. Cold may be a factor, dampness of climate. Recently we've been working on something called ley lines—sort of a connect-the-dots of reported hauntings, which indicates there may be a grid of electromagnetic force lines around the earth where hauntings are more likely to occur. Interestingly, Stonehenge and other stone megaliths, as well as a number of ancient churches fall along the grid, suggesting that in archaic times the power of such a line may have been felt by the surrounding peoples."

"If that's the case," Devon said, "there should be more ghosts in cold, damp climates than there are in hot desert regions."

"It certainly seems that way. Great Britain, for example, and of course, your New England experience would certainly fit the parameters."

"But you don't think this is just a *haunting,*" Devon said, picking up the train of his thoughts.

"In a haunting, the sequence of events never changes. The apparition makes the same journey again and again, retracing the moments exactly as they occurred. Your encounter suggests something different. If the two phenomena are linked—and given the fact that a child is the root of both occurrences, I highly suspect they are—then the assumption is that the spirit in question is able to move from place to place as well as cause physical manifestations of his outrage. If that is the case, then what we have is indeed an apparition in the truest sense of the word. Possibly a very malevolent one."

"What do you mean by 'physical manifestation of his outrage'?" Jonathan asked as he shifted in his chair. Devon wondered if some of her nervousness had begun to rub off on him.

"I'm speaking of the fire."

"The fire?" His deep voice rose a little. "You believe Florian may have started the fire?"

"What do you believe?"

"That it was electrical. The house was a hundred years old."

"And completely remodeled," Devon countered. "Maybe Florian used his power to overload the circuits."

Jonathan looked skeptical. "Is that possible, Doctor?"

"It is highly uncommon to come in contact with an entity who can command such a colossal psychic force. It is, however, quite possible."

Jonathan fell silent. The clock on Linderman's desk seemed to tick a little louder.

"In your newest publication," Devon said, "you mentioned a connection between anxiety and psychic perception." She swallowed against the dryness in her throat. Her heart was still beating a little too fast. "In the past, I suffered quite severely from this condition. Could you explain how that might have affected what happened in Stafford?"

"Is that what you were feeling here today?"

She wet her lips. "Yes."

"Even as we speak, I presume."

"Is it that obvious?"

"Yes, my dear, I'm afraid it is. As to how it may affect psychic phenomena, we haven't enough research on the subject to know. At this stage, it's merely an hypothesis—one I personally favor. Coupled with the right-mindedness you most surely have developed from your writing, I'd say there's a very good chance your perceptions are often quite strong."

"Is someone studying that now?"

"Laboratory testing for extrasensory perception has met with limited success, I'm afraid. It takes hours of tedious experimenting to achieve the repeatability demanded by the scientific community in order to accept the phenomenon as genuine. Personally, I prefer competent, repeated and observed natural phenomenon."

"Considering the elusive nature of the subject," Jonathan said, "I can see where that makes sense."

Linderman nodded. "It's frustrating really. We know it's there. Millions of people experience it every day, and yet we can't figure out how it works, or even why. It's rather like trying to nail chocolate pudding to the wall."

"But my anxiety may have been a conduit," Devon persisted, "an avenue for knowing what happened in the house."

"It may have enhanced your clairvoyance—enabling you to sense what happened by means of a document or some other object in the house which contained the information."

"Not very likely."

"Or you might have known through psychometry—touching an object which has trapped the psychic energy of the trauma; or even by retrocognition—your mind simply traveling backwards in time to see and relive what happened in the house—kind of like watching an old movie."

Devon frowned. "I'm beginning to get an idea of just how uncertain all of this is."

"To make things even more confusing, you might have found out by telepathy—in which case you perceived what happened from someone in the house who knew the story."

"I don't think anyone knows."

"Theoretically, the spirits know," Jonathan pointed out.

"That's correct, Mr. Stafford, assuming they're true apparitions."

"It's all so complicated. Will we ever really know what happened?"

"Probably not, but it doesn't really matter. What matters is that during a psychic experience you discovered a young boy's death at the hands of his father and a young woman's physical abuse. Your research has so far upheld your discovery, which forces us to conclude that Florian Stafford may well be a malevolent spirit, one who may be, for reasons only he knows for certain, entrapping the souls of at least two of his victims—and that he might be dangerous."

"Dangerous?" Jonathan leaned forward in his chair, his expression suddenly alert.

"Need I remind you what happened to your son?"

Jonathan's face grew a shade paler beneath his swarthy skin.

"I'm not trying to frighten you, Mr. Stafford. I'm only examining some of the possibilities you came here to discuss." Linderman leaned back in his chair and looked down at the note pad resting across his lap. "Who currently resides in the house?"

Jonathan settled back once more. "Ada and Edgar Meeks. They manage the inn, and assuming certain conditions are met, they'll eventually be the owners. They've been living there for the past several years."

"And they've reported no incidents?"

"Not that I know of."

"Elwood Dobbs thinks they might just be keeping things quiet," Devon said to Jonathan, then turned to Linderman. "He's a handyman in Stafford who occasionally works on the house. He says there've been a number of ghost stories involving both the Stafford mansions over the years."

Linderman assessed her for a moment. "I sense a certain urgency in you, Ms. James, a determination to somehow deal with this problem. May I ask what it is you plan to do?"

She didn't falter. "I want to release Bernard and Annie. If my perceptions are correct, then they've asked me to help them. I feel a deep responsibility for their trust. I intend to do what they've asked."

"I was afraid you were going to say that. What do you propose?"

"Whatever she's planning," Jonathan broke in, "she isn't going to do it on her own. Not if there's the slightest chance it may be dangerous."

"We were hoping you might be able to tell us what to do," Devon said.

Linderman tapped his pencil on his note pad. His thick gray brows were drawn together in a pensive frown. "In some cases, parapsychologists have used what's called *appeasement.* In a building over the site of an ancient grave, for example. The supposition is that if the spirits are willing to accept some token of the current user's goodwill, they will desist in whatever unwanted activity they've been engaged in."

"Florian isn't likely to be appeased," Devon said darkly.

"So I gather. My advice is to contact a medium—not some quack, mind you, but someone with legitimate talent.

You're going to need to reach this entity. You're going to have to let him know that you know what he has done. You'll have to make him face the facts and to convince him to go on. Once he has, the others will be free."

Devon sat up straighter. "There's a woman named Sara Stone. She works at the Insight Book Store. A friend of mine has been pressing me to meet her."

"I know Mrs. Stone, at least by reputation. I believe she's quite legitimate. She's worked on a number of cases, some as far away as California."

"Then we'll go see her," Jonathan said.

"My advice, exactly."

At last Devon started to relax. The interview was almost over and as nervous as she had been, it hadn't been as bad as all that.

"Thank you, Dr. Linderman." Extending her hand, she rose from her chair and so did Jonathan. "We really appreciate your time." Jonathan shook hands, too.

"One more thing," Linderman added, stopping them as they turned to leave. "As I said, I don't want to frighten you, but if this entity—Florian—is as powerful as I suspect, there's a very good chance he's holding not only his victims, but also the people who live in the house."

"Edgar and Ada Meeks?" The skepticism returned to Jonathan's voice. "What are you talking about?"

"What I'm talking about, Mr. Stafford, is possession. It's an ugly word, as well it should be. Fortunately, most of us have the power to keep out unwanted spirits. It isn't difficult really, it just takes the will. But some of us are vulnerable. People who suffer from drug and alcohol abuse, those fraught with emotional instability, paranoia—people who suffer undue stress and the resulting depression or anxiety."

Unconsciously, Devon's hold grew tighter on Jonathan's

hand. "You're saying Florian might be able to gain some sort of hold over me." That same thought had occurred to her that night in the house. It had occurred again as she had tried to leave.

"As with everything we've talked about, I'm only saying it's possible. Assuming our postulations are correct, what we have here is an entity trapped in a vortex of incredible emotional force. If you don't feel you're strong enough—if you have the slightest doubt about yourself or your ability to control this situation—I advise you to turn your back on this matter before it goes one step farther."

"I can't do that."

"Then at least consider letting Mr. Stafford and Mrs. Stone proceed without you."

"It isn't an option," Devon said stubbornly.

Jonathan took her arm, his grasp a little too firm. "Thank you, Doctor. Devon and I will discuss what you've told us. You've been incredibly helpful. Thank you for seeing us."

"I hope you'll let me know the outcome. If I weren't so heavily committed, I believe I should like very much to go along on this one."

"We'll let you know," Devon promised.

"Good-bye, Doctor." Jonathan led her outside and closed the door.

Devon turned to face him. "I actually think you're becoming convinced."

"I'll be convinced the day I meet my dead uncle. In the meantime, I've promised to keep an open mind. Which means I have to face the fact that my son is in a wheelchair and Francis Linderman believes Florian Stafford may have had something to do with it. Now you're involved. I don't want anything happening to you."

"I'm going through with this, Jonathan."

"Not if I won't let you. I own that house, remember? You won't set one foot inside unless I say so." He jerked open the door to the limo, which had just rolled up to the curb.

Devon got in, angry and drained and feeling the bite of his words. "Damn you." She slid away from him as he got in and closed the door. Tears stung the backs of her eyes. "I have to do this, don't you see—I have to. You said you understood. You said—" Her voice broke on the last word, and she swallowed against the ache in her throat.

Jonathan sighed into the warm interior of the car. His hand came up to her chin, turning her to face him. "I'm sorry. You're right. This is your project—you have to see it through. If I were you, I'd feel exactly the same."

"Then you'll tell Ada Meeks to let me into the house?"

"I'll tell her. I'm returning the receipt books she sent to my accountant. I'll drop a note in the package. But I want you to promise you won't go in there without me—at least not at night."

Devon rolled her eyes. "Are you kidding? If I could avoid it, I wouldn't go back there at all."

Jonathan put his arm around her shoulders and settled her against him, then leaned over and kissed her. "Let's go home."

"Aren't you going back to the office?"

"Most of the day is already shot. I'll stop and pick up the paperwork I need to finish, and take it home."

"To my place?"

Gray-blue eyes fixed on her face. "Unless you've got plans."

"I plan to snuggle up with you in front of a nice warm

fire and forget anything and everything I ever heard about ghosts."

"At least for tonight," he put in.

Devon sighed wearily. "At least for tonight."

Twenty-one

"You're awfully pensive this evening." Jonathan toyed with a strand of Devon's silky blond hair. Lying on the sofa in her apartment in front of a slow-burning fire, he cradled her spoon-fashion in front of him. Earlier they had made love. They had showered together, pulled on robes—his now with its own special hook on her bathroom door—then come into the living room to read and relax.

"Am I?"

He nodded, though she couldn't see him. "Want to tell me about it?" Beneath the fluffy yellow terry, he felt her tense.

"Not really."

"Mind if I take a guess?"

She turned to look at him over her shoulder while he absently stroked the curve of her hip. He liked the way she was built, lean and racy. He liked her height and the graceful way she moved. He liked the way they fit together like two interlocking pieces of a puzzle, two meshing cogs on a wheel.

"It's nothing important, really."

"No?" He traced her jawline with his finger, thinking of other things about her he liked. The way she cared about people, the warmth in her eyes when she looked at his son, the way she made him forget his troubles and enjoy life in the present. She had forced him back into the stream of life, made him feel alive as he hadn't in years.

"I don't suppose this 'nothing' could have anything to do with the 'nothing' you didn't want to discuss with Dr. Linderman—the sexual experience you had at the inn?"

Her brow arched in surprise at his perception. "I might have only imagined it."

"Dr. Linderman doesn't seem to think so."

"I really don't want to talk about it . . . especially not with you."

"Why not? Are you afraid I won't believe you?"

"No. It's just that . . . that I was in bed with Michael at the time."

Jonathan bent his head and kissed the place behind her ear. "I know you had a life before I met you, Devon. It doesn't thrill me to think of you with Galveston, but that's in the past. I'd like to know what happened."

Devon sighed and sat up turning to face him. "Maybe it really was nothing. The fact is I'm not sure." Using as little detail as possible, she told him about the hands she had felt. Big hands, rough but gentle. "When it was over, I sensed something about him . . . or it . . . or whatever it was. I remember thinking he was a foreigner, olive-skinned, and for a moment, I imagined he was my lover."

"I don't blame you," Jonathan teased, working to lighten the moment. "He had to be better than Galveston."

Devon laughed softly, and he felt her tension ease. "It was very sensuous, Jonathan. I felt worshipped. Loved. Of course, at the time I thought it was just some sort of erotic fantasy. Later I wondered about it, but when I turned up nothing to account for another man's presence in the house, I thought I'd been right in the first place and it was just an illusion."

"You're certain it wasn't Florian? Linderman said an apparition could materialize in different forms."

"It wasn't Florian. Whoever—whatever—this was, I sensed tenderness and caring. I sensed nothing but evil from Florian."

A chill swept down Jonathan's spine. This whole thing still seemed insane. Grisly and surreal and totally out of the realm of possibility. And yet there was evidence to the contrary he couldn't ignore. He had agreed to help Devon. To do that, he had to accept her premise: that there was some sort of presence in the house. He had to accept what had happened between Florian and Annie—and the brutal tragic death of Florian's son. If he did, then he also had to accept that this might also be real.

"Whether it happened or not," Jonathan finally said, "I don't want you worrying about it. It doesn't change anything between us, and it isn't involved in what you've set out to do. At least at this point we've got no reason to think it is."

Devon sank back down on the sofa beside him. "I suppose you're right. Besides, it could have been any number of things. Maybe it was just the tension in the atmosphere of the house. Maybe I got several different things mixed up."

"Maybe." He didn't remind her that her other perceptions had already been corroborated on several different levels. So far, she hadn't been wrong. "I want to ask you a favor."

She tilted her head back against his chest and looked up at him through a sweep of dark gold lashes. With her high cheekbones, and soft coral lips, she was lovely. Achingly, heartstoppingly lovely.

"What?"

"We've got a little over a week until Christmas. Both of

us have shopping left to do and holiday decorations to buy. I want you to hold off on all of this until after Christmas." The first of the year would be better, but he didn't want to press his luck. "You could work on *Traces* a little, but mostly we could spend the time together, make the most of the holidays."

"You're going to decorate your apartment?"

"I'll be hiring someone to come in. It's important for Alex, and to tell you the truth, it just wouldn't be Christmas without a tree. I could arrange for someone to decorate your place, too."

Devon turned excitedly in his direction, propping her elbows on his chest. "Why don't we do the decorating ourselves? Alex could help us on the weekends. I know he'd enjoy it."

Jonathan mulled the idea over. Except for his occasional chance to cook, it had been years since he'd done anything quite so domestic. He smiled. "All right. We'll go shopping tomorrow after work. The florist has a tree reserved for me; I'll have him get a smaller one for you. We'll buy strings of colored lights—"

"Little tiny white ones," Devon corrected, "they look so old-fashioned . . . like small flickering candles."

"All right, little tiny white ones. Colored glass balls okay?"

She nodded. "And tinsel, of course."

"Of course." He smiled, caught up in her excitement. "What would any self-respecting Christmas tree be without tinsel?"

Devon slid her arms around his neck. "That sounds wonderful." She bent down and kissed him.

It did sound wonderful. And romantic. And domestic.

And permanent. Just like the hook she'd installed on the bathroom door to hold his robe.

It was the first time he had thought about it quite that way. The first time his mind had begun to examine the long-term consequences of his growing involvement. Was a permanent relationship really what he wanted? Would it fit into his busy life, or allow him time for Alex and his constantly growing responsibilities?

As much as he wanted her, as much as he liked her, in many ways even admired her—as much as he cared for her—he had never intended to get in quite this deep. Was he ready for that kind of commitment? In the weeks since he had started seeing Devon, his desk was piled high with paperwork he couldn't quite get to. Meetings had been postponed—he had even been late to the office.

His marriage to Rebecca had been ruined by his trying to merge a personal relationship with the responsibilities involved in running a hundred-and-fifty-year-old family business. And there was Alex to consider. He didn't want to bring a woman into his son's life, let the boy grow fond of her, maybe even come to love her, and then lose her as Alex had his mother.

Jonathan rested his head against the arm of the sofa, and Devon snuggled against his chest. Wherever their relationship was headed, now wasn't the time to worry about it. Christmas was just a few days away, Devon was excited about it, and so was his son. As Devon had agreed to do with the problems that plagued her, he would put off the ones plaguing him. When Christmas was over, he would review his options, consider his responsibilities, and decide the best course for everyone.

He wondered if the decision he would make would also be the best one for himself.

* * *

The holidays for Devon were something out of a Christmas story. Jonathan bought armloads of glittering decorations. Both of their apartments bloomed with poinsettias, and the fragrance of pine and woodsmoke scented the air. Over the weekend, when Alex came home, they made popcorn balls together, then greased their hands and pulled taffy. Jonathan did most of the cooking, thank God. Though he had never made candy—and few of the other holiday treats—she was amazed at how well they all turned out.

While Jonathan worked in the kitchen, Devon made pinecone centerpieces for the table and Alex strung cranberries, which they used along with shiny gold balls to decorate the pine boughs over the mantel.

"This is great, Dad," Alex said, "why haven't we done this before?"

Devon smiled, loving the closeness, the sharing. She hoped they'd be repeating the newly formed tradition again next year.

"Probably because it's a helluva lot of work," Jonathan grumbled, shoving a huge armload of presents beneath the tree. But Devon could see he was enjoying the spirit of the holidays as much as she was.

They spent the week finishing the last of the Christmas shopping, wrapping packages, and making arrangements for spending Christmas together with their families. Christy called to arrange a meeting with Sara Stone, but true to her word, Devon put the appointment off until the Wednesday following Christmas.

"Okay," Christy grudgingly agreed, "but I want to be there."

"I hoped you would. I'll feel more comfortable since you two are friends, and besides, I want you to meet Jonathan."

"He's coming with you?"

"Yes."

"Fantastic. I can't wait to meet him."

And so the appointment was set for seven o'clock the following Wednesday evening. Alex would be back at the clinic, and Jonathan would be home from work. Only one other item kept the subject of the Stafford Inn from disappearing completely beneath the holiday cheer. Letters from former guests began to arrive in response to the mailing they had done.

Most of the people who replied, said simply that their stay had been moderately pleasant. None of them raved about the inn, and two of them emphatically complained about the dismal unfriendly atmosphere in the house.

"And I thought Mrs. Meeks was making a success of the place," Jonathan grumbled one night as he read a stack of the letters.

"In a way she is. With the advertising she's done, you said yourself the place is usually full. It's just that she gets very little repeat business."

"And you think it's the house itself, rather than Mrs. Meeks's unpleasant attitude?"

"I think the two are connected."

"For her sake, I almost hope so."

Two days later, in a new batch of replies, Devon found something from a man in Scranton, Pennsylvania, a response card that looked more than a little intriguing. *Won't be back,* the card read. *Awake half the night. Some kid crying. The place was supposed to be for adults only!*

When she showed the card to Jonathan, his sleek black brows drew together. "Interesting . . . considering Ada

Meeks wouldn't let a kid through the front door if it meant two months' worth of business—except her son, of course."

"Ada has a child?"

"Grown. Gone away to college. Not a likely candidate for keeping the guests awake."

"No, not likely. So you think this is worth following up?"

"In terms of validating your book, every lead is worth following. But working under the assumptions we've already made, I think it's a safe bet the crying noises had something to do with Bernard."

Devon felt a surge of excitement, followed by one of warmth. That was her thinking exactly, but it was nice to have Jonathan there to back her up. "Shall I call and arrange an appointment?"

"After Christmas," he reminded her. "Just pull out the cards you think may be worth investigating and set them aside. In the meantime, I'm dying for a persimmon cookie."

Devon smiled. "They're almost out of the oven." Then she pretended to frown. "I don't know . . . maybe you should skip them. I wouldn't want you getting fat."

Jonathan slid an arm around her waist and hauled her against him. "We can always go into the bedroom and work off a few extra calories."

Thinking of the cookies, she started to protest. Instead, she pulled away from him and went into the kitchen. Once the tray was removed from the oven, she returned to the living room, walked up and slipped her arms around his neck. "I think you're right, Jonathan, it's time you got some exercise."

Christmas Eve they spent with Devon's parents. Alex went with them, and her mother fell in love with the child on sight. She stuffed him with cookies and candy and fussed over him endlessly.

"He's such a darling little boy," Eunice said, bringing Alex a second helping of mincemeat pie, setting it down in front of him on the white linen tablecloth. "You know, Alex, if things had worked out differently, Devon might have had a little boy just about your age." She sighed wistfully, and flashed Devon a meaningful glance. "I've always wanted a grandson."

"I never see my Gramma Winston," Alex said. "She sends me nice presents though."

Gramma Winston, Rebecca's mother. Nearly as big a socialite as her daughter had been.

"Sometimes Grampa Winston comes by on Sundays, but not very often."

"Well, you can come see me anytime you like." Eunice smiled at Alex. Her thin face was flushed with warmth.

Devon's mother had always loved children. Devon had known she hoped for grandchildren; she just hadn't known how important it was.

"This pie is delicious," Jonathan said, smoothly stepping in to change the subject. "Maybe even better than your pumpkin."

Eunice beamed. They had already eaten a huge Christmas Eve supper: peach-glazed ham, fresh peas and carrots, mounds of mashed potatoes drenched in butter and swimming in her mother's special country-style gravy, and of course homemade dinner rolls. After they had finished their pie, they moved into the living room to open their presents, and the floor was quickly obscured by mountains of crumpled wrapping paper, dozens of red and green satin bows, and stacks of empty cardboard boxes.

Devon lavished all sorts of extravagances upon her parents—the latest in kitchen appliances, a new sport coat for her dad, a new robe and slippers for her mom. Also the cashmere shawl and meerschaum pipe she had purchased. They gave her a pair of gold earrings and a white angora sweater she had wistfully eyed several months earlier on a shopping excursion with her mother.

"I love them, Mom, Dad." She leaned over and hugged them.

Jonathan seemed surprised to find under the tree a gift from Devon's parents for himself as well as one for Alex, though he had purchased each of them something. He was even more surprised when he opened his to find a beautiful hand-knit scarf that matched the overcoat he'd been wearing on his previous visit. Alex got a pair of red hand-knit mittens.

"These are great," the little boy said, obviously pleased that someone had gone to so much trouble just for him. "Thanks a lot."

All in all, the evening was a tremendous success, and Jonathan and Devon could easily see the Fitzsimmonses held high hopes for their growing relationship. That after they left, Jonathan seemed pensive, even a little bit edgy, she forced herself to ignore.

Christmas Day went much the same. Since Alex was home from the clinic, Devon spent the rest of Christmas Eve at her apartment, but Jonathan arrived to pick her up at ten the following morning for their trip out to the Hamptons. By that time, Alex had already opened the huge stack of gifts Santa had placed beneath the tree, and Jonathan had opened his son's gifts to him as well. Devon had hoped Jonathan might ask her to join them, but he hadn't.

He kissed her cheek as he settled her beside him in the

back seat of the limo. Alex sat on the opposite side so he could look out the window.

"Dad loved his present," Alex said, beaming. He was dressed in a V-necked sweater and brown corduroy pants. Jonathan had on slacks and a dark blue jacket, while Devon had chosen a pair of camel slacks, a cream silk blouse and a Ralph Lauren brown tweed jacket. The effect was feminine yet tailored.

"I'm sure he did. Your picture was very impressive."

"Thank you for helping him with it," Jonathan said.

"Alex did all of the work. Besides, I enjoyed it. We both had fun, didn't we, Andy?"

"Yeah, Dad." He grinned. "Devon taught me a lot. I wish she could keep coming to the clinic."

Devon could see by Jonathan's expression, that wasn't a very good idea. "I'm awfully busy, Alex. Maybe we can get together some weekend when you're home."

Jonathan seemed satisfied with that. She could almost feel him relax.

"I thought you and I would open our gifts this evening," he said, "when we get back to the city. Alex is spending the night with his cousins." The promise in his gray-blue eyes banished the chill she'd felt from him earlier.

"That sounds perfect."

"Look, Dad, it's snowing!" Alex's small hands splayed on the window of the car. Outside, huge white flakes had begun to drift down.

Jonathan leaned forward to get a better look. "A white Christmas."

"I love it when it snows," Alex said with growing excitement.

"Me, too," Devon agreed, almost as excited as he was.

Henry piped up from the driver's seat. "I just 'ope it don't give us problems getting 'ome."

But it didn't look like it was going to storm badly enough for that.

Instead, all the way to Long Island, the snow continued to fall gently, merely whitening the landscape. The streets remained relatively clear, and the trip to Southampton continued with merciful ease.

When they turned off Route 27, made their way through town, and finally reached Meadow Lane, the glowing yellow lights of the big white contemporary house seemed a beacon in the storm. Henry pulled up in front, Devon got out, Jonathan got out carrying Alex, and they all ran in. Alex's chair and the presents were brought in while Jonathan introduced Devon to his sister Maddie and her husband Stephen, then to each of their three boys, Thomas, Frederick, and Winifred.

"It's so nice to meet you all. I've really been looking forward to it."

"We've been looking forward to meeting you, too," Maddie replied for all of them; then Jonathan whisked Devon away.

For the holidays, the house had been completely decorated in red and white. The tree was huge and heavily decorated, with big red balls hanging from the branches. The windows had Christmas scenes painted in white, and there were pine boughs and wreaths on all the tables, all done up with big red bows.

It was elegant, yet charming, done in the best possible taste. Obviously it was the work of Jonathan's sister, who radiated style from the top of her glossy black hair slicked back in a tight chignon, to the soles of her expensive flat black patent-leather shoes.

"Jonathan's told me a good deal about you," Maddie said, once Jonathan left them alone. She didn't bother to hide her shrewd appraisal, and Devon felt her face grow warm. What exactly had Jonathan said?

"I hope it was good."

"Very good. My brother thinks a great deal of you."

That was nice to hear and even better to know that he had said so to his sister. "I think a great deal of him, too."

"Do you?"

Devon didn't miss the protective gleam in his younger sister's striking blue eyes. She was dressed in a pair of red velour stretch pants that were banded under the foot in the latest fashion. A matching red velour top, embroidered and studded with diamonds, completed the expensive, modish outfit. Her skin was smooth and as dark as Jonathan's, complementing her high carved cheekbones and full red mouth.

"Yes. The time we've spent together has been wonderful."

"I'm glad to hear it. Jonathan's endured more than his share of hardship. I wouldn't want to see him hurt again."

What about me? Devon thought, *I'm the one who's likely to get hurt.* But she didn't say so.

Instead, they made pleasant conversation and eventually Devon found herself coming to like Jonathan's outspoken sister. Her husband Stephen was gallant to the point of appearing almost foolish and obviously in love with her. Their three little boys were a treasure.

"Excuse me, little sister," Jonathan said, returning to where they sat in front of the fire a few minutes later. Christmas carols played softly on the stereo and one of the children was singing along. "If you don't mind, I think I'll steal Devon away for a moment."

Maddie flashed a knowing smile as Jonathan took Devon's

arm and guided her toward a small high-ceilinged room with a wall of windows facing the beach. On another day, it would have been sunny. The room had probably been designed for reading or sewing.

"I believe you know my aunt Stell." He squeezed Devon's hand as they moved into the room. The old woman sat in front of the window, watching the snow drift down onto the sand along the shore. She didn't turn at first, just kept watching the patterns in the billowing white, the way the wind swept it first one way then the other.

"Aunt Stell?" Jonathan repeated softly, moving toward her, and finally she turned.

"Jonathan." She smiled as her frail arms reached for him. Jonathan bent over, and Aunt Stell hugged him. Jonathan hugged her back.

"I was sleeping. I didn't realize you had come."

"I brought a friend, Aunt Stell, Devon James. I believe you two have met."

Aunt Stell peered around his wide shoulders, saw Devon standing beside him, and smiled.

"Hello, my dear, it's good to see you again."

Devon reached forward and clasped the old woman's outstretched hand. It felt thin and small, but warm and alive with a strength that surpassed her fragile looks.

"It's good to see you, too, Aunt Stell."

Jonathan pulled up a couple of chairs and the two of them sat down beside her.

"Alex came with you?" Stell asked.

"He's been waiting for you to wake up."

"How is he?"

"Fine."

Aunt Stell's mouth thinned. "He is hardly fine, Jonathan. He's still in that damnable chair. Now answer my question."

Jonathan grumbled something beneath his breath, but the look he flashed his aunt was one of admiration. "About the same. I've given Doctor Raymond six more months, then I'm taking him home. After that . . . I just don't know."

"You mustn't give up." Stell patted his fine dark hand. "There's a way to reach that child, we just have to find it."

Jonathan nodded.

"And you, Devon, how is your work progressing? You haven't let this young rogue stop you?"

Devon smiled. "As a matter of fact, Jonathan's been helping."

"Well, good for him. It's certainly way past time."

"Jonathan was worried about Alex." Devon found herself defending him. "He was afraid the newspapers might get involved the way they did the last time."

Aunt Stell's silver brows drew together. "I suppose that is something to consider. I worry about him so."

They talked for a while, the conversation easy and pleasant. Devon knew the subject of Annie Stafford would not be popular with either Stell or Jonathan, and yet her opportunities were limited; she felt she had to ask.

"I was wondering, Aunt Stell, if we could talk just a little bit more about Annie."

Jonathan stiffened a little, but didn't try to stop her.

Aunt Stell frowned again. "I suppose if Jonathan has decided to help, then I must continue to do the same."

Devon inched her chair a little closer. "The last time we were together, you said something about Annie that's been on my mind ever since."

"What was that, dear?"

"You said that in the end she was happy. I've thought a lot about that. She seemed so alone . . . I mean she never had a husband or children. How could she have been happy?"

"Annie did want children and no, she never had them. I suppose I should have told you the day you came to see me, but the subject seemed so unpleasant . . . Annie never had children because she couldn't. She got pregnant with Florian's child when she was fifteen. Florian arranged an abortion. In those days, it was illegal. He took her to a woman who was willing, for a price, to protect his good name. But, oh, she made a mess of things. Annie nearly died. As it was, she ended up sterile."

The air hissed from Jonathan's lungs. "Damn." He shook his head, his face lined with disgust. "I never knew very much about her. Just that she was a recluse who lived alone in the house. Who would have guessed the sort of nightmare she had lived through?"

"But you said she was happy," Devon pressed. "Do you think there might have been someone in her life . . . a man perhaps . . . someone who loved her?" It was the only explanation she'd been able to come up with for the man with the gentle hands. Annie was blond, so was Devon. If Florian had thought Alex was Bernie, maybe someone had mistaken her for Annie.

"I've told you all I intend to. What my cousin did with her life after she moved away from Florian is her own affair. I've told you as much as I have because you already knew most of it, and because Florian was an evil monster who deserves to be remembered for exactly what he was. As for the rest, I gave Annie my word I'd never repeat what she told me, and I never will. If she wanted someone to know, she wouldn't have hidden her diary."

"Her diary?" Devon leaned forward. "Annie kept a diary?"

"From the time she was a little girl. But it's lost now. Gone forever, and to tell you the truth, I'm glad. She deserves to keep her few happy memories and be left to rest in peace."

Devon couldn't have agreed more. But had Annie really found the peace she deserved—or did her soul remain shackled to the house at 25 Church Street?

"But there *was* someone?" Devon pressed, though she knew she shouldn't.

Aunt Stell just smiled and turned to look back out the window.

"Aunt Stell?" Jonathan said softly. His aunt just sat there, her body gently rocking as if she sat in her favorite high-backed chair.

"Merry Christmas, Aunt Stell," Devon said, squeezing the old woman's hand and feeling a little bit guilty.

Aunt Stell turned her silver-gray head and looked at her kindly. "Merry Christmas," she said. "My nephew's a very lucky man." She turned to stare back out the window.

They left the room in silence and quietly closed the door. "I shouldn't have brought it up," Devon said as they walked along the hall.

"Yesterday, I might have agreed." Devon looked up at him in surprise. "To be honest, after listening to what she had to say, I realize you were right. I *had* been underestimating her. She's a bright, intelligent woman. Her age hasn't changed that. I'm not even completely convinced this thing she does—this staring out the window to end a conversation—isn't just a very shrewd trick."

Devon laughed softly. "I've had the same thought myself."

"As far back as I can remember, she's loved to sit and rock in her old cane-backed chair. She told me once that her father bought her a red and white spotted rocking horse one year for Christmas when she was a little girl. She used to sit in front of the window and rock on that horse for hours. Years later, when she moved back into the old Stafford mansion, she found it up in the attic. Alex used to rock on it just the way Aunt Stell did when she was a little girl."

"Does she still have it?"

Jonathan shook his head. "Unfortunately, it was destroyed in the fire. I think Aunt Stell was more upset about losing that old rocking horse than she was about losing the house."

"Another of Florian's victims."

"Maybe. As far as I'm concerned, even if he didn't start the fire, the bastard deserves to burn in hell for what he's done. If that's where your efforts will send him, then I hope I can be of some help."

They walked arm and arm into the living room, where by unspoken agreement the subject was dropped. It was Christmas Day, after all, a time of celebration.

And the mood in the house was indeed joyous. Devon felt the warmth of the Stafford family almost from the moment of her arrival, discovering to her relief that it didn't take her long to fit in. Jonathan must have sensed the same thing about her, but unlike Devon, who rejoiced in the fact, Jonathan seemed uneasy about it. She wondered if he was worried for Alex, who clung to her hand off and on through most of the day.

When they left the house, Maddie and Stephen both hugged her good-bye at the door, and Maddie gave her brother an especially warm embrace.

"This was the best Christmas we've had in years. And

the first time in a long time you and I have been able to talk."

"It's been wonderful. Maybe we can do it again next year."

"I'm planning on it. Only this time, I expect you to join us in England."

He smiled. "When will you be going home?"

"Right after New Year's. We've enjoyed ourselves, the kids have had a ball, but it's time to go home."

"Yes, I suppose it is." He hugged her again. "I'm going to miss you."

Maddie glanced at Devon. "Maybe not as much as you think." She flashed a hopeful smile.

Jonathan said nothing, and Devon wondered what he was thinking.

They returned to his apartment early that evening, and he surprised her by carrying her into the bedroom, peeling off her clothes, and taking her straight to bed. He was wildly passionate, almost desperate in his need for her, and Devon responded to that need, the way she always did.

Several hours later, in front of the fire, they exchanged their Christmas gifts. Devon gave Jonathan a lapis and diamond bezel for his watch. The glow in his eyes said he loved it. His gift to her was a single two-carat diamond solitaire suspended on a thin gold chain.

"I love it, Jonathan. It's beautiful." He kissed the nape of her neck as he fastened the tiny jeweled clasp.

"I thought it would suit you." He stepped back to admire it nestled against the hollow of her throat. "And it does."

They ate a late supper of leftover turkey they had brought back from the Hamptons, then went back to bed. Jonathan's lovemaking seemed even more passionate, and Devon wondered uneasily why lately his need for her seemed to swell.

Before they fell asleep, he told her he had to make a trip to California for a couple of days to check on a problem at Pacific American.

"I tried my best to postpone it until after the first of the year, but I just can't put it off any longer."

Devon didn't bother to hide her disappointment. "Will you be back by Wednesday? We're supposed to have our meeting with Sara Stone."

He smiled that charming smile of his. "A house full of demons couldn't keep me away."

Devon fell asleep in his arms, but when she woke up, Jonathan was gone.

Twenty-two

The days dragged till Wednesday. A full-blown storm set in, blanketing the city, causing endless snarls of traffic. Jonathan called only once. He was trapped in meetings, he said, with hardly a moment to himself. Devon didn't completely believe him. There was something in his voice, something guarded and distant. Ever since Christmas Eve, she had felt him pulling away from her, and the shining memories of the warm romantic hours they had spent together during the holidays seemed a little dimmer than before.

On Wednesday afternoon, he called again. He was running late. He would have to meet her at the bookstore. He offered to send Henry to pick her up, but she told him it would be easier just to take a cab.

She was dressed in a pair of brown tweed slacks beneath a cable-knit brown turtleneck sweater, a heavy antique gold chain belt slung low on her hips. Her feet were warmed by soft knee-high kidskin boots. Devon grabbed her brown leather Anne Klein bag, and the silver-wrapped package that was Christy's Christmas present—they had been too busy to get together sooner. She rushed out the door.

After a cab ride that was just a little too exciting in the heavily falling snow, she arrived at the Insight Book Store to find Christy waiting for her just inside the door. The women hugged, exchanged gifts, though they didn't take time to open them, then Christy glanced back toward the door.

"Where's Jonathan?"

"He's running late." Devon tried to smile, but it came out forced. "I'm sure he'll be here any minute."

Christy's black eyes ran over her face, discovering the hint of uncertainty. "You two aren't having problems, are you? I thought things had been going great."

Devon sighed. "I think he's getting nervous, feeling trapped . . . I don't know."

"The old 'Oh, my God, what have I gotten myself into?' syndrome. Damn men. They're all such—"

"I know, they're all such bastards."

"All except Francisco, of course." Christy actually blushed.

Devon couldn't believe it. "You're in love with him!"

"What if I am? I'm in love with them all, in the beginning."

Devon eyed her shrewdly. The sparkle in her eyes was a little bit brighter, the bloom in her cheeks a little pinker than if it had just been the cold. "Not like this, you aren't. That little Italian must really be something."

Christy's expression turned serious. "Actually, he is. He's kind and considerate, intelligent and fun. I'm hoping he'll ask me to marry him."

Devon leaned over and hugged her. "Then I hope so, too."

"What about Jonathan?"

"What about him?"

"Do you want to marry him?"

Devon sighed. "I didn't. Not in the beginning. Now that

I've gotten to know him, I can't think of anyone I'd rather spend the rest of my life with."

"But you don't think that's the way Jonathan sees things."

"No . . . at least not lately. Ever since Christmas, he's been . . . I don't know . . . withdrawn or something."

"Well, you never know, maybe he'll come to his senses."

"Maybe."

"Maybe he already has." Christy's glance went over Devon's shoulder just as the door came open, ringing the bell at the top.

"Jonathan." Devon turned toward him and for an instant neither of them moved. He stood there as tall and imposing as ever, his unusual gray-blue eyes running over her, his face one moment forbidding, unreachable, the next moment softening, warming, his reluctance melting away. Then he stepped toward her and Devon rushed into his arms.

"I've missed you," she said. "I've missed you so much."

"I've missed you, too," he said, his voice thick and husky. Then he kissed her, long and hard, and some of her fears fell away.

From a few feet behind them, she heard Christy clear her throat. Even at that, Jonathan's hungry kiss lingered. When they finally broke free, Devon turned to her friend and smiled. "Jonathan, this is my best friend, Christy Papaopolis."

"Hello, Christy. It's nice to meet you at last."

"Devon's told me all about you," Christy said.

"Did she?" He cocked a black brow that looked entirely too wicked.

"Well, maybe not quite all."

"I certainly hope not."

Devon flushed and Christy laughed. They made idle conversation for a moment. Jonathan spoke briefly about his trip, and the weather he'd encountered on the way in from the airport. Eventually, their interest turned to the reason they had come.

"I suppose we'd better get going," Christy said. "Sara will be wondering where we are."

"I was wondering about that myself." Jonathan surveyed their ominous surroundings. "God, this place gives me the creeps."

"I don't like it either," Devon said. "Unfortunately, if we want to see Mrs. Stone, we'll have to put up with it."

"Well, I won't have to." Christy grinned. "Now that Jonathan's here, I can leave."

"But I thought you'd be staying."

"You don't really mind, do you? Francisco is waiting at my apartment, and you two don't really need me."

"No, I don't suppose we do."

"Good. I'll take you back to meet Sara then I'm out of here. I'll call you first thing in the morning."

Ignoring the musty smell of incense and the eerie glow of flickering candles, they made their way to the back of the bookstore. Christy knocked lightly on a narrow wooden door, and Sara Stone pulled it open.

"I've rounded up our strays, Sara."

Devon extended a hand. "Hello, Mrs. Stone, I'm Devon James, and this is Jonathan Stafford." Sara Stone was a woman in her fifties. Average height, average weight, gray-streaked medium brown hair. She had pleasant, nondescript features. Only her eyes, an astonishing golden brown flecked with an even lighter gold, separated her from a thousand other middle-aged women, that and the way those eyes seemed to drill a hole right through you. They gave the unmistakable impression that to lie to Sara Stone would be a worthless waste of time. Sara would know the truth.

"And I'm pleased to meet you, Ms. James." The graying woman smiled, and her average features somehow looked less average. "I've read all of your books."

"You have?"

"Why, yes. Is that so incredible? Or is a psychic just supposed to read Anne Rice or Stephen King?"

Devon laughed softly. "I guess I never gave it much thought."

"And you, Mr. Stafford. I've been reading about you in the papers. Your support of children's orthopedic medicine has been laudable. Didn't I see somewhere recently that Stafford family donations were responsible for an entire new wing at University Hospital?"

"I'm happy to say that is so."

"Bye, Devon," Christy put in, easing away from them with a Cheshire-cat smile. "It was good to meet you, Jonathan." She left them standing in the open office doorway.

Sara motioned them in, her lips curving up in a smile of welcome. "I hope you'll both call me Sara. Welcome to my humble abode."

It was rather humble, being in the back room of Nathaniel Talbot's musty old bookstore, but as they stepped inside, they were pleased to discover there was nothing dark or forbidding about it. Just old three-drawer files, a scarred oak desk that had seen better days, and three old oak chairs positioned in front of it. The calendar showing each month's astrology sign was the only thing that remotely connected the world of the metaphysical with simple, unimposing, Sara Stone.

"You're aware that Christina has already told me a good

deal about what happened to you at the inn," Sara told them as soon as they were seated. "I'm not here to convince you of the truth one way or another, or to impress you with what I might be able to sense. I'm here to help you solve your problem—if you decide you have faith in me, and if that's what you want."

"You come highly recommended, Mrs. Stone," Jonathan said. "Dr. Francis Linderman over at Princeton."

"Dr. Linderman, yes." She nodded sagely. "We've never met, but I've read his work. As a matter of fact, I'm eagerly awaiting his next book. I believe it's due out any day now."

"*Parapsychology: The Study of Psychic Phenomena.* Devon and I were fortunate to receive an early copy. I'll see that you get one, too."

"Why, thank you. That would be wonderful."

"Sara," Devon broke in, "I'm afraid I'm not quite clear on something you said earlier. You called yourself a psychic. Christy said you were a trance medium. I don't think I understand the difference."

"The difference simply lies in the way I use my psychic gift. You see each of us has different abilities, or at least our strengths seem to lie in different areas. A trance medium has the ability to contact entities which are, for the most part, unreachable by most people. Unlike a channeler—whose scope may be broader and, as far as many of us are concerned, they often lack credibility—what I learn is usually verifiable. Names, dates, general information about the time in which the spirit might have lived. I've been successful in aiding distressed souls in a goodly number of cases—that is my gift. But I certainly couldn't tell you your future, or even relate your past."

"That's a relief," Jonathan said wryly, a corner of his mouth curving up.

"Actually, the future is almost impossible to predict, and the further away, the more difficult the task becomes."

"Assuming the possibility exists, why is that?" Jonathan asked.

"Choice, Mr. Stafford. Every choice we make changes the course of the future. Compound that element by minutes, hours, days, years, and the future becomes quite hazy."

"You're saying that even if there is such a thing as fate, we all have a large amount of control over it."

"Yes, that's exactly what I'm saying."

"You called these entities *distressed*," Devon said, bringing the conversation full circle.

"That's right. Most souls wish to go beyond, but some of them seem to have lost their way. I send them on with kindness. A lost person deserves kindness."

"Not this lost person," Jonathan said darkly.

"Remember, Mr. Stafford, every life teaches a lesson. Florian committed a heinous crime—several crimes—and for that in another life he will pay. It all balances out over the course of time."

Thinking of the good and evil in each of us, Devon wondered if Sara might not be right. "When people come to you as we are now, what do you usually recommend?"

"In many instances, people seek me out with tales of a haunting. They've heard chains rattling, footsteps on the stairs, that sort of thing. Sometimes they've actually seen an apparition, but most of the time they simply have this overwhelming *feeling* that someone is there."

"That's the way I felt," Devon said. "Completely overwhelmed—and absolutely certain something was there."

"Yes, well that's the sort of story I'm usually faced with."

"And your recommendation?" Jonathan asked.

"I tell them the first thing they need to do is determine

whether these occurrences might have a rational explanation. If the person makes a valid attempt to investigate but still turns up nothing, and the problem continues, we seek help in the form of organizations devoted to the study of psychic phenomena. Groups like the American Society for Psychical Research, right here in New York, or the Psychical Research Foundation in Carrollton, Georgia. On the West Coast we have the Southern California Society for Psychical Research in Los Angeles and the parapsychology program at John F. Kennedy University in San Francisco. Unfortunately all of them are in need of funding, which limits their capacity to help, but if the case shows enough merit, they will sometimes come in for study."

"And they work directly with you?" Jonathan asked.

"Not in the beginning. First they call in geologists, engineers, experts in explosives, a dozen different people to run every conceivable test you can imagine. They're looking for natural phenomena—methane, electricity, vapors, sewer gas, natural gas, electromagnetic fields—there are dozens of avenues of explanation that must be eliminated first."

"And step two?"

"The foundation brings in some of their own people. They set up tripods, automatic flashes, infrared cameras. They take as much time as they can to physically examine the scene."

"Are you suggesting we do some of those things?"

"No I'm not. I believe Ms. James's research has eliminated most doubt that the entity is there." She turned her attention to Devon. "I would, however, like to ask you some questions."

"All right." Devon shifted a bit in her chair. So far she was a lot less nervous than she had been in Linderman's office, but the tension nevertheless was there. She answered

Sara's questions as concisely as possible, filling in the gaps in the story Christy had already told her. When she had finished, Sara sat pensively, her hands steepled in front of her on the desk.

"I believe your intuitions—the perceptions you made at the house, Devon, are sound. Florian's guilt for the crimes he has committed have likely confused him, kept him earthbound. It's highly possible, as you believe, that he is holding Annie and little Bernie on the physical plane with him. If that is the case, then we must free them. Since they have reached out to you, our best chance is to go into the house together."

Devon's chest grew tight. She had expected something like this, yet part of her had hoped it would not come.

"When?" Jonathan asked.

"I prefer to work at night. My sensitivities seem to be strongest then."

Devon's pulse increased till it thrummed loudly in her ears. Her uneasiness must have shown, because when Jonathan glanced in her direction, his smooth black brows drew together in a frown.

"Is there a chance you could do this alone?" he asked Sara.

"Possibly." Her golden brown eyes swung to Devon. "If that is what you wish."

Devon wetted her lips. "No . . . I want to be there. I have to."

"How will we know if you've actually made contact?" Jonathan asked, with the first note of skepticism he had revealed.

"If this apparition has the will to hold other spirits earthbound, he'll be a powerful force to reckon with. If that is the case, you will know. As a matter of fact, I must caution you that such a force can be extremely dangerous."

"That's what Linderman said."

"I'm afraid it's true. There may well be physical manifestations of at least a portion of that power. It is certainly something to consider, should you decide to go through with this."

"We've already decided," Devon said staunchly. "We just need to decide when."

Sara pulled open a battered oak drawer. Its squeal of protest splintered the quiet in the room. She drew out a small black calendar and flipped it open. "I'm committed through the middle of next week, but I think we should get on with this as soon as possible. From what you've said, several people may have already been hurt, and the contact between Devon and Florian has already been established. How does Friday a week suit you?"

"Jonathan?" Devon turned to face him.

"I'll clear my calendar, and see that any guest reservations Mrs. Meeks has accepted are canceled."

"All right, then it's settled." Sara wrote the date in her book, closed it, and came to her feet.

Jonathan shoved back his chair and stood up, then helped Devon to stand. He draped her camel-hair coat across her shoulders and pulled on his cashmere overcoat.

"Thank you for your time, Mrs. Stone," he said.

"Good-bye, Sara." Devon walked past Jonathan out the door, and they made their way down the long, narrow dimly lit book-lined corridors toward the front of the store. They had almost reached the door when the bell clattered loudly and Henry burst through the opening, snow flying in small white flecks off his coat.

"Sorry, guv'nor, but somethin' dreadful 'as 'appened. It's Alex, sir. The 'ospital just phoned."

Jonathan froze. "Alex? What is it?"

"Reporters everywhere. Someone must have leaked Ms. James's ghost story. Apparently the blighters put two and two together and come up with Alex as the link."

"Is he all right?"

" 'Fraid not, sir. Seems they set upon 'im in the playroom. Shook 'im up pretty bad. 'E's gone into convulsions."

"Dear God," Devon whispered.

"I've got to go to him." Jonathan started forward, but Henry stopped him with a hand on his arm.

" 'Fraid there's more bad news, sir. It's your aunt, Mr. Stafford. She's had a 'eart attack. They've taken her to the 'ospital in Mystic."

"I-Is she all right?" Devon's own heart slammed against her ribs. At the sound of her voice, Jonathan turned. She had never seen such seething emotion, such raw, uncompromising pain. In the flickering glow of the candles his angry expression made him look almost demonic.

"This is your fault—all of it! I tried to tell you this would happen. I tried to make you see. But all you cared about was writing your damnable story. Because of you, I ignored my responsibilites. I let my work slide. I blinded myself to what I knew almost surely would happen. Because of you, my son is back in a hospital bed and God only knows what will happen to my aunt."

Jonathan glanced around at the flickering candles, the dark occult posters on the wall, and his arm swept out like the blade of a sword. "Look at this place. What the hell am I doing in a place like this? Why am I listening to all of this garbage? I should never have gotten involved in this. Look what's come of it—it's destroying my family!"

"Jonathan, please, I never meant to hurt them. I never—"

"I don't want to hear it. Not another word. Not this time." He turned away from her. "I'll send Henry back to pick you up just as soon as I reach the hospital. He'll see you safely home."

There was finality in his dark expression, condemnation in the unforgiving set to his jaw. His eyes were flat, gray, and hard. Whatever course he'd been debating, Devon had no doubt he had just made his choice.

Her bottom lip trembled, but she forced her eyes to his face. "I'm sorry. Maybe someday you'll know just how sorry I am." Inside, her heart was breaking, tearing her apart. She hoped he wouldn't notice the over-bright sheen of her eyes, the pulse that fluttered at the base of her throat. He started to walk away, and it was all she could do not to run to him, beg him to forgive her.

Instead she spoke softly to his driver. "Don't worry about me, Henry. I got here on my own. I can get home the same way."

"Sir?" Henry said.

"If that's the way she wants it." And then he was gone.

Devon stared after them out the window. The snow swirled around the limousine as it pulled away from the curb, then Henry was racing off into traffic, swallowed up by the blaring autos and the fury of the storm.

It took every ounce of her will to pull open the door and step out on the curb. Snowflakes flurried around her as she raised her arm to a passing cab. Her bones felt leaden, her chest tight. A heavy pulse pounded in her ears. She didn't remember the cab ride home. She didn't remember paying the fare or riding the elevator up to her apartment. All she could think of was getting to the phone in her living room, dialing the Woodland Clinic.

"I'm sorry, miss," said the voice on the end of the line, "we've been instructed not to give out any information on Alex Stafford." The woman was polite but determined, and no amount of pleading could change her mind.

Devon hung up the phone, dialed information in Mystic with trembling fingers, and got the number of the local hospital. A little more helpful than the clinic, they told her Estell Stafford Meredith's condition was critical. She was confined to intensive care.

Devon set the receiver back in its cradle, still hearing the dull click of the line going dead and thinking that was exactly the way she felt. Dull and lifeless. She felt guilty and grief-stricken, and the pain in her heart was unbearable.

Jonathan had tried to tell her. He had tried to bribe her. He had reasoned. He had begged her not to continue. He had predicted dire consequences for himself and his son, but she hadn't believed him.

Now she had lost him. And she knew without doubt, he would never return. Numb with heartbreak and pain, awash with guilt and remorse, she made her way into the bedroom like a woman in a trance. She thought about what Sara Stone had said about the future, about choices and how each of the choices we made changed the direction of our lives. If she could only undo things, make different choices. But she knew it was too late.

Devon toyed with the tasteless mashed potatoes clumped in a corner of the frozen TV dinner she forced herself to eat. It was New Year's Eve. All over America and most of the world, people were celebrating the arrival of the New Year.

Devon hadn't even been able to make herself turn on the television. She couldn't bear to watch the descending ball at Times Square usher in the New Year. She knew only too well the heartache the coming months would bring.

Instead she called the Woodland Clinic for the twenty-second time and this time was told that Alex Stafford was now in good condition. The danger to Alex was past.

Devon sank down in the chair, relief washing over her. Immediately, she dialed the hospital in Mystic, though she had called once earlier in the day.

"Can you give me an update on the condition of Estell Stafford Meredith?" she asked.

The nurse thumbed through the records on her desk. Devon could hear her shuffling papers. "I'll have to ring you through to Dr. Rineman." Always before they had merely responded by saying Stell's condition remained critical. Had something happened? Devon waited tensely for the doctor to pick up the phone.

"Are you related to the patient?" he asked, his voice low and alarmingly calm.

"No, we're just friends. My name is Devon James."

"I'm very sorry, Ms. James, but Mrs. Meredith passed away at six o'clock this evening."

"Oh, my God." A hard lump swelled in Devon's throat. She wanted to ask if there might be some mistake, but in her heart she knew there was not. "Th-Thank you, Dr. Rineman. I'm sorry for the trouble."

"No trouble, Ms. James. I wish it hadn't been such bad news."

"So do I."

Devon hung up the phone and started to cry. She put her head down on the desk and sobbed until her eyes were red and swollen, but she couldn't stop blaming herself. Several hours later, she dialed Jonathan's home number, but got only his answering machine. She left a message there, and left one with the service at his office, but she knew he wouldn't return them. Just as she knew that he would never forgive her for what she had done.

That she would never forgive herself.

On Sunday, Christy called, but Devon didn't want to see her. Christy was happy and bubbling with news of her engagement to Francisco. Devon knew her dismal mood would take some of that joy away, so instead she thanked Christy for the lovely lingerie she had received from her for Christmas, not telling her it was a size too big.

On Monday, she called Jonathan's office again, and this time Dee Wills came on the line. "I'm sorry, Ms. James. Jonathan won't be in this week."

"Did you give him my message?"

There was an uncomfortable pause. "He's been terribly busy."

Devon bit her lip to stifle a sob of despair. "Can you tell me when the funeral is scheduled?"

"It's Wednesday at one o'clock. Graveside services. They'll be held at the cemetery behind the Methodist Church in Stafford."

"Thank you." Devon softly hung up the phone. She wasn't sure how long she sat there. She only knew she wasn't able to work and she wasn't able to sleep. Crying didn't seem to help either, but she couldn't seem to stop.

On Tuesday, she was so restless and weary from her endless weeping and the lost dismal days in her apartment, she left the house and caught a cab out front. Taking Christy's present back was as good an excuse as any to get out in the fresh air, even if it was still snowy and cold.

At Saks, employees were busily removing the last of the Christmas decorations. The glittering tinsel and shiny glass balls reminded her of the wonderful days she had spent with Jonathan. Only now the sparkling foil had begun to tarnish, and a few of the shiny glass ornaments had been smashed. It seemed appropriate somehow, since her own bright shiny world had come tumbling down.

At Saks, Devon pushed through the after-Christmas shoppers on her way to the lingerie counter and ran head-on into a tall man walking rapidly in the opposite direction.

"Sorry," he said as he bent down to pick up the lingerie box she had dropped.

"Is that you, Michael?" She stepped back to look at him as he returned the box.

"Devon." He grinned. "I wondered when our paths would finally cross."

"Saks Fifth Avenue wouldn't have been my first guess," she said, working for lightness. "More likely a rubber chicken dinner at a Sheraton or Marriott."

"Oh, I don't know, we both like expensive clothes."

She couldn't argue with that. "I suppose that's true."

"So how are you? You haven't been sick, have you? You're looking a little bit pale."

"Not exactly." She smiled with false brightness. "Actually, I'm fine. What about you? Are you dating again, seeing anyone special?"

Michael's face lit up, making him look younger. "As a matter of fact, I've been seeing Caroline Holcomb. You remember her, don't you—J. P. Holcomb's daughter?"

"Ah, you mean as in the wealthy New Haven Holcombs. How could I possibly forget?"

He grinned again, and she remembered with affection that there were times that he could be charming. "Not jealous, are you? You know if things aren't working out with you and Stafford, you and I could always—"

"Caroline's really a very nice girl," Devon said, discovering she actually meant it. And now that she thought of them together, possibly a very good match for Michael. "I'm happy for you. I hope things work out."

"Remember what I said."

"I'll keep it in mind." But she had no such intention. Whatever she had felt for Michael Galveston was as dead as poor Aunt Stell. "Good-bye, Michael."

He leaned over and bussed her cheek. "Good-bye, Devon."

Twenty-three

"Don't forget your overcoat." Dee Wills held it up so Jonathan could slip it on over his spotless black suit. Absently, he slid his arm in one sleeve, but he was too tall for her to lift it over his shoulders. Eventually he got it on, and started toward the elevator door. His face was the same expressionless mask he had come in with earlier that morning.

"Anything special you want me to do while you're gone?" Dee asked. It was the day of his aunt Stell's funeral. She wished she could go with him, just to lend her support, but she knew she was more valuable in the office.

"What?" he replied absently. He looked so unbearably tired her heart went out to him.

"I said is there anything special you want me to do?"

"As a matter of fact there is." He pushed a strand of wavy black hair off his face with the back of his hand. "You can call that secretary friend of yours over at Tri-Star Marine. I want to know who decided to use that stuff in the tabloids against us. The bastard has cost us a damned good customer, and I want to know who he is."

The Carstairs account. The gossip in the papers had been the final card Tri-Star needed to steal Holidex Industries' biggest account. Who would have figured a huge corporation could be swayed by something like that?

But Tri-Star had blown the incident all out of proportion, hinting at the lunacy of a man like Jonathan Stafford, the president of a giant corporation, being involved in the investigation of family ghosts. The truth was, Carstairs had been looking for an excuse to defect. They believed Tri-Star's Kelovar plastic might just out-perform the old tried and true, stamped and cast-metal fittings Holidex supplied.

The breach had been coming, probably would have happened anyway. But happening now, on top of everything else, it was just one more nail in the coffin of Jonathan's ill-fated relationship with Devon James.

"Any particular calls you want returned?" Dee asked. Certainly none of those from Ms. James. Jonathan had ignored them, instructed her to do the same, and for the most part she had.

"No. Just put everyone off until tomorrow."

"Are you sure you don't need a couple more days? It wouldn't hurt for you to get a little rest, you know." He'd been up day and night since Alex's traumatic relapse. The child had bounced back faster than the doctors had at first expected, but just when that horizon began to clear, his beloved aunt had died. A woman who had been his surrogate mother, in some ways closer to him than his own mother ever was.

"Too much to do. I'll be in first thing tomorrow morning."

And too much on your mind, Dee silently added. It was obvious to Dee, if it wasn't to Jonathan, that the pain he was suffering was as much a result of his feelings for Devon James as it was for the loss of his aunt. Maybe he didn't know it, but the fact was, Jonathan had fallen head over heels in love with the woman. Because of what had happened, he had ruthlessly banished her from his life and he intended to keep it that way.

And yet he was hurting. It was there in every line of his face, in the rigid set of his jaw. Worry etched his forehead and regret darkened his eyes. Dee wished she could comfort him, but there wasn't really anything she could do. Eventually, Jonathan would get through this, just as he always did. But what price would he pay? How much more life would go out of him? How much more guarded and remote would he be to the next woman who came along—if there ever was another.

Dee sighed as she watched him, standing there so tall and alone waiting for the elevator doors to slide open. Family pride and a sense of responsibility seeped from every pore in Jonathan's body. They were the foundation of his life, the very marrow in his bones. Now with all that had happened, he felt he had abandoned his responsibilities by falling in love with Devon.

Dee wished there was a way to make him see he also had a responsibility to himself.

The elevator bell rang, signaling its arrival. Jonathan started to walk in.

"Jonathan, wait! I almost forgot." Dee turned away from him and hurried into her office, returning a few moments later with a small packet of envelopes, faded with time, tied up with an equally faded narrow satin ribbon. "I found these on the floor beside your desk. They must have been in that box that came in yesterday with some of your aunt Stell's belongings." Estell Stafford Meredith had kept letters and mementoes in her bedroom at the little yellow house in Stafford. The majority of her things were stored in one of the family homes she had once lived in, but a few things she had kept with her. "It's just a stack of old letters, but somehow I hated to see them separated from the rest of her things."

Jonathan crossed to where Dee stood holding the packet of letters and took it from her hands.

"I'll see they're put back with the others. Thanks, Dee."

"Take care, Jonathan."

But he only nodded. As he strode to the elevator, his fingers tightened around the letters. Dee wondered if he intended to read them.

Sitting in the back seat of the limo, Jonathan rode beneath flat gray clouds along the narrow paved road leading into Stafford. The snowstorm had ended, leaving the ground white and frozen, but the wind was only a breeze, and the day was not too bitterly cold.

Alex sat on the car seat beside him, staring out at the passing landscape. Alex was a miniature version of himself, in a new black suit and shiny black leather shoes. The color had returned to his small son's cheeks, and he looked healthy again. Only the news of his aunt Stell's death had hindered his recovery.

At first Jonathan had been afraid to tell him. Then he worried that the shock of accidentally finding out might be worse than hearing the news broken gently. Alex had cried when he'd heard, but nothing else untoward had happened, and Jonathan felt the little boy's tears were a healthy sign. Alex hadn't cried in years. Not until Devon had come along.

Devon. Just the whisper of her name at the edges of his mind made his mouth go dry and his stomach ball into a hard tight knot. Every day since he had left her standing in that dismal bookstore, he had thought of her. He could see her lovely green eyes, remember the softness of her lips beneath his. He remembered the way they had trembled when she'd heard the news about Alex, the way her eyes had glazed with tears when he had accused her of being to blame. He knew he had hurt her. He wondered if she had any idea how badly she had hurt him.

Jonathan clamped his jaw. It was over between them. He had faced that fact the moment he'd heard the news about his son. Once in the past, he had put his work before his family and it had left his son bound to a wheelchair.

This time it was Devon. She had awakened longings in him, made him feel things he didn't want to feel, want things he couldn't have. For a moment, he had forgotten his responsibilities.

Alex had suffered for it.

Aunt Stell was dead.

Of course, he couldn't blame Devon for the death of his aunt. He had over-reacted that day, assuming some connection between Alex's relapse and Aunt Stell's heart attack. He shouldn't have. Aunt Stell had been sick off and on for years. Hearing of Alex's relapse might have brought on the attack, but even that was doubtful. He had faced that fact and regretted the way he had handled things, but it was over and done with. Jonathan no longer blamed Devon, which meant that in some nebulous way he blamed himself.

Now that his father was gone, he was the head of the family. The man ultimately accountable for everything that happened to the people he loved. Maybe if he had spent less time with Devon, more time checking on his aunt . . .

He sighed and leaned back against the seat. As usual, he was being too hard on himself. Just as he had been too hard on Devon.

The limousine rolled up in front of the Methodist Church and Jonathan got out carrying Alex. Henry got the wheelchair out of the trunk, and as soon as the boy was comfortably wrapped in a warm plaid blanket, Jonathan pushed the chair ahead of him along the freshly shoveled walkway toward the cemetery in the rear. A green-striped canopy covered the fresh mound of frozen earth. Jonathan absently thought how difficult it must have been to dig up. His aunt's brass casket sat above the grave, the entire top covered in yellow roses.

Aunt Stell's favorite color. Devon's favorite, too, came the unwanted thought from out of nowhere. His aunt had always loved roses. He would never know how Devon felt about the fragrant blooms.

From the corner of his eye, Jonathan caught Maddie's approach. She was dressed severely in black, as was Stephen, though he wore a red-striped tie. Jonathan had never seen the children looking more somber.

Jonathan bent to hug Maddie, shook Stephen's hand, then guided Alex's chair, through the burgeoning throng of people, to the front row of seats that faced the grave. Huge overhead heaters worked to banish the chill, but nevertheless it was there, lurking in the corners of his heart and mind.

From another recess came the dim awareness of the growing number of people around him. The ladies who had lived with Aunt Stell in her pretty yellow house, old Elwood Dobbs, her friend for the last twenty years, Ginny Griggs, the elderly woman who ran Stafford's general store. Beulah Davis was there, at ninety-two, Aunt Stell's oldest acquaintance. But there were young people, too. People she had done charity work with, people who had driven all the way out from Manhattan. It made him proud of her, proud of his family.

It made him sad to think that he had lost one of them.

Jonathan sat down on the cold metal chair. The minister, Reverend Perkins, a short, stout little man wearing wire-rimmed spectacles, stepped up to the podium on the opposite side of the casket. He shuffled the papers in front of him and waited for the hush to settle in.

"Dear Friends. We are gathered here today to pay our respects and say a final farewell to a very great lady, Estell Stafford Meredith. Aunt Stell, as most of us called her, passed away on December thirty-first of this year at the age of eighty-one. She never saw the New Year, but in her long and full life, she saw many other grand and happy things."

With a glance at his notes, he spoke of the way the world had changed since Estell's childhood, the way she had adapted to those changes, reveled in them—the way she had traveled far and wide, but had never forgotten the tiny town she grew up in. As a friend of Stell's for more than forty years, the minister cleared his throat against a thread of emotion that had crept into his voice.

"For those of us who grieve," he said, "let us find comfort in the Twenty-third Psalm."

Jonathan bowed his head. Beside him, Alex bent his small head forward and steepled his fingers in the attitude of prayer.

"The Lord is my Shepherd; I shall not want. He maketh me lie down in green pastures; He leadeth me beside the still waters. He restoreth my soul."

Jonathan didn't catch what came next, just the familiar cadence of the words, then more praise for a woman who had lived many long and prosperous years. There were words of her kindness, her charity, her concern and help for others. An old church friend sang "Amazing Grace," and the pure sweet notes caused a tightness in his throat.

A woman behind him sobbed softly, and Maddie wept

quietly beside him. Alex sniffed back tears, and Jonathan knew he worked hard to hold them away. They were all going to miss her, but they would go on. Life would go on.

And even as he grieved, Jonathan realized in a way he envied her. His aunt's life had been rich and full. She had lived and loved every day of it, every moment. Stell had grabbed onto life whenever she'd been given the chance.

He thought of Devon. Could he say the same for himself?

"Dad?"

Jonathan leaned close so he could hear him. "What is it, son?"

"Look." Alex pointed toward the small snow-covered knoll beneath a barren maple tree. "Dad, it's Miss James."

His heart constricted at the sound of her name. His breath caught, squeezed inside in his chest.

"She's crying, Dad. I'll bet she misses Aunt Stell, too."

Even though she stood some distance away, he could see the white handkerchief she occasionally dabbed at her eyes. It stood in sharp contrast to her black wool suit, wide-brimmed black hat, and the long black coat that flapped open in the breeze. She was staring at the coffin, her face almost as pale as the handkerchief she held and the snow at her feet. She looked so alone, so forlorn—exactly the way he had felt since he had been without her.

"I feel sorry for her, Dad. She doesn't have anyone to sit with."

Jonathan's gaze swung back up the hill. She didn't belong up there alone. It wasn't right, somehow. In her own way, she had always been alone; she shouldn't have to suffer that fate here. He searched her face, saw the anguish there, saw the pain, and felt his own despair in the hollow thudding of his heart. She looked fragile and vulnerable, yet regal somehow. Like an errant queen removed from a chessboard.

She needed her knights to protect her. Her castle to go home to.

Instead she stood there by herself, the outsider she had always been, and just seeing her that way wrenched a hard knot inside him. She shouldn't be alone, not now, not with him so near. Devon belonged down there with the rest of them. She belonged with the family.

It hit him like a blow, hit him so hard his mind reeled with the implications. He felt staggered with the knowledge, stunned beyond anything he had known. The truth overwhelmed him—and yet it set him free. Devon belonged with his family because she was *part* of his family. Somehow, some way she had earned a place among them, and it belonged to her just as surely as it did to Alex or Maddie. To Stephen or the children. What had happened didn't matter. Members of a family often disagreed. You didn't turn them away for it. You loved them in spite of it.

Just the way he loved Devon.

The minister began a eulogy, a story of warmth and laughter, gifts that Aunt Stell had so easily shared. Jonathan rose from his seat, and the minister stopped speaking. His brow shot up at the unexpected interruption.

"I need a moment," Jonathan told him. "I'd appreciate it if you would wait."

A murmur drifted through the crowd, but Jonathan didn't care. His course was set. He had never felt more certain of anything in his life.

Devon stood on the hill looking down at the gravesite. She could barely hear the minister's words; they faded in and out with the shifting crowd around him. Then she realized the little man had stopped speaking. Jonathan was standing, saying something she couldn't hear. When the minister nodded, Jonathan made his way to the aisle and started walking in her direction. Devon heard the buzz of the crowd around him, shifting nervously, and her apprehension began to build.

Surely he wasn't so angry he would make a scene, come up the hill and ask her to leave? Devon paled at the notion and swayed on her feet. *Oh, my God.* She paled even more as she watched him walking toward her, his eyes searching, coming to rest on her face. He was bundled against the cold, his collar turned up so the bottom of his face was hidden. She couldn't really see him, but each of his long purposeful strides told her she had guessed his purpose exactly.

Dear God in heaven. Jonathan please don't do this. She wanted to turn and flee. She wanted to disappear, to vanish into the chilly air like the smoke in the chimney of the house across the street. Instead she held her ground. There was nothing for it now but to face him, even if people were staring, all of them looking in their direction, some of them whispering, some of them pointing. She closed her eyes and willed her lips to stop trembling, the weakness to leave her knees.

Jonathan was almost there now. Just a few more long-legged strides and he would be facing her at the top of the hill. Knowing what was to come, feeling the burning humiliation wash over her though he hadn't yet said the words, she still drank in the sight of him. Tall, so very tall. The fine dark skin, the smooth black brows over eyes so compelling, that they could warm her with only a glance. Would she ever feel whole again without him? Be able to fill the terrible empty void he had left inside her heart?

He stopped in front of her but he didn't speak. She

couldn't read the look in his eyes, the strange expression on his face.

"I-I had to come, Jonathan. Please don't be angry." Tears burned the backs of her eyes, she didn't know how long she could keep them from falling. She hated him seeing her like this, so raw, so exposed.

"I'm not angry." Jonathan just looked at her. His eyes moved over her face, studying it as if he were comparing it to the picture he carried in his mind.

Devon's hands were shaking. She stilled them against the fabric of her coat. She had prayed that he wouldn't see her. That she could stand up here on the knoll, pay her respects, mourn her friend's loss and leave. Instead, she had to face him, confront all her longings . . . her shame. She blinked at the wetness in her eyes and it slowly slid down her cheeks.

"I never meant to hurt her. I can't bear it, Jonathan, to think that I was the cause, that if I hadn't—"

"Don't," he said, his voice rough and husky. The blue of his eyes seemed to reach her very soul. "Don't say it. Don't even think it." Then he was reaching for her, his hard arms going around her, drawing her against him, cradling her wet cheek against his shoulder.

"You had nothing to do with this; it wasn't your fault." She didn't understand why he was holding her, but she didn't care. "Aunt Stell's been sick for years," he said softly. "We should have been expecting this."

The tears came in earnest then, Devon sobbing softly against his neck.

"Listen to me—this wasn't your fault."

Devon just clung to him, feeling the heat of his body, the familiar abrasion of his heavy woolen coat against her cheek.

"I had to come, Jonathan." She had never questioned her coming, not from the moment she had first heard the news. Estell Stafford Meredith had befriended her, helped her when she needed it. She wasn't about to abandon a friend.

"I should have known you would be here. I'm glad you came."

"You are?"

"Very glad."

She turned her face up to his. "I'm so sorry, Jonathan. I don't know if it matters, but I wanted you to know."

He said nothing for a moment, but a look of tenderness crossed his face. "It matters. We'll talk about all of this later. For now, just give me your hand."

She did, and he tucked it into the crook of his arm. They started back down the hill, and when they reached the bottom, he ushered her through the crowd. Maddie had moved over one chair, leaving a place for Devon to sit beside him. Alex smiled up at her from the opposite side.

Devon turned to Jonathan. "I brought something for her." Her eyes slid over to the grave. Fingers trembling, fumbling in the pocket of her coat, Devon pulled out a small carved wooden rocking horse, white-painted with tiny red dots. "I saw it in a department store window. I wanted her to have it."

She saw the muscles in Jonathan's throat constrict. He only nodded. Devon took a step toward the casket, then another. She laid the tiny wooden rocking horse on top of the blanket of pale yellow roses. When she turned to look at Jonathan, she caught the sheen of moisture in his eyes.

He glanced away for a moment, then took her hand and guided her into the chair beside him. "You can finish your eulogy, Reverend," he said softly. "Part of my family had not yet arrived. They're all here now."

Devon looked up at him, saw the tenderness in his eyes. His handsome face was glowing with pride and possession, and for the third time that day, she cried.

"How did you get here?" Standing once more at the top of the knoll—the service had been completed, condolences given and received—Jonathan kept Devon close beside him, his arm protectively around her waist. God, it felt good to have her there.

"I hired a car and driver. He's parked right over there." She pointed toward the street out in front of the church. "I suppose I ought to be getting back."

Jonathan shook his head. "I'll talk to him. See he's taken care of and send him on his way. You can ride home with Alex and me." The little boy sat in his wheelchair beside them. When Alex grinned his approval, Devon smiled back at him.

"All right."

They loaded Alex's chair into the trunk of the car and said their good-byes to Maddie, Stephen, and the children.

"Take care of him, Devon," Maddie said, giving her an extra warm hug. "I think he's finally figured out what he wants."

Devon smiled, but her face still looked pale and lined with uncertainty. "Good-bye, Maddie."

Damn, if only he'd been able to see things more clearly, figure things out before both of them got hurt.

"Good-bye, Sis." Jonathan hugged his sister one last time. After Aunt Stell's heart attack, the St. Giles family had postponed their return to London. They would be leaving tomorrow. Jonathan waved to them as they climbed into the Bentley that had carried them there from the Hamptons, then he took Devon's hand.

"Let's go home." There was so much he wanted to say, so much that needed saying. Why was it so difficult? Why couldn't he just tell her the way he felt?

Though Devon said nothing, some of her tension seemed to ease. He lifted Alex into the back of the limo, helped Devon in, then climbed in beside her. They spoke little on the way back to the city. Devon was watching him occasionally from the corner of her eye. Alex was quietly subdued but obviously glad to have her there. As for himself, he kept a very firm hold on her hand.

"Can you join us for dinner?" he asked. It wasn't what he wanted to say, but the powerful emotions that seethed inside him stifled the words he longed to speak.

Devon's eyes searched his face. "If you're sure that's what you want."

"It's part of what I want. The truth is, I was hoping you might stay over."

"Stay over?"

"Yes."

"At your house?"

"Yes."

She glanced down at Alex, whose attention was focused on the sketch pad he balanced on his lap. When she looked back at Jonathan, her big green eyes asked the unspoken question, *What about Alex?* "I don't think that's a very good idea. I'm surprised you do."

She was more wary than ever, and he cursed himself for having made her that way. He was rarely at a loss for words, but they had certainly abandoned him now.

"Maybe we should ask Alex?" he said with forced lightness. "He thinks the world of you, I don't think he would mind."

Devon flushed prettily, as he had known she would. "Jonathan, I don't think you know what you're doing."

"I know what I'm doing. It's taken me a helluva lot longer than it should have to figure it out, but believe me, this time I know."

She forced a tremulous smile. "I'd love to join you for supper, but I don't want to stay."

His insides clenched, yet what had he expected? "All right, if that's the way you want it. It's just that I've missed you so damned much." Why didn't he just tell her he loved her? Why was it so damned hard to say the words? Because it was all so new to him. Because he didn't know for certain how *she* felt. And after all that had happened between them, he was afraid to find out.

Devon's fingers meshed with his, easing his worries a little. "I've missed you, too."

Since Devon's black wool suit looked entirely too uncomfortable, Jonathan had Henry stop by her apartment to pick up a change of clothes, then they went home to his apartment. While Devon went into the bathroom to pull on slacks and a cable-knit sweater, Alex wheeled himself over to where Jonathan stood in the living room.

"If it's okay, Dad, I think I'll go draw until it's time for dinner." His sketch pad rested in his lap.

"That's a good idea, son. Maybe after you've finished, Devon can give you a few more pointers on your work."

"That'd be great, Dad." As he wheeled himself off toward the game room, Jonathan went in search of Maria to let her know there would be three of them for supper.

When he returned to the living room, he found Devon in front of the window, watching the lights of the city against the backdrop of darkness. Muted sounds of a plane in the distance followed tiny red blinking beacons. As Jonathan came up behind her, he slid his arms around her waist and eased her back against his chest. She smelled like orange blossoms, and he could feel the silky strands of her hair against his cheek.

"God, I'm glad you're here." He kissed the side of her neck, then turned her in his arms until she faced him. Her eyes searched his, he read the tension, the uncertainty.

"Are you?"

"Yes."

"Even after all that's happened?"

"None of that matters now."

"Doesn't it? There's a gulf between us, Jonathan, you saw it from the start. My work, my beliefs—your family, your responsibilities. They've clashed before, they might clash again."

"I don't care. Besides, once you've finished your book, this will all be behind us."

"I haven't worked on it since this happened. I'm not certain I will again."

"I'm not asking you to quit."

"What if something else happens?"

"Nothing's going to happen. Alex knows about your project. The papers know. What could possibly happen?"

"I don't know, but something might. You've got to face the possibility."

"I don't care, dammit." He gripped her shoulders. "Can't you see it doesn't matter? What matters is you and me—what we feel for each other."

Green eyes probed gray-blue. "And what is that, Jonathan? What is it we feel?"

Love, he thought, *I'm in love with you.* But he had never said the words, not even to Rebecca, not and really meant them. And as hard as he tried, he could not say them now. "This," he said instead, his mouth coming down over hers as he pulled her into his arms. This was the way he would show her, let her know the way he felt. Devon slid her arms around his neck and kissed him back, melting against him, opening her mouth to let his tongue slide inside. Then he was lifting her into his arms, striding off toward the bedroom.

"Jonathan, wait! We can't do this. What about Alex?"

He stopped midstride, looked down at her flushed face, felt his own rapid heartbeat and the unrelenting hardness of his arousal.

"Damn." He took a deep breath and slowly released it. "For a moment, I forgot where I was. Christ, all I can think of is how bad I want you."

She kissed him again, her arms still clinging to his neck. "I want you, too, Jonathan. No matter what happens, I probably always will."

Jonathan let go of her legs and she slid the length of his body. They kissed long and hard, both of them trembling by the time they had finished.

Devon pulled away first. "I want you Jonathan, but maybe it's better this way. Maybe it would be best for both of us if we took a day or two to think things over."

"No. There's nothing to think about. You belong with me, surely you can see that."

"There are other considerations and we both know it. Let me go home, take some time to sort things out."

"You want to go home—fine. As soon as we've finished eating dinner, I'll put Alex to bed and take you there myself. But I'm coming in. I'm taking you to bed, and I'm going to make love to you until you shout the walls down."

Her eyes widened at that, then she smiled. "With an offer like that, how could a girl resist?"

Jonathan smiled, too. His hand came up to cradle her cheek. "A lot of this is my fault. I blamed you for something you weren't responsible for, for doing something you had to do. I should have stood by you. I want you to know—it'll never happen again."

She only shook her head. "You can't know that for sure."

"Can't I?"

Devon turned away from him and moved closer to the window. "I'm frightened, Jonathan."

He brushed the hair back from her cheek. "Don't be." He bent his head and kissed the side of her neck, but Devon turned away.

"You can't know how I felt when you walked out of that bookstore. I've never felt like that—never. I wanted to die, Jonathan. I can't stand to think of suffering that kind of pain again."

"You won't have to. I promise you."

"I don't believe you. I don't think you can make that promise."

Jonathan caught her arm and pulled her closer. "I know I overreacted. Did you ever think I might have been just as frightened as you are?"

"You? What could you possibly be afraid of?"

He cupped her face with his hand. "Loving you . . . losing you. I'm in love with you, Devon. I knew it the moment I saw you standing on the hill. I knew without doubt, without reservation. I love you and I always will."

Devon's green eyes softened, glistened with the sheen of tears. "I love you, too, Jonathan." Then she was in his arms, holding him, kissing him, clinging to him and making his heart feel lighter than it had in years.

"I love you," he repeated. "I think I have for a very long time."

The rest of the evening passed in a haze of soft words and glances, gentle touches that meant more than a whole night of loving. After dinner, Devon helped Alex with his drawing, then Jonathan took her home.

Once they reached her apartment, the last of Devon's reserve fell away and she kissed him with all the tenderness she had felt for him before any of this had happened. Jonathan carried her into the bedroom, gently undressed her, and through the long hours of the night, they made love. Slow, passionate love. To Jonathan's way of thinking, more beautiful than any that had gone before.

They slept in each other's arms, and in the predawn hours when he awoke, he found her cradled spoon fashion against him. He groaned at his painful arousal, pressed hard against her bottom, and wondered how he could possibly be so hot for her after the hours they had spent in bed.

Then again, it was always that way between them. He ran his hands along her body, cupped a smooth, well-formed breast, and felt her nipple grow hard beneath his hand. Shifting his position on the bed, he eased her legs apart, found her damp enough to accept him, and slid himself inside.

"Uumm," Devon moaned softly, moving to accommodate his thick length, parting her legs to give him better access. "What a lovely way to wake up."

"I'm glad you like it." He kissed the nape of her neck, stroked and caressed her breasts until he had her trembling, then gripped her hips and began to move slowly inside her. Fresh heat flooded his loins, and the feel of Devon's rhythmic movements hotly matching his own made him swell and harden even more.

"Wench," he whispered, his teeth nipping her shoulder. He shifted again and drew her up on her knees, keeping himself inside her, following her up, his loins pressed hard against the soft round curve of her buttocks. He pulled out most of the way then thrust home. Devon moaned and arched her back. Her tousled blond hair was falling over her shoulder, her tongue running wetly across her lips.

Jonathan drove into her again and again. He gripped her bottom, felt the tension in her body, felt her straining to meet each of his demands, and knew his release loomed near. It came hard and fast behind Devon's, his loins pulsing, the pleasure nearly unbearable. Devon cried out his name, and he tightened his hold, spilling his seed hotly inside her, as his body constricted in a second spasm of pleasure.

He found himself wishing the seed would take root and Devon would bear him a child. Alex's arrival had been unplanned, and after Becky's death, he had never given the idea of a family much consideration. Now he realized how much he wanted exactly that. He wasn't too old and neither was Devon. The knowledge warmed him as nothing else could have and made him more determined than ever to set things right between them. Time and caring were all they needed. And to be sure he had won Devon's heart.

Still deep inside her, he pulled her down on the bed beside him, lifted damp strands of pale blond hair away from her cheek and kissed her. Devon smiled softly as he cradled her against him and they drifted back to sleep.

"Jonathan?"

"Uh-huh," he answered sleepily. They were still in her bed, the sun barely up. Devon knew Jonathan would be leaving soon for his office.

"I'm destroying the notes I've made on my book."

Jonathan's eyes flew open at that. He propped himself up on the bed. "Like hell you are."

"I've been thinking things over. I don't want anyone else hurt by this. It just isn't worth it."

"We've talked about this. The damage has already been done. Alex knows about your research, so do the papers. You never meant anyone harm. I know how much this means to you, that you're fighting your own private demons. I think we should see this thing through."

"I almost lost you, Jonathan. I don't want to take that chance again."

"You aren't going to lose me. You mean everything to me, Devon. Everything. I'm not about to let you go."

"What if something else happens? What if someone else gets hurt?"

"We'll face that problem when and if it comes—and we'll face it together."

"I don't know, Jonathan . . ."

"I do." He lifted her chin with his fingers. "I want you to see this through."

"Are you sure?"

"Very sure." Tossing back the covers, he swung his long legs to the side of the bed then crossed the room naked to where his clothes had been thrown over a chair. Reaching into the pocket of his shirt, he fished something out and returned to the place beside her. "There's something I've been meaning to show you."

"What is it?"

He handed her the faded yellow envelope. "A letter from

Annie Stafford to my aunt, written in 1940. I found it among a packet of letters that belonged to my aunt. Stell was living with her husband in Boston at the time. Annie had moved back into the house on Church Street, apparently she'd been living there for several years."

"What does it say?"

He took the envelope from her hand, pulled out the fragile, thin sheet of paper, unfolded it, and handed it back to her.

"Dear Stell," Devon read aloud, sitting up straighter on the bed. "I know it's been far too long since I've written. Believe it or not, I've wanted to, but I've been so busy, I've scarcely had the time. I know what you're thinking—busy doing what? Well, the truth is, a wonderful thing has happened. I've met someone. I know, I know, I said it could never happen—not to me! But he's marvelous, Stell, the most wonderful man in the world. Of course, I'm not exactly certain what he thinks of me, but he is kind to me, and he often seeks out my company. I've always been so lonely. Now . . . well . . . I'm holding such great hopes, Stell."

The letter said little more about the man Annie had met, mostly there was news about what was happening in Stafford, about friends Annie and Stell had in common, the children of friends and whom each of them had married. There wasn't much of interest in the balance of the letter. It was the reference to the man Annie had met that Devon found intriguing, as Jonathan had known she would.

"This must have been what Aunt Stell meant about Annie being happy. Maybe she and the man fell in love."

"Maybe."

"Maybe he was the man in the yellow room. The dark

foreign man." She leaned over and kissed him softly on the mouth. "Thank you for this, Jonathan."

"I knew you would want to see it . . . which reminds me, what's happened with Sara Stone?"

"I'm not sure. The last time I talked to her, I told her about Alex's relapse . . . and about Aunt Stell. I told her I'd have to get back in touch."

"Then do it."

"I'm not sure she's still planning to meet us on Friday night."

"If she isn't, set it up for a night the following week."

"You know, Jonathan, if this works out—if Sara can really reach Annie and little Bernard, this whole thing could soon be over."

"Whatever happens, this isn't going to pull us apart. Not this time. I'm not going to let it."

Twenty-four

Instead of going into the office, Jonathan took Thursday off. Alex stayed home from the clinic, and the three of them spent the day together. It was a wonderful, magical time of loving touches and meaningful glances. Of giving and receiving, of listening and sharing. Though Jonathan said little about their renewed relationship to Alex, the little boy's joy at having her there shone in his bright blue eyes, and Devon had never felt more at home than she did with the two of them.

That afternoon, she phoned Sara Stone, but wasn't able to reach her. Devon left a message with Nathan Talbot, but he told her Sara wasn't expected back until sometime Friday afternoon. It looked as though their confrontation with Florian Stafford would have to wait.

Jonathan went back to work on Friday, and Alex went back to the clinic. At one o'clock Friday afternoon, Devon got a phone call from Sara Stone.

"Is everything set for tonight?" Sara asked.

"Tonight? But I thought you'd decided to cancel, since we'd left things up in the air."

"Not unless you want to. My evening's open. I've got something to do along the way, so I'd rather find my own transportation, but I'll be happy to meet you there."

"What time?"

"How's eight o'clock?"

Devon chewed her lip. Jonathan thought the appointment had been postponed. He had gone to Franklin Lakes for a meeting with Holidex Industries. She wasn't sure he'd be finished in time to meet her in Stafford. On the other hand, maybe it was better if he didn't. There was no way to know if Sara would be any more successful than Zhadar. Jonathan hated this sort of thing, and Devon's project had been the thorn in their relationship from the start. Maybe she could have everything over and done with before he knew where she had gone. Leaving him out of it, might just be better for everyone.

"All right, I'll meet you in front of the Stafford Inn at eight o'clock."

"I might be a little bit late, but don't give up on me. I'll be there."

"Can you find the place all right?"

"Shouldn't be a problem. The directions you gave me seem simple enough."

"Good. Then I'll see you there." Devon hung up the phone feeling a burst of nervous energy. She paced the floor of her apartment, then went over her notes until it was time to leave.

At the last minute, she decided to call Jonathan's apartment to leave a message for him on his answering machine. She didn't want him worrying about where she was, and by the time he got home, it wouldn't matter anyway. It would be too late for him to join her. She would probably be finished and well on her way back home.

Devon hung up the phone just as the voice of the driver she had hired came over the intercom. Devon answered the call, grabbed up her purse and raced anxiously downstairs. She had dressed warmly in her brown tweed slacks and kidskin boots and she left in time to arrive in Stafford well before dark. She wanted to walk the grounds of the old Stafford mansion. After tonight, she hoped she wouldn't be returning to Stafford for a while. She had meant to do this earlier but something had always come up. At last she would have her chance.

With her nerves already on edge, the trip to Stafford seemed to take twice as long as it should have, but in truth they arrived right on schedule.

"I'll need to stop at the Stafford Inn," she told the same young, brown-haired man who had driven her up to see Elwood Dobbs. She needed to see Ada Meeks, since she hadn't called the woman before she left Manhattan. She didn't want the woman phoning Jonathan.

"Looks like this is the place." The driver pulled up to the curb in front of the house, which was just as grimly impressive as it always was. No wind blew through the tall, thin cypress trees, but the ominous feeling the house exuded still gripped her.

"I won't be long." The driver pulled open her door and she stepped out onto the sidewalk. She started to walk toward the house, then stopped and turned back. "I'm only going a block or so, down to the old Stafford mansion and back. It isn't that cold, and the walk will do me good. In the meantime, why don't you go get something to eat? I won't be returning to the city until at least nine o'clock. As long as you're back here by then, that should be fine."

"Thank you, Ms. James." The young man grinned. "I'm sure I can find something to do to entertain myself."

That taken care of, Devon headed up the narrow cement

walkway, toward the Corinthian columns that lined the overhanging porch, and she pressed the doorbell. The chimes echoed dully, just as they had before. The peephole in the center of the ornately carved front door swung open. A moment later, Ada Meeks pulled open the door.

"Hello, Mrs. Meeks. I'm not sure you remember me, but I'm Devon James."

"I know who you are," she said, her voice surly and gruff. She wore her calico apron over an old print housedress. Her gray-brown hair was pulled back in a bun.

"I-I just wanted to remind you we'd be here at eight."

"That's what Mr. Stafford said when he called last week." She glanced over Devon's shoulder. "He coming?"

"I'm not really sure," she lied. "It depends on whether he gets out of his meeting in time."

"Anyone else coming?"

"I'm meeting a woman named Sara Stone. First I'm going over to the old Stafford mansion. I want to see what's left over there."

"Nothing there but a bunch of falling-down walls. Some of the second story's still standing. Not a good idea to go up there, though."

"No, I don't suppose it is."

"This is all a bunch a hooey, ya know. Isn't a word of truth to any of it."

"Well, I believe there is."

"You believe in ghosts, is that it?"

"Yes, I suppose I do."

Ada harrumphed. "Hooey, I say. All you're doing is causing trouble and costing me a whole night's lodging. Mr. Stafford must have lost his mind, letting you dredge all this stuff up."

Devon lifted her chin. "I'll be back here at eight. Good-bye, Mrs. Meeks." She turned and crossed the porch, descended the stairs and headed down the walkway. Ada stared after her; Devon knew it though she didn't turn to look. Finally the older woman closed the door.

Releasing the breath she'd been holding, Devon rounded the corner of the block and continued down the sidewalk. The houses on the street were all very old, but most of them had been well cared for. Huge leafless trees dominated many of the front yards along the way. Remnants of the latest snow clung to the clawlike exposed roots but had melted off the branches. The air was brisk, but with the sun peeking out from between passing clouds, it wasn't all that cold.

Devon glanced ahead of her. Halfway down the middle of the next block, the houses vanished. A barren field stretched to the cross street, enclosed by an old-fashioned wrought-iron fence. In the middle of the field, the blackened crumbling walls of the old Stafford mansion rose up from the weeds like a monument to the lords of darkness.

Devon shivered. She could almost see the bright orange flames leaping into the cold night sky, hear the crash of burning timber. Just as Ada had said, a portion of the mansion remained, the windows nothing more than gaping holes. Bricks from the chimneys were lying in crumbling piles along the walls.

Fighting down her growing trepidation, Devon started toward the gate that led to the burned-out shell. All the way there, it was eerily silent. The old gate creaked as she pushed it open, then fell as quiet as the rest. She almost wished the wind would blow, rustle the branches on the barren tree near a side door she could see hanging loose from its hinges. Instead she heard nothing but the crunching of an occasional patch of snow beneath her feet, the snapping of a twig as she moved it out of the way to walk past.

The house, once a magnificent two-story white-walled structure, had originally been built of wood. Now remnants of a later coat of plaster clung to patches of exposed chicken wire. There were blackened fallen beams and piles of charred tumbled-down wood. Since the front door was blocked by debris, Devon rounded the corner toward the door she had spotted at the side. The door, once ornate, was now weathered and peeling. She pushed on it, it resisted for a moment, then with the sound of grinding wood, it swung open.

Though the whole place made her uneasy, she wasn't really afraid. So far, she'd sensed none of the overwhelming terror she had known at the Stafford Inn. For a moment, she stood quietly outside the door, working to open her mind, to absorb any lingering emotions she might be able to feel, any clues to the past that might come to her.

Nothing.

Braver, now that she had made the initial confrontation and nothing untoward had happened, she stepped inside the shell of the house. It wasn't really dark inside. The roof was mostly gone, some of the walls were down. She saw only shadows and smoke-blackened hallways. She made her way along them, stepping carefully, avoiding the soot and the mud. Her heart was beating faster now, her nerves strung a little bit tighter. She didn't like being in there, yet weeks ago she had made up her mind to investigate the old place. She intended to see it through.

Ignoring the moldy smell of dampness, and the faint, smoky odor of charred wood, Devon continued along the hall, rounded a corner and stepped out into an open, roofless area that appeared to have been part of the entry. The house must have been splendid in its day. What was left of the staircase was broad and spiraled upward to a wide, open hall.

Devon crossed to it then stood beside the banister. Taking a long deep breath, she released it slowly, trying to clear her mind, to open it up, to *feel* what might have happened. She closed her eyes and still felt nothing, but when something rustled in the passage behind her, Devon's heart speeded up.

"Is someone there?" she called out, searching the dim rays of light that faded in and out when the clouds overhead obscured the sun. "Hello. Is anyone here?"

Nothing but the echo of her voice returned the question. Devon's palms began to sweat. She heard another shuffling, possibly the sound of footfalls, but she couldn't be sure. From off to her left came a scraping noise, a grinding, something heavy, she thought, something moving along the walls.

And it was moving in her direction.

Devon's pulse thundered in her ears. She turned toward the passage she had come through, her steps unsteady as she hurried back through the shadows. She had almost reached the door when a high-pitched scream tore through the house.

"Dear God," she whispered, as her heart went slamming hard against her ribs. When she heard footsteps behind her in the passage, she turned in time to catch a movement from the corner of her eye. Devon gasped as something blunt struck the side of her head. She cried out in pain, her shoulder hit the wall, and she went down. The last thing she remembered was a tiny rustling sound near her feet. Dimly she recognized the skittering of a rat, then the pain took over and her mind spun into darkness.

* * *

"Where is she, Ada?"

Ada Meeks shifted nervously. "Down to the next block. She wanted to see the old place . . . the old mansion. She hasn't come back yet."

"How long has she been gone?" Jonathan asked. He stood in the entry, having just arrived at the house.

"Hour, maybe."

"Dammit, it's dark outside. I'd better go get her."

Jonathan left the inn, intending to walk the block and a half to the ruins of the house, but he was anxious to find Devon. Besides, it was dark and getting windy. If Devon had been gone that long, she was bound to be cold. He climbed back into the limo and had Henry drive him down.

"Leave it running," he said as he got out in front of the mansion. "I won't be long." He stepped out onto the sidewalk and pushed open the old iron gate that led to the house. The wind felt icy against his face so he turned up the collar of his coat.

Devon must be freezing out here, he thought, his temper rising again as he imagined her coming here without him. If he hadn't called his answering machine just minutes after she had left her message, he wouldn't have known where she was until it was too late.

"Damned stubborn woman," he muttered as he followed her tracks through the snow and the weeds to the door at the side of the mansion. Surely she hadn't gone in.

But her tracks said she had. Looking at the dilapidated state of the house, Jonathan cursed her. And himself. He should have had the damned thing leveled years ago. It was a danger, a liability a family like the Staffords could ill afford. He made a mental note to take care of it as soon as he got back to his office.

"Devon, it's Jonathan—where are you?" He listened,

heard no reply. "Devon? Are you in here?" Still no reply. He should have known she wouldn't be in there after dark. She must have gone somewhere else. "Devon?" he called one last time just to be sure, then a few feet down the hallway someone groaned.

"Devon!" In the dim, cloud-streaked light of the moon, Jonathan ran down the passage. Devon was groaning softly, trying to sit up. Jonathan knelt beside her and folded her gently into his arms.

"Easy, love." His heart was thundering, his breath coming fast. God, he would never forget the sinking in the pit of his stomach when he had seen her lying there in the shadows.

Devon's eyes searched his face. "Jonathan . . ." Then her arms went around his neck and she clung to him.

"I'm right here, love. Just take it easy."

"Thank God," she said.

Silently, he already had. "Are you all right?"

"Yes, yes, I think so."

He felt her icy fingers against his neck, her body shivering against the cold. "You're freezing." He helped her climb to her feet. "What the hell happened?"

"I-I don't know. Let's get out of here."

"Dammit, you shouldn't be here in the first place." He pulled her coat more closely around her, hoping it would lessen the chill.

Devon looked a little embarrassed. "I didn't intend to come inside, but . . ."

"But as usual, you just couldn't stay out of trouble."

She smiled weakly as they stepped out of the house into the cold night air. "Something like that. How did you know where I was?"

"Ada told me. Are you sure you're okay?"

Her fingers probed the bump on the side of her head. "I've got a lump the size of an apple. Other than that, I'm fine."

"What happened?"

"I'm not exactly sure. I heard something. Movements. Footsteps, maybe. Then this blood-curdling scream. God, it was awful. I started running back toward the door, but something hit me on the head."

Jonathan stiffened. "I didn't see anything, not a timber or an object that might have fallen."

"It wasn't anything like that . . . at least I don't think so."

"Florian? You think it could have been Florian? Surely he couldn't be here."

"I don't know. I didn't sense anything. I just heard noises, and I got scared. I started back the way I came but I never made it." She shivered again, so cold it was all she could do to keep her teeth from chattering.

Jonathan lifted her into his arms. "You should have called me. I wanted to come with you. If I'd been here, this wouldn't have happened."

"I'm sorry. I just hated for you to get involved in all of this again."

"As long as you're involved, I'm involved. Right now, I'm taking you home. I want the doctor to have a look at that bump on your head."

Devon chewed her lip. This time *she* had been the one to suffer the consequences of her work. From the very beginning she had worried about the terrible power Florian Stafford might wield. She had been afraid he might hurt her. She touched the bump on her head. What might have happened if Jonathan hadn't come when he did?

"What about Sara Stone?" she asked.

"I'll see she's well-paid for her trouble. We can meet with her some other time . . . if that's still what you want."

"I-I'm not sure anymore." She was weakening, taking the easy way out. But she could still hear that horrible, bone-chilling scream. It sounded almost . . . *human.*

Devon shifted in Jonathan's arms as he pulled open the old wrought-iron gate. Her hold was still tight around his neck. *Human,* she thought again, once more recalling the sound. What if that was exactly what it had been? she suddenly thought. Not Florian Stafford. Not some evil spirit. But someone paid to scare her? Someone willing to go to any length to stop her from completing this project.

Someone like Jonathan.

Devon shivered, and this time not from the cold. When they reached the car, Jonathan helped her climb in. The heater was running full blast, thank God, and in minutes she started to thaw. Henry drove around for a moment while Jonathan rubbed the feeling back into her hands and feet. Then he ordered Henry back to the inn.

"I'll have Ada tell Sara Stone we couldn't make it . . . at least not tonight. All right?"

Devon stiffened. Thoughts that hadn't surfaced in weeks began to roll through her mind. Articles about Jonathan's ruthlessness in business. Jonathan's outrageous offer of money, the man he had hired who broke into Dr. Townsend's office, Jonathan's anger at her visits to his son. She thought of Alex's setback at the clinic, of Aunt Stell's death.

An even older memory appeared. Rebecca Winston Stafford, killed in a freak auto accident. An accident that left the Stafford fortune intact. Jonathan had obtained the custody of his son. She wished she had read the details.

Devon felt another chill, its icy tendrils sliding down her

spine. She remembered thinking once that she wasn't afraid of Jonathan. That he would never really hurt her.

Or would he?

He had told her he loved her. Had he meant it? She had wanted to believe him so badly.

He had encouraged her when she wanted to quit, but he had done that before. Was it just a diversion? Dear God, her head hurt so badly she couldn't think!

The car pulled up in front of the inn, and Jonathan popped open the door. "I'll only be a minute."

"Wait—" Devon caught his arm. "I'm going with you."

"But I thought . . . after what happened—"

"Sara will be here at eight. The house is empty. I'm seeing this through."

"I don't think that's a good idea. At least not tonight. You've only been here a couple of hours and look what's already happened."

"I don't care. I want this over and done."

He looked at her long and hard. "So do I."

Devon stepped out of the car and Henry turned off the engine. With the wind beginning to wail, bending the tall cypress trees, and a sliver of moon streaking the roof from between passing clouds, the house looked much as it had the first night she had been there.

Devon wet her lips. Her head still pounded from the blow, and her heart thudded dully. It didn't matter. Nothing mattered but going inside and facing up to whatever it was she would find. Facing up to herself.

Ada let them in, grumbling as she had before, making ugly noises in her throat and casting Devon dark sidelong glances. At Jonathan's instruction, the older woman shuffled off toward her quarters in the rear, leaving Devon and Jonathan alone in the salon. Devon glanced around her. It was warm in the house, for which she was grateful, but the heat enhanced the moldy smell of the damp, aging wood. The old brass lamp with the red-fringed shade cast a dim yellow glow into the room, and the battered grandfather clock ticked loudly from the end of the hall.

"I don't feel anything," Jonathan said. "How about you?"

How *did* she feel? Her palms were damp. Her heart was pulsing sluggishly, almost painfully. She felt weighted down and oppressed. "I'm not sure." She wasn't sure what she felt, but she was certain she felt something. "I want to go upstairs."

"Why don't we wait for Sara?"

"No. I want to go up for a moment or two by myself."

"No," he said. "You went to the mansion alone and look what happened. I'm coming up with you."

"Ten minutes. That's all I'm asking. If anything happens—anything at all, I'll come right back down."

"I don't like this, Devon. This wasn't part of our plan."

Plans change, she thought. After what had happened in the old burned-out house, she wasn't sure about Jonathan. But she needed to do this. She had to.

"Stay here and wait for Sara," she said. "If I'm not back down in the next ten minutes, you can come up and get me."

"You can count on that."

Devon reached over and cupped his cheek. *Don't let it be him,* she thought, and felt an ache rise up in her throat. She loved him so much. But what did he really feel for her? Every doubt she'd ever had, rode on her shoulders as she climbed the first flight of stairs. The second floor hall was lit by small brass wall sconces, but only very dimly. The doors to the guest rooms were closed; no light came from beneath. She moved past them nervously, pausing for a moment in front of one of them, reaching out to touch the frame, not really knowing why she did it.

This was Mary's room, she suddenly knew. Florian had once shared it with her, but later Mary had slept there by herself. A feeling of loneliness washed over her . . . and sorrow. It must have been what Mary felt whenever she went into that room.

Devon nervously wet her lips. She continued down the hall and up the narrow stairs that led to the pair of third-floor attic bedrooms. The door to the yellow room was closed, and blackness seeped from beneath. She had hoped Ada would have left on a lamp. Her heart beat faster now. The blood went pumping freely through her veins. Beads of perspiration dampened her temples as she turned the small brass doorknob and stepped into the darkness. Devon groped along the wall beside the door, searching for the overhead light, but her fumbling hand found nothing.

"Damn," she whispered into the silence, then something moved in the room. It all happened so quickly. Someone stepped from behind the door, grabbed her around the waist, and clamped a hand over her mouth.

Dear God, no! Devon thought wildly, thrashing against the arm that tightened like an iron band around her. She had been right about what had happened in the ruins, right about her attacker being human!

God in heaven, had she also been right about Jonathan?

She thrashed even harder, tried to kick and bite him, but the man only tightened his hold.

"You'd better listen, lady, and listen good," a harsh voice warned. "You're gonna stop snooping into other people's business and you're gonna stop now. You don't, and that lump on your head will seem like a mosquito bite—you hear me?"

The hand around her mouth nearly cut off her air supply. She worked to nod her head.

"I tried to scare you away. I figured you might think it was that ghost of yours, but no, you had to keep at it. Well, I know where you live, lady. You give up your crazy notions—you stay away from this house—and I'll leave you alone." He squeezed off her air. "You got it?"

Gagging against the tightness, she gave him another shaky nod.

He let go of the arm around her waist and she felt him reach behind her. From the corner of her eye, she saw him lift the broken shaft of an old iron curtain rod. Devon tried to scream as he swung it down toward the back of her head. At the last possible second, she twisted in his grasp. Her hand came up to stop the blow. She screamed as the door swung wide and Jonathan stood framed in the opening.

"Devon!" He stepped into the room, taking in the situation in an instant. His leg shot up, striking toward her, knocking the rod from the man's outstretched hand. With a single quick turn, his powerful arm drove forward, and the heel of his hand caught the man beneath the chin, sending him crashing to his knees. Another quick blow and the man went down with a harsh grunt of pain.

"Jonathan," Devon whispered. Hard arms went around her, pulling her close, holding her against the wall of his chest.

"Devon, for God's sake what the hell's going on?" His body felt rigid with tension, steely with muscles that hadn't let go.

"He's the man who attacked me in the ruins."

"But I thought . . ." Still holding onto her, Jonathan flicked on the overhead light, then leaned over the man on the floor. Devon noticed that her attacker wore a black knit ski mask. Jonathan grabbed it and jerked it from his head, eliciting a grunt of pain as the man's skull thumped hard against the floor.

"Who is he?" Her voice still sounded shaky.

"Louis Meeks. Ada Meeks's son." His expression grim, Jonathan grabbed the front of the man's shirt and hauled him to his feet. He was sandy-haired, tall and lanky, but young and solidly built. A man in his early twenties. "Did Ada put you up to this?" The man just groaned. "I want to know, dammit. Are Ada and Edgar behind this?"

His head lolled back on his shoulder. He shook it as if to clear the pain. "It-it was my idea. I knew my mother was worried about the bad publicity. I knew if she and my dad couldn't keep the damned place rented, couldn't make a go of it, you wouldn't sell it to them."

Jonathan looked over at Devon. "It's in the contract of sale. They've got to make this place profitable and keep it that way for a period of five years. If they do, I've agreed to deed the place over to them. There are restrictions on the usage—it's got to be kept in its original condition, but other than that the house would be theirs."

"Then you weren't involved—you knew nothing about this."

"Of course not. Surely you didn't think I had anything—"

Devon blinked against the sudden sting of tears. "I wasn't sure what to believe."

Jonathan let go of Louis Meeks, who sank back down on the floor. Jonathan pulled her into his arms. "I love you, dammit. I'm not going to let anyone hurt you."

"I wanted to believe that. More than you'll ever know. It's just that so much has happened."

"I love you," Jonathan said with conviction, and this time she knew without doubt that he meant it. "I love you so damned much." His arms tightened around her. They stood there like that, neither of them willing to give up his hold on the other until a groan from the man on the floor put the moment to an end.

Jonathan dragged Louis Meeks to his feet. "Call the police," he said to Devon. "This bastard is going to jail."

Devon looked at the tall young man. His head hung forward in abject despair, his shoulders sagged, and a lock of sandy hair fell over his forehead. Without his ski mask, he didn't look nearly so ferocious, just very young and very miserable. She looked at him harder, saw the sallow cast to his skin, the glazed look in his eyes.

"How long have you been staying in the house?" she asked.

"Ever since school got out." He stared down at the floor. "About a month, I guess."

"You were going to college?"

"I'm a senior. I was supposed to graduate this year."

"Why didn't you go back to school when the semester started up again?"

He shrugged his shoulders. "I don't know. I meant to, but after awhile, I just didn't feel like going back."

"Let's take him downstairs," Devon suggested. "I want to talk to his mother."

"You could have been seriously injured, Devon. The man's got to pay for what he's done."

"I'm not sure he's responsible."

"What the hell do you mean?"

"Look at him, Jonathan. There's something wrong with him."

Jonathan gripped the boy's chin and carefully surveyed his face, turning it from side to side and studying his hazel eyes. "Are you taking drugs, Louis?"

"No, Mr. Stafford. I swear I never fool with the stuff." But his pupils were open and vacant, and his skin looked waxy and bloated.

"It's the house," Devon said. "His mother's skin and eyes look the same. I noticed it the first time I came here." She glanced around the room, feeling the thickness in the air, the heavy oppression, then she walked over to the attic window. Below her, the rose garden thrust bare thorny branches into the icy air. Their silence was louder than a scream of protest.

Devon shivered. "Florian's here," she said softly. "I can feel him."

"Are you sure?"

"I'm sure."

All of them stood motionless, listening to the whistle of the wind. Though the window was closed and tightly latched, a sudden chill swept in, so cold it raised goosebumps over their flesh, and Devon started to shiver.

"Good God, do you feel that?"

"I feel it," she said.

The windows rattled, then the table beside them began a violent shaking, tilting and turning, dancing a macabre rhythm on each of its four wicker legs.

"It's him," Devon whispered. "It's Florian." She shuddered against the cold. "And I think he's very, very angry."

Twenty-five

Devon screamed as a violent force shoved her hard against the wall, knocking a small gilt-framed picture onto the floor with a clatter.

Jonathan gripped her hand. "Come on. We're getting the hell out of here."

She started to protest, but her head throbbed until her vision blurred and her knees had begun to feel weak. Besides, the look in Jonathan's eyes warned her it wouldn't do a bit of good.

"You're not up to this," he said, dragging her into the hallway. He glanced back into the room. "I'm not sure I am."

"B-But what about Sara Stone?"

"Ada can tell her we've gone. You can call and explain things tomorrow."

"I've got to see this through, Jonathan."

"Did you see what happened in there? Dammit, I don't want you hurt!"

He must have seen her indecision, the way her fear warred with her resolve. His hand came up to her cheek. "I know how important this is. We'll come back. I promise."

A wave of dizziness swept over her, and Devon nodded. With an arm around her waist, Jonathan forced a dazed

Louis Meeks down the two flights of stairs to the first floor of the mansion then off to his parents' small apartment in the rear.

Neither Jonathan nor Devon mentioned the unsettling occurrences in the yellow room and, strangely enough, neither did Louis. While the young man sat in silence, Jonathan told his parents what had happened at the old Stafford mansion, described his attack on Devon upstairs, and finished by pointing to the bruises on her face.

Ada and Edgar looked stunned. Their expressions were clearly proof that Louis had acted on his own.

"He was so worried. He only wanted to help us, Mr. Stafford." Ada's thick fingers nervously twisted the calico apron over her dress. "He never really meant to hurt her. Louis would never hurt anyone."

"But the fact is, he did hurt her. He might have injured Devon badly."

"We'll make it up to you somehow," Edgar Meeks said in a rare display of emotion. He was a thin-boned man who rarely left his overstuffed chair in front of the television, a wisp of a man Jonathan had only spoken to on one or two occasions. "Please don't send our boy to jail."

"I'll think about it." Jonathan fixed hard gray eyes on Louis Meeks. "I'll speak to Devon, and together we'll decide what to do. We'll let you know our decision."

He and Devon left the house. Devon was leaning on him for support, her nerves shattered, her heart still pounding erratically. Jonathan sent the car and driver she had hired back to the city. Henry held open the door so they could climb into the rear of the limo.

Jonathan gripped her hand. "I'm sorry things didn't work out, but we knew this wouldn't be easy."

"Thank God you were here. I don't know what might

have happened if you hadn't found me lying out there in the cold. And later . . . upstairs . . ." She shivered. "I'm so glad you felt him, got to see those things happen with your own two eyes."

"I saw them, all right. I'm not exactly sure *what* I saw, but I definitely saw something."

"And felt something?"

Jonathan reassuringly squeezed her hand. "I felt it. Whatever it was, I've never felt anything quite like it."

With a sigh of relief Devon relaxed against him. It wasn't over—not by any means. But Jonathan had experienced enough to know she had told him the truth. On the way back home, they talked about the attack she had suffered at the old Stafford mansion and the suspicions she had harbored.

"I jumped to conclusions," she admitted. "All I could think of were the things I had read about you, the death of your wife, the ruthless things the papers said you had done."

"I'm not a saint, Devon. I never will be. But I don't go out of my way to hurt people. And as much as I wanted to protect my family, I would never have hurt you." Jonathan answered all of her questions, even explained the details of his wife's accident, telling her it had happened one day after she had left the country club.

"She got a little tipsy, not really drunk, I don't think. That wouldn't have been like her. In any case, Becky wasn't wearing her seat belt. A child ran in front of the car, she swerved into a van that was parked along the street, and her door flew open. She was thrown from the vehicle and her head hit the curb. The blow killed her instantly."

"I should have known you had nothing to do with her death. In my heart, I did."

"You can trust me, Devon. In the past I've let you down. It won't happen again."

"I believe you. If I hadn't been so upset, I would have thought things through and come to that conclusion. I love you, Jonathan."

He leaned over and kissed her. She wondered if he could feel the tension that still shimmered through her body. They rode a while in silence, each of them lost in thoughts of what had happened in the house.

"Are you sure you want to go back?" Jonathan finally asked, breaking into the silence.

"I have to, Jonathan. You must know that. I want this whole thing over. I want to put it behind us—once and for all." Devon leaned back against the gray leather seat, her hands unconsciously clenching together.

"Even if you do, even if you find some way to reach Florian, I'm not sure this will end."

Devon sat up straighter. "What do you mean?"

"You've still got your book to write. This whole affair will be stirred up all over again."

Devon laced her fingers into his, a faint smile playing on her lips. "My book isn't going to be a problem. Now that I've had time to think things over, I've decided to do what I should have done in the first place."

Jonathan cocked a sleek black brow. "Which is?"

"I'm a fiction writer, Jonathan. I don't write true-life stories. I'm going to write a *novel* based on my research and the psychic experience I had that night at the inn. I'll change all of the names and all of the places. By the time my book is published, no one will remember any of the gossip, and even if they do, the characters will be so different no one will vaguely associate the story with you."

Jonathan's worried look softened. "Are you sure that's what you want?"

"It's exactly what I want. I've still got a lot of loose ends to tie up . . . and God alone knows what may happen when we go back there with Sara Stone, but whatever occurs, I'm convinced this is the answer to all of our prayers. Maybe even little Bernard and Annie's."

Jonathan said nothing for the longest time. Then, "Thank you." He gave her a tender, loving kiss then eased her down in the seat, cradling her head in his lap. "How are you feeling?"

Devon's breath came out slowly. Now that they were away from the house, the events of the evening had all begun rushing back in. The truth was, she felt nervous, and worried, and more than a little bit frightened. She kept thinking of the force it had taken to shove her up against that wall. But she didn't dare tell Jonathan that. He might not let her go back in.

"My head is pounding. I'm scratched and bruised. Other than that, I feel fine."

"That bump still looks nasty. I'll put a cold compress on it when we get home."

She smiled softly. Even as tense as she was, she couldn't help thinking of several other things she hoped he would do when they got home.

As they sped along the road, Jonathan worked to keep the conversation light, telling her several clever anecdotes about Alex, and eventually she began to relax. "How did your meeting at Holidex go today?" she asked him as the limo neared the city.

She felt the rumble of his chest then Jonathan actually grinned. "Ammonia."

"Ammonia? What in the world are you talking about?"

"I'm talking about Kelovar plastic. The flaw is ammonia. The damned stuff practically disintegrates when it's saturated with bird droppings."

Devon sat up on the seat. "You've got to be kidding." He shook his head and grinned even broader. There was a tiny dimple inside his left cheek, just like the one Alex had. Devon had never seen it. "I don't believe it."

"I swear it's the truth. That's the reason my meeting got finished so quickly. Wayne and Debra, Carl Murphy and Barbara Mills down at the lab—they all did one helluva job. By the end of next week, Tri-Star will know what we've found out—everyone in the boat-building business will know."

Devon laughed softly, and Jonathan laughed, too. "Guess what else?"

"What?"

"I did a little checking of my own on our friends at Tri-Star Marine. The guy responsible for leaking all that ghost stuff about us was the chairman of the board, Wallace Conner, but the brains behind the moves the company's been making is a VP named Collin Dorsey. From what I hear, he's hell on wheels."

Devon eyed him warily. "What are you going to do to him?"

"Do to him? What I did to him was hire him. I'm going to groom him for my job—or at least a portion of it. We've been in meetings for several days now. The guy is incredible. The first man I've met I've had enough confidence in to shift some of the burden away from myself. Once he's settled into the operation, I'll have a lot more time to spend with my family."

Devon watched him from beneath her lashes, curious just

where she might fit into that picture. "That's wonderful, Jonathan."

"Yes, it is." He eased her down in his lap and smoothed the hair away from her cheeks. "As soon as you're feeling better, I intend to show you exactly how wonderful it is."

Devon pulled his mouth down to hers for a deep, lingering kiss. "Show me now," she said.

Devon woke up Saturday morning in the middle of Jonathan's big king-sized bed. Her hand groped the indentation where he had slept, but he wasn't there. The sheets had long since grown cold. Only the trace of his lime after shave hinted at the fact he had been there. And the dampness from their loving that still lingered between her legs.

Devon smiled at the thought and forced herself up from the pillow. She winced and then groaned. The lump on her head began to throb. Her body was still sore from Louis Meeks's attack. Refusing to dwell on those ugly thoughts, she pushed herself up from the bed and grabbed her robe. Since it was Saturday, Jonathan must have gone to pick up Alex.

Padding into the bathroom, she showered, washed and dried her hair, put on some makeup, then dressed in slacks and a sweater. Walking toward the kitchen for a desperately needed cup of coffee, she heard voices down the hall coming from the game room. One of the voices was Alex's, the other Jonathan's. She walked in that direction, but halted just outside the door when she heard what they were discussing.

"You and Devon," Alex was saying, "you were up in Stafford last night?" He was sitting in his wheelchair next to the sofa, as Jonathan squatted on his haunches at his side.

"Yes."

"And you saw the man in the flames?" Alex asked.

"We didn't exactly see him."

"Did he talk to you?"

"Not exactly, but we both believe he was there. The man in the flames died a long time ago, Alex, but he got lost on his way up to heaven."

"You said he thought I was his son."

"That's right. His own little boy died, and Florian missed him. He got confused that night you were there. He thought you were his son, Bernard."

"Before, you didn't believe me." There was a note of accusation in Alex's small voice. "No one believed me." He sniffed a couple of times then tears rolled down his cheeks. Jonathan reached over and hugged him, drawing the child against his chest.

"I made a mistake, son. So did the doctors. I realize now that what you saw was real. I didn't think it was fair not to tell you."

"Then you believe me? You really believe me? You don't think I just made it up?"

"No, son, I don't. I was wrong, Alex. Grown-ups make mistakes, too."

His cheeks still damp, he looked into his father's handsome face. "I tried to pretend it was a dream, Dad. I thought that would make you happy. But I knew it wasn't. Devon said she believed me. She was the only one."

"Devon's very smart, Alex. That's why I'm going to ask her to marry me. What do you think about that?"

Alex looked pensive, and Devon held her breath. "Would she be my mom?"

"If you wanted her to be."

"I would, Dad. I'd love it."

"I would, too, son. I love her very much."

"And I love both of you," Devon said from the open doorway. When she stepped into the room, Alex turned in her direction, a broad grin lighting his thin dark face.

"Did you hear that, Dad?"

Devon sucked in a breath at the sight of him. She blinked, then blinked again, staring at the small boy in amazement. "Jonathan . . . ?"

"What is it?" he asked. But at the stunned expression on her face, he turned a worried look on his son. For a moment, all three of them just stood there. Alex was smiling. Devon and Jonathan were staring.

"What's the matter, Dad?" Alex finally asked, his thin face crumpling, "You're crying."

"Am I?" Jonathan's big dark hand came up to touch the wetness on his cheek. "Yes, I guess I am."

"But you never cry."

Jonathan smiled softly. "Maybe I'm crying because you're standing up in your wheelchair."

"Oh, Andy." As Devon hurried toward them, Alex looked down at himself in astonishment.

"I am. I am standing up!" But even as he said the words, his short thin legs began to wobble. Jonathan scooped him into his arms before he could topple back down in his chair.

"It's going to take time, son. Your legs are weak. It's been three long years since you've used them. But if you can stand, you can walk."

Alex wrapped his arms around his father's strong neck. "I can, Dad, I know I can."

"I know it, too." Devon reached over and hugged him.

"Dad?"

"Yes, son?"

"If I can walk, can I come home?"

The muscles in Jonathan's throat constricted. "You can come home, son. You better believe, you can come home."

Devon called Sara Stone the following morning. She apologized for the trouble Sara had gone to. Then Devon explained in detail about Louis Meeks's attacks and what had happened at the Stafford Inn.

"It isn't the first time something like this has occurred," Sara said. "Florian's an incredibly powerful presence. He's influencing all of their minds. He's dangerous, not just to you but to anyone who threatens his domain. It's imperative we reach him as soon as possible."

Devon wet her lips. Her hold grew tighter on the phone. "Jonathan has forbidden Mrs. Meeks to rent out any of the rooms. He's afraid someone might get hurt. We can go back whenever you're ready."

"Then I suggest we go tonight," Sara said.

"W-What time?"

"As I said before, I prefer to work after dark. Say nine o'clock? I'd prefer to meet you there."

"All right." Devon hung up the phone, already nervous and uneasy.

Jonathan saw it the minute she entered the room. "You've spoken to Sara Stone," he said.

Devon nodded. "She thinks we should return to the house as soon as we can. She wants to meet us tonight."

"Tonight! But that's impossible. You're still not feeling well, you need more time—"

"Every minute we drag this out is only making things worse. I want to get this over with."

Jonathan raked a hand through his thick black hair. "I hate this whole damned business."

"So do I." She rested her hand on his arm. "Let's make it end."

Jonathan eyed her a moment. When he spoke, his breath came out a little ragged. "All right, we'll go back tonight. And God help us all."

They drove through a pouring rain that froze on the windshield and set all of their nerves on edge. The wind howled in the trees, leaves and papers whipped in front of the headlights, but they reached the inn right on schedule. At Jonathan's insistence, Ada, Edgar, and Louis had left the house, though they'd been instructed to leave some of the lights burning.

Setting his drenched umbrella on the porch, Jonathan used his key to let himself in, then ushered Devon in through the wide carved front door.

"All right?" he asked as he helped her out of her rain-dampened overcoat.

Devon nodded, but her eyes slid away from his to survey the room. "Every time I come here I dislike this place a little more." Just in the time they had been gone, the sense of oppression in the house seemed to have swelled. Even Jonathan felt it. She could tell by the way his arm went protectively around her waist, the way his eyes kept searching the darkened corners.

"Are you sure you're up to this?" he asked for at least the fourth time.

Devon forced down a sense of dread. Her chest felt tight, her palms damp, but she had come this far, she wasn't about to quit. "I'm fine."

Sara Stone arrived at exactly nine o'clock, ringing the dull old chimes then stepping past them into the foyer. She was dressed in a simple beige dress beneath a sturdy brown wool coat, and her feet were encased in serviceable brown lace-up shoes. She returned their smile of welcome.

"Thank you for coming," Devon said to her.

"Yes, we're extremely glad you're here."

"I wanted to come. A case like this is highly unusual, one never knows what knowledge might be unearthed, and if, in the process, I can be of some help . . ." Sara broke off and glanced around the room, taking in the worn Oriental carpet, the old brass floor lamp with its faded red-fringed shade. She stepped away from them, walking slowly, her golden eyes searching, scanning, seeing something no one else saw. "You were right about this place," she said softly. "There is definitely something here . . ."

Devon's pulse speeded up. She had prayed that Sara would feel the same things she had. Now that she heard the confirming words, Devon's throat went dry. She was tense and nervous, yet her body felt weary and battered, even as the blood pumped through her veins. "I feel it, too. Even stronger tonight than it was the time before."

Sara shrugged out of her coat, laid it over the arm of an overstuffed chair, and began to wander around the room. She touched the burgundy horsehair sofa, picked up a small brass snuffbox, then a gilt-edged leather bound book that rested on the Hepplewhite table.

In the hall, she examined the old mahogany-framed pictures Devon had seen the first time she had come to the house. Sara's attention swung to Devon, who stood next to Jonathan in the doorway to the salon.

"It's Florian you're sensing," Sara said to her. "He feels the threat. He knows you've come for the others."

"Is he downstairs?" Jonathan asked softly. "Is he here with us now?"

Sara's all-knowing eyes fixed on his face. "He is everywhere."

Devon froze. A chill of apprehension went racing along her spine. "What should we do?"

"Why don't you show me the yellow room? Let's see if his presence is stronger up there."

Jonathan took Devon's hand and crossed the room toward the stairs. Still leading the way, he climbed to the second-floor landing, then up the narrow stairs that led to the third-floor attic bedrooms. Light fled into the yellow room from the open doorway, but aside from that single beam, it was dark. Jonathan reached for the switch to the overhead fixture, but Sara caught his arm.

"Let me get to know him a little." She stepped past him into the darkness. Devon walked behind her, and Jonathan followed them in.

Just as Sara seemed to, Devon sensed Florian's powerful presence, stronger here, the oppression nearly overwhelming. In the dim yellow light streaming into the room, Jonathan's tall frame felt comforting beside her. One of his hands rested at her waist, the other came up to gently brush her cheek.

Devon started, jolted by the sudden realization it wasn't Jonathan's hand at all.

"There's someone else," she said, swallowing hard, her pulse pounding faster as she guessed whose gentle touch it had been. "Another man, someone other than Florian."

"Yes . . ." Sara continued to prowl the room, touching one object after another, as she had done before. A staghorn-handled letter opener that sat atop the wicker desk in the corner, a tiny silver pillbox, a small oval picture. "This one watches out for her . . . for Annie. You remind him of her."

"Who is he?" Jonathan asked.

In the thin beam of light, Sara shook her head. "I don't know. He's her protector. He loves her . . . and he hates Florian."

"Yes . . ." Devon was beginning to feel the second presence more strongly.

"Are the others here?" Jonathan asked. "Annie and little Bernard?"

"Not here. Not in this room." Sara moved silently forward. "He won't let them near us. They're reaching out to us, but they don't have the strength to fight him . . . not like the other one does. That one is very strong. But Bernie and Annie are waiting close by."

"Florian has that kind of power?" Jonathan asked.

For a moment Sara didn't answer. When she did, her voice sounded hollow and strained. "There is madness here . . . And possession . . . It happened after the boy died. Florian's grief was so strong . . . one led to the other."

The pressure of Jonathan's hand at her waist grew more firm. "An entity within an entity," he said with what might have been awe.

"That is why he is so evil . . . why he is so strong."

"What now?" Jonathan asked.

In answer, Sara sank down on the foot of the bed. Hands resting loosely in her lap, she took several deep breaths and released them slowly. The quiet in the room felt thick enough to slice. Devon's palms were moist. Sara continued her deep breathing and it finally evened out. Her head slumped forward. Her shoulders were sagging a bit as she calmed herself into a state of deep relaxation so that she might better reach Florian.

Sara was calm. Almost serene. As for Devon, her nerves were as brittle as old candle wax. Her body was so tightly strung it seemed it might snap at the slightest word. It occurred to her that in an opposite way her tension was creating a state similar to the one Sara was experiencing with her calm—the same heightened awareness Devon had experienced before.

"Florian?" Sara called into the darkness. "I know you are here."

There was a faint rustling. It could have been the wind in the trees, mice in the closets. Devon knew it was not.

"We have come so that you may go on." The windows rattled, maybe this time it was the wind. "You must listen. You must know that what we tell you is the truth."

"It's grown cold," Jonathan said from beside her, his muscles suddenly tense, "just like the last time. It was warm just a minute ago, now it's icy cold."

Devon shivered and Jonathan's arm went around her shoulders. The chill was undeniable. An icy gust surrounded them, pervaded their clothing and made goosebumps crawl along their flesh.

"You must listen, Florian."

The closet door swung open so hard it crashed against the wall. Devon jumped, and Jonathan's hold on her grew tighter. Her chest felt leaden. The air was so heavy she had to open her mouth to draw in deeper breaths.

Beside her, Jonathan shifted, his senses coming more alert. "Creosote," he said as the rancid smell washed over them.

"I-I smelled it the night I stayed here." Suddenly dizzy, Devon swayed a little on her feet.

Jonathan glanced down at her. "All right?"

She only nodded, but he caught the movement. Still, in the glow of light from the hall, his face looked grim.

"Florian?" Sara said. "You must try to understand. You

are no longer of this world. You died a great many years ago. Bernard and Annie . . . they are dead, too."

From across the room, the bathroom door swung open with a force that sent it reverberating against the wall.

"Jesus!" Jonathan dragged Devon back a step. The faucets squeaked as they turned, then the crash of gushing water spattered against the sink and the bathtub.

"Florian, you must listen." Outside the window, the rain had stopped and moonlight began to stream in through the panes. In the silver glow, Devon gasped as the small round table in the corner tilted sideways and the wicker lamp atop it crashed to the floor. On the desk, the dark green blotter shifted, Devon caught the flash of metal, then the blade of the letter opener flew past them, slamming into the wall behind them, burying the blade to the hilt.

"That's it." Jonathan gripped Devon's arm. "We're getting out of here."

"No!" Devon jerked away. "I'm staying. I've got to."

"Speak to him, Devon," Sara's voice floated toward them from the darkness. "Tell him what you know."

Devon reached for Jonathan's hand, gripped it, and took a deep steadying breath. "I was here before, Florian. I wasn't sure about you then, but I am now. I know all your secrets. I know what happened to your son."

All three doors in the room slammed closed and then opened again. Devon's knees went weak, but she stood her ground. "I know you killed him. I know it was an accident, that you didn't mean to hurt him. But Bernie is dead. You must face up to it, accept what you have done."

A loud rapping against the pipes echoed into the room, the sound so shrill it hurt her ears. A bright yellow flash of electricity leaped with a hiss from the sockets on every wall.

"Dammit, Devon, I want you out of here."

"I know about Annie," she said, ignoring him. "I know what you did to her. I know how you beat her . . . how you raped her. You hurt her, Florian." Glass shattered as a small crystal vase lifted off the desk and hurled against the opposite wall.

"You'll have a chance to atone," Sara put in. "Take it, Florian. Leave this place of sorrow and go on."

Devon cried out at the sudden pressure against her throat. She stumbled backwards, fighting her unseen attacker, slammed hard against the wall and began to struggle for breath.

"Devon!" Jonathan reached for her but an instant later his body flew backwards against the wall.

There was an eerie, whirling sound, a clap like the echo of thunder, and as quickly as the unseen force had closed around her throat, she was freed. Jonathan came up beside her just as a roaring wind swept through the room, knocking the pictures off the walls, clearing the top of the desk with a wailing clatter, hurling a small fringed carpet into the air. Devon screamed as a glass-framed portrait flew past and shattered against the bathroom doorframe. Jonathan clutched her against him, and her fingers curled around the lapel of his coat.

"If you won't leave for yourself," Sara said, "do it for the children. If you ever loved them, give them this chance to go on."

As fast as the howling wind had erupted, the house fell silent. Painfully, eerily silent. No sound came but the scrape of branches against the windowpanes, the drip of the now turned-off faucets. Devon held her breath.

A second clap of thunder broke over the house and the

air crackled with a shot of electricity that raised the hair on her arms.

"Get down!" Jonathan jerked her down to a crouch on the floor, ducked his head beneath his arm, and protected her with his body as the glass in the windows shattered and flew into the room. The splintering shards were landing with a clatter all around them. The wind outside followed the broken glass into the house, and the hiss of scraping branches grew louder.

"Sara!" Devon called out as they came back to their feet. She was trembling all over, her breathing short and ragged. Her neck would most surely carry bruises.

"I'm all right," Sara called back to them.

"What's that?" Jonathan strained toward a new sound sweeping into the darkness. At first a low, mournful keening, the chilling sound grew and echoed until Devon clamped her hands over her ears to hold the pain-filled vibrations at bay. Then it changed. "It sounds like . . ."

"Weeping," Devon said softly as the noise grew louder. Anguished, pitiful, heartwrenching sobs that cut through the night and beyond. "Dear God." Devon's own heart wrenched at the agony that sliced through the room like a scythe. The terrible, mindless pain hovered, drawing them in, making each of them feel a little of the awful anguish Florian must have suffered. Then it began to fade. In seconds, Devon strained to hear it, but only the faintest remnant remained, and even that, sounded very far away.

Once more there was only silence.

"He's gone." Sara's voice had returned to normal. Devon heard her movements as she came to her feet off the bed.

"Yes." Devon wiped at a tear that trickled down her cheek. In the aftermath of quiet, another feeling surfaced, this one sweeping over her like a warm summer rain. It lingered only a moment, but it filled her with gladness and a joy so profound an ache rose up in her throat.

"Bernard and Annie are gone," Jonathan said, and she knew he must have felt it, too.

"Thanks be to God," Sara said.

No one moved for the longest time. Then Jonathan took Devon's hand.

"We can go now," she said softly and he nodded. None of them spoke as they wearily descended the stairs. What was there to say?

Sara touched Devon's arm, the women quietly embraced, then Sara left the house. Standing in the foyer, with their arms wrapped tightly around each other, Jonathan and Devon watched her descend the stairs and travel the narrow sidewalk to her car.

The children were free, Florian had conquered his demon, and Devon had conquered her own.

"What about Louis Meeks?" she finally asked Jonathan, once Sara had driven away. "You won't call the police, will you?"

"No."

She glanced around her. "It feels different in here now. Almost peaceful."

"Yes. Maybe people will enjoy coming here now."

Devon smiled up at him. "I'm sure they will." Then she took his hand and started walking toward the rear of the house.

"Where are we going?" Reluctantly, he let her lead him.

She turned to him and her smile grew softer. "I know where Annie's diary is."

Twenty-six

Outside the house, Devon headed straight for the rose garden she had seen from the upstairs window each time she had been to the house. There was a large ancient-looking bush in one corner. Its trunk was thick and gnarled. Long stout thorns protected it from intruders. The ground beneath it was damp, but there was no snow around it. Devon knelt and began to dig up the earth.

"Here, let me do that." Jonathan came to her side, carrying a small metal trowel. He dug where Devon pointed as she wiped the dirt from her hands on a tissue, but when he hit something solid, he set the trowel away. Digging more carefully now, he felt around the edges, dug a little more, and finally pulled out a small rectangular package wrapped in dirt-encrusted oilskins.

Devon examined the package, then pulled the string that tied it together and carefully unfolded the cloth from around it.

There were three separate volumes, all old and faded. Once they had been gleaming red leather, beautifully trimmed in gold. Ignoring the first volume, she opened the one marked with the Roman numeral II, which she guessed would represent the middle years of Annie's life. Inside, she found the name Anna Mae Stafford inscribed in beautiful blue letters.

Devon skimmed the pages until she found the first reference to the identity of the man she hoped to learn more of.

"Here it is. November 1, 1939."

Today I am forty. I had planned to celebrate with a few of my friends, but an unexpected storm is raging. I sit huddled in front of the fire, chilled to the marrow, but strangely enough, as I glance out the window, I see the gardener I hired just yesterday. He is bent over the weeds in the rose garden, tugging them from their stubborn hold on the earth with a vengeance. He seems not to notice the cold.

It pleases me to watch him working. As big and strong as he is, at first I was hesitant to employ him, but there was a gentleness in his bold dark eyes, for all his massive size and seemingly endless strength. His name is Sergio Baptiste. He tells me that he is Portuguese. His English is broken but he tries very hard to speak correctly. Mr. Baptiste is not a handsome man, and yet there is something about him. Maybe it is loneliness. I guess I must recognize in others what I know so well myself.

Devon skimmed the pages, moving forward through the book. "April 20, 1940."

I am teaching Serge to read. He is such a proud man. I know what asking me to help has cost him. Yet, in truth it is I who am humbled, I who gain the most from the hours in the evening we spend together working. If truth be known, I dread the day he will no longer need me.

Devon skipped ahead. "May 22, 1942."

I know, my beloved Serge, how strongly you feel about this wretched war, but in my heart I cannot say I am sorry you must remain at home. At forty-eight you may be too old to fight, yet you are the most virile man I have ever seen. I only have to see you working shirtless in the garden to know longings I have never known. To feel things I had long believed did not exist. To know in my heart that I love you. Merciful God, if only I had the courage to tell you.

Devon glanced up at Jonathan, fighting an ache in her throat. She thumbed through several more pages. "Look, Jonathan. This page is empty. It's the only blank page in the book."

"It's dated September 21, 1943. Read what it says the next day."

"There's only a few short lines." *I wrote nothing yesterday for there are not words on this earth to describe the way you have made me feel. When you came to me last night, my world began anew. Never will I forget the gift of love that you have given to me.*

"I'm not sure we should read any more," Devon said softly.

"I don't think we need to."

But the book had fallen open to a page a little farther on. "July 15, 1958." *My beautiful, wonderful Serge. So many years have I loved you. So many years have you guarded that love, never demanding, always protective, wanting only what is best for me. I would shout my love, if you would but let me. I do not care that you have no money, that your work is tending the flowers in my garden, that you nurture them with the same loving care that you nurture me. No matter the course of our lives and beyond, I will always be there for you, and I know you will be there for me. You are the husband of my heart and I am your wife. What God has joined together, let no man put asunder.*

Devon closed the book and held it against her heart. She brushed a tear from her cheek.

Jonathan cleared his throat, but his voice remained a little husky. "What do you want to do with them?" He held up the other two volumes.

"Put them back where they were. She just wanted someone to know the way she felt."

Jonathan only nodded. He wrapped the oilcloth back around the small leatherbound books, placed them back beneath the rose bush and covered them over with earth.

"They're together now," he said softly.

"Yes." Devon turned to look up at him. "Now may they rest in peace."

Epilogue

"Are you sure you're feeling up to this?" Jonathan took Devon's hand and helped her over the rail and onto the deck of his sixty-foot Hatteras sailboat.

"I'm fine. I haven't had a bout of morning sickness in weeks; a little fresh air won't hurt me."

Jonathan rested a hand on the small round swell below her navel. She was five months pregnant, but she still didn't show very much.

"The seas are nice and smooth," he said, "but the wind's coming up. Are you sure you'll be all right?"

He was always so protective, more so now that she carried his baby. "For God's sake, Jonathan, the boat is sixty feet long. It's got every piece of navigational equipment money can buy, three cabins, and two bathrooms. It isn't like I'm going sailing in some canoe."

His lips twitched into a smile. "Two heads," he corrected. "On a ship, they aren't called bathrooms, they're called heads."

"I know." But she smiled at him just the same, liking the way the salty breeze ruffled his glossy black hair. The sun shone brightly, huge puffy clouds drifting across an azure sky, and with her windbreaker on, it wasn't even cold. From the moment of their arrival, Devon had been enjoying herself immensely.

"Hey, Dad, look at this!" That from Alex, who raced toward them from down on the pier clutching something in his hand. His recovery had taken time and a lot of hard work, but once the child believed he could walk again, his therapy had progressed fairly quickly.

He climbed over the rail and roared up beside them. "Look!"

"What is it?" Jonathan asked.

"A conch shell." Proudly he held up his hand. "The lady down at the souvenir shop gave it to me for drawing her picture."

"It's beautiful, Andy."

"I'm going to set it on a piece of fishnet and make a drawing of it."

"That's called a still-life." Devon examined the beautiful white conch shell with its glistening pink throat, then held it to her ear. "I'd love to see the picture when it's finished."

Alex beamed. "I'm making it for you, Mom."

Devon's heart turned over. "Thank you, Andy." But he didn't need to bother with the drawing; he had given her so much joy already.

"Let's get goin', Dad."

"Good idea," Jonathan agreed. "How about casting off the stern line? Think you can handle it?"

"Aye, aye, Captain." He ran toward the rear of the boat as Jonathan and Devon made their way to the wheel. Once Alex stood clear, Jonathan ordered the deckhand, a college student named Peter McKenzie, to cast off the bow line, then Jonathan threw the 120-horsepower Ford diesel engine into reverse. Easing the stern away from the dock until it was well clear of the boat in front of him, he slipped the lever into forward, and the boat began to chug away. Once they had cleared the harbor, they would put up the sails.

Devon watched Alex, who stood transfixed at the rail looking at the wake slicing the foaming blue water.

"He's such a wonderful little boy."

"It's a good thing you think so, Mrs. Stafford, since you're going to have another wonderful one just like him in about four more months." Jonathan bent over and kissed the side of her neck. "I can just imagine the trouble two of them can get into."

Devon leaned against him. Her breasts, a little fuller since her pregnancy, pressed provocatively against his chest. "If you can stand two, how about three or four?"

Jonathan chuckled, but his hand came up to caress the fullness. "Your mother would certainly approve."

So far everyone had been thrilled at the news of her pregnancy. Christy had sent her a pair of Venetian lace booties from Italy, where she and her husband Francisco were spending the summer. Both her agent, Marcia Winters, and her editor, Evelyn Frankie, had been a little bit worried at first, thinking it might take too much time away from her writing, but with *Traces* on the *New York Times* bestseller list, they remained optimistic about the future. Then yesterday Devon had turned in the completed manuscript for *The Silent Rose.*

"My mother loves children even more than I do," Devon said. "I'm lucky to have her."

"I'm the one who's lucky." Jonathan turned her into his arms and gave her a quick hard kiss. "And of course your adoring public."

"Speaking of which, Marcia called this morning while you were in the shower. Alex was in such a hurry for us to get going, I forgot to tell you."

"What did she say? Did she like the manuscript?"

"She said she stayed up until midnight reading it. She says *The Silent Rose* is my best book yet."

"I never doubted it for a moment."

Devon arched a brow. "Not even when you offered me all that money not to write it?"

"Not after you turned me down."

"Not even when you read about me in Dr. Townsend's file?"

"Not for more than a moment or two."

"Not even when I barged in on you and Tanaka in a fit of temper that day in your gym?"

"Especially not then."

"Why not?"

"Because that's the moment I first fell in love with you."

Devon turned her head to look up at him. "Really?"

"Uh-huh. When Tanaka called you my fire-breathing angel."

Devon smiled softly, and leaned against her husband's broad chest. As the boat slipped between the buoys, leaving the harbor behind, she appreciated more than ever the name he had chosen for his beautiful new sailboat. It was painted in big red letters just below where Alex stood at the stern watching the wake fan out from the gleaming white hull.

Tenshi. Angel.

Devon smiled again to think of it. She was hardly that, but the word warmed her heart and spoke of a long and happy future.

Tenshi. It was Jonathan who was the angel—a tall dark angel who could sometimes be fearsome, but he was always protective and at times could be achingly gentle. Every day she said a prayer of thanks for him.

But she knew without doubt that the greatest gift of all was that fate had somehow destined the three of them to be brought together. Fate and *The Silent Rose.*

AUTHOR'S NOTE

Though Devon's story is fiction, the events that led the author to write this novel are not. There is indeed a bed and breakfast in New England which resembles the Stafford Inn, and while spending a night there, the author experienced many of the bizarre incidents Devon James experienced and discovered many of the same shocking truths.

With a degree in Anthropology from the University of California and long a student of Parapsychology, Kasey Mars believes that under unusual circumstances, anyone can experience psychic phenomena. Unlike Devon, most of us simply choose to ignore them. Sometimes fate intercedes, changing the course of events until we no longer can ignore them.

Put a Little Romance in Your Life With
Janelle Taylor

__Anything for Love	0-8217-4992-7	$5.99US/$6.99CAN
__Forever Ecstasy	0-8217-5241-3	$5.99US/$6.99CAN
__Fortune's Flames	0-8217-5450-5	$5.99US/$6.99CAN
__Destiny's Temptress	0-8217-5448-3	$5.99US/$6.99CAN
__Love Me With Fury	0-8217-5452-1	$5.99US/$6.99CAN
__First Love, Wild Love	0-8217-5277-4	$5.99US/$6.99CAN
__Kiss of the Night Wind	0-8217-5279-0	$5.99US/$6.99CAN
__Love With a Stranger	0-8217-5416-5	$6.99US/$8.50CAN
__Forbidden Ecstasy	0-8217-5278-2	$5.99US/$6.99CAN
__Defiant Ecstasy	0-8217-5447-5	$5.99US/$6.99CAN
__Follow the Wind	0-8217-5449-1	$5.99US/$6.99CAN
__Wild Winds	0-8217-6026-2	$6.99US/$8.50CAN
__Defiant Hearts	0-8217-5563-3	$6.50US/$8.00CAN
__Golden Torment	0-8217-5451-3	$5.99US/$6.99CAN
__Bittersweet Ecstasy	0-8217-5445-9	$5.99US/$6.99CAN
__Taking Chances	0-8217-4259-0	$4.50US/$5.50CAN
__By Candlelight	0-8217-5703-2	$6.99US/$8.50CAN
__Chase the Wind	0-8217-4740-1	$5.99US/$6.99CAN
__Destiny Mine	0-8217-5185-9	$5.99US/$6.99CAN
__Midnight Secrets	0-8217-5280-4	$5.99US/$6.99CAN
__Sweet Savage Heart	0-8217-5276-6	$5.99US/$6.99CAN
__Moonbeams and Magic	0-7860-0184-4	$5.99US/$6.99CAN
__Brazen Ecstasy	0-8217-5446-7	$5.99US/$6.99CAN

Call toll free **1-888-345-BOOK** to order by phone or use this coupon to order by mail.

Name ______________________________________

Address ____________________________________

City ____________________ State ________ Zip ____________

Please send me the books I have checked above.

I am enclosing $____________

Plus postage and handling* $____________

Sales tax (in New York and Tennessee) $____________

Total amount enclosed $____________

*Add $2.50 for the first book and $.50 for each additional book.

Send check or money order (no cash or CODs) to:

Kensington Publishing Corp., 850 Third Avenue, New York, NY 10022

Prices and Numbers subject to change without notice.

All orders subject to availability.

Check out our website at **www.kensingtonbooks.com**

Put a Little Romance in Your Life With

Fern Michaels

__Dear Emily	0-8217-5676-1	$6.99US/$8.50CAN
__Sara's Song	0-8217-5856-X	$6.99US/$8.50CAN
__Wish List	0-8217-5228-6	$6.99US/$7.99CAN
__Vegas Rich	0-8217-5594-3	$6.99US/$8.50CAN
__Vegas Heat	0-8217-5758-X	$6.99US/$8.50CAN
__Vegas Sunrise	1-55817-5983-3	$6.99US/$8.50CAN
__Whitefire	0-8217-5638-9	$6.99US/$8.50CAN

Call toll free **1-888-345-BOOK** to order by phone or use this coupon to order by mail.

Name____

Address______________________________________

City ____________________ State ________Zip______________

Please send me the books I have checked above.

I am enclosing $____________

Plus postage and handling* $____________

Sales tax (in New York and Tennessee) $____________

Total amount enclosed $____________

*Add $2.50 for the first book and $.50 for each additional book.

Send check or money order (no cash or CODs) to:

Kensington Publishing Corp., 850 Third Avenue, New York, NY 10022

Prices and Numbers subject to change without notice.

All orders subject to availability.

Check out our website at **www.kensingtonbooks.com**

Celebrate Romance With Two of Today's Hottest Authors

Meagan McKinney

__The Fortune Hunter	$6.50US/$8.00CAN	0-8217-6037-8
__Gentle from the Night	$5.99US/$7.50CAN	0-8217-5803-9
__A Man to Slay Dragons	$5.99US/$6.99CAN	0-8217-5345-2
__My Wicked Enchantress	$5.99US/$7.50CAN	0-8217-5661-3
__No Choice but Surrender	$5.99US/$7.50CAN	0-8217-5859-4

Meryl Sawyer

__Half Moon Bay	$6.50US/$8.00CAN	0-8217-6144-7
__The Hideaway	$5.99US/$7.50CAN	0-8217-5780-6
__Tempting Fate	$6.50US/$8.00CAN	0-8217-5858-6
__Unforgettable	$6.50US/$8.00CAN	0-8217-5564-1

Call toll free **1-888-345-BOOK** to order by phone or use this coupon to order by mail.

Name ______________________________________

Address ____________________________________

City ____________________ State ________ Zip ______________

Please send me the books I have checked above.

I am enclosing $__________

Plus postage and handling* $__________

Sales tax (in New York and Tennessee) $__________

Total amount enclosed $__________

*Add $2.50 for the first book and $.50 for each additional book.

Send check or money order (no cash or CODs) to:

Kensington Publishing Corp., 850 Third Avenue, New York, NY 10022

Prices and Numbers subject to change without notice.

All orders subject to availability.

Check out our website at **www.kensingtonbooks.com**